COUNTING *On* YOU

J. C. REED
JACKIE STEELE

COUNTING ON YOU

Cover art by Larissa Klein

Editing by Elaine York/Allusion Graphics, LLC/Publishing & Book Formatting

ISBN: 1546638253
ISBN-13: 978-1546638254

COUNTING On YOU

DEDICATION

This book is for those who believe in love. Here's to believing in the magic of the moment, finding love in all the wrong places, and never giving up on your wildest dreams.

PROLOGUE

Vicky

"FUCKING HELL," I mutter, frozen to the spot.

The guy in front of me is standing in front of a mirror, his naked ass on full display.

His back is rippled with muscles; his chest is broad, and even from my sideways position in the doorway, I can see the well-defined six-pack beneath the taut skin.

My gaze skims over his broad biceps and lingers on the tattoo on the back of his neck. It looks like a snake engrossed in a battle with a lion. It's powerful and fascinating in a scary kind of way. As though he's one or the other and fighting his demons that are about to come to life.

His back is sexy as hell, but I think the most beautiful part of him is his ass. It looks like it's been carved out of marble.

Oh, wait.

My eyes widen and my jaw drops open as I realize what he's doing.

His hand is on his dick. There is no denying it. You can see his hard-on, the veins on his shaft, the slow movement as his hand goes back and forth.

Oh. My. God.

He's jerking off, his face drawn in concentration. The shock at the picture before me is short but intense.

But there's more than shock.

A wave of heat travels down my abdomen and settles between my legs. I can feel myself vibrating down there, my lady parts clenching and unclenching with sudden want.

It's not like I haven't seen a dick before. It's the mixture of it all—his dark hair, muscular body, and the fact that he seems to be enjoying himself way too much—that's turning my insides into jelly, and I don't like it one bit.

He must not have heard me because he neither

turns his head, nor does he stop stroking himself.

"Jesus. Get a frigging room," I call out, my voice a little too breathy.

His hand freezes in its movement. He turns around and shoots me an unfazed smile. "I'm taking care of basic needs here, if you don't mind."

His gaze meets mine, and my breath catches in my throat. His eyes, a dark shade of brown, are hooded, giving me the kind of bedroom look that screams he's not in the least ashamed of having been found jerking off.

For a second, I think I see surprise on his face, but the fleeting impression is gone before I can fully grasp it.

His brows shoot up as his eyes pierce through me, shimmering with challenge. "Want to join in, or why else are you still staring?"

Heat rushes to my face.

Jerk.

"Why would you think I'd—" My voice breaks as utter humiliation and blinding rage render me speechless.

I peer from his eyes to his cock. His hand is still wrapped around it. Instead of deflating, I think it's just gotten even bigger, the veins pronounced, the crown glimmering with moisture.

The temperature's just increased tenfold.

Either that, or a complete stranger has just made me lose it.

Peeling my gaze away from him, albeit unwillingly, I cover my eyes with my hand to block the image of his glorious cock. "Who says something like that to a stranger?"

His raucous laughter rings behind me as I slam the door shut and press my back against it, taking slow, labored breaths.

Okay, Sullivan.

This so did not happen.

"Jesus." I rub my eyes hard, as though to wipe away the image of his naked body, but that's not possible.

The harder I try, the clearer I can see his huge dick in his hand. Who has a dick like that? Thick, engorged, and oh, so wet.

The slick sound of his hand moving up and down rings in my ears. Was it as loud before? Or has he just resumed his action?

Pressing my ear against the door, I hold my breath and think I can hear his hard breathing.

God, those low, deep moans are sexy.

I move back down the hall, focused on getting away as fast as possible, and open another door by accident.

It's a bedroom with clothes scattered across the bed.

Men's clothes.

Men's shoes litter the floor.

The scent of aftershave lingers in the air.

"Changed your mind after all?" The voice is deep and husky. For a moment, I'm immobilized as he continues, "I think bedrooms are a bit overrated, but what the hell? If that's your thing, I'm up for it."

It's the same guy.

I turn to face him, my gaze strangely drawn south, and find that a thin towel is wrapped around his hips, covering his junk.

I let out an exasperated snort.

It's really tiny. The towel, that is.

Not his tool.

That one's about the biggest I've ever seen, counting TV and Internet pop-ups.

I don't want to gawk, and yet I find my gaze glued to the clearly defined bulge beneath that towel.

In the bright light spilling in through the large bay windows, I can see everything. There's no denying he still has a raging erection, as though pleasuring himself wasn't nearly enough to still his sexual appetite.

"Seriously?" I ask, pointing to the towel. "Can't you put something on?" My voice sounds strangled, breathy, which I attribute to the fact that I'm highly uncomfortable standing in front of a hot guy built like a Greek god and hung like a donkey.

"What's so important that you had to interrupt?"

"I interrupted?" My jaw drops, and white hot flashes of anger begin to cloud my vision. "Oh, you're talking about your date with your right hand. Sorry about that." I smirk. "What are you doing here?"

His brows shoot up. "Here?"

"Yes, here, in my apartment."

Ignoring my question, he squeezes past me, his erection coming dangerously close to my abdomen. From up close, he smells of sandalwood and raw manliness.

My breath catches in my throat.

It takes all my willpower not to jump a few steps back to put some distance between us.

He retrieves another white towel from his suitcase and wipes his face with it.

Every fiber of my body is heating up at the sight of his naked back. Bruce is tall and a bit skinny. This guy is built like a boxer: tall with broad shoulders and hard muscles in places I didn't know existed.

As he turns to regard me, I notice the color of his eyes.

Deep brown and broody with long, dark lashes.

They're the sort of eyes that make you feel like you're the only woman in his world.

It's a pity I didn't get the chance to watch him finish the act earlier.

Why would I think something like that?

I can feel my cheeks burning. I wouldn't be surprised to find that my face has just turned a similar shade to our counselor's hair color.

The guy steps in front of me, eyeing me with curiosity. He's standing too close for comfort, sucking the oxygen right out of the air. "What makes you think this is your apartment?" His voice is low and nonchalant, as though we're sitting in a café engaged in small talk about the weather. No sign of nervousness at all that he's just exposed himself to a stranger.

"The form in my folder says so."

"The form?" The corners of his lips twitch. "What does it say?"

"2B." I scan the room again, suddenly uncertain. "What apartment is this?"

"2B." He frowns, but for some reason I think I see amusement in his eyes. "Clearly a mistake."

"No doubt." I stare him down. "Why don't you start packing up again? Because I'm pretty sure this is my place."

"Is that so?" He crosses his arms over his imposing chest. I try not to stare at his bulging biceps, but it's hard. "I'm not leaving."

My anger flares. "This is my apartment. You've made a mistake."

"I assure you I haven't. I've been here since this morning. Even had a counselor stop by to ensure I was comfortable." His lips twitch again. I don't know why his statement sounds dirty, but this isn't the time to probe.

My eyes widen and my legs begin to shake just a little bit. "Are you saying you're staying here?"

"Yes, that's what I'm saying." He cocks his head to the side. "I assume you're the love addict who's going to be my roommate? My counselor told me a little bit about you."

Love addict?

I open my mouth, but no sound comes out.

In all honesty, what could I possibly reply?

The fact that he's just called me a love addict is too much.

Turning around, I bolt down the hallway as quickly as I can, then grab my luggage and head for the elevator.

It has to be a mistake.

It has to be a fatal mistake. There's no way anyone would shack me up with a guy.

I *can't* live with a guy, not even for therapy purposes.

1

Kaiden

Three days earlier

My life sucks.

I'm not a sex addict. Honestly, I'm not. That word makes me cringe. I'm not even sure why I'm here, but apparently the board thinks my healthy sex life is spiraling out of control...

Well, they're wrong.

It's not an addiction if I enjoy every minute of it.

It's not an addiction if I love what I do.

But tell that to the thick-sculled fatties with no sense of humor on my board.

"This is a catastrophe for the company," Ben, one

of the six board members, says. "We've already lost two million in revenue." He slaps the paper for effect, then looks up, his gray-blue eyes meeting mine. "This cannot go on, Kaiden."

I cringe at the last word. Only my friends and family are allowed to call me Kaiden, and they never do so lightly.

"What do you expect me to say?" I shrug. "That I'll give up my private life to make you happy?"

There is a short silence.

My brother, Chase, leans forward.

Now, let me tell you something about my brother.

He's a kickass attorney. He's proven himself on numerous occasions. Whenever either of us needed to get out of a sticky situation, he always knew what to do.

Except, now I'm not so sure.

There's a frown on his face, and he takes too long to reply. Either he's preparing for a long speech, or worse, he agrees with the board.

For the sake of our friendship, I hope it's the first option.

"Chase." My sharp tone conveys a warning I hope he's clever enough to heed.

He turns to me and exhales a long sigh. "Kade, they're right." I stare at him with a mixture of shock and anger. "You've painted the company in a bad light."

"Et tu, Brute?" My mouth tightens in a line.

Again I'm reminded that we thrive on opposites.

I may have been adopted, but growing up in the same household and being closer than real brothers, I would have thought Chase would agree with me for once.

I guess I was wrong.

"Those are serious accusations," Chase continues. "As your attorney, I can tell you this could ruin your career. Your life. The woman in question—" Chase waves his hand to Ben. "—what's her name?"

"Brenda," Ben says.

"Brenda went to the tabloids," Chase says, as though I'm not familiar with the outcome of my last sexcapade. "This 365-day, non-stop sex calendar of yours is earning serious attention right now—and not in a good way. We can't afford for it to draw any more attention or else we'll end up losing important deals and clients. If you don't stop, we'll soon be facing a crisis."

"You're all a buzzkill."

When I came up with the idea of a 365-day, non-stop sex calendar, I didn't realize it would be such a rewarding challenge. My best friend, Cash Boyd, owner of the famous Club 69 establishments, couldn't agree more. In fact, he's the one who's been more concerned that I make it than even I am. He's my wingman. Sometimes I wish my brother would be more like him rather than have the brain of an attorney.

It's not an easy task, let me tell you that.

In a city of one million women, half of them are married. A small percentage is gay, widowed or retired. That's already a small pool. What I'm looking for is the small percentage (of an already small pool) that actually wants to stay single and enjoys sex without any sort of commitment. The kind that just wants to have fun.

I admit, that's my favorite kind of woman.

Unfortunately, they're not easy to find. The majority are romantics pining for "The One." I call them the "deluded lunatics."

Maybe it's because I don't fall in love.

The only two things I've ever loved are my work and the way my dick always seems to know what to do.

I just don't like the drama, the pleading, having to stifle a woman's hope that someday we'll be in a relationship. For the life of me, I cannot see myself depending on someone to make me happy, to let someone so close to me that I would have to trust her.

Which is why I'm always being upfront with every woman I meet before I invite her back to my place:

The only relationship I have is with my cock.

That's another reason why I started the calendar in the first place.

The way I see it, I'm doing women a favor. They learn from me. I live to please them and treat them well. That's one of the most important rules I set up.

I even love going down on them if I know they're clean.

I'm not doing men though. I'm as straight as a cannon and love to dive into deep places that are warm, moist, and welcoming, like a hot apple pie fresh from the oven.

"I can assure you she had fun. And she never asked for money," I say.

"Yet." Chase sighs. "She hasn't asked for money *yet*. But once she learns that you take photographs of all your conquests, she'll want a payout. In the meantime, she'll go to every rag magazine that wants her and can earn her media coverage."

"She won't." I let out a chuckle because I *know* Brenda. I know what she really wants.

Remember the kinds of women you should never

go for? Yeah, she falls into one of those categories.

"You can't know that." Chase interlinks his fingers as he stares me down. "Did you get her written permission to take photographs?"

I exhale. "No, but it's not like I'm publishing and selling the snapshot of a *face* on the Internet."

"Does she know that?"

I groan.

What's the big deal? The snapshots I take are there to help me remember the women I've bedded. They aren't even dirty, unless the woman in question wants them to be.

I always make sure I never photograph below the waist unless I'm asked to.

"For now," Chase keeps saying. "But the moment your other conquests come forward, that's the moment your entire life will go downhill."

I drape my arm over the chair and lean back, thinking. Brenda was into me a bit too much. I gave in and slept with her in a moment of weak judgment. Once she realized we'd never walk down the aisle, the claws came out.

At last, I draw a deep breath as I realize that maybe that makes her unpredictable. "All right, little brother. What do you recommend we do?"

"You mean what we recommend *you* do?"

Another board member, Vince, chimes in. He's the oldest in the room. His hair is streaked with gleaming silver. I've seen him around a few times, but I've no idea what he actually does in the company. Investors and shareholders shouldn't have the kind of power he has.

"There was a meeting yesterday." Ben ignores the glances I throw at my brother and continues, "It's been decided that you'll attend the LAA Center. It's the only place that will help save your reputation which, as I'm sure you know, is our reputation, too."

The LAA Center?

I snort.

"I'm not a sex addict."

Ben sighs. "We've already discussed all other options. You have no choice. You either check yourself in or you retire. It's that simple."

With that he gets up. "Your choice, Kaiden," he throws at me in the kind of voice I'd like to punch right out of him. "Your therapy starts tomorrow. If you're not there, you can kiss your seat goodbye. For the sake of our friendship, we recommend you do as we say."

I stare at him, my anger flaring up. "May I remind you that I built this company from scratch?" I point my finger to each of the six board members, including my brother. "You wouldn't be sitting here if it weren't for me."

Ben nods his head as if he saw that coming. "We're all aware of your hard work, Kaiden. But your company wouldn't exist if it weren't for our shares, connections, and support. Right now, you're risking our investment and reputations for a bit of a good ol' roll in the hay, so to speak." He stares me down, which doesn't have quite the threatening effect I'm sure he's going for.

"It's still my private life," I mumble, irritated.

"That may be true, but we won't let you ruin the very company you and your brother worked so hard to build." His expression softens. "Your father and I were friends long before you were born. Remember our agreement before we agreed to invest in your business?" He pauses, but not long enough to give me a chance to reply. "We want you to get better."

Better?

I snort.

Frankly, I've never felt better. The sex is ah-mazing. Like rip-your-clothes-off-amazing. Imagine you could have all the food you wanted. Now imagine that what you got is so deliciously and mouthwateringly melty you'd instantly lick your fingers—that's sex to me. Just give me a woman with hips and something to grab onto so that it doesn't feel like I'm fucking a blowup doll. Give me a pair of tits—any size, any shape—I can push my face, or cock, in between, and I'm happy and ready to go.

"I'm doing very well, thanks for asking," I say.

He shoots me a hard stare before he gets up, followed by the other board members. Only my brother remains seated.

As soon as the door closes behind them, I stand and walk to the bar.

"It's not even ten a.m., Kade," Chase says.

"It probably is...in Australia."

I grab a bottle of whiskey and two glasses before I return to the table.

My hand's slightly shaking as I pour the golden liquid into two tumblers, spilling a drop.

My anger flares up again. "It's a fucking mess. I'm far too young and sexy to retire. Besides, they need me because I'm the only one who knows how to run my company the way it should be run. It's not my fault they're thick-skulled brutes, with their only interest being fluffing up their savings accounts rather than expanding this business. Sometimes I wish I didn't have to ask for investors...that I'd never sold the shares to start up."

"But you did," Chase says. "Nothing you can do

about that now."

"Obviously, I have to have some patience and understanding, what with most of them being past sixty and counting," I say, ignoring him.

His lips twitch in understanding. "You can't expect people who have no idea what Snapchat, Instagram, Twitter, and the likes are, to get you."

"Obviously," I mutter. I turn around in a dramatic manner. "I'll tell you a secret. I do actually know what's going on."

"Please enlighten me."

"They're bored with their lives because nothing ever happens, which makes them jealous of me."

That's right.

They're jealous of *me*.

Jealous because they're married and stuck in their boring routine.

Jealous because they think they have left their best years behind and miss their old, carefree days.

Divorce is always an option, but not when it's already their second and third marriage.

"They love their mansions, their Botoxed wives, but they still think the grass is greener on the other side," I continue. "That's because the grass is greener on my side. Not my fault though. You can't have it all. Even I know it, which is why I do have a set of rules."

"Rules?" Chase's brows shoot up. "What rules?"

I smile at him knowingly. As much as I love my brother, some things aren't meant for his prude ears.

Some of my rules:

I never do repeats. Ever. I'm fairly proud of that. If you're a prude, don't ask me what my magic number is because it's only a number. To you, anyway.

I don't hire prostitutes or sex workers or strippers. And I don't do married women or religious fanatics or virgins—not because they're not hot, but because I have my own standards. These types of women get too invested in the idea of marrying, and I have no time for healing their broken hearts. I'm not a lifeboat, either. I don't save anyone from their mundane lives.

I don't do love...or commitment. As such, I avoid women who are looking for the white picket fence, or a rock on their ring finger. I'm a business strategist and marketing expert who always keeps things uncomplicated, because commitment = mess, which equals drama, which equals trouble.

My point is: don't ask me for my phone number. Don't tell me you're married, or want kids. Don't ask me how many women I fucked before you, just like I won't ask you how many breaths you've taken in this little thing called life.

To me, it doesn't matter.

You may think I'm a manwhore.

I assure you, I'm not.

"Let's just say," I respond in response to his inquiring look. "I just like to give back the enjoyment and learn from experience the same way you would read a book and savor each and every nuance of it."

"Just do it, Kade," Chase says quietly. "It's only for six weeks."

Smiling coldly, I push a glass across the table toward him. "What about my game plan?"

"What about it?"

I wave my hand. "Don't tell me it's all been in vain. I only have a few women left."

He stares at me with no sense of humor. "How many are we talking about?"

I lift my hand. He stares at my three fingers. "Jesus, dude. I'm surprised you haven't caught an STD yet."

"I'm not stupid. You know how careful I am." I lean back, lifting the glass to my lips, but I don't take a sip yet.

"You know what? Forget I even said that. I don't

want to know." He shakes his head and releases a sigh. "Look, I'm not judging you, all right? You're my brother and no matter what you do, it's your business and I'll always have your back. But..." He wets his lips, hesitating, probably choosing his words. "Please, just do the six-week program. After that... resume whatever you were doing before, just be more discreet about it. Fuck, I'll even be your wingman. Anything, as long as I can keep you out of trouble."

I give a little snort.

Chase being my wingman would be the worst thing that could happen to me. He's married and ready to be a father.

"Do you know what you're asking me to do?" I ask.

"I..."

"No, answer the question, Chase. Do you know what you're expecting of me?" I ask sharply. "You request that my dick go on hiatus. That's not human. It's fucking immoral. Fucking torture. I wouldn't expect that from my worst enemy."

"Look, if monks can do it, you can do it."

"I'm not a monk. I'm an adult with a healthy appetite for sex."

Chase holds out his hand, a knowing smile

playing on his lips. "I get it. You need it."

I cringe at his choice of words.

He makes me sound like I *need* sex in a bad way.

"I'm not a sex addict, all right," I say. "I just enjoy it. That's all it is. A hobby, if you have to define it. Like I said to the board before, I like the workout, the challenge, and the chase because I'm a man of many aspirations. As long as I have a goal in sight, I like to sweep right in and finish it in one fast ride. See things through, so to say. I said that to the company board. My honesty didn't help my case. They had little understanding for my "sex escapades" as they called my little encounters. This ultimatum is not fair."

"I think it might be understandable," Chase says. "You didn't go a day without sex in the past year."

"That's because I want to reach my goal."

Chase shakes his head. "You are at the top of the world right now, Kade. The company has never done so well and you want to throw it all away. For what? For some fun? Why don't you give it a break for a few weeks?" His eyes narrow at my viperous glance. "Days, then?"

"Are you asking me to break a promise?"

"A pointless promise you made to yourself? Yes, I am." He regards me for a few seconds, his anger visible in the way his fingers clutch at the glass. "Just do it, bro. How you do it, when you do it, with whom, it's none of my business. Lie your way through. I don't care. Honestly, I just want to see your ass at the rehab center tomorrow."

The door opens.

We both look up at my new assistant, Miranda, striding in, a folder tucked beneath her arm. Her hair is piled high on her head, and she's wearing a sexy dress.

"Oh, sorry," she says. "I thought the conference room was empty."

Chase gives her a short nod of his head. "That's fine. We were about to finish up anyway."

She drops an easygoing smile. Her entire posture is nervous, as if it was her first day, even though Miranda has been working for me for three months now. I understand her nervousness, but I also think she has a bit of a crush on me.

I wink at her, which earns me a strange glance from Chase.

"Can I bring you anything?" she asks.

"We're fine," Chase says.

"Actually, I'd love some coffee."

Chase shoots me a warning glance, which I shrug off.

"Coming right up." Miranda leaves, closing the door behind her.

"Seriously?" Chase mumbles.

"What?"

"You haven't even started therapy yet."

"I never said I would." I shrug my shoulders. "Jesus. It's just coffee. I wasn't planning on fucking her while sipping it."

He shakes his head again then gets up, grabbing his jacket in the progress. He lifts his briefcase, hesitating. "Tomorrow, Kade. You're taking the private jet tonight."

With that, he storms out, leaving me alone.

I pour myself another glass of whisky, nursing it slowly.

Why can't the damn therapy start in three days so I get to finish what I've been working so hard to complete for a full year?

Would it count if I fucked three ladies today rather than one a day?

I grab my glass and walk over to the window. Below me, people are swarming like ants. I don't turn around as the door behind me opens, the click clack of high heels following the enticing scent of fresh coffee.

"Is there anything else I can do for you?" Miranda

asks.

I turn around and regard her with the kind of smile I know will melt her panties in a heartbeat. "As a matter of fact, there is. Would you care to join me for lunch?

2

Vicky

Three months earlier

AN OPEN LETTER TO JANE AUSTEN

Dear Jane,

For the last two hundred years or so, your delightful words have etched their way into every young woman's buoyant heart hoping for a bit of romance in her life. Your books have given us hope. They've made us dream, but after spending years of my life looking for my Mr. Darcy, I've come to realize you were a romantic, just like the rest of us, and the path ahead isn't as fluffy as you made it out to be. For all I know, Mr. Darcy may always remain a beautiful dream (preferably one with lots of sex in it, because I'm not getting very much of that lately.) However, I will never give up dreaming because, even if Mr. Darcy doesn't exist, maybe some day Mr. Darcy's poorer and less sexy brother will trudge along. I'm definitely game for giving *him* a try.

Yours affectionately,
Vicky Sullivan

Two months earlier

AN OPEN LETTER TO JANE AUSTEN

Dear Jane,

I think I've found him—my own Mr. Darcy. Actually, I'm quite sure of it. While we haven't met at some uptight ball, like Elizabeth, Starbucks isn't so bad a place either. He spilled hot coffee on me (I'm sporting a small scar, but who am I to complain when we're talking about true love here) and then he asked me to have a cup of coffee with him the next day. So far, we've only gone on two dates, and no se*...uhm, lovemaking, but my heart's already confident. He's the one. We might not be Elizabeth and Mr. Darcy in the sense that we don't talk much, but in the silence surrounding us, we say everything.

Yours affectionately,
Vicky Sullivan

"ARE YOU FUCKING kidding me?" I mutter under my breath as soon as the bus pulls onto a potholed road. Looking out of the window, the only thing I can make out is a vast space of trees, sand, and water, and yet more water. It feels as if I'm part of another world even though that is impossible. We are as deep in North Carolina as one can get.

Throughout our drive, I spied a few shops, the Pea Island National Wildlife Refuge, and even caught a glimpse of the Fort Raleigh National Historic Site. It sure feels like we're far away from civilization, fumes, and traffic, but the driver keeps assuring me we're only "a stone's throw" away from the buzzing nightlife.

I should have clarified his interpretation of the term "buzzing nightlife."

Roanoke Island is beautiful. I've read tourists are all over this place, but right now it feels more like a death sentence than a blissful oasis. On top of the seclusion, the clouds are as dark and ominous as the feelings inside me and the dread of losing myself.

Okay. I'm not going to panic. I refuse to. I'm

going to stay on this tiny island for only six weeks.
Six weeks.

Forty-two days.

1008 hours.

It should be as easy as pie. Except, I have the
feeling it won't be.

It's going to be a fucking disaster, that's what it is.

"What are you in here for?" A voice disrupts my
thoughts.

I turn my head.

A young woman is sitting behind me in the half-
empty bus, her expensive fragrance wafting over.
Apart from me and her, there are eight other
women—all ranging from their mid-twenties to their
forties, all of them miserable looking. Or maybe
that's just reflection, and I'm only seeing what I
want to see.

Most of them are dressed in casual clothes, except
for the one behind me. She's wearing a short dress
and high heels—I glimpsed at her attire when she
asked the driver to stop several times. Something
about her having a weak bladder. She's the reason
we're late. In fact, very late, which has diminished
my hope of figuring out how to file a complaint
immediately upon our arrival.

I barely give her another glance as my attention

focuses back on the scenery outside the window.

"To be honest, I still have no idea," I mumble more to myself than to her.

That's half the truth.

Theoretically, I know what I did was wrong when the judge court-ordered me to this place.

Theoretically, too, I know they were all exaggerating when they claimed I broke into Bruce's home. What I did was most certainly *not* breaking and entering.

I lift my hand to the glass and draw an invisible heart, my mind wandering back to the person who's responsible for this.

"I don't belong here," I find myself whispering. "It's all a big misunderstanding."

"That's what everyone says before they hit rock bottom." She lets out a knowing laugh a moment before she slides into the empty seat beside me. A pale hand moves past me, hovering in mid-air. "I'm Sylvie, by the way. Sylvie Holton."

I shake her hand. "Just Vicky."

"This place is going to be amazing," the girl continues, oblivious to my wish to be left alone.

"How do you know?" I narrow my eyes to regard her closer. Her long, blonde hair looks like a cascade of bright sunshine over her naked shoulders. Her eyes, blue and wide, are staring at me, full of curiosity and something else: knowledge.

As though she's been here before.

"I just know." She lets out a laugh, and I instantly know she's one of those people who seem to laugh and smile all the time. I've always admired optimists and their ability to see the positive in the aftermath of drama. That's a skill I haven't mastered yet. "That, and my research has dug up a few things."

"Yeah?" I pull up my brows in interest.

"Yeah," she replies matter-of-factly.

My curiosity is piqued. "What did you found out?"

"For starters, they've just reopened some of the historical centers," she says with a soft smile, like that's supposed to tell me something. "This place actually gets a lot of tourist attraction, but since there are going to be renovations in the next few weeks, the place will be closed to the public before summer, which is why they've turned one of the historical buildings into a temporary rehab center." The words pour out of her like a waterfall. Jesus. She can talk fast without breathing. I can barely keep up with her.

"Good for us," she continues. "I've always wanted to have a whole island to myself." Her eyes light up.

I don't think the renovations plan was included with the info leaflet they sent me as a means of making it look like I had a choice in coming here. And I sure didn't take it upon myself to find out much about the place after the hearing.

My eyes narrow as I give her a critical glance. Her eyes are framed by heavy eyeliner. She's wearing fake eyelashes. Her whole posture is relaxed. Too relaxed for someone who is about to enter this kind of facility. She's styled as though she's about to join a party. She wears expensive designer shoes. And isn't she the one with tons of bags? The driver could barely cram them inside.

Maybe she's one of the counselors?

"Are you about to start working here?" I ask, unable to control the sudden mistrust seeping into my voice.

"I wish." She lets out a hearty laugh. "But no, I'm here to get therapy." She eyes me, amused. "Like you."

I cringe at the word.

She says it like it's not a big deal.

I give a sigh, curiosity rising within me.

"You don't seem too bothered by this," I state. "What are you in here for?

"I came of my own free will."

"Right." It makes so much sense, and yet it doesn't. "I didn't know that was even possible." I draw my eyebrows up in surprise, then give a short nod. "Well, good for you. So, you can leave anytime, right?"

"Yeah, but who would do that?"

"Yeah, who would do that?" I make a face. How anyone could choose to stay of their own will is beyond me.

"Do you know where you'll be placed?"

"No idea. And right now, I'm not sure I want to know." I shrug and turn my head back to the window, eyeing the unknown territory and ignoring the pangs of desperation washing over me.

I wish they had let me keep my phone.

The very phone I had to hand in before we boarded the bus from New York to North Carolina. The only thing that would have kept me connected to the world, my real world. Now it's gone, a figment of my past. Gone along with pictures of Bruce. His texts. The possibility of checking his updates on Facebook to see if he's online and what he's up to.

Bruce.

My heart slams against my ribcage.

If only I could get in touch with him.

Oh, wait.

A thought hits me.

If Sylvie can leave anytime, maybe she'll send a secret message to Bruce for me. Maybe she'll become a sort of messenger. I'll ask for nothing major. Just to know if he's okay and that he's received the long text I sent right before they confiscated my phone.

The thought makes me giddy with excitement.

"Sylvie, right?" I ask to be sure I got the name right, which earns me a small nod. "You said you could leave anytime?"

"Yeah," she replies and adds quickly, "I hope they'll place us together in the same group so we can support each other."

"That would be great," I say with a sudden rush of excitement. "It would be a lot of fun if we could get to know this place together and help each other out."

For example, by texting certain people, which I don't mention just yet.

"I'm not sure we can roam freely, what with the renovations under way," she says thoughtfully.

"Of course." I nod my head. "But maybe they'll make an exception to ensure we're not bored to death."

She lets out a loud, hearty laugh that has everyone turning their heads toward us, and I can't help but realize I like her. Maybe we'll be friends.

It wouldn't be so bad to have an ally in a place like this, especially when my new friend is going to help bring Bruce and me together.

"I doubt that's even possible. My job is already boring as shit," Sylvie says. "I'm a business strategist. You?"

My stomach relaxes before tightening into knots again. "I'm a nurse..."

That's how I met him, I want to tell her.

Bruce.

He was visiting his elderly gran after New Year's Eve, and she introduced me to him. A few weeks later, I ran into him again at Starbucks, and he invited me for coffee.

God, I miss him.

I can't wait for the whole thing to be over and get back to my old life.

"Look." Sylvie moves her arm past me and points a long index finger to the window. "We're here."

I follow her line of vision. As I make out the shapes, my smile dies on my lips and my frown deepens.

Ahead of us is a white building. It's expensive and big. And frigging ancient.

It must be at least two hundred years old. At least from the look of it.

Please let it not be *it*.

Please.

I shudder at the thought of sleeping in an old bed. It's an irrational fear I have. Like the fear of never meeting someone who'll love me and want to grow old together. Or ending up all alone with only a couple of cats as company. Nothing against cats. I love them, but let's face it, they're not always exciting company.

It's the same fear—the fear of losing someone—that got me in trouble with the judge. In my humble opinion, it's nothing that reading a self-help book couldn't solve.

They didn't have to send me to rehab.

There, I just said it.

It's an ugly word.

Rehab.

I associate it with needle marks on arms, yellow-stained faces, and moody alcoholics. To be honest, I'm sure being branded a love addict isn't worse. It's not like I follow Bruce everywhere and have to know what he is doing every *minute* of the day.

It's simply enough if I know what he's doing every day.

3

Vicky

IF I AM BEING honest, I know that sneaking into Bruce's home was wrong. But in my defense, I had a very good reason. One that comes in the form of a six-foot-tall, ice hockey player who has a crazy ex and a smile to die for.

When he didn't reply to my messages, I seriously thought he had gone missing and that I'd be doing him a favor by tracking him down. For all I knew, his ex might have killed him and buried him in her backyard. He had told me on several occasions that she was jealous of him dating me, so much so that she even slashed his tires and set his sports equipment on fire.

The judge showed no understanding for any of my reasons.

Zero. Zip. Nada.

She went completely overboard when she called my behavior sort of stalk-ish and even had the nerve to tell me that I was addicted. The thought that my love for Bruce had turned into an obsession was so absurd, I laughed in her face, which did not amuse her.

But can you blame me?

Addicted to love?

I snort, which earns me a curious glance from the blonde sitting in front of me.

People are addicted to books. They're addicted to caffeine. To alcohol or drugs. But to love? Sweet, tender love?

How can someone love too much?

But apparently when you violate your restraining orders three times, they have no sense of humor. It wasn't even my fault. The first two times, *he* texted me and wanted to hook up while continuing to keep our relationship a secret. The third time...I thought I was doing him a favor by protecting him from his crazy ex.

If you were to ask me why I went to such great lengths to violate my restraining order knowing that I would get in trouble, I would answer:

1) I love him.
2) He needs me.
3) We belong together even though "forces are standing against us."

The last two points were his words, not mine, right before he broke up with me.

He even defined our love as "star-crossed" and claimed he'd be with me if "the circumstances were ideal."

Point is: I'm not planning on letting a stupid therapy center ruin what we have.

I stare out of the window. At least it's not cold out here, and the world hasn't ended.

Located off the northeast coast of North Carolina, this place is still near land. About four hundred years ago, a colony got lost and settled here. Even now, no one knows what happened, but it's all very tragic and mysterious. It's as if Roanoke Island is some kind of undiscovered Bermuda Triangle no one knows about. Roads are not marked well, and from what I hear from the driver, the GPS is spotty, at best.

Sure, I'm going to miss my phone.

All right, I have a confession to make.

Maybe I do have a bit of stalking tendencies. Maybe thoughts about Bruce have been consuming me lately. And maybe I do think of him all the time. But I'm sure I don't need therapy to control "those urges," which make me wonder all kinds of things such as whether he's thinking of me.

To me, it's all-the-more proof that I love him.

As we near the building, the chatter around us increases in volume. At last, the bus halts and a woman holding a microphone in her hand gets up. Her hair, dyed a scarlet red, makes it hard to guess her age. I realize it's the same woman who took my papers when I boarded the bus. She must have traveled with us.

"Ladies and gentlemen," she starts, and I bite on the inside of my cheek. There are no men on the bus, so I assume it's one of the many standardized speeches she is going to hold. "Welcome to the LAA Center."

She pauses for effect.

It works.

Everyone is sitting so still you could drop a pin and hear it.

"This is going to be your sanctuary for the next few weeks. It's a place where we don't judge you. A place that will offer you redemption. With the help of the finest psychologists and renowned... blah...blah...blah."

My mind trails off.

I'm far away mentally, thinking of Bruce.

What's he doing right now?

I hope he isn't back with his ex. I'm pretty sure she's the one responsible for my restraining order...she and Bruce's mom.

I've barely caught fragments of the woman's long talk when people stand, and I follow suit. Everyone seems excited, like they're about to go on a trip to the Bahamas.

Everyone but me.

In my opinion, they're crazy, not me.

I don't belong here, and I can't wait to get the hell out.

Stepping out of the bus, I inhale the humid scent of the earth and the wind ruffling the leaves.

The air is crisp. Clear. It does nothing to improve my opinion of this place.

Holding my handbag in one hand, I drag my suitcase behind me, which I packed lightly because I'm convinced I'm not going to stay for long. The crowd seems to know what to do, so I trudge behind, up the broad path that snakes all the way to what looks like a mansion from the late nineteenth century. I'm not particularly into architecture, but even I can't deny that this place is both scary and imposing.

The large, wooden doors open into a huge reception area.

I stop to stare.

My first impression wasn't wrong.

Even though the building is very old, the architectural design still looks intact, but the walls smell of paint.

There is hope that we haven't entered the nineteenth century yet. Maybe the furnishings aren't that old either.

Like a mattress or bed, for example.

Or else I'll be forced to sleep on the floor. Because there's no way I'll sleep on a mattress that's absorbed the sweat of a hundred other people.

The redhead has stepped on a small podium in the entrance hall, from where she seems hell bent on continuing her speech, her hand extending toward the rows of brown boxes stacked on a long table.

"Please grab a welcome package," she says. "It contains all the information you'll need as well as your therapy plan. We're giving you the day to explore and acquaint yourself with the premises, so there won't be any lessons. You're expected to drop by your appointed counselor tomorrow at ten a.m. sharp. I wish you all a good time and hope to see everyone again."

She *hopes*?

What does she think might happen? That we steal the bus and drive back wherever we came from?

On second thought, that isn't such a bad idea.

A soft tug on my shoulder catches my attention. It's Sylvie again.

"Are you okay?" she asks, her perfectly shaped eyebrows slightly raised. Her hand is clutching a thick folder, and I realize I was so engrossed in my thoughts that I didn't even notice people are busying themselves with picking up their itinerary.

I shrug. "Yeah. Why?"

"You seem kind of zoned out." She eyes me, amused. "You're not scheming to break out already, are you?"

My face seems to catch fire. God, I'm such a bad liar that I don't even try to answer that one. "I'm just tired."

"Good," she says. "Because I would strongly advise against it."

"Out of curiosity, why?"

She shoots me a warning look and lowers her voice conspiratorially, which I'm pretty sure isn't necessary. "I've heard people who aren't complying are sent abroad to a mental institution. Compared to what's going on over there, this is Heaven."

She pauses for effect. I don't want to point out the obvious—that since it's all hearsay, she can't know whether people are being sent abroad. And even if they were, maybe that place isn't worse than this one.

"Yeah." She pats my arm knowingly, misinterpreting my silence for dread. "It sounds awful, I know. Besides, I would hate to see you leaving so soon. We have to work in teams, and I think we'll be a perfect match."

"Don't worry about me. I wasn't going to run," I say, my already bad mood plummeting further. "I'm looking forward to joining the cult."

She lets out a laugh. "It's not that bad." Her gaze moves to my empty hands, lingering there. "So, where are you staying?"

"No idea. Time to find out." As I walk over to the table to find my folder, Sylvie follows closely behind. She's basically breathing down my neck. I find the one that says "Vicky" and rip off the envelope that's glued to the box.

Anticipation and fear intermingle as I begin to read.

"Apartment 2B." I scan the text quickly to absorb as much information as I can. "You?"

"Apartment 4C," she replies, her voice oozing disappointment. "I guess we're not staying in the same room after all."

She sounds so thwarted I actually feel bad for her. "Doesn't mean we can't work together."

"True." She lifts her suitcase and exhales a small sigh. "Okay. I'll see you when I see you." She hesitates, as though there's more she'd like to say but then decides otherwise. After another sigh, she walks off.

"See you in a bit," I call out after her.

Sighing, I press my folder against my chest, clutching at it as though it's my safety net. But the motion does nothing to take away the tension and the dark thoughts at being on my own in this place.

Under different circumstances, I would have asked Sylvie for her number to make sure we keep in touch. I guess she would have done the same.

But these aren't ordinary circumstances.

I'm here because my emotions aren't what people would call "ordinary love" either.

According to the judge, who court-ordered the therapy, I need to be here to learn how to stop my "obsessive compulsive stalking disorder."

I'm going to prove to her that I don't need this BS.

My love for Bruce is real.

It really is—even if people don't understand the depth of my emotions.

Why can't they just see it? I'm Juliet to Romeo. Elizabeth to Fitzwilliam.

Maybe Bruce and I are star-crossed lovers after all, but I know that what I'm feeling is real. And there is no way that I'm going to let them pierce their invisible daggers into my heart and tell me what I can or cannot feel.

I won't let some idiot with a medical certificate declare that I'm addicted to love.

***

The building boasts a total of twenty apartments and plenty of space.

According to the leaflet, this used to be a popular attraction with visitors before it was remodeled to fit the needs of the acclaimed LAA Center.

My new home is situated in the west wing on the

second floor. I find the key in my box and unlock the door, silently praying that my new roommate is going to be as easygoing as Sylvie. The last thing I need is someone who's difficult to live with.

I close the door behind me with my foot and then drop the box onto the table in the hall, next to a beautiful arrangement of flowers.

The apartment is much smaller than I expected, but it's clean and the furniture looks fairly new. I kick off my shoes and squeeze out of my jacket, ready to explore the place.

It's seriously not as bad as I thought.

The living room is dominated by a cream, leather couch that's covered with pillows. There's no TV, but a bookcase filled to the brim with classics adorns one of the walls, and there's even a leather reading chair strategically placed next to a floor-to-ceiling window overlooking the woods outside. I plop down to test it and sigh with delight as I realize this is going to be my favorite place. I know I'll spend hours in this chair, immersed in a book, or maybe even daydreaming about a time when Bruce and I will have overcome all obstacles and finally be together.

Reluctantly, I eventually get up to inspect the rest of the apartment.

According to the brochure, the adjacent room is

my bedroom—small, smelling of fresh linen and yet another flower arrangement. Walking along the hallway, I enter the kitchen, which is barely larger than a cupboard.

Out of curiosity, I open the fridge and find it stocked with fruit, flavored water, low-fat yogurt—all fresh produce and other healthy stuff, but nothing microwavable and no ready meals.

Too bad I can't cook. However, I would definitely learn if it helped me get Bruce back.

I grab a bottle of flavored water and lean my head against the fridge, closing my eyes for a few seconds.

My heart pounds hard at the thought of Bruce.

What is he doing right now?

Does he regret the situation I'm in?

He went to great lengths to keep our relationship secret from his rich family when he could have given up on us and taken an easier path—go for someone his family would have approved of. That, in itself, is all the proof I need that Bruce's feelings for me are indeed real.

He might not be a man of many words, but a woman's gut feeling is never wrong.

You just have to look at a guy's body language.

And facts. Like the fact that he invited me over, even after ending things with me, giving the excuse that he's afraid of getting hurt. While I might not understand his motivations, I do believe his proclamation that someday we'll have a future together.

As I return from the kitchen, I get confused in the hallway. There are so many doors, I can't remember which one is my bedroom. I know I should be knocking and yet I find myself trying each handle.

All are locked.

I continue down the hallway and try the handle of the last one.

It's unlocked. I push it open.

My heart drops.

A scream escapes my chest.

My feet are frozen to the spot.

This isn't my bedroom.

The person standing before me doesn't look female.

It's a guy.

A hot guy with his pants gathered in a heap at his feet.

4

Vicky

"FUCKING HELL," I MUTTER, frozen to the spot.

The guy in front of me is standing in front of a mirror, his naked ass on full display.

His back is rippled with muscles; his chest is broad, and even from my sideways position in the doorway, I can see the well-defined six-pack beneath the taut skin.

My gaze skims over his broad biceps and lingers on the tattoo on the back of his neck. It looks like a snake engrossed in a battle with a lion. It's powerful and fascinating in a scary kind of way. As though he's one or the other and fighting his demons that are about to come to life.

His back is sexy as hell, but I think the most beautiful part of him is his ass. It looks like it's been carved out of marble.

Oh, wait.

My eyes widen and my jaw drops open as I realize what he's doing.

His hand is on his dick. There is no denying it. You can see his hard-on, the veins on his shaft, the slow movement as his hand goes back and forth.

Oh. My. God.

He's jerking off, his face drawn in concentration. The shock at the picture before me is short but intense.

But there's more than shock.

A wave of heat travels down my abdomen and settles between my legs. I can feel myself vibrating down there, my lady parts clenching and unclenching with sudden want.

It's not like I haven't seen a dick before. It's the mixture of it all—his dark hair, muscular body, and the fact that he seems to be enjoying himself way too much—that's turning my insides into jelly, and I don't like it one bit.

He must not have heard me because he neither

turns his head, nor does he stop stroking himself.

"Jesus. Get a frigging room," I call out, my voice a little too breathy.

His hand freezes in its movement. He turns around and shoots me an unfazed smile. "I'm taking care of basic needs here, if you don't mind."

His gaze meets mine, and my breath catches in my throat. His eyes, a dark shade of brown, are hooded, giving me the kind of bedroom look that screams he's not in the least ashamed of having been found jerking off.

For a second, I think I see surprise on his face, but the fleeting impression is gone before I can fully grasp it.

His brows shoot up as his eyes pierce through me, shimmering with challenge. "Want to join in, or why else are you still staring?"

Heat rushes to my face.

Jerk.

"Why would you think I'd—" My voice breaks as utter humiliation and blinding rage render me speechless.

I peer from his eyes to his cock. His hand is still wrapped around it. Instead of deflating, I think it's just gotten even bigger, the veins pronounced, the crown glimmering with moisture.

The temperature's just increased tenfold.

Either that, or a complete stranger has just made me lose it.

Peeling my gaze away from him, albeit unwillingly, I cover my eyes with my hand to block the image of his glorious cock. "Who says something like that to a stranger?"

His raucous laughter rings behind me as I slam the door shut and press my back against it, taking slow, labored breaths.

Okay, Sullivan.

This so did not happen.

"Jesus." I rub my eyes hard, as though to wipe away the image of his naked body, but that's not possible.

The harder I try, the clearer I can see his huge dick in his hand. Who has a dick like that? Thick, engorged, and oh, so wet.

The slick sound of his hand moving up and down rings in my ears. Was it as loud before? Or has he just resumed his action?

Pressing my ear against the door, I hold my breath and think I can hear his hard breathing.

God, those low, deep moans are sexy.

I move back down the hall, focused on getting away as fast as possible, and open another door by accident.

It's a bedroom with clothes scattered across the bed.

Men's clothes.

Men's shoes litter the floor.

The scent of aftershave lingers in the air.

"Changed your mind after all?" The voice is deep and husky. For a moment, I'm immobilized as he continues, "I think bedrooms are a bit overrated, but what the hell? If that's your thing, I'm up for it."

It's the same guy.

I turn to face him, my gaze strangely drawn south, and find that a thin towel is wrapped around his hips, covering his junk.

I let out an exasperated snort.

It's really tiny. The towel, that is.

Not his tool.

That one's about the biggest I've ever seen, counting TV and Internet pop-ups.

I don't want to gawk, and yet I find my gaze glued to the clearly defined bulge beneath that towel.

In the bright light spilling in through the large bay windows, I can see everything. There's no denying he still has a raging erection, as though pleasuring himself wasn't nearly enough to still his sexual appetite.

"Seriously?" I ask, pointing to the towel. "Can't you put something on?" My voice sounds strangled, breathy, which I attribute to the fact that I'm highly uncomfortable standing in front of a hot guy built like a Greek god and hung like a donkey.

"What's so important that you had to interrupt?"

"I interrupted?" My jaw drops, and white hot flashes of anger begin to cloud my vision. "Oh, you're talking about your date with your right hand. Sorry about that." I smirk. "What are you doing here?"

His brows shoot up. "Here?"

"Yes, here, in my apartment."

Ignoring my question, he squeezes past me, his erection coming dangerously close to my abdomen. From up close, he smells of sandalwood and raw manliness.

My breath catches in my throat.

It takes all my willpower not to jump a few steps back to put some distance between us.

He retrieves another white towel from his suitcase and wipes his face with it.

Every fiber of my body is heating up at the sight of his naked back. Bruce is tall and a bit skinny. This guy is built like a boxer: tall with broad shoulders and hard muscles in places I didn't know existed.

As he turns to regard me, I notice the color of his eyes.

Deep brown and broody with long, dark lashes.

They're the sort of eyes that make you feel like you're the only woman in his world.

It's a pity I didn't get the chance to watch him finish the act earlier.

Why would I think something like that?

I can feel my cheeks burning. I wouldn't be surprised to find that my face has just turned a similar shade to our counselor's hair color.

The guy steps in front of me, eyeing me with curiosity. He's standing too close for comfort, sucking the oxygen right out of the air. "What makes you think this is your apartment?" His voice is low and nonchalant, as though we're sitting in a café engaged in small talk about the weather. No sign of nervousness at all that he's just exposed himself to a stranger.

"The form in my folder says so."

"The form?" The corners of his lips twitch. "What does it say?"

"2B." I scan the room again, suddenly uncertain. "What apartment is this?"

"2B." He frowns, but for some reason I think I see amusement in his eyes. "Clearly a mistake."

"No doubt." I stare him down. "Why don't you start packing up again? Because I'm pretty sure this is my place."

"Is that so?" He crosses his arms over his imposing chest. I try not to stare at his bulging biceps, but it's hard. "I'm not leaving."

My anger flares. "This is my apartment. You've made a mistake."

"I assure you I haven't. I've been here since this morning. Even had a counselor stop by to ensure I was comfortable." His lips twitch again. I don't know why his statement sounds dirty, but this isn't the time to probe.

My eyes widen and my legs begin to shake just a little bit. "Are you saying you're staying here?"

"Yes, that's what I'm saying." He cocks his head to the side. "I assume you're the love addict who's going to be my roommate? My counselor told me a little bit about you."

Love addict?

I open my mouth, but no sound comes out.

In all honesty, what could I possibly reply?

The fact that he's just called me a love addict is too much.

Turning around, I bolt down the hallway as quickly as I can, then grab my luggage and head for the elevator.

It has to be a mistake.

It has to be a fatal mistake. There's no way anyone would shack me up with a guy.

I *can't* live with another guy, not even for therapy purposes.

My heart belongs to Bruce only. He's the first man I'll ever move in with.

Bruce with his dark brown eyes and soft smile.

Bruce who loves me and would never be such a jerk to me.

5

Vicky

IT FEELS AS THOUGH it takes me forever to reach the reception area, and twice as long to find my way back to the redhead who's engrossed in small talk with a group of new arrivals.

As I wait for her to acknowledge my presence, I make out her name:

Marlene Elijah.

"Excuse me?"

She turns her head away from the group and for a moment, confusion crosses her face.

She has no idea who I am.

"We met ten minutes ago," I say to refresh her memory. Her face remains blank. The woman's clearly overworked. Either that, or her facial recognition abilities suck. "I think you guys made a mistake. I'm supposed to share my apartment with a girl, but there's a guy in there."

Her frown deepens as she regards me. I can almost see her brain trying to place me. "What's your apartment number?"

"2B."

"And you are?"

"Vicky Sullivan."

Her manicured finger trails down the names on her list and begins to tap against one row at the bottom of the page. After a short pause, she glances up with a smile.

"Not a mistake, I'm afraid. Your roommate is Kaiden Wright."

I stare at her, completely dumbfounded. She can't have said what I think she just said. Someone made a mistake somewhere. After all, this is the LAA Center.

Hello?

The Love Addicts Anonymous Center.

"But..." I shake my head. "I'm supposed to be here to get help."

For...

There, I can't even say the words.

LOVE ADDICTION.

It sounds so ugly. Sickening. Like an infectious disease.

Marlene doesn't look at me full of pity or wrath. She smiles kindly, as if my supposed condition is something she's dealing with on a regular basis.

"I'm pleased to say that we've placed you in our newest therapy program." At my horrified expression, she pats my upper arm. "At first it might seem inconvenient that you've been paired with a male, but don't worry. We know what we're doing. Kade is going to be your partner. You'll make a great team."

"But he is male," I protest.

Doesn't she get the magnitude of it all?

I *can't* engage with a stranger in the kind of things Bruce and I should be experiencing, like living together and going to therapy.

This is just wrong.

"Correct." She nods her head. Her glance sweeps to the waiting group behind her, and I realize I'm about to lose her. "You're going to help each other. Isn't that great?"

It's immoral and wrong on so many levels, I can't

even begin to describe it. "Is that even allowed?"

"If you want to come out of this experience stronger and more independent, you need to triumph over your demons," she says, her smile fading a little. "Living with him is going to be a test. And yes, I realize that it may seem somewhat unheard of, but this is our newest therapy plan which, without a single doubt, is going to be very successful." She gives my hand a comforting squeeze. "Don't worry. You will receive all the support you need." She pauses for a second, as if unsure whether to throw in more information or not. Eventually, she leans forward, close enough to whisper so no one but me can hear her.

"Personally, I think it's a bit counterproductive." She smirks. "But I'm not the one who develops the therapy plans. It might help you to know that you two don't suffer from the same kind of addiction."

"Yeah?" The tension falls off a bit. "What is he here for?"

Drugs? Games? Sounds about right.

Maybe he's one of those people who work too much.

I can deal with a workaholic.

"I'm not supposed to tell, but what the hell?" Marlene laughs. "You're partners. You'll find out

70

soon enough, right?"

Now she's really made me curious.

I nod my head, impatiently waiting for her big revelation.

When nothing comes I prompt, "What is it, Marlene?"

"Kade is our newest sex addict," she says gently, as if he had an addiction to little, furry bunnies.

I stare at her, open-mouthed.

A sex addict?

What the hell have I gotten myself into?

I burst out in laughter.

A sex addiction makes so much sense. Why didn't I think of that? After all, he wasn't exactly stroking little bunnies in that bathroom. Besides, who in their right mind can't control their urge to jerk off in the knowledge that someone could barge in any minute?

"Do you have a problem with that?" Marlene asks. Her smile is gone; her tone is hard, on edge. Maybe this was all a test...which I've just failed, and she'll report back to the judge.

I might never see Bruce again.

"No." I clear my throat. "Not at all. You can rest assured that I'll do my best."

"Good. You'll find everything you need to know in your leaflet. Now, if you'll excuse me." With that, she turns her attention back to the group, dismissing me.

Heading back to my apartment, I barely notice the blonde bumping into me.

"Sorry." I look up. It takes me a second or two to remember her name.

"They placed me in the wrong apartment," Sylvie says.

"Me, too."

Her features relax a little. "No way. Are you saying that—"

"That I've been paired with a guy? Yes."

"Holy shit," she mutters, then clasps a hand over her mouth. "Have you talked to someone? Are they really okay with this?"

I nod my head. "Apparently, yes." At her mortified expression, I laugh. "But you haven't heard the best part yet."

6

Kaiden

MY GRIP ON THE razor tightens as I start to move it down the side of my face, leaving a smooth line behind. I rinse the razor under the cold water and bring it back up to my face, holding it close to my skin.

I stare at myself in the mirror, but it's not me who I see.

It's the vexed stare of my new roommate.

Damn.

It's been at least half an hour since the bathroom incident, but I'm still worked up like a goddamn teenager in heat.

My counselor mentioned her name, but I can't remember. I can't even focus on racking my brain to find that tidbit of information. All I can think about is how hot she is.

My head is pounding, and fuck, my hands are still shaking.

It's not fear that's squeezing my chest in her clutches. It's pure, raw need and anticipation, all fueled by the knowledge that I'll be seeing a lot of her.

A lot.

I'm not even sure why I'm surprised, but I am.

When I arrived two days ago, I was told that I'd be partnered up with a woman. Apparently, sex addicts are now paired with love addicts. I was told something about knowing that a girl is obsessive and clingy being a huge turn-off and usually...I would agree.

As soon as I hear the word commitment, my dick goes all limp. Limp like floppy, soft, put on your PJs and go straight under the covers because there's not going to be any action tonight, ma'am.

The only thing worse than obsessive and clingy is doing the same woman twice.

I never do twice. That's almost a relationship.

I do one hook-up per woman; strictly one hook-up only.

And lots of fucking, preferably in all kinds of shades and flavors.

I aim to please, and I aim to return the favor, but I don't do commitment. Not once; not twice. Never. The mere thought of a woman asking for my phone number causes my entire body to break out in a cold sweat.

In my opinion, there's nothing wrong with being different than the rest.

But good gracious...my new roommate is a goddamn nutcase.

And most importantly, she's hot.

If love were a cake, she would be the icing on it.

There is no denying I would fuck her in a heartbeat if the chance presented itself.

Her hair, long and curly, moved down past her breasts. Her breasts bounced as she stormed out. I could instantly tell from the way they moved that they were real. And I'm pretty sure she is a natural redhead, too. Even though I don't really have a type, redheads with their fiery temperament and milky complexions are my weakness.

Secretly, they've always been my favorite kind.

There's a fire burning inside them that can never

be stifled.

I bet she's so wild in bed she'd let me continue to fuck her even after the bed breaks, which, judging from the quality of the mattress in my bedroom, won't stand a chance once I get down and dirty.

Something tells me she isn't going to be quite as easy to get, though. She carries an air of dignity and aloofness, as if she's used to keeping guys at arm's length.

It could be my imagination though.

Could she be a nun?

I so would do one, love addict or not. Except…she can't be. She has a confidence about her that not every woman possesses.

I think of her fiery, hazel eyes and feel my cock hardening again.

Goddammit.

A door opening and closing registers in the periphery of my mind, then footsteps—light and wary.

It's *her.*

I know it with certainty because of the way my body reacts. Every muscle tenses and my heart begins to pump more blood directly to my crotch.

Maybe she's changed her mind and is about to ask for a little merry welcome party in my bedroom.

The possibility gets me excited, makes me realize maybe this place isn't as bad as I initially thought.

The footsteps stop in front of my door. There's a slight pause, as if she's hesitating, plucking up the courage.

Finally, a knock—strong for a woman her size.

With a grin, I jump up, but as I open the door, I know with certainty that our little party will never happen.

The surprise is short, but it wipes my grin right off my face.

Fuck, the angry frown on her face makes her even more beautiful. She doesn't turn her head away. She doesn't glance at my dick or at my chest, two of my best features. Her eyes are focused solely on mine—penetrating and intense, and a hell of a lot challenging.

"Can you please, for the love of God, put something on?" she says with disdain, as if my nakedness is annoying, something to be avoided.

She even sounds bored.

"Why?"

She scowls, her gaze not leaving mine. "Because it's rude to run around naked."

I cock my head to the side, taking her in from head to toe. I cannot help but smile. "What are you?"

"What am I?"

"A nun?"

For a moment, she seems taken aback. "I'm sorry?"

"Are you a nun?"

She stares at me blankly before her brows shoot upward. "Wow. You're a jerk with a capital J. What are you going to ask me next? Whether I'm the maid? Because I bet that's the fantasy playing now right before your eyes."

I let out a snort.

She has no idea.

Really, I just can't help myself. She isn't just hot; she's funny, too. That's a sexy combination.

"Well, are you?" I prompt.

She scowls. "No, obviously."

"That's too bad." I cross my arms over my chest as I regard her with the kind of look that's melted many panties. "I've been wondering if you're—"

"A nun? Into women? Something like that?" She looks at me, her hazel eyes shimmering with anger. "Why? Because I don't like seeing you naked? Big newsflash. I'm none of those things. I'm just not impressed, that's all."

"Huh." Sounds like she'll be panting my name by the end of the week.

"Yeah." She nods her head, as though to convince herself of the ridiculous statement she's just made.

"How come?" I take in her posture, the way she glares at me. Her perfume, a blend of roses, wafts past me, and I force myself not to inhale too deeply. In fact, I'm fighting the urge not to lean over and bury my nose into her skin, then lick my way down her neck to her breasts.

"You seriously believe everyone wants to see you naked?" The annoyance is gone, replaced with disbelief.

I cross my arms over my chest, unable to stop the hint of a smile creeping over my face. "Not everyone, no. But I'm sure most want to, you included."

She lets out a snort. "Well, you're wrong, buddy. No woman with her head safely screwed on and a modicum of self-respect would want to unless she had no choice."

"I can assure you most of them plead with me to take off my clothes." I grin at her. "So, why are you here again?"

"I'm here to get treatment, just like you, even though I'm not...I'm not a..." she trails off as she waves her hand at me, "you know, I'm not like you."

The silence that follows is long and peaceful. Unlike her gaze, which is wild and doubtful and a little rebellious.

I realize she's waiting for me to say something, but I'm not going to help her out by declaring that she's not a nutcase or that she doesn't belong here.

"No, that's not what I meant. Why are you here right now, standing in front of my bedroom door?"

"I want to talk," she says.

"I'm not going to move out if that's what you're here for."

"I know. And I don't expect you to." She pauses, not returning my smile as she takes a long breath. "As strange as it may sound, apparently, we've been roomed together on purpose. So..." She trails off again, biting her lip as she eyes her hands. For a second, I can't help but wonder if she'd slap me if I sucked that lower lip of hers between my teeth. But the opportunity vanishes the moment she looks up again, her expression softer.

She really has the most beautiful eyes. Almond shaped. Framed by full lashes. Only the slightest hint of eyeliner and mascara. "Look, you can jerk off as much as you want. Honestly, I don't care what you do. But if we're to make this work—"

"Will," I cut in.

She frowns. "Huh?"

"You made it sound like there's a possibility that

we might fail. But we're not going to. We *are* living together. We *will* make it work. Just pointing out a fact."

Not least because there's no chance in Hell I'm losing my chair on the company board.

Her features harden again; her eyes are ablaze with fury. Whatever thought's riding her, it's riding her hard. "Just be finished in ten. I'll be waiting in the living room."

Her mouth stays open as if to say more, then she closes it, but her gaze lingers on my neck. "You might want to do something about the bleeding," she says eventually.

"What?"

She spins around, slamming the door behind her.

I reach up to my neck and realize there's blood on my fingers. I must have been so engrossed in my thoughts of her that I cut myself while finishing up shaving and didn't even realize it.

Fuck.

I didn't even feel the pain.

***

Thinking back, our little conversation was kind of hot.

And she even encouraged me to finish up. At least in my mind she did when she gave me ten minutes to finish up shaving

Maybe I should listen to her and finish what I started.

My hand travels south, and I exhale a sharp breath in surprise. I'm still completely hard. Our little confrontation has turned me on. My grip tightens around my cock, but I can't bring myself to resume the action.

I'm so close to my goal—too close. After my assistant, I managed to squeeze in the neighbor right before heading for rehab.

One more conquest, and my 365-day, non-stop sex calendar is complete.

The truth hits me like a train.

Damn.

Why am I stuck with a sexy nutcase as my roommate? The rules are clear: all other patients are completely off-limits.

I even had to sign a damn admissions release that I'd abide by those rules.

Talk about callous and unfair.

But what if she hasn't signed hers yet?

The rules would be broken by only one of the parties involved in the tryst, so it would be a "glass half-full/half-empty" kind of situation.

It's a possibility, far-fetched, wild, and forbidden, but I decide I like it. Therapy is supposed to start tomorrow. What's one broken rule before treatment has started? You can't break something that she hasn't agreed to yet.

They would understand.

We've already been labeled as addicts so we're not here for the free coffee, right? We're here to get help. I bet they even *expect* us to have a relapse or two along the way to recovery.

I'm so absorbed in my own thoughts that I barely register the footsteps thudding down the hallway.

The knock on my door startles me.

"Jesus. How long does it take you to get done?" she mutters, probably thinking I can't hear her through the closed door.

More knocking, louder this time.

Good grief.

Is she trying to break down the door?

"Why the fuck can't you just give me a few moments?" I yell, trying to sound angry, but I can't help the amusement creeping into my voice.

"Your ten minutes are over."

I groan, more out of desperation than out of frustration. "Another minute."

"Don't keep me waiting."

Bossy much?

The steps retreat.

This is going to be interesting.

***

As soon as I enter the living room, her relaxed expression turns into another frown.

"What took you so long?" She scans my white robe. "Is this what you call dressed?"

"Which one do you want me to answer first?"

"Sorry?"

"You asked two questions," I explain patiently. "Which one do you want answered first?"

The slightest hint of a smile tugs at the corners of her luscious lips. "I'm just saying you should put in more effort if you're sharing your apartment with someone. Wearing proper clothing is one of those things that doesn't require much effort on anyone's part."

"What's wrong with my robe?" I glance down, my hand brushing over the white fabric.

"It's called having manners."

"Are you implying that I don't have any?" I wink. "Sweetheart, if you knew me, you wouldn't make such a statement. This is a major trade up. I'm usually naked."

"Naked?" She draws out the word. At the same time, her gaze is drawn to my lap. "Yes. I sleep naked, I cook naked, and I fuck naked, if you have to know."

"Whoa. Hold your horses." She holds up a hand to stop me from saying more and lets out another long breath. "Jeez. I knew you were a sex addict, but seriously, there's no need to go into detail."

I cringe at the way she emphasizes the last word. She makes it sound like I'm some kind of perverted fuck who fucks the entire day.

"I'm not a sex addict." The words come out more defensive than intended. Fuck, I hate how weak it makes me sound. But more than that, I'm annoyed by the fact that she just managed to make me want to justify my actions.

I shouldn't feel the need to explain my life, and yet in her presence the word "denial" springs to mind.

"That's not what I've been told," she says.

"Well, they're wrong."

Our gazes lock in a fierce battle.

She isn't afraid of making eye contact, I notice.

She isn't shy, either.

So, why doesn't she want me to touch her in all the good places, like most women do?

"What do you want?" I slump down on the couch, still eyeing her.

"A chat."

"About what?"

"About ground rules." She shrugs her shoulders. "It won't take long," she adds as she catches my alarmed glance. "Now that it's clear we're expected to share this apartment, we need to discuss how—"

"The answer is no." I jump to my feet again. "I didn't come here to be told by a woman what I can or can't do."

"But—" She leans forward and her frown deepens. "—you haven't heard me out yet."

"True. But you see, I know what women want from me, and the answer is no. Are you done?" I make a point to take a step toward the door.

To be honest, I'm enjoying myself. I enjoy winding her up.

Her face distorts into anger, just as I expected. "That's so sexist of you. You have no idea what I'll ask of you."

"Believe it or not, I do. You'll want what all other women want."

"Again, so sexist. But you're wrong."

No woman has ever called me a sexist. "What are you saying?"

"You got it all wrong," she repeats.

I take a step toward her, my gaze buried in her blazing eyes. "Let me prove that I'm right. If I make a correct guess, I want you to go out with me."

Shock crosses her features. I can see it in the way her eyes widen the moment her mind processes the meaning of my words. At last, she leans back, the shock replaced with surprise. "You want to go out with me?"

Surprise and complete disbelief.

What's so hard to believe that yes, I'd take her out to dinner and then I'd rock both the bed and her world?

"Yes," I say slowly.

She frowns. "Why?"

"To get to know you better." Among many things.

"We barely met half an hour ago."

"That's correct." I've taken out women I knew for less than ten minutes, so half an hour is pretty long for me.

She frowns again, and her confusion deepens. "I don't get it. Why would you ask me?"

"Because you'd like it." Not just dinner, but everything else I have to offer.

"You don't know me well enough to say that I'd like it or *you*." She bites down on her lip. "I honestly don't know why you'd ask me. Besides, there's nowhere to go, really. If you're familiar with the renovation plans, you surely know that everything within a mile is closed."

My smile turns into a grin. She hasn't said no yet.

To be more precise, she's absolutely not adverse to the idea, and she doesn't seem to know about the "don't fuck other patients" rule either.

"Is that the only thing you're concerned about? That I won't find a suitable place to take you out?"

"No." She leans back and flips a strand of hair out of her eyes. "I've got another one for you. How about my boyfriend's waiting for me at home."

She's playing the boyfriend card. Haven't heard this one in a while.

"A boyfriend I really love and never want to hurt," she adds, her eyes challenging me. "I appreciate the offer, though. I'm sure you mean well, but really, no, thanks, I can't."

My lips twitch. She eyes me with mistrust. "What's so funny?"

"I'm just playing with you," I say. "Even if I wanted to, we couldn't date. There are way too many rules here. Dating a fellow addict breaks a couple of them."

She frowns as she processes my words. "Rules?"

"You didn't know?" My smile widens at her alarmed expression.

"No one mentioned anything to me."

"You got a folder, right?" I gesture with my hands to outline the size of it. "Big, brown. Probably weighs more than a stack of magazines."

"Like that one?" She points her finger to the box she must have dropped near the door.

"Exactly. Pretty much like that one. Now, do yourself a favor, roomie, and have a look inside. Better yet, skip all the info and orientation leaflets and get straight to the book. Turn to page ninety and read the second paragraph, which mentions no dating, among a few other things."

She stares at me for a few moments, her eyes narrowed. "Why did you ask me out if you knew that it's against the rules?"

"I wanted to see your reaction."

"Right. You did that." She bites down on her lip. She looks kind of cute when she does it. Her teeth are white and perfect, but not in the fake veneers kind of way. It makes me want to suck her lower lip into my mouth to get a first taste of her. To feel her teeth on my skin. Press her hips against mine so she can feel that I'm getting hard for her.

"Are you sure you're not a nun?" I ask.

"Do I *look* like a nun?" Her frown is back in place.

"Maybe."

I don't know why I keep wanting to wind her up, but it sure works.

"Well, I am most certainly not." Her eyebrows raise an inch as she tilts her head. Her posture is rigid. I wonder what it would take to get her to relax. "You know you've asked me twice already? One more time and it'll make you sound kind of creepy."

I shrug my shoulders. "It was just a question. Someone told me something about a nun joining us." That's a little lie, one I want her to believe.

"Well, it's not me."

"Clearly," I say. "So, if you're not a nun, what is it that you do when you're not in rehab?

There is a short pause before she replies, "I'm a nurse."

My heart skips a beat.

I've never done a nurse. Or, have I? No, I don't think so.

The realization hits me like a soft, relaxing breeze. I *knew* there was going to be some benefit to visiting this place.

"A nurse?" I can barely control the enthusiasm

seeping into my tone.

"Yes." She draws out the word.

"Cool." I lean back, eyeing her. "Must be interesting to see lots of naked people."

"I don't, really. I work in a nursing home." For the first time, I can see a hint of a smile on her face. "Bet that's not your kind."

"I don't have a kind."

"Right." Her gaze moves away from me as she begins to play with something in her hand.

It's a Darth Vader keychain.

"Nice accessory," I say pointing to her hand. "Can I see it?"

She hesitates for a moment before she stretches out her hand, long enough to let me get a better look, but not close enough to let me touch it.

"It was a gift from my little brother," she says almost apologetically and pulls back again.

"He has great taste."

"He's nine."

She offers me a soft, almost apologetic smile. Her hand brushes over the length of her skirt. It's impatience, I assume, but I can't be sure.

She's unlike any other woman I've met before—cagey, almost hostile.

Judging from her posture—all rigid, her gaze

glued to the rug beneath our feet, her perfect teeth gently chewing on that full lower lip of hers—I can sense there's something she wants to say but doesn't know how to say it without sounding rude.

"What?" I prompt.

She looks up, and her eyes meet mine again. "Are you really a sex addict?"

"Why are you asking?" I cock my head to the side. "Is it because I asked you out? You know it was a joke, right? Something that people laugh about and don't take seriously."

"I know. It's just..." She takes a deep breath and waves her hand, looking for words. "In spite of your obvious preference to run around naked, you don't look like a sex addict to me."

"You don't look like a love addict, either, and yet here you are, stuck in this place with me."

She nods her head. "Fair enough."

I regard her amused. "Out of interest, what do you think a sex addict should look like?"

She shrugs. "Bald. In his forties, I guess. Maybe someone with a few divorces behind him, because no woman is good enough for him so he feels unloved and has channeled that emptiness into his sex life. Definitely someone older than you."

"You seem to have a very clear picture of a sex

addict. Who's judgmental now?" I grin at her. "To answer your question, you don't have to worry that I'll come running to your bedroom door in the middle of the night and force myself on you. I'm not that kind of guy."

She looks embarrassed at my insinuation. "I wasn't worried about that."

"Good," I say. "But just so you know, I'm not a sex addict. People keep insisting that I am, but I'm not. Honestly, I'm not."

"Why do they insist that you are, then?"

"I don't know," I say. "Honestly, it's not an addiction if I love what I do. I could stop whenever I wanted, but why would I want to?"

"That makes sense." Laughter erupts from her throat. And, wow. She really has the most beautiful laughter. Pearly, infectious, coming from the heart. Everything about her seems real, unlike all the fake women back home who are after my money.

"You're good." She laughs again before growing silent. "Look, honestly, I don't really care what you are or what you do. You could have slept with half of the female population in the world, and I wouldn't care. I want to go home, meaning all I care about is getting this whole thing over and done with. The only reason I wanted to talk is to ask you not to clog the sink with hair and not—" she points at my crotch "—don't touch my things, not my food, not my private stuff, and particularly not after you've touched *yourself*."

Why does her reference to me jerking off make her sound so damn hot?

Ignoring the sudden stirring in my crotch, I grant her an innocent smile. "That's all?"

"I think so. I'm not looking to hook up with anyone. I'm not interested in getting into more trouble than I'm already in."

"Done deal, roomie."

There is a short, heavy silence.

She opens her mouth, then closes it again, surprise apparent in her face. "You're fine with it? No arguing? No questions? No complaints? Just like that? Because you said—"

"I know what I said, and the answer's yes."

She leans back, all tension gone, but I can feel the waves of suspicion wafting from her. "Why?"

"What do you mean 'why'?" I frown in mock annoyance. "Can't your roommate be friendly with you and agree to your rules for the sake of building a good relationship?"

"Wow. You're serious then?"

"Absolutely. Now, talking to me wasn't so hard,

was it?"

"No, it wasn't." Her skirt rides up a few inches as she crosses her leg. The way she's leaned back gives me a good view of her breasts straining against the thin fabric of her top. God, it's hard not to stare at them and imagine all sorts of things I could do to her naked body.

"It's all settled then," she continues, completely oblivious to the thoughts I'm harboring this instant. "You stay on your side, and I'll stay on mine. And if you could slip into something less discomforting," she breaks off as she catches my face, then adds quickly, "or not. That's totally fine, too."

"You're really pushing your luck, you know that?" I say, amused. "But alright, if it helps you feel more at ease around me, I'll slip into something 'less discomforting.' Even though I've got to say, I still don't get what's wrong with it." I consider getting up, then decide against it. For one, I'd rather be in her company than in the confines of my bedroom, unsure what to do with myself outside of my office. And then there's the tiny inconvenience in my pants. I don't think she'd appreciate seeing another hard-on—at least, not quite yet.

"It's called having manners."

"You keep mentioning that." I wink. "Let's not go

there again."

"I don't know a lot about you." She shrugs. "So, obviously, I wouldn't know if you had any or not."

"Then let's change that, shall we?" I stretch out my hand over the table. "My name's Kaiden Wright, but you may call me Kade. Obviously, I'm your new roommate."

"Victoria Sullivan. Usually no nickname, but you can call me Vicky." She takes my hand and gives it a firm shake. "Nice to meet you."

"Likewise, Vicky."

I let her name roll off my tongue, realizing that it's both sweet and innocent, and somehow fits her perfectly.

In spite of her firm grip, her hand feels soft inside mine. I marvel at the way it fits like it was made to feel perfect against my skin. She looks into my eyes, and for a moment I think I can see a sparkle that wasn't there before. Her lips part, and her gaze lowers to my mouth the way it does when women have their own naughty thoughts about me and think they're being discreet about it.

I would have held on much longer if she didn't let go.

As she settles back against the sofa, her eyes grow distant. It must be something I said or did. I comb my memory to find the thing that's turned her distant again.

And then it hits me.

It's not me. It's about someone else.

I watch her start playing with the keychain again. "He must be pretty special if you don't want to upset him."

Vicky looks up, her irises widening, surprise written on her face. "How did you guess?"

I shrug my shoulders. "Judging from the fact that this is not exactly a vacation, it was either that you're recovering from a bad relationship or that you're here to get rid of him. Call it a wild guess, but I don't think it's the latter."

"He has nothing to do with it." She wets her lips, and for the first time I see nervousness and something else—vulnerability—flicker across her face.

I wouldn't usually pursue the issue, but with her it's different. It's partly entertaining, partly interesting, and partly, to my surprise, I find that I care somehow.

"You're not here because of him?" I ask.

"I'm here because I violated my restraining order that ordered me to keep away from him."

I lean back. It's my turn to be stunned. I never

expected her to be so frank.

"I take it you're a professional stalker?"

She lets out a fake laugh. "I'm anything but that." Her laugh grows silent, the words soft. "It's all a big misunderstanding. That's all it is."

My body tenses at the way she says the words. As if she's grown tired of having to repeat them over and over again. Vulnerability stains her voice, her stance, even the air surrounding her.

It makes me want to touch her, to hold her hand in mine and make her laugh again, which is absurd. I'm not someone who likes to comfort. Heck, I usually don't give a damn.

Her hands brush over her skirt, and then she gets up. "I should get going."

I rise with her. "Want me to help you find your way around?"

"I don't think that's necessary, but thanks." She offers me a weak smile.

"You sure?"

"Yeah. Definitely."

"Your room is—"

"—the first door down the hall. I know," Vicky says, interrupting me.

"That's correct. I took the bigger room, seeing that I arrived first. First-come, first-served, dibs, and all that." I offer her a smile, but she doesn't return it.

"I don't mind. I prefer the smaller one anyway." Her gaze travels to the front of my robe.

With a soft groan, she lifts up the box. I take it out of her hands. "Come on. Let me help you."

I follow her down the hall and we reach her room. I open the door for her and step aside to let her past. She steps inside, barely giving me a second glance as she hauls her luggage into a corner. As she turns around, I pass her the box. Our hands touch again and her last words echo in my mind.

"To hell with them, Vicky," I whisper. "I believe you. If you say that it's all a misunderstanding, then that's all it is."

I don't know what just made me say that, but it feels true.

For whatever stupid reason, I believe her.

"You are?" Surprise replaces the weariness. I expect her to withdraw her hand, but she doesn't.

"Why not? I'm not the person to judge you. Right?"

My gaze meets hers again, and in that moment, something happens. I don't know what it is, except that it feels like a vault's just opened. It's deep, intense, and a hell of a lot intimate. As my eyes zoom in on her, I know she feels the same way.

We're standing near the door. She pulls back and places her hand on the handle. It's my clue to leave. I know it is, and yet I find myself glued to the spot, fighting the sudden want to stay.

She places the box onto the table and then she turns around. "Thank you."

"For what?"

She shrugs. "For making it all so easy, I guess."

I let out a chuckle. "Don't get your hopes up. I'm not doing it for you. I'm selfish and incredibly vain and really need my beauty sleep. A yelling, angry roomie wouldn't be in my best interest."

Her lips twitch. "Okay. I don't want to hold you back longer than necessary."

Turning around, I head out the door. She closes it behind me when I remember her ugly accessory. I can't leave without making a last impression.

"Hey, Stalker!"

The door opens again and her head pops out. "Yeah?"

I put on my most serious expression. "May the Force be with you!"

She frowns, confused. Finally, as my words sink in, her lips start quivering, and then a laugh erupts from her chest.

It's really addictive.

Her lips. Her eyes. Most of all, her laugh. I love people who can laugh like that. Open. Full of life.

"May the Force be with you, too, Panty-chaser."

I can feel her gaze on me as I head down the hall, realizing I like it. I like her. But most importantly, I want her.

The little, sexy nurse.

7

Vicky

Dear Jane,

This may sound silly at first, but would you say that Elizabeth is suffering from a love addiction just because she loves Mr. Darcy? I don't think so. See, my dilemma is that I'm very much in love with someone. I *know* he loves me. I *know* he wants to be with me. I *know* he's afraid of disclosing the magnitude of his feelings, which is the only reason why he's not replying to any of my messages. I also *know* I'm in rehab because his ex is trying to ruin his life.

She's trying to ruin our relationship. She and his over protective mom. Because there's no way he would do this of his own will.

But I won't let them.

As tiresome and inconvenient as it may be, I've got to say that I've reached a crossroads in my life. It's either give up or fight for us.

I'm not ready yet to give up what we have because I truly believe that we belong together. A restraining order won't stop me. People may not see what we have, they may call me crazy, but I know our connection is special. I know that if I love hard, fight hard, the reward will be great.

When darkness prevails, love remains.

I truly hope so.

Yours affectionately,
Vicky Sullivan

***

Shit.

I think I've just reached the lowest point in my life.

As I stumble out of the counselor's office into the hall, tripping over my own two feet, someone almost hits me. My stomach is churning; the urge of emptying my stomach overwhelms me. Inside my mind I know that I'm in denial, and yet I can't quite grasp the meaning of it all as her words keep coming at me like an echo.

"You need to accept that your feelings for Bruce are unhealthy."

Unhealthy.

That's what my counselor said when I mentioned how often I think about Bruce, and I didn't even admit the full extent.

Bruce is constantly on my mind.

Like. All. The. Time.

Even now, flashes of Bruce keep circling before my eyes.

His smile. His eyes. His happiness whenever his team scores a win.

How can she, the counselor, the judge, everyone, be so wrong?

The fact that I can't see him, haven't heard from him in what feels like an eternity, is too much.

The smell of coffee hits my nose as I stumble into the canteen. There are only a few tables, but most are occupied, the unfamiliar faces as grim as mine. Without a doubt, they want to be here as much as I do.

Which is not at all.

"Hey, Vicky. Over here."

I turn in the direction of the voice calling my name and spy Sylvie waving from a corner booth on the east side. She's wearing a short dress and cowboy boots that draw attention to her long, tanned legs.

I make my way toward her.

"Coffee?" Without waiting for my answer, she pushes her cup toward me.

"No, thanks." I grimace at the strong smell.

"Not a fan?"

"It's not that." I press my fingers against my temples in a futile attempt at easing the tension inside my skull. "I'm kind of sick."

Which is an understatement.

I feel like I'm being squeezed into a can of sardines where even talking requires Herculean effort.

"How's the coffee?" I ask.

"Worth trying, I guess. But it's nothing like my usual blend back home. Or a good bottle of wine." She leans over and pats my arm conspiratorially. "You're coming straight from your counselor's office, right?"

I narrow my eyes at her. "How do you know?"

"I can tell from the way you look." She grimaces. "I had my meeting yesterday and it wasn't pleasant. I locked myself up inside my room and had a whole bottle of wine. I'm surprised you didn't have the same idea."

"They serve wine here?"

She grins. "Of course they do. We're not exactly alcoholics, are we?"

"Not yet."

"Yeah, I'm pretty sure that counselor of mine could turn me into one in no time."

I laugh, feeling the tension slowly lifting off my shoulders. "God, I wish someone had told me about this place yesterday. I would have claimed the whole bar."

"There goes my plan of keeping this little secret all to myself. I should learn to keep my big mouth shut." She joins in my laughter. "I'll get you some tea. Wait here. Don't move from the spot."

Before I can protest, Sylvie's gone. I lean back in my seat and close my eyes for a few moments. When I open them again, I take in the surroundings. The walls are painted in yellow and green tones. Pictures of early settlements adorn the walls, and there's a large grandfather clock in the far corner, its unnerving noise carrying over.

Sylvie takes her sweet time, during which more patients arrive. I scan their faces, but there's no sight of Kade.

I realize I haven't seen him since yesterday. A wave of disappointment washes over me, even though I don't understand my reaction one bit. I close my eyes again, waiting for Bruce's familiar face to flash before me. Instead, I find myself smiling as I remember my conversation with Kade.

He's so different from Bruce.

In some strange way, he reminds me of my little brother and his inability to stay serious, which can be both irritating and endearing.

"I bet they're not rated PG-13." Sylvie's voice draws me back.

I open my eyes in time to see her sliding back into her seat. On the table are two cups of tea and a bowl of fries.

"What?"

"Your thoughts. You looked all flushed and were miles away," she clarifies and pushes a cup of tea toward me. "Try this. It will make you feel better."

Judging from the color and strong smell, it's an herbal blend. I wrap my hands around the cup, warming my hands because it's too hot to drink. "You didn't have to get me anything."

"I wanted to. You're my only friend here, and there will come a day when I'll hit rock bottom and need you." She pushes the bowl with fries toward me.

"Fries at ten in the morning?"

She shrugs and pops a fry into her mouth. "They're one of a kind." She motions to the bowl again. Hesitantly, I grab one and take a bite, expecting my nausea to hit me with full force. The flavor is strong, oily with the slightest hint of chili. I swallow and realize I feel better.

"You're right. They're good," I say.

"They're the best," Sylvie agrees. "They probably serve good food so we don't want to leave."

I snort. "Like that would ever happen."

Sylvie shrugs her shoulders. "It's not that bad here, you'll see. Not when they serve fries like these.

I cock my head. "That little statement might apply to you because you're here of your own free will. Me, on the other hand—" I grimace "—not so much. I bet your counselor serves you coffee—the delicious, creamy kind."

"He actually does," she says slowly. "Why? How's yours?"

"My counselor went right for the jugular without even thinking about offering me anything first. No sign of coffee whatsoever." I stir sugar into the tea and take a tentative sip, realizing it's still too hot to drink without burning my tongue. "This new therapy plan sucks. They should set up a vote whether we want to work together with a guy, because as far as I'm aware, I should still be allowed to voice my opinion."

"I don't think this place works that way."

"No, it doesn't. But one can hope."

"Your first session was really bad, huh?" Sylvie says after a pause.

"It was. It was worse than bad," I say. "I didn't take kindly to her words, and she didn't take kindly to mine. I wouldn't be surprised to find myself kicked out."

"What happened?" Flicking her long hair back, Sylvie leans forward until I'm sure no one can hear us.

Under different circumstances, her

inquisitiveness would have annoyed me, but those aren't usual circumstances. I feel lonely. Stuck in a place that scares me. I need a friend.

And if I'm to be absolutely honest, I'm happy to have someone to talk to. Someone to conspire with, especially when said new friend will assist me with my plan of getting in touch with Bruce.

"She said my feelings weren't real," I say.

"Wow. Those were her exact words?"

"No, but I'm sure that's what she meant to say." Pausing, I take a deep breath and release it slowly, considering my words. "She said my love for my boyfriend wasn't healthy. I'm ashamed to say that I overreacted. I actually blew a gasket."

Her eyebrows shoot up, her incredulous expression inviting me to go on.

"I might have screamed a little," I say. "Actually, make that a lot. And I'm not even the screaming type."

Sylvie eyes me as I stuff another fry into my mouth. "How did she take it?"

"To be honest, she was quite composed. As if she expected such a reaction from me." I shrug my shoulders. "Her reply was that I'm in denial, which was the point where I stormed out, slamming the door behind me, and skipped my first mandatory lesson. Like I said, I wouldn't be surprised if they kicked me out."

"They won't do that because of a little disagreement," Sylvie says.

"It was a little more than that." My words come out so low for a moment I'm not even sure I spoke them. "Things were...heated. I told her that her therapy plan sucked and that she could shove it. I also might have told her that I didn't need therapy and that she might need it more than I do, among other things." My hands close around the cup. I bite my lip hard to stifle the growing sense of helplessness inside me. "I don't feel like we got along. At this point, I think I'd be better off switching counselors. Do you think they'd let me do that?"

Sylvie remains silent for a moment. "I don't think so. But hey, it's her job to help you. I'm sure she knows what she's doing."

"Maybe," I mumble. "That is, if they let me stay after my fight with her."

Which I don't even want to. But if it's the only way Bruce and I will be together again, then so be it.

"I don't think anyone's ever been kicked out." She grabs my hand over the table and squeezes it. "At this point, you need to stay positive and have faith.

Just keep your head up and see what happens. Trust that everything happens for your own good and you'll be surprised with the outcome."

"I'm trying." I look up, my eyes burning. There's a tight sensation in my chest, but the tears don't come because underneath it all I still feel angry.

Angry that nobody's getting me.

Angry that hurdle after hurdle keeps stopping me from being with Bruce.

"How come you're here of your own will?" I ask.

"That's pure coincidence." She waves her hand good-humoredly, as if she saw the question coming. "When my best friend broke up with her boyfriend, I bought her a therapy plan as a gift to help her move on from him. But they worked things out. She had no need for it, so I thought why not use it for myself?"

I laugh, my worries almost forgotten. "Why would you do that?"

"What? Getting her a therapy gift card or using it for myself?" She shrugs her shoulders. "I meant well. Obviously I was happy for them to reconcile, but it wasn't exactly cheap. Besides, I heard nothing but great things about this place. Maybe it was just curiosity. Or the fact that my love life's a mess. The truth is, I think everyone needs therapy in some way or another."

That's a strange statement.

"How so?" I lean forward, eager to hear more.

"I always seem to attract the wrong man," Sylvie says. "Every guy I go for either doesn't want to enter any sort of commitment or just not with me. There must be something wrong with me."

I stare at her. Sylvie's beautiful. With her perfect teeth and her symmetrical features, she could easily pass as a model. Her skin is tanned and glowing—the kind of complexion I've always wanted rather than my pale, freckled skin. In addition, she's tall and slender, with the kind of body you only ever see on a Victoria's Secret runway. And then there's the straight, glossy, blonde hair of hers that looks so natural it can't possibly be.

"I'm twenty-four and I can't keep a guy committed to me for long," she continues. "Last year I had a relationship with my married boss, and then I found out he lied to me. I thought he and his wife were separated, but obviously, that wasn't the case. Long story short, he fired me when she found out about the affair." She draws a long breath and shakes her head grimly. "Just so you know, I'm not a cheater. I really didn't know. Now, I'm with someone I love, but he keeps telling me he isn't ready for commitment."

Leave out the married guy account, and her story sounds so much like mine. I don't know what to tell her, so I keep quiet and wait for her to continue.

Sylvie grabs her cup, her hands clasping it. "It seems my life's dominated by patterns that keep repeating themselves over and over again. No matter what I do, I can't make it stop. So here I am with the hope of getting the bad luck that's been following me out of my system and finally settle down with someone who takes me seriously and wants the same thing." Her gaze shoots up to me, and her gloomy expression instantly lifts. "What about you? Why are you here?"

"Pretty much the same. I've been single most of my life, not because I hate dating. It's just hard to find the right guy."

Sylvie giggles as she raises her cup to her lips and takes a sip. "Come on. What's the real reason? I know you're not in for being single. No one gets therapy for that."

She doesn't look like she's going to drop the topic, and I'm not sure I want her to. Taking my sweet time, I take a sip of my tea and grimace at the bitter aftertaste it leaves in my mouth. "Well, there's this guy."

"I knew it," she shouts with a little too much enthusiasm.

"It's not really a secret." I avert my gaze from Sylvie and peer out of the window. But instead of seeing the water and the beautiful backdrop of woods, it's Bruce I see. "I think I was about five years old when I first realized that all I wanted was to get married. I want the white-picket-fence type of life. Have two kids. Grow old with someone who loves me. I know I'm not old enough to think that it'll never happen, but recently all my friends from college seem to have started to settle down. Every day I go through my mail, I seem to see a wedding invitation popping up. And did I mention that my younger sister got engaged? I feel like such a failure."

"Why?"

I bite my lip hard.

Why indeed?

"I don't know," I say slowly. "Maybe because my sister has it all. A kid, a house, a great boyfriend who will soon be her husband. For a while, I couldn't stop the feeling that I was running out of time; that I'd never find someone to fall in love with. That's when I met Bruce, and everything changed. We started to date, but then his family found out about us and he broke it off with me." I turn my head back to Sylvie and meet her questioning frown. "His mother doesn't like me."

"Doesn't surprise me at all. Protective moms can be like that."

"Yeah. Except, she wants him to get back with his ex. His ex, who I'll have to stress is rich. Her parents are friends with his, so it's all perfect."

"Well, she can't force him, can she?"

I take a breath, pausing to calm the sudden tightness in my chest. "No, she can't. But his mom is influential and has a real shot at being the next mayor."

"So?"

"So, compared to her, and his family, in general, I'm ordinary. You need to understand that his family has a long family history of politicians that spans generations. It's the reason we used to meet in secret in the first place. She wasn't supposed to find out."

"I still don't see how that landed you in here."

I nod slowly, understanding her confusion. "He never told anyone that we were dating, and I didn't know. If I had, I wouldn't have turned up at his parents' house for a surprise visit on Valentine's Day. His mom arrived early and thought I was an intruder. I tried to explain. I told her that we were dating. She called him, but he denied it." I clear my throat to get rid of the lump that seems to have cut off my air supply. "She thinks I'm someone he met in college who's still crushing on him and has been following him around."

"Wow." Sylvie looks horrified. "What a coward."

"He had a good reason for lying," I defend him quickly. "You don't know his family. They're crazy controlling. His mom and his ex demanded that he file a restraining order against me."

"So, let me get this straight. You both were dating, and yet he had a restraining order filed against you?" She sounds partly upset, which is understandable given that she doesn't know Bruce.

I know how this makes me sound. Like a weak woman.

"They forced him." My voice comes out low, choked.

"How do you know?"

"He told me." I grab the spoon and start to stir the tea furiously until some of the liquid spills onto the table. "He's apologized like a thousand times. He says he's going to tell them when the time's right."

"What's wrong with now?"

"Because, like I said, his mom is running for mayor and—" Breaking off, I turn my head away, hit by the same train of hurt, confusion, and turmoil I just can't seem to get rid of ever since that fateful day. "Officially, like whenever he's mentioned in the papers, he's still dating his ex. He told me he'd get that sorted out so I agreed to continue to see him. We met in secret. Unfortunately, his ex saw us and went straight to his mom, weaving a story about how I was still stalking Bruce. They filed another report and before I could even realize what was happening, I was told that I had broken my restraining order. But Bruce continued to want to meet up." I meet her frown. "He said he needed me and I told him I would always be there for him. It went on for a few weeks. Until...he stopped replying to my texts."

I fall silent.

My heartbeat speeds up as I recall the events that changed my life.

"I didn't know what happened. Call it my gut feeling, something felt wrong. Days passed and no reply came. Finally, after about two weeks of not hearing from him, I couldn't wait any longer, so I decided to pay him a visit, even if that meant sneaking into his parents' house, knowing that I would really be breaking my restraining order again."

"You..." Sylvie cuts me off, shaking her head.

"Yeah, I know." Grimacing, I peer down at my hand and realize I've been clutching at the cup so hard, my knuckles have turned white beneath my skin. "It was a stupid move. I don't even know what I was thinking, sneaking in through the back door. But to be honest, I may have been a bit drunk that day." I release the cup before it snaps into countless pieces and go on, ready to get the whole story out. "In my defense, it was my birthday; I was drunk, and like I said, I had this bad feeling. Besides, I didn't break in. The door was open, so...anyway, as you can probably imagine, it all went wrong. He wasn't even there that day, but his ex was, and his mom." Catching Sylvie's frown, I hurry to add, "They're friends, and his mom really likes her. They're like this huge, perfect family."

"What happened?" Sylvie asks impatiently.

"The cops arrived, and they treated me like I was a criminal." I groan inwardly, annoyed with myself for making such a bad decision when I should have known better. "It's my fault, really. I should have insisted that Bruce make our relationship official and tell them the truth. Instead, I played along. I just couldn't out him. I loved him that much. So, now I'm here, taking responsibility for my actions. Crazy, huh?"

I don't expect an answer. I don't need anyone telling me that I was a fool in love. I know that damn well.

Sylvie and I remain quiet for a few seconds. But the silence isn't uncomfortable; it's cleansing, lifting the fog that seems to have been clouding my mind for too long. She leans back, sucking in the air in a long, deep breath.

"Wow," she says. "Why would you want to be with someone who doesn't tell their family about you?" A pang of anger flashes across her face. "Sorry. I don't want to meddle in your affairs, but this...this makes me angry. You seem like a good person and he treats you like a toy he can play with. I mean, who does he think he is?"

I shrug my shoulders, feeling oddly defensive of him. "He has a good reason, I'm sure. His parents are rich. His mom's in the paper all the time. I just don't fit in. So—" I shrug again, my words eluding me.

Crap.

How can I explain it? The feeling of betrayal. The desperate need to believe his excuses. Is believing lies easier than acknowledging the truth?

I don't want to lose him—that's it. That's what keeps me trapped in a vicious cycle.

"I so want to punch that fucker. I hope you gave his ass a good kicking."

I laugh. "Actually, I didn't. I chose to forgive him."

Sylvie's mouth drops open. "No!"

"Yeah, I did," I say, shifting uncomfortably in my seat. "Right after the court order, he called me on a friend's phone, saying that the situation at home was heated and tense. And I gave him one more chance. He said he was going to sort it out and that once I'm out of here, he'll take me out."

Sylvie starts to shake her head again. "How can you do that?" She sounds so shocked, I can barely contain a laugh.

"Because I love him, silly."

I meet her eyes and see pity reflected in them. Her concern causes another lump in my throat.

"That's why you need this place." Her words sound so resolute, I almost believe them. "Sorry, that came out wrong. I didn't mean to imply that you're crazy. It's just—"

"It's fine." I take a deep breath. "I'm sure he misses me and something good will come out of this experience. I want to leave everything behind—the fear, the anguish—and start anew. I want to come out stronger. I want to prove to him that we can beat

121

this. We'll start over again, but this time everything will be different. That's what he said. That's what I choose to believe, too."

She looks at me for a long time. "You know there's nothing wrong with you, right? He's the one who should be held accountable for this mess."

I turn my head away. That's what my counselor said this morning, right before I began a shouting marathon.

"How's your roommate?" I ask.

The change in topic isn't subtle, but Sylvie bites.

"Don't get me started." She laughs.

"What's that supposed to mean?"

"He's a designer, and so playing for the other team," Sylvie says with the kind of excitement that's usually reserved for Prada warehouse sales. "When I complimented him on his work, he asked me to help him create a custom clothing line and even invited me to a runway event as a guest."

"Oh." I say, surprised. "So, he doesn't run around naked?"

The words make it out before I can stop them.

She lets out another laugh. "Hell, no." Her face lights up as realization sinks in. "Are you saying yours does?"

"Aren't they all?" I swallow. "Sex addicts, I

mean."

"No. Mine definitely doesn't take off his clothes more than is necessary." Her eyes narrow as a soft smile plays her lips. "Looks like someone's messing with you."

"He's not—"

"Well, I hope he didn't ask you out, because that would be so totally against the rules," Sylvie says.

Rules.

I forgot the rules.

As if reading my mind, Sylvie frowns. "Don't tell me you haven't read them yet?"

"I forgot, alright."

"You need to read them." She leans forward in a conspiratorial way. "My counselor told me at the end of my session that they're pretty strict about it."

"I broke off my first therapy session, so she probably didn't get the chance to remind me. Why? What's the most important rule?"

"You're not allowed to fuck your roommate. Obviously."

"Oh." Obviously.

Kade's almost naked body pops into my mind.

"Between me and you, I think it's an experiment." She drops her voice further. "You haven't slept with him, have you? Because if you have, you're both in so much trouble."

"No. God, no." I let out a noise that remotely sounds like laughter, but it comes out a bit too shrill. Heat begins to scorch my cheeks. I was so close to saying yes when he asked me out.

Too close, and I don't even know him.

"Vicky?" Sylvie's voice snaps me out of my thoughts.

I smile at her. "Don't worry about me. He's not my type," I say, my voice a bit too breathy. "Even though he's funny, easygoing, and..."

Hot.

And built like a rock star god. But he's still not my type.

Or, is he?

Shut up. Shut up.

"He's okay. Just okay. In a friends kind of way." I add quickly, "But let's say someone broke the rules, what's the worst thing that could happen? Being grounded or what?" I take another sip of my tea and almost choke on it. Now that's cold, it's way too spicy and burning my throat.

"Should you decide to break the rules, they'll transfer you abroad and the treatment will take at least twice as long. I've heard they'll even subject you to controlled visits afterwards."

"Oh."

Sounds like a load of BS to me. I mean, this is a treatment center, not exactly Guantanamo Bay.

"But you didn't sleep with him, so there's nothing to worry about," Sylvie says as she eyes my cup of tea. "Are you ready for the big tour? I bet you haven't seen the communal kitchen yet."

8

Kaiden

SHE MAY BE JUST a woman, but to me she's paradise in a place that's Hell.

For the last three days, I've fought to get into a routine while mainly doing four things: eat, sleep, attend sessions with my counselor, and work out. My thoughts, however, have been occupied by the many ways I want to have her, be inside her, stilling my thirst that stretches as deep as a canyon. Every time I pass her room, I fight the very real urge to knock down her door so I can kiss her and carry her to my bed, where she should be.

A distraction is what I need—if only to clear my mind, get rid of the thoughts that have been plaguing me day and night. Thoughts that make no sense. Usually, I'm not someone who's wasting his breath on a woman when there's no way I'm hooking up with her as long as there's a chance that I'm losing my seat on the company board. And yet here I am, fantasizing about a woman I've known less than three days.

A woman I can't even say I like.

According to my schedule, love addicts have their therapy sessions in the morning. Ours are in the afternoon.

As soon as the door to the apartment closes, I check the hall to make sure she's gone and indeed find no sign of her. Satisfied, I settle on the sofa in the living room and speed-dial the one number I know won't let me down.

Cash might not be as responsible and word-savvy as my brother, but as a club owner and my best friend, he always knows what I need: a quick pep talk.

After three rings, he picks up. His voice is heavy with sleep, as if I've just woken him up. "Kade? Is that you?"

"Who else would it be?"

"I didn't realize you'd be calling so soon. I thought you'd be busy fucking all the nurses, and *then* calling to tell me all about it."

"Yeah, I thought so, too, but life has a way of fucking up your plans when you least expect it." As I fall silent, I make out the hushed voice of a woman.

I frown.

"Do you have someone over?" Oh, wait. It's not one voice. It's two. I lean back, a wry smile on my face as I realize what I'm missing. "Am I interrupting your threesome?"

"No. To be honest, I expected your call. Give me a sec to get rid of them." Hushed voices again and steps. Eventually, the sound of a door closing and a heavy chair being moved.

"Please don't tell me your ass is back in California," Cash is back on.

I let out a laugh. "Come on, man. I may be many things, but I'm not stupid enough to lose my seat. I worked my ass off for that company. I sure as fuck won't be walking away just to chase some pussy. I'm not sure though how I feel about you having a party of three while I'm gone."

"It wasn't a party. I crashed a wedding and decided to take my dessert home."

"Two, huh?" I shake my head even though he

can't see me. "Make sure to wear a condom. Otherwise you'll soon be paying for child support. Not that you couldn't afford it."

He lets out a laugh. "So, what's up?"

"Not much. I'm good. Really good."

"Yeah?" He sounds unconvinced.

"Once I'm done here, I might be quitting my job to become a counselor." My words are rewarded with dead silence, so I continue, "My first group session was nice. Lots of handholding. Plenty of support and understanding. I've come to realize I have a lot of issues and that I haven't been the real me in a long time. My point is, having so much meaningless sex is blocking my spiritual path and yours as well. You should give rehab a try."

"Are you bullshitting me right now? There's no way you'd give up your sex life."

I let out a laugh as I imagine my best friend's shocked expression. "Damn right I wouldn't. I was just quoting my counselor." I lean back against the sofa and prop my legs up on the table. "So, buddy, is the other half of the world doing okay without me?"

"Obviously, you're being sorely missed, but I've vowed to make you proud. I was doing fine before you called." There's the unmistakable sound of a glass being set down on the table. "I gather you managed to sneak in your phone."

"Thanks to your invaluable advice, I did."

Cash came up with the idea of hiding it in my boxers, assuring me that no one would pat me down. My boxers are tight enough without my smartphone, so the even more defined bulge earned me a few interested looks, but no one dared make a comment.

"How are you holding up?" Cash asks.

I grimace. "I'm not going to pretend it's been smooth sailing so far."

"No shit?" The hint of amusement is unmistakable. "Are there no good-looking women to keep your mind occupied?"

"It's not *that*. It's worse. There's plenty of them; I'm just not allowed to fuck any."

Cash laughs. "Come on, man. Don't tell me you didn't see that one coming."

"Yeah, I did, but that doesn't mean I'm okay with it." I take a sip of my soda and wince at the sweet taste. "I feel like I'm being prepared for the end of times."

"No, Kade, it's not the Rapture. Six weeks are nothing, you'll see."

"It still feels that way. Six weeks feels like six centuries for my cock." I move over to the kitchen and grab a bottle of water. "It's barely been seventy-two hours and I'm already feeling like a thirsty man in the desert. They won't even hook me up with a porn channel. Heck, some magazines would do."

"Why don't you use your imagination?" Cash asks.

I grimace. "You know me. I'm not particularly good at jerking off, all alone with nothing but my imagination. I may be good at my job, but I'd rather go for the real deal rather than imagine it." I cock my head to the side. "Maybe I've had too many women, but no one long enough to recall a face."

Or a particular body.

However, last night, when I jerked off, it was her I thought of.

Her face, her eyes. All in precise detail.

She has such a pretty mouth, all soft lips and little freckles on her nose. I imagined the way she moves, as if she owns the world, and the way she frowns.

Her shoulders are petite and rounded; her skin is the color of alabaster.

She has wide hips and a tight, perky ass.

Her legs look strong, as if she used to be a dancer. Judging from the way she moves, it sure would make sense. I so would do a dancer right now.

My cock stiffens, reminding me that I'm in desperate need of sex.

"You might be right," Cash says.

"And it doesn't exactly help that I have a living arrangement situation."

"Which is?"

"I'm roomed with a woman."

"You're roomed with a woman?" Cash asks in disbelief.

"Yeah."

There's a short silence. "No way. You're bullshitting me."

"I've been assigned a new roommate," I say slowly. "The rehab's freshest meat, for the next six weeks. We're basically sleeping wall to wall."

"Get out." I wince as Cash lets out a roaring laugh. "Oh, shit. You're serious?"

"Yes, I am," I say, irritated that my best friend finds my dilemma funny.

"Dude, I'm so glad I'm not you. That sounds like a nightmare."

"She's a lot of things. A nightmare is definitely one of them."

"You think she's hot."

"Like you wouldn't believe it." I close my eyes, and the image of her red hair brushing her shoulders flashes before my eyes. "Under any other circumstances, I would fuck her."

"Why don't you?"

"Because she's crazy."

"That's your kind," Cash says. "I don't think you've ever done normal."

"Not that kind," I reply. "She's like batshit crazy."

"How crazy are we talking about?"

"Let me think." I pause and think back to all the crazy shit that's ever happened in my life. "Remember when I stopped giving out my phone number because of that woman who kept calling and went on to stalk me for nearly a year?"

"You mean Joanna?"

"You still know her name?" I ask, surprised.

"Hell, yeah, I do. She worked the bar at one of my clubs. As I recall, I explicitly told you not to fuck her. I told you she had issues, but you wouldn't listen."

"You weren't explicit enough," I say with a smile. "Anyway, this one's just like her. A stalker."

"You're saying that—"

"—I'm roomed with a fucking love addict."

"Shit," Cash says slowly after a pause. "No sex addict, then. I feel for you."

"Sex couldn't be further from her mind. But the problem lies elsewhere: she's into someone else. So even if I wanted to, she would not be interested," I say. "Bro, I'm facing a crisis here. I need to hook up with someone. And quick before I lose my fucking mind."

"What do you need?"

"Good question." I lean against the fridge. "Do you think you can arrange something to make this all a little easier on me? You know, get me out of here for a couple hours."

He lets out another roaring laugh. "Are we talking about breaking you out? Already? You've barely been in there for what—three days?"

"Come on. We're only talking about an hour or two. Let's hit a club. Meet some chicks. Have a few drinks. Help me get the chance to finish my 365-day, non-stop sex calendar. I only skipped yesterday, so it doesn't really count. I'm so close."

"How close?" I can hear the excitement in his voice.

"Just one left, and you'll hear the dong."

"Damn. You've really gone through with it?" Cash's voice echoes through the line, heavy with disbelief. "I thought you gave up long ago."

"A bet is a bet. Do I look like someone who's ready to lose?"

"I didn't think you would take it so seriously."

"Well, I have. So don't waste the five hundred bucks you owe me because I'm almost ready to pick up my check."

"Almost," Cash says, laughing. "Alright. I'm going to help. You still have your pho: 2?"

"I wouldn't be talking to you if I didn't."

"Good, don't lose it. I can arrange for a driver to pick you up this Friday."

"Why Friday?"

"I'm opening another club. There's someone I want you to meet. She's a new dancer I hired last week. I think you'll like her. You're absolutely her type: young, rich, and an asshole."

I let the asshole comment slide, because to be honest, I don't care what Cash thinks of me.

"If you weren't a club owner, you'd probably make a good pimp, you know?"

"That wouldn't be my career choice."

"What would be?" I ask, interested, and take another gulp of my drink.

"Making great movies and asking you to be the lead actor." The dirty connotation is unmistakable. I shouldn't have mentioned the missing porn channel.

I grimace. "I love sex, but I wouldn't want to make money off of it. Give it a few more days here though, and I might be telling you a different story."

"Two more days and you'll have your fun."

"Thanks. I owe you big time."

"Yeah, you do. I'm most certainly not doing this for free. I mean, let's face it, the 365 days are up. But I'll help under one condition."

"Which is?"

"I want you to fuck your roommate."

My heart speeds up as Vicky's image flashes before my eyes. "What if I don't want to do that?"

There's a short pause, but the silence is ominous, heavy with the promise of bad news.

"Then you'll lose the bet." I open my mouth to protest, but Cash continues, "As you might recall, when we made that bet, we also agreed that I'd get the chance to point to anyone and you'd have to fuck her. Well, I haven't used that card yet. So, here's my condition: I want her to be the last on the list. It goes without saying that any women you might have in between don't count. Including the dancer I'll arrange for you to meet."

"I don't know," I say, hesitating. This could work. Besides, I'm not one to say 'no' to a challenge.

"It shouldn't be too difficult," Cash says. "Most women dig bad boys. However, my gut feeling tells me that's not what she needs. Patience is not your best virtue, so, me being your best friend and all, I suggest you play the friends card. Do we have a deal?"

I let the thought sink in for a moment.

Cash might be spot on about her.

I close my eyes and take a breath. "I can take all the time I need?" I ask warily.

"Of course."

This can't be too hard.

A woman like her is in desperate need of romance and love, and I know exactly how to lavish attention on her. Besides, I can plan this carefully, make her want me with everything she's got, and then strike on the last day, right before I leave this place.

I nod. "Deal, it is. If she needs nice, I can be nice."

"And, Kade? I want proof."

I let out a snort. "As if I'd ever cheat my way into winning a bet."

"You never know. Remember the time we played cards and you kept on winning? I'll just say, trust is earned."

"That's old news. I was twenty and in desperate need of quick money, seeing that I was going through a losing streak."

"Who's to say you're honest now?" There is another pause. "You can come up with any kind of proof you want, as long as it's believable."

"Don't worry about that. I'll come up with something," I say and end our conversation.

One hour later, I'm in my room, devising my plan.

9

Vicky

I SCAN MY NEW room.

Clothes are arranged in the closet: check

Bed made: check

Furniture dusted: check

Everything looks in its right place, except for the box in the corner. For the life of me, I just can't open it to retrieve its contents. It's too much of a reminder that I'm a patient in this place, and my mind just refuses to accept it.

Sylvie was right about one thing.

My initial fears that I'd be kicked out on the first

day were unreasonable.

I spent the day in knots, waiting for the call to come. When nothing happened—no letter of transfer, no complaint filed against me—I checked in with the therapist on the following morning. She acted like nothing happened.

Except for the odd glance she threw at me whenever I mentioned Bruce, she kept most remarks to herself, and we focused on my feelings and childhood, which was fine.

I didn't really want to talk about Bruce, and she didn't seem very keen on it, either.

I've been here for five days, during which I've only attended the morning sessions with my therapist. I'm too afraid of others' judgment and am not ready for a group meeting.

Luckily, it's not mandatory.

"If I didn't know any better, I'd say you're avoiding me." A deep voice startles me.

I turn around and find Kade standing next to my bed.

My breath catches in my throat and heat shoots up my neck, as if he's just caught me doing something naughty.

Which is ridiculous.

I frown, ready to spit fire at him for bursting into

my room uninvited. And yet all I can think about is—

Wow, he looks hot.

Dressed in a black shirt and jeans that hang low on his hips, with his dark hair falling into his face, he looks sexy, but with a dangerous touch.

Yes, I've been trying to avoid him—successfully so. There's something about this man that makes me want to hide from him. He's too full of himself, too rash, and maybe I do find him attractive just a little bit, even though he really isn't my type.

I thought I could go on like this for as long as we're forced to live together.

Fat chance.

"I've been hanging out with a friend," I reply, my voice a bit too breathy.

Which is only partly the truth. While I'm seeing Sylvie every day after the morning session, I like to spend my afternoons reading in the rehab's own library rather than seek out all the creative arts or sports activities on offer.

"You're a Jane Austen fan," Kade says and picks up the book arranged on my pillow. It's a little thing my mom gave me, the edges almost falling apart. I still remember the first day my mom read it to me. I was five and into fairytales and even harbored the stupid dream of marrying a prince.

"Don't touch my things." I snatch the book out of his hands and press it against my heart.

"You didn't strike me as the literary kind."

"Well, I am. Not that it's any of your business." I frown at his choice of words. I should be insulted, but for some reason, I'm not quite.

Not when he looks so damn hot. It's like he's taking up the room and stealing all the air to breathe.

"Fair enough." He holds out his hands in a peace gesture and starts walking around, completely violating my privacy by examining all the books I brought with me.

Every part of my body is on high alert, expecting another snarky remark.

"You arrange all your books alphabetically," Kade says.

"Who doesn't?"

"I don't." He glances at me over his shoulder. "You've turned this into a nice place. Gave it a little personality," he says as he keeps looking around, his gaze settling on my bed.

He doesn't need to say what he's thinking.

I can see it. It's right there, in the tightness in his jeans.

My heartbeat spikes unnecessarily.

"Why are you here, Kade?"

I can feel the heat seeping deep into my bones. He turns his back to me, giving me a few seconds to check him out.

At least he's clothed, the black shirt stretching over his broad shoulders. As he moves to face me, the muscles beneath stretch it farther, and I can't help but think of the tattoo adorning his back, beckoning to me to lift up his shirt and touch it.

"What? Can't your roommate check in with you to make sure you're still alive?"

I stare at him. "I'm not suicidal."

His eyes sparkle with something I can't read. "Good. You didn't strike me as the weak type either. I'm glad I got one thing right."

The compliment is indistinguishable, and I have absolutely no idea what to make of it. "It took you five days to come looking. I can't imagine how long it'd take you to arrange a search party. If I were suicidal, I'd be long dead and you'd have found me hanging from the ceiling."

I don't know why I just said that, but it's definitely too late to take it all back.

"So uncreative." His lips twitch. "In that case, I'll make sure to check up on you more often." His gaze sweeps over the floor and remains stuck on the info box in the corner. "Still haven't unboxed your manual yet?"

"No time."

"Interesting." He turns back to me, his dark eyes piercing right through me. "You're a rebel."

I frown. WTF? Is he psychoanalyzing me? He can't be. I open my mouth but before I can come up with a reply, he says, "Don't worry. I find your neuroses entertaining."

I take a deep breath, then another. "You can stop psychoanalyzing me, Dr. Phil. I have no intention of getting to know you, so I'm not going to return the favor and ask anything about you. There's no point in the game you're playing."

"Some people spend a lifetime in here, and they might get bored." He points his thumb at himself. "Like me."

"Luckily, people don't have to." I shrug. "I don't know about you, but I have no plans for staying longer than my allotted time."

"Me neither, but you never know. What if we're incurable, according to them?" I can sense a change in subject as he begins to inspect the pin board I've hung up on the wall.

He scans the dozen photos—little Polaroid snapshots I took over the years. "Nice collection you have here. I gather this is *him*, the player."

"He's not a player." I frown, annoyed with his words and by his curiosity. "That's my boyfriend we're talking about."

"He still looks like a player, if you ask me."

"You don't know him," I snap.

"You're right. I don't know him. Half of my friends are players, and I know one when I see one."

"Well, you're wrong." My voice comes out sharp. I'm almost ready to grab a hold of his arm and drag him the hell out of my room before he makes me say something I might come to regret. Luckily, he turns around and puts some distance between himself and the pin board.

"How long have you two been together?" He crosses his arms over his chest and regards me with a hint of amusement in his eyes. It's so condescending, I'm fighting hard not to kick his arrogant ass right out of my bedroom.

"Long enough to know that he loves me and that you're being a pain in the ass."

He cocks his head to me. "Snarky."

"Stop communicating your conclusions drawn from bad judgment."

"Why?"

"Why what?" Closing my eyes, I take a deep

145

breath and force myself to hold it before I release it. "You're really starting to piss me off. I'm reaching the maximum point of pisstivity."

"I don't think that's a word," Kade says.

My face grows hot as he turns back to my pin board and doesn't just inspect one of the photos.

No, he's actually removing it from the pin board to look at it.

It's a snapshot of my sister and me, taken not too long ago when my life wasn't the mess it currently is.

"Your best friend, I assume?" Kade says with a playful smile and a little too much enthusiasm.

I don't know why, but his words make my heart slam in my chest. I can't help the pang of jealousy shooting through me. It makes no sense whatsoever.

"That's my sister."

"She's hot."

Of course he had to say that. She is. She damn is. But he doesn't need to acknowledge it.

"And taken," I answer before his dirty mind can take off in a specific direction. "She's getting married in two months."

"Pity. The male population will lose another beautiful woman. Do you happen to have another sister, by any chance?"

I roll my eyes at him. "Is there a reason why

you're here, except to annoy the hell out of me?"

"As a matter of fact, yes, there is." He leans against my tiny desk, taking his sweet time with a reply. "I need your opinion."

I narrow my eyes at him because I don't trust him one bit. "On what?"

"On women, obviously." He regards me with that unnerving grin of his. "This might take a while. You might want to take a seat."

Making myself comfortable around him is the last thing I want to do. I cross my arms over my chest. "Why don't you get to the point? I haven't got all day."

"Right. Since you're so busy, I'll make sure to call your assistant to set up an appointment next time."

That sarcasm of his is driving me insane. He's lucky I'm not the argumentative type.

"Kade." My tone carries a warning, which he doesn't seem to want to register.

He motions to my bed. "Really, I might need some time. Come on. It's just a conversation; I'm not going to bite. I want to hear your opinion."

He grabs my hand, his long fingers encircling mine. I flinch a little at the way his skin feels against mine—warm, intimate, so very good. His expression remains unfazed, and I realize my strange reaction to him is not reciprocated.

His hand pulls gently, forcing me to sit.

"Okay." I do as requested, but only because I really need him to stop touching me.

Without waiting for my invitation, he sits down next to me, his thigh brushing mine. My body stiffens.

He's too close—so close I can smell the manly blend of his aftershave.

My skin prickles. My lungs fight against the sudden lack of oxygen. I can feel him with every fiber of my body. My skin is tingling, catching fire under his burning gaze. My shallow breathing comes so loud, I'm sure he can hear it.

"Okay, so don't laugh," he starts, his magnetic eyes piercing through me. "With so much time on my hands, I feel like I have to get productive before I go crazy. I've been thinking about writing a book about sex experiences. Not just mine, but in general. Do you think people would be interested in reading it?"

His casual tone helps me relax a little. I brush a hand over my skirt before I reply.

"I don't know," I say earnestly. "Why do you think I might know what other people want to read?"

"I just thought you could answer the question,

considering that you read books."

A laugh escapes my throat. His reasoning makes no sense whatsoever. "Me? I'm not interested in porn. Because that's exactly what you would write, right?"

If he caught the subtle insult, he doesn't react to it.

"No. More along the lines of a sex-help book. You know, share a little of my wisdom, spice up personal lives, and help people have fuller experiences."

"Obviously, you're talking about your perception," I say, and add at his confused expression. "I mean, how do you even know if you're good in bed and that your girlfriends feel the same way?"

His eyes narrow and the air between us cools down a few degrees. "Because I am."

A hot blush shoots up my neck and spreads to my cheeks.

I should so shut up right now. And yet I just can't keep my mouth closed.

"Yeah, but how do you know they're not faking it?"

"I could show you, and then you could communicate your opinion on the matter," Kade says coolly.

My heart stops. Literally stops, only to jolt back into action faster than before. Of course he would suggest something like this.

He's a sex addict, Vicky. What did you expect?

He catches my expression and his lips break out in a gorgeous smile. "I'm joking. I didn't mean it in a literal way."

That stings a little bit, which is irrational given that I *don't* want him to want to sleep with me.

"Why don't you ask another sex addict?" I ask. "Surely there's someone better suited than me to answer the question."

He shakes his head slowly. "There isn't, or I wouldn't be asking you. Haven't you noticed that most sex addicts in this place are male? And the few female ones are out of my preferred age range."

I shake my head. "Still, why me?"

"As I said, you're the literary kind. I also really want my first reader to be...well, you know when you said you were a rebel?"

"Actually, you said that."

He nods his head. "I need someone like that. I need someone who's brutally honest and can communicate it as it is. That's you. The snarky one. Did you know your name Vicky comes from Viking?"

I want to point out that I'm anything but snarky

and my name has nothing to do with Vikings, but I just bite my tongue lest I confirm his assumption that I might be a bit snarky.

"Okay." I shift in my seat. "Before I answer, let me get something off my chest. I have two concerns. First, I'm not sure you ought to write a book when you haven't finished therapy yet. You getting treated for your sex addiction while trying to help others with their sex life, isn't that a bit of a paradox?"

"Possibly. I definitely see your point." He nods his head again, his eyes scanning my face. "So, will you read it?"

I groan. "Will you leave me alone if I say yes?"

His lips curve upwards. "I can't guarantee it, but chances are I'll stop bothering you."

"Alright. I'll do it. But only under one condition." I hold up one finger. "Stop analyzing me. I'm already being scrutinized by my therapist during my sessions. I don't need you to continue her work during my spare time as well."

"I'm just pointing out positive qualities as I go along. Consider them compliments." His arms wrap around me, gently squeezing me to his chest. His sudden hug catches me off-guard, and for a second I forget to breathe.

I know he's only being friendly, but in the privacy

of my bedroom, it feels like so much more than that.

Releasing me, he catches my glance, completely oblivious to my confusion. "Thanks. I really appreciate it."

I shrug, way too aware of his presence. "I don't mind."

Under his glance, I feel hot.

Aroused.

Naked.

He's sitting so close to me, I can feel the warmth of his body seeping into my skin, making me wonder what it'd feel like if I pressed my lips against his.

I swallow.

You can't be attracted to him.

"If you're going to write a book while you're here, how are you going to do it without a computer?" I ask.

"There are three computers in the entertainment room," Kade says.

My heartbeat picks up in speed. "There's an entertainment room?"

And computers?

"Yeah." He stares at me, amused. "It's hard to miss it when you're in group therapy right next to it." His grin widens. "Oh, wait. You haven't attended group therapy yet, right? I haven't seen you."

I ignore his remark as my mind keeps circling around the most important thing. "Do they have WiFi?" I ask breathlessly.

"No. No Internet, if that's what you were hoping for. You're not supposed to have any contact with the outside world."

The air swooshes right out of my lungs in a sigh of defeat. "The whole rehab thing sucks. No phones, no Internet. We're basically cut off from civilization. Can they even do that? I mean, even prisons have Internet. I feel like I'm trapped in the Middle Ages..." My voice trails off.

"Yeah, but with better food and medical care," Kade says.

I can't help the feeling that he's not really taking me seriously.

"Whatever," I mutter. "I'm so sick of being here. There's nothing to do. There aren't even good books in the library."

"Is that where you've been hiding from me?"

His question sounds like a statement.

His remark is spot on, and definitely the kind of conversation I want him to drop. Ignoring his rhetorical question, I turn away.

"Look." He lets out a long breath. "Now, I don't do this for everyone, but I think I have what you need."

I turn back to him. "What do you mean?"

His hand squeezes inside his pocket. My eyes widen as he pulls out a tiny phone. "You can use it to get online."

"You have a phone?" I stare at him, almost choking on my words.

"As you can see, I do."

Wow.

This is my chance. Who would have thought the insufferable guy would turn out to be my lifesaver?

"How?" I mumble.

He flashes me a grin. "Let's say I'm well connected, and I know where to hide stuff." His hand points to his jeans and he raises his brows meaningfully.

I'm pretty sure he's not talking about his jeans.

"Oh, my God. You did not hide it in your underwear!"

"I did, and I had to flirt with the security guard to make sure she wouldn't pat me down," he says smugly.

"Of course, you would." I stare at the phone, fighting the urge to snatch it out of his hands, lock myself in the bathroom, and see what Bruce has been up to. "What else did you hide?" I ask, even though I'm not interested.

"Well, do you want to borrow it or not?" Kade asks, and in that moment I sort of want to hug him.

"Yes," I croak.

"You can have it for one hour." He drops the phone on my bed. As I reach for it, he puts his hand over mine. "In exchange for having dinner with me."

"You are asking me out again?" I stare up at him, my breath catching. "Seriously?"

He shrugs his shoulders. "It's not a date."

"What do you call it then?"

"Two friends eating?" He winks.

"I'm not sure we're allowed to do that, Kade. It would look like two roommates on a date."

"What? We're not allowed to eat?" He laughs.

"What if I don't want to go?"

"Then you can't have my phone," Kade says coolly.

I shake my head. "You play dirty."

"I play fair."

I sigh, unsure how to proceed next. My gaze turns back to the phone again. I want it so badly, I've no idea why I'm making such a big deal out of having dinner with the guy. Like he says, it's just food. "It's just dinner, right? Because I told you I have a boyfriend."

"I don't see him anywhere here."

"I'm not a cheater." I can feel my hesitation dissolving into thin air and flying right out of the window.

"I never thought you were." He heaves a long, exasperated sigh. "Look, Vicky, I don't know you, but I just put myself out on a limb for you to make you feel better. I need to know that you're not going to screw me over. So, do you want the phone or not? If not, just forget I even offered."

I eye him for a moment, unsure whether I can really trust him not to screw *me* over. Eventually, I let out the breath I didn't even know I had been holding. "Okay, I'm going for it. And—" I catch his glance and reward him with a smile, "—I'm not going to betray your trust. Just make sure you don't betray mine."

"We're partners in crime." He hands me the phone. "Nobody but you can know about it. Understood? We can't afford to lose it."

We.

A rock forms in the pit of my stomach at the word. When did things take this particular turn? I mean, one moment I could barely stand the guy and the next we're plotting and breaking rules together.

I nod, and for a moment we just stare at each

other in silent agreement. His expression is softer now, fearful even. I can't blame him. Being in rehab, cut off from the world, a phone is that one thing that can save lives. It sure does mine. Every day that passes, I feel like I'm dying without it. It's not just about Bruce. I also miss my family.

I need to be in touch with the outside world to stop feeling as though I'm slowly losing my mind.

"Being discreet about it goes without saying," I say. "In fact, I've absolutely no intention of leaving this room while using it."

"Good." He gestures at the phone and gets up. "It's unlocked. And so you know, I cleaned it."

I look up only to see he's almost at the door, his hand on the handle.

"Kade?"

"Yeah, Stalker?"

"Thank you."

He shoots me a devilish grin that's so handsome I almost forget what I'm about to do. "Don't thank me yet, Viking. You still owe me dinner." He presses the handle, calling over his shoulder, "By the way, don't let the photos bother you."

"What photos?" I ask, but he's already gone, the door closing behind him.

Sighing, I let myself sink against the pillows as

anticipation courses through me. I can feel it coursing through my body from my feet to my fingertips. It's thick and prickling like a warm spring fountain. One hour...it's not a lot, but those sixty minutes will grant me enough time to check up on all the people who matter to me.

I'm giddy with excitement at the prospect of finding out what Bruce is doing.

If he's replied to my emails.

Maybe he's even talked to his mother and changed her mind about us.

My fingers swipe over the screen a couple times until a text conversation pops up. It's from last year, but its content is not what's causing my breath to catch in my throat.

My eyes remain glued to a photo.

It's a picture of a dick.

It's huge and thick. And so very familiar.

Oh, wait, is that Kade's cock?

I stare at the pic, ignoring the short conversation with a woman, and then scroll down to another picture. This one is of her breasts pushed up so high I wouldn't be surprised to find she could rest her chin on them.

"Gross," I mutter and scroll back to his dick.

This is like a train wreck. You know you shouldn't

be staring, and yet you can't peel your gaze away from it.

The familiar heat from before returns, pooling between my legs, making me wonder how it would feel inside me.

10

Kaiden

VICKY.

Such an ordinary name for a woman who looks anything but ordinary. The day's been hot and dry, perfect for a date. For the first time in my life, I actually put some thought into the way I dress for a woman and give myself the obligatory once-over in the mirror.

My eyes are bloodshot from the lack of sleep and the drinks I had last night. My hair is still wet from the shower, the dark curls falling deep into my face.

I've been told on more than one occasion that I

look like a celebrity. I have even had random people on the street approach me for an autograph, mistaking me for a famous actor whose name I couldn't be bothered to remember. Honestly, I don't see the resemblance to any celebrity, but if people claim so, then who knows? Maybe we're related. I wouldn't be surprised, considering that I've never known my birth parents.

Absentmindedly, I brush my fingers through my hair, wondering whether to cut it. Women dig the two or three extra inches in all instances. They like my dark brown eyes and haunted look. They say they love my cocky smile, but underneath it, I can be serious as fuck.

Planning. Scheming. That's what I'm good at.

Getting Vicky into my bed is my newest goal.

The plan is to do it in an old-fashioned way—have dinner, get her invested in me.

The more I think about it, the more I want her to be the last one in my 365-day, non-stop sex calendar. Cash was right to demand that I sleep with her. Get her out of my system.

She knows that fucking your roommate is not allowed, so that might make the task at hand harder, but not impossible.

The faint sound of a door opening and closing

echoes. I turn around just in time to see her entering the living room, her hand clutching my phone like it's a rare commodity.

"As good as new." Smiling, she hands it to me. "I even gave it a good scrub."

"There was no need. Believe it or not, I'm pretty meticulous when it comes to hygiene. I clean up after I finish everything. My brother calls it OCD."

Her groomed eyebrows shoot up as she asks in surprise, "OCD?"

"Yes. Even addicts suffer from it."

"I thought you weren't an addict."

The fact that she seems to have warmed up to me a little bit, and no longer looks like she wants to rip my head off, doesn't escape me.

"I'm not." I point at the phone in her open hand. "Why don't you keep it for now?"

She opens her mouth, then closes it again, seemingly at a loss for words. I turn back to the mirror hanging on the wall and regard her through my reflection. "Do you think I should cut my hair?"

"You're vain, aren't you?" She laughs, the sound both innocent and sexy as hell.

"Why? Because you always seem to find me standing in front of a mirror?"

"I know, right?" She laughs again and takes a step

toward me.

The ice queen is melting.

I chuckle, inwardly pleased with the progress a little gesture has made. "Since I've got all the time in the world, I thought I could take a little more care of myself."

"There's nothing wrong with taking care of yourself. Just be careful that you don't fall in love with your image or the mirror might end up glued to your chest." Her smile widens and there's a sparkle in her eyes.

She isn't just snarky; she also has a sense of humor. I find that I like that about her.

"I don't think I can," I say honestly.

"What?"

"Fall in love."

"Why's that? Are you incapable of loving or—"

"No. I mean, I don't think I could fall in love with myself. You see, I like it soft and warm, with a little moisture in all the right places."

The double entendre is obvious.

She stares at me, and then she throws her head back and laughs. "Do women fall for your kind of crap?"

"Always." Her laugh is so infectious, I can't help but join in. "So, what do you think? Cutting or not cutting?"

"Let me see." She takes another step forward and stretches out her hand, her fingers lingering inches from my face. "May I?"

I nod my head to signal my agreement.

She shifts behind me, her fingers raking through my hair, gingerly at first, then with more determination, each stroke sending electricity through me. And fuck, I can feel myself hardening again. She takes another step, this time to the left, to inspect the side. Standing so close, I catch a whiff of her perfume. It's rather heavy for a woman her size, but it's decadent and sexy, as if the vulnerability she displays is nothing but a disguise.

It's the kind of fragrance I want to linger on my pillows.

"When I was younger, I used to cut my father's hair," she says. "He always used to say that I was better than any hairstylist he's ever met. Back then, he was the best hairdresser in Jacksonville."

"Jacksonville? Is that where you are from?"

"No." She lets her hand drop, making me miss her touch instantly. "I'm from Portland."

She steps back and I turn to regard her. Her face is drawn in thought. "I think shorter would look good on you."

"How short are we talking about?"

"Buddhist style."

I frown until I catch the hint of a grin and the mischievous glint in her eyes.

"You're messing with me," I state the obvious.

"Wait here." In the mirror, I see her heading out. A few seconds later, she returns holding a pair of scissors. "Who's joking now?"

"You want to cut my hair?" I ask, surprised. "Now?"

"Yeah, now. What are you afraid of, big boy? That I might ruin your look?"

"I'm not worried. But we have a date."

Her expression hardens. "You said dinner."

Fuck!

I could slap myself for making such a rookie mistake.

"I meant dinner. Obviously, we're not allowed to have dates." I let my gaze brush over her. She's wearing jeans and a shirt that look like they've been through the laundry a few times too many. "Is that what you're going to wear?"

"I didn't think you were being serious about having dinner," she says. "This is my lounge wear."

"My phone doesn't come for free." I take in her confusion. She's torn about this. If I don't play my cards right, I'll lose her.

"Where do you want to go anyway? There's nothing around here."

"I'm not spilling my secrets to everyone."

She narrows her eyes. "Why do I have the feeling it involves breaking the rules?"

"Probably, but definitely not more than you using my phone." I wink, expecting a laugh, but she doesn't seem to acknowledge my attempt at breaking through the sudden tension.

"I'm still not sure this is a good idea," Vicky says.

I throw up my hands in mock surrender. "Fine. Forget about it. But it's the last time I let you use my phone."

She keeps silent for a few seconds, but her thoughts are written on her face. This phone is probably like a lifeboat to her; it keeps her glued to the asshole she's in love with, robbing her of any chance of seeing him for what he is.

I've barely finished drawing my conclusion when she places her hand on my shoulder. Before I can figure out what the fuck she's doing now, she's pushed up on her toes, her lips coming dangerously close to my ear as she whispers, "Relax, I never said no. Only that I'm not sure it's a good idea, not with this haircut of yours. I'm not leaving with someone looking so—"

Frowning, she waves her hand in my face, looking for the right word.

Fuck it!

My hair's like my dick—it's perfect. No woman's ever found anything to fault.

"What's wrong with it?" I ask.

"It's not about what's wrong with it," Vicky says slowly. "It's more the fact that you need it. New phase. New look. That's what my dad used to say whenever people were having a hard time. He said going for a new haircut and reinventing yourself helps to shed old behavior and make room for the new. Now, sit down. You'll like it."

"As long as you don't leave me bald," I mumble.

She lets out a laugh. "You can't reject the possible."

"Yeah, I might go bald. At sixty. I'll probably even rock it."

"Vain. That's what you are." She rolls her eyes and motions for me to sit on the sofa. I do as she instructs and realize that I enjoy our banter way more than I should.

"Wait," I say as the scissors come dangerously close to my face. "What cut are you going to give me?"

"Where's your trust?" She smiles sweetly and lifts the scissors. "Any last wishes? You know, once it's gone, it'll take weeks to grow back."

I close my eyes and take a deep breath, but relaxation is the last thing on my mind. Her hands are soft, her expert fingers determined as she rakes them through my hair. I can't help but wonder how they'd feel on my dick.

"Just don't make me regret it," I say.

11

Kaiden

"HOW MUCH LONGER is this going to take?" I ask.

I don't know how much time has passed, but it sure feels like my hair's been at Vicky's mercy for hours. The sound of scissors cutting is making me nervous. And it's not helping that Vicky keeps making those tiny noises—half irritation, half delight.

Either she's having a hell of a time, or she's on the verge of giving up.

Several times, I tried to steal a peek at the mirror, but she caught me and covered it with my jacket.

Vicky insisted that I don't look.

She wants my new haircut to be a surprise. I'm not sure how I should feel about that, but I like the touch of her hands on my skin. It's soft and feminine, the strokes determined, as if she's used to touching people.

I don't want to tell her, but she really has wonderful hands. Some hands are rough, others are harried. Hers are like heaven. They seem to know how to send a tingle down my spine and make me want to peel her clothes off her body.

The fact that I'm glued to this chair, able to do none of the things I want to do to her because I can't afford to scare her away, amplifies my anxiety.

"How much longer?" I ask for the umpteenth time.

"You got somewhere to go? Places to see?"

"No, I'm just concerned we'll be starving if we don't get going soon."

She lets out a laugh at my half-ass attempt at a comeback. "I'm about to create art here. You can't hurry it. Trust me, you'll like it."

Why the hell does she keep saying that?

"I'm sure I'd like everything at this point," I mumble.

"You'll have to because there's no going back

now." She runs her hands through my hair again. The motion travels through my body, straight to my groin, and I'm barely able to stifle the groan in my throat. "Besides, this is trendy."

My brows shoot up at the covert insult. "And my previous cut wasn't?"

She lets out another tinkling laugh. "Let's put it this way...this was long overdue."

Eventually, the scissors drop on the table and Vicky removes my jacket from the mirror, revealing my reflection.

My heart gives a jolt.

That's a hell of a cut.

I'm almost unrecognizable.

My hair is still long enough to fall into my face, bringing out my strong features, but the back is shorter. I never figured such a cut would suit me.

"What do you think?" she asks and bites her lip, as though nervous.

"I think it's bearable." I reach for the pair of scissors. "Now you've got to let me cut your hair."

"Hell, no. Not before you watch a few instructional videos on YouTube." Her eyes twinkle.

"Don't need to. I can assure you I'm quite the expert myself," I say. "Just tie your hair in a ponytail and I'll take it from there."

"Oh, my God." She snatches the scissors from my hand, keeping it at a safe distance.

For a moment, I'm tempted to try to snatch it back just to get a little closer to her, but then decide this isn't the time.

She's not ready for it yet.

I get up to inspect myself in the mirror.

The more I look, the more I decide that I like it.

I run my hand through my hair and then turn to catch her expression as I ask, "What do *you* think?"

"I think you look sexy."

"You do?"

Her eyes linger on my mouth. I know what she's thinking. Under different circumstances, I'd just go for it. But instead, I fight the urge to kiss her and let the moment pass.

"Yeah, I do." Her cheeks flush a little and she looks away.

She's attracted to me. In spite of whatever she's trying to make herself believe, her body gives her away.

The thought brings a smile to my face. "Have you ever thought about opening a salon?"

"Why would I?"

I shrug my shoulders. "You're not half bad at this. Besides, you'll already have a returning customer."

"I don't think I could."

"Why not? I tip well. You could probably earn a living from my tips alone."

She shakes her head, but her eyes glaze over, as though the thought has already occurred to her but she'd decided not to pursue it further. "For starters, I love my job."

"The one at the nursing home?"

"That one." She catches my glance. "It's hard, but I like working with old people. I know what most people say about old folks, but..." There's a challenging glint in her eyes. Defiance, like the people in her life have often questioned her choice of work and she's determined to show them. I grimace, and she laughs. "Oh, my God, you, too? Please don't tell me you hate the elderly."

"Sorry," I say and grimace again. "It's not hate, per se. But I can't help it. I find old people unbearable. I work in marketing, but when I was younger, at the beginning of my career, I interned in a call center for insurance stuff, and I hated it. You can't reason with them. Can't come to an agreement. We had this policy that expected us to keep every conversation under three minutes. Have you ever tried that? It's impossible. Just because they've lived through more stuff than we have, they think we ought to listen to their stories I don't give a fuck about."

"Well, I have a different opinion on that." She brushes a strand of hair back and her jaw sets stubbornly. "Sure, their stories are longwinded and often suit no purpose, and yes, they can be unreasonable, but I like them. I think there's something to learn from each and every one of them."

I frown. "Why?"

"What do you mean by why?" She mirrors my frown, and I sense our first disagreement—one of many. "They're dealing with the aftermath of losing friends and family. Every day, they struggle with being alone because their grown-up kids and grandkids can't be bothered to visit them. Now, this doesn't apply to everyone, but most of them are forgotten, which is a pity. We have so much to learn from their experiences."

"Like what?" I ask, unimpressed.

"Like to treasure life and learn from past mistakes. You wouldn't believe the stories they could tell you if you only cared to listen. I've learned that challenges make couples stronger and that love doesn't need to be searched for. That you can't force it. That love at first sight exists. I've heard so many

174

love stories that I know I want it for myself. I want to get married, grow old togeth .."

Staring at her, I wait for repulsion to wash over me, but nothing happens.

"You have your boyfriend," I point out.

"Yeah. I have Bruce." She turns her head away, and in that instant I know something's going on between them, and it's not pretty. Her posture's rigid and there's a strained expression on her face.

She looks upset—I can see it in her eyes.

"Did I say something wrong?" I ask carefully.

She shakes her head. "I'm going to get dressed." With that, she storms out.

12

Vicky

AN OPEN LETTER TO JANE AUSTEN

Dear Jane,

I think we have a lot in common, even though centuries separate us. Honestly, I know it's just fiction, but I believe that every word you wrote in your books is part of your life experience coming from the deepest recesses of your soul. In your book, Mr. Darcy shows little interest in Elizabeth Bennet. In fact, he refuses to dance with her. I guess that was the expression you used for the today's slang term "hook up." My Bruce doesn't like to dance with me, either. He has yet to reply to any of my ten emails. He's probably too busy at work. Is it wrong that I opened a fake Facebook account so that I can spy on him? Is it wrong that I used a Victoria's Secret model's face as my profile picture? As it happens, I have sent him a friend request. Fingers crossed he'll accept it.

Lots of Love,
Vicky Sullivan

P.S. I know *Catfish* would have a field trip with this one. If it helps, I do think we (the model and I) look a bit alike depending on whom you're asking, and obviously lots of good lighting.

***

Sneaking out of the LAA Center building is much easier than I thought. In fact, it might be the easiest thing I've ever done. There are no security guards. The reception area is unmanned. It pretty much involves just walking out the door and no one giving a damn about it.

From outside, almost all windows are lit, including Kade's and my apartment, left to look as though we just stepped outside and would be right back. It suits the purpose of fooling anyone who might come checking on us, even though I'm pretty sure no one will bother.

When Kade suggested we walk the small distance to the intersection, I agreed, which I shouldn't have.

"Where are we going, Kade?" I ask for the third time in what feels like at least twenty minutes. "There's no restaurant nearby."

Or on the island.

I glance at the moon rising between the clouds. Night is about to fall, and I really don't want to be walking around a deserted street in an unfamiliar place.

If Kade isn't careful, someone is going to see us and report us.

"Where is your trust?" He shoots me a cocky smile, repeating my previous choice of words.

"If you're thinking about dragging me into the woods and raping me, you should know that I took a self-defense class, and I'm not afraid to kick your ass."

He stops and turns to face me. "Let me get this straight. You're a stalker, a fighter, and a rebel."

"I'm not a fighter."

"No?" His gaze sweeps over my body appreciatively. "What is it that you do? Karate? Jiu-jitsu? Pillow fights, maybe?"

I stick out my tongue. "It's kickboxing, asshole. And I know the best place to hit you to take you down. If I were you, I would be careful what you say next."

"No need. You hit me pretty well when you stepped out in that red dress." He gives me another glance and shakes his head. "Wow. I just want to strip you naked."

My heart skips a beat.

Shit.

He did not say that!

Why the hell did I put on a tight dress?

It's a bold shade of red, too.

"This is how I dress every day," I lie.

179

"It's a nice cocktail dress, without a doubt," he says. "I'll have my hands full beating the competition off."

I give him a little shove. "I'm not going to cheat on Bruce. Not with you, not with anyone. We'll have dinner, as agreed, but I'm only doing this because you gave me no choice."

"Not because you like me?" His eyebrows shoot up, and I close my eyes, letting out a groan. I know how it sounds, and it's wrong on so many levels. "Okay, you gave me a choice. The thing is, I need that phone. I need to make sure he's okay."

"Stalking him much?"

"Shut up," I say with more anger than I actually feel. "I don't need your judgment. What the hell is it you do when you're not thinking of sex, Kade?"

"A few weeks ago? Or right now? Let me think." He remains silent for a few moments. "A few weeks ago, I would have said, nothing. Now, however, I'm trying to become a writer." He seems so earnest, I find myself laughing. "I should tell you that I've started writing a journal while you were squeezing into this exquisite little thing." He points at my dress. "And, get this. I think I'm going to turn it into a story. Less of a memoir and more of a—" He taps a finger against his lips, looking for the right word.

Oh, this is going to be good.

"A story?" I prompt. "About what, for crying out loud?"

"About a man who's a sex addict and—" He breaks off as he catches my grin. "I'm not talking about myself, obviously."

"Obviously. I can't wait to read it," I say sarcastically. "All three hundred pages of a dick's sexcapades. I hope you have a thick skin."

He lets out a laugh. "Trust me. I have. The only thin skin is the one that's pulsing between my legs."

I don't know why, but a hot sensation builds between my legs.

"Gross," I say and resume walking, putting some distance between us. He catches up with me in no time.

"You saw the picture." It's more a statement than a question.

"No, I didn't see your cock." The lie comes out all wrong. "I mean, I can only assume you'd have a picture of a cock on your phone. Not that I know what you're talking about. Obviously."

He lets out a laugh.

It's irritating, but at the same time also sexy and captivating.

"I wouldn't have lent you my phone if I had

known you'd be bothered by it."

"Nothing scares me," I say. "As a nurse, I've seen plenty of naked people in my life."

"I knew it." His smile is back in place, and I realize he smiles a lot. As though life isn't so bad, and there's always something to laugh about. I like that attitude in people. Come to think of it, I like Kade's smile. But if he isn't being careful, it's going to stay stuck forever. "You're one hot nurse. I bet the guys flashed everything they had to get your attention."

"That's a preposterous assumption. I—" I shake my head. "People don't do that."

"Trust me, guys do." His fingers entangle with mine, and with a soft tug he guides me to the other side of the street. "The driver's here."

"What—" My words die at the back of my throat as I notice the black limousine blending in with the shadows. I might not be versed in riding luxury cars, but I'm not seeing one for the first time. My sister's birthday parties always involve renting something that you usually only see in auto magazines.

"What the hell, Kade?" I turn my head to him. "You want us to break out?"

"I want us to go out." He smiles, his white teeth building a strong contrast to the darkness surrounding us. "We'll be back before they even notice we were gone."

I close my eyes and force air into my burning lungs. "This can't be happening. This isn't what I agreed to at all."

"You have no choice," Kade whispers behind me and opens the door. "The driver's booked. I can't back out of this just as much as you can't. And I'll gladly remind you that you already said yes. There's definitely no going back on your word."

I groan. "Again, if I so much as find myself in a strange situation, I swear I'll—"

"You'll kick me where it counts so I may never have kids," he finishes for me. "Got the memo."

"Those weren't my exact words, but yes, that's pretty much the plan."

He motions at the car again. This time, I can sense his impatience. With a defeated sigh, I get in, settling on the backseat.

The fact that I didn't put up much of a fight pisses me off, and yet I went along with whatever Kade has in mind.

It's because of Bruce.

Out of my periphery, I see the driver watching us in the mirror.

The way Kade settles next to me, his thigh glued

to mine, even though there's enough space to lie down and not touch each other, it looks like we're a normal, dating couple.

Couple.

Where the hell did that come from?

"Fine. I hope I'm not going to regret this," I say, repeating his words.

"I don't see why you would. There will be drinks, fun. Heck, you can even call Bruce and rub it in his arrogant face."

I let the arrogant part slip as my pulse picks up speed. Maybe all's not lost.

Back in my room, I used Kade's phone to check if Bruce had replied. Instead of an email, I found that he had unfriended me on Facebook. His actions hurt, but what hurt me more was the discovery that he had accepted my catfish account's friend request.

Is Bruce into blondes like most guys are said to be?

"How did you get this drive?" I ask.

"A friend?" Kade half asks, half states.

"He has to be a really good friend if he sends a limo."

He shrugs. "I guess everyone has a price. People's loyalty can be bought."

I'm not sure I wholly agree with that, but I let it

slide.

"I can't believe the driver even found this place. Whoever hired him must be rich."

"Cash Boyd." Kade raises his eyebrows at my clueless face. "You don't know him?"

I shake my head. "Should I?"

"Club 69."

That doesn't ring a bell either.

"Cash is probably the richest nightclub owner in the world. He's in the magazines all the time," Kade elaborates, which earns him another clueless expression from me. "Where the hell have you been living, Vicky?"

"If you want to make fun of me because I don't read the kind of magazines you're probably referring to, then please, go ahead. Be my guest. I don't mind."

I don't feel that I've been missing out just because I don't frequent clubs or don't know who the hell his friend is. That just isn't me.

I stare at him, challenging him to start ridiculing me. But he doesn't.

The car takes off and I turn to the window, looking at the woods passing us by even though it's too dark to make out more than the trees and branches' silhouettes.

"You know what? I won't," Kade says. "I'm going to shut up and pretend I never asked." He opens a drawer and pulls out a bottle, examining it shortly before lifting it up to show me the label. "Drinks?"

"Thanks, but I'll pass. I get drunk easily."

In the reflection of the tinted window, I see him inclining his head. His expression is the same one he used on me before. "This is a five-hundred dollar bottle, baby. And it's free, courtesy of my friend. Are you telling me in all honesty that you're not interested in trying a drop?"

Turning to him, I eye the bottle, wondering how people can justify spending so much money on a bottle of wine. Then again, they can afford it and probably don't know what else to do with their money.

I do feel a bit thirsty, and I haven't had wine in a long time.

"What's the harm, right? I'll have half a glass."

"Good choice." He retrieves two wine glasses from a cabinet and places them on a small counter before pouring the wine.

"That's more than enough," I say, signaling him when to stop.

He hands me my glass and lifts his. "Here's to us breaking all the rules."

I nod my head and take a sip, then another.

Damn.

That's one good wine and definitely worth its price tag.

13

Vicky

"You didn't say we were going to a club opening."
I stare at the rows and rows of people gathered
outside Club 69.

"Must have slipped my mind. Now, come on,"
Kade says with a wink.

In spite of my usual dislike for clubs and huge
crowds, I'm excited. The place is huge with a
luxurious flair—not in the slightest the kind of places
Bruce took me to.

There's a red carpet spread outside, leading from
the long line of limousines to the open doors with

ushers dressed in black suits parked outside. I can't help but notice that even the crowd is dressed to the nines.

"Are you sure we'll even get inside?" I ask, eyeing the ushers who seem to be very picky. Not only do they check IDs, they also have a list. "Those bouncers look like they beat people for a living."

"What's up with all the questions, Vicky? Don't you trust me?"

I heave an exasperated sigh. "When you said you wanted to go out, I assumed you'd pick a small, private place where we wouldn't be seen by half of the world. Not that." I point my finger to the photographers camped outside, eager to take pictures of whoever might look remotely famous. "If one of them takes a picture of us just by mistake, we might end up in the papers. If Bruce's mom sees me, she'll have a reason to put me away for good. I could lose my job, and the judge might—"

I almost choke on my breath. It's such a long shot, and yet I can't help the sudden panic shooting through me.

Kade's arm is heavy on my shoulder as he spins me around to look at him. My breath catches in my throat. He's way too close, his lips within reach.

I inhale a shallow breath, my gaze glued to his

mouth, and I can't help but wonder if he tastes as good as he looks.

But mostly it's his eyes that are doing strange things to me.

They are wild and beautiful. If one glance can undo me, what would happen to me if I had him naked and at my disposal? Could I stop myself from kissing him? Would the warm, fuzzy feeling inside me evaporate or turn into the raging volcano I can feel bubbling beneath the surface?

What the hell are you doing, Vicky?

I freeze and bite my lip, unsure how to fight the attraction I seem to be feeling for him even though I'm very much in love with Bruce.

"I said everything will be fine," Kade says, misinterpreting my hesitation. "I've got us covered." He lets go of me and squeezes out of his jacket, handing it to me. "Put it on."

No question, no offer—just a plain request that leaves no room for discussion.

"But..."

"It's for your own safety," Kade says, his tone a little sharper.

I should argue with him because no woman should ever let a man dictate what to do. And yet I just clamp my mouth shut and let him help me into his jacket, then pull the collar around my face.

Once done, he watches me, seemingly pleased with the result. "Nobody will recognize you like this."

I want to point out that wearing a red dress underneath his black and very manly jacket might make me look a bit like a drag queen. At least his jacket is way too big on me. It's almost as long as my dress.

"I look like a wannabe thug." I laugh at the thought. Then again, the notion isn't quite so ridiculous, given that I have a restraining order, which I've violated...and probably will violate again.

"I wouldn't have said thug. More like a hot chick taking the walk of shame."

I give him a little shove that sends him laughing.

"What about you?" I ask. "Someone might recognize you."

"Don't worry about me. I can always pretend it was my brother," Kade says.

"Do you look alike?"

"I wouldn't say that," he mumbles and helps me out of the limousine. His hand is on the small of my back, but his body is slightly turned away from me. I want to pursue the topic, but I can sense his caginess and decide against it.

He guides me across the red carpet and heads straight to the bouncers, cutting the long line. I'm pretty sure a few cuss words are addressed at us, but Kade doesn't seem to notice. Either that, or he really doesn't care.

As we reach the bouncers—all eight of them look like they've been members of the steroid overuse club—I begin to doubt Kade's sanity.

Those guys are large. I wouldn't want to get in trouble with them. And they certainly look pissed that someone wouldn't honor the line.

Every muscle in my body tenses as one of them takes a menacing step forward. "Your names?"

"Wright," Kade replies. "Kade Wright. Cash Boyd is expecting us."

"And her?" He points to me.

"She's my plus one." Kade's arm moves around me and pulls me a little closer.

I'm instantly aware of his hard body and intoxicating scent. I should push him back, get the hell away from this guy who's so different from Bruce, and yet all I do is close my eyes for a moment to inhale the scent of his aftershave.

"Give me a sec."

I watch in astonishment as the bouncer talks into his headphone, then begins to swipe his large fingers furiously over his iPad. I lift on my toes to get a better look and catch a glimpse of photos.

Within seconds, he opens the belt and nods his head. "You're clear."

"About time," Kade mutters.

Another guard hands us wristbands. I peer at the purple color with gold dots and the cursive writing that reads "VIP."

Wow.

I've never been a VIP in my life.

I don't think I've ever even met one.

"You were right." Kade's lips twitch as he motions me through the open door. "They're extremely hostile. Now we'll have to find a way to sneak in through the staff kitchen. I suggest we pretend that we work here."

I roll my eyes. "Are you always a goof?"

"Only when I'm around you." His fingers curl around mine. "Shall we?"

I nod my head, interweaving my fingers with his, and let him guide me.

The club's like a maze. The stairs lead to a basement, which is poorly populated. The few patrons are nursing drinks at the imposing bar area. Kade leads us up another flight of stairs into an open area with a busy bar and a dancing circle that seems to have been carved out of glass. The music is so loud, I don't even try to ask him where we're headed as he takes us to the top floor that overlooks the entire area below.

My head swirls from the LED starlight ceiling. Even the walls seem to glow. And there are way too many mirrors. Passing one, I stop briefly to shrug out of Kade's jacket and hand it back to him.

"If you're not being careful, you'll lose your jaw," Kade whispers in my ear. "I'd hate to miss your beautiful mouth."

His statement comes out of the blue, and I've no idea what to make of it. But this isn't the time to ponder over his enigmatic comment.

"This place is so cool." I spin to face him. "I love it here. Why didn't you tell me it was going to be this awesome?"

He lets out a chuckle, his eyes meeting mine. "Wait until you taste the drinks and see the live band."

Girls in skimpy shorts and tops brush past us, holding serving trays. Like the bottles they're carrying, they look expensive—expensive hair, expensive makeup.

One of them eyes Kade up and down. Even though I really don't care if he hooks up with her,

I'm so not going to wait for her to make her move.

I turn around, pointing my finger to the top floor. "I want to see what's up there."

"Sure."

We fight our way through the crowd, past the bar until we stop in front of another bouncer guarding the entrance that says "VIP AREA." I expect him to inspect our wristbands. Instead, he shifts in front of us and asks in the kind of tone that makes me want to run as fast as I can, "The password?"

"If life is a party, don't waste it by asking stupid questions," Kade says, unfazed.

My heart gives a jolt.

What sort of answer is that?

Is he *trying* to get our asses thrown out or whacked or whatever it is this guy does to annoying clientele?

Holding my breath, I turn to the bouncer, expecting to see a red face and veins popping out. But he just nods and steps aside, making room for us.

We ascend the narrow stairs. Only when I think we're safe do I ask the obvious. "*That* was the password?"

"Yeah. Cash has a penchant for the theatrical. I think you two would get along."

"Maybe," I say, even though I highly doubt it. From the looks of this place, Cash is a very rich man, meaning he and I probably have nothing in common.

The top floor is even better than the other levels combined with its own bar area, a lounge area, and a gaming room. On the west side is a huge veranda that overlooks the people below, their bodies writhing to the rhythm of the music. Near the bar, dancers sway their half-naked bodies around poles.

"That's his style, too?" I laugh and shake my head.

"Those aren't strippers, if that's what you're implying." Kade's eyes remain glued to one of the girls with her breasts almost spilling out of her corset. A double D, without a doubt. "They're dancers. Real professionals who get jobs in music videos and tour with pop stars."

I snort and when one of them does a split, I say, "The only thing they have in common with dancers is that they do love an audience."

I know I sound bitter, but I can't help myself. They're gorgeous and sure know how to use their perfect bodies. I can't blame Kade for gawking just as much as I can't blame them for gawking at him.

As if on cue, a stunning blonde heads straight for

us, balancing on six-inch stilettos that make her almost as tall as Kade. Her flowing hair brushes the front of her top, emphasizing the generous cleavage that can't possibly be natural.

She is a beautiful woman with a confidence that stems from getting plenty of male attention. As she joins his side, her hand settles on Kade's shoulder, resting there naturally as she pulls her leg up, brushing the front of his pants.

The movement looks straight out of a Robin Thicke music video.

It pisses me off for no reason.

As she struts her way to another guest, I realize Kade's gaze is glued to her. I don't like the look.

His expression is hooded, lips parted, and I realize he wants to fuck her.

"It didn't take you long to get our newest star's attention," a voice says.

I spin around and stare up at the guy dressed in a suit. And not just any suit. Thanks to my sister's obsession with fashion magazines, I'm pretty sure he's wearing this season's Armani. Judging from the gold Rolex clasped around his wrist, the two meaty bouncers guarding his left and right, and his hot but arrogant features, I wouldn't be surprised if he was a celebrity or someone important.

"How's it going, Cash?" Kade draws his friend into a brief hug.

This is Cash?

The nightclub owner?

I've seen my fair share of beautiful men but have never fallen in love with one. Those two are out of this world with the kind of brashness that screams hot sex. Even though Cash screams luxury designer clothing and Kade looks kind of boyish rugged in his jeans and a shirt, both share that something special that seems to draw every woman's look to them.

And they're all staring—the dancers and the guests alike.

Even I find myself staring. Their faces as exquisite, their bodies chiseled to perfection as though they've been Photoshopped. But it's their attitude that pulls you in, fills you with the wish to find out more about them, and makes you want to touch them.

I bet every woman in the club would want to take at least one of them home.

I can see that now. I can see it from the way they flick their hair back, push their breasts out, lick their lips, stop their conversations—and just stare.

Away from rehab, having just entered his natural habitat, it's easy to forget who he really is. It's hard not to really see him and acknowledge that he's hot.

It has been ages since I've last had sex.

The thought hits me like a bucket of cold water.

It must be the alcohol, even though deep down I know it's not the truth.

"I see you were able to break out." Cash's voice draws me back. The two friends are standing shoulder at shoulder, staring at the new dancer. "So, hot or not?" he asks Kade.

"I think this one might be your best yet."

"You can have her. I've got a room set up for you, which..." His voice trails off as he catches Kade's glance at me.

I'm not a tall, half-naked dancer with legs that reach up to the sky, which is probably the reason why he didn't notice me before.

"It's okay." I gesture with my hand a little too enthusiastically, and it looks as though I'm swatting at an annoying fly. "Don't mind me listening in. You were saying you've set up a room for him and—" I encourage him to finish.

Cash raises a brow, and his mouth breaks into a smile as he takes a step forward. "And you are?"

I peer all the way up and realize his eyes are impossibly green and piercing. He looks feral, almost wild. Before I can open my mouth, Kade says,

"A friend. Leave it at that."

Kade's hand travels down my spine and settles on the small of my back, and for a moment I fear he's going to pull me against him. But his hand just rests there, the pressure a little too hard. "Vicky, this is Cash. Cash, this is Vicky."

"Nice to meet you." I grab Cash's outstretched hand, feeling his gaze on me, and give it a strong shake.

He doesn't release my hand as his glance travels down my dress and settles on my breasts. They're not as generously sized as the dancers', but my backside and hips, which always used to carry the extra fat, really make up for it. Eventually, he addresses Kade. "Is this...?"

Kade goes rigid. I peer up at him and see his set jaw. "Actually, Vicky needs to make a call. Do you mind if she uses your office?"

I regard him, unsure whether to call him out on his lie, then decide against it. Maybe he's trying to get rid of me so he can hook up with the dancer, in which case I sure won't be standing in his way.

"Sure." Cash nods his head. "Follow me." He smirks apologetically. "Don't pay attention to the naked walls. The club renovations took longer than expected, and I didn't get to finish the office. But the basics are there."

"Give us a moment," Kade says as soon as we've reached the office.

Cash hesitates for a moment but then leaves, closing the door behind him.

"Feel free to take all the time you need," Kade says. "Just do me a favor and don't run away. We need to be back before breakfast."

"I wasn't planning on running away." I settle into Cash's leather chair. "You booked this ride before you asked me to tag along. Why?"

"Why?" Kade's expression is blank.

"Why are you doing this?" I elaborate. "You didn't have to. Obviously, your friend had very specific plans for you tonight. And I'm—"

I struggle to find the right expression, but all that pops into my mind is 'spare baggage.'

He smiles gently. "We're friends. That's what friends do. They support each other."

"But you barely know me." I brush my hair back, confused.

"And?"

"You're supposed to be my partner, to help me get over my addiction." I shake my head.

"I think I'm doing a great job so far. Don't you?"

I laugh. "You can't be serious. All you've done so

far was help me break the rules. You're taking risks for me even though you're raising the odds of you being caught. I just want to know why."

"It's no big deal, Vicky. I see that you miss him and that you really need to hear from him. What am I supposed to do? Stop you from having feelings? Leave you in pain?" He circles the chair and places his hands on my shoulders. Even though my back's turned to him and I can't read his features, I can feel his soft expression. Strange as it may sound, he understands me.

"Look, I don't know if this asshole deserves you," Kade continues. "I don't know if this whole rehab thing works. All I know is that I hear you crying at night. You're shedding tears over a guy who's probably not worth it, and it's none of my business. But seeing you hiding in that smelly old library day in, day out, reading old marine books, wasting your life, that is my business. As your friend, I've made it my priority to look after you. So, here you are."

I let out a laugh. "You're right. The library's a bit stuffy, and the book collection sucks. It's either historical, non-fiction or books about sailing and marine life. Don't even get me started on the addiction stuff. There's no romance; nothing exciting to read. Given the lack of choice, the marine stuff is almost bearable."

His fingers brush the nape of my neck, massaging gently. The last few months' pressure begins to lift almost instantly.

"What will you do when you've finished them all?"

"I don't know. Read your first draft, I guess." I close my eyes and lean into his hands, swallowing down the moan in my throat. His fingers are pure magic, which doesn't come as a surprise considering the rest of him is just as good. "I'm sorry, Kade. I'm doing a terrible job of looking after you."

"I'm doing good." He stops his massage abruptly and pulls back. I should feel relief, but instead I find myself pouting with disappointment. "Okay, I'll leave you to it. Do whatever you need to do. You have—" he looks at his watch, "—three hours left."

That's a lot of time to catch up on Bruce.

I watch him heading for the door, a part of me not wanting him to leave. "Kade?" I take a deep breath and let it out slowly. "I don't know how to thank you. Right now, you might be the only friend I have. Not even my family understands me."

I expect him to make fun of me, crack a joke, anything I've come to expect from him. But he doesn't.

From the door, he looks at me for a long time before he says, "I do care about you. That's all."

I want to say something, but I can't say what I'm thinking—that I like him, too, even though I shouldn't.

Instead, I keep quiet as I watch him leave.

14

Vicky

Dear Jane,

Bruce accepted my fake friend request within hours. I should be happy, but I'm not. I'm both angry and hurt. Within a few minutes he sent two messages to the fake profile while ignoring the ones I had sent.

My heart is hurting as I think of him, and a part of me can't help but wonder if he's into her—the model. She's hot, but not *that* hot. On a second thought, she looks like a gnarly, anorexic stick. Is that what he wants?

Obviously, I can't reply to him and call him out on it. The only purpose of creating a fake account was to spy on him, find out what he's been doing. Not for him to ask me—the person behind the fake profile—out.

I don't know what to think. I don't know if I should be angry and offended, or hurt and just put up with it. In retrospect, I should never have chosen a Victoria's Secret model, but then he'd probably not have accepted an ugly person's friend request, would he?

The messages were mostly harmless, except for the fact that he calls her beautiful and sexy. He wants to meet her and has invited her to a horse racing thing his family is always attending.

He's never invited me to join them.

I don't have to tell you how much that breaks my heart.

But surprisingly, somehow there's also strength and a little hope that maybe he suspects that I'm behind the fake account.

Even though a part of me wants to know more, if only to see how far he'd go, I'm going to delete the fake account. Not today, but as soon as rehab's over.

I've also decided to swallow my pain and not confront him.

I'm sure Lizzy Bennet's heart was broken countless times before Mr. Darcy proposed. I might not be a Victoria's Secret model, but surely inner values count just as much, and I have plenty of those.

Lots of love,
Vicky Sullivan

***

I bury my head between my hands. My breath becomes labored. My head is pounding. This day has officially turned into one of the worst days of my life.

"Can I buy you a drink?" A guy in his forties slides into the seat next to me.

I raise my head and nod my head in agreement. "Sure, why not."

"Another drink for the lady." He gestures to the barman, probably mentally high-fiving himself at the prospect of a sure thing.

"Where's your boyfriend?" he asks as the barman slides a glass of vodka on the rocks across the counter.

At home, drooling over a Victoria's Secret model who doesn't even know he exists.

"Not here," I mutter and bring the glass to my lips, readying myself to take a generous, numbing gulp when a strong grip holds my hand in place. "What the—" I turn around angrily and see Kade leaning over me.

His breath is close to my face—warm, moist, and deliciously sexy. I stare at his lips, wondering what he'd do if I just pressed my mouth against his.

"What the fuck are you doing, Vicky?" Kade's voice is sharp, menacing. And holy hell, he's angry. "I've just spent the last half hour looking for you. When the bouncer said you left the office, I thought you had run away. Do you have any idea how much you scared me?"

I laugh. "Why would I want to run away?"

"That's the question I kept asking myself when I couldn't find you." He yanks the glass out of my hand, spilling a few drops in the process, and places it on the counter with a little too much force.

"You shouldn't have worried." I peer at my vodka, wondering how much of it it'd take to push Bruce into the proverbial filing cabinet of my mind.

Or force him into complete oblivion.

"Hey, back off, dude. She's with me," the guy says, his fingers wrapping around mine.

"Get your fucking hands off of her," Kade roars.

"Is he your boyfriend?" the guy asks.

I know I should be lying for the sake of getting rid of him and returning the peace. But I can't. It's clear Bruce would rather be with someone else. This stranger's attention is like a balm to my wounded soul.

I shake my head. "No. He's my roommate."

"Let's head to my place, then." The guy's grip on

my hand tightens, and I realize I should have lied.

Kade's jaw sets. Before I can tell the guy that I'm not interested, Kade slams his fist into his face, sending him flying backwards. "I said get your fucking fingers off of her before I break them."

"Kade." I step in front of him as I watch the guy stumble to his feet, his hand pressed against his nose. "He was just buying me a drink."

"And you decided to thank him by fucking him?" Kade almost spits out the words.

He's so angry I almost laugh. The hypocrisy is ridiculous. Wasn't he planning on fucking the blonde dancer when he hadn't even bought her a drink?

"Why not?" I yell at him. "I'm not exactly a virgin."

"What about Bruce? I thought you were going to be faithful to him."

"Bruce." I let out a laugh. "You mean the guy who wants to fuck a stick?" I laugh again at his confused expression, my veins boiling from the two glasses of vodka and the adrenaline coursing through them. "Relax, dude. We're all adults here. Why don't you go fuck your hot little dancer who you pretend isn't a stripper? What? You thought I didn't see you eyeing her up and down?"

"I barely noticed her, Vicky," Kade says, his tone suddenly calm and sincere.

Oh, he's a good liar, this one. He might just give Bruce a run for his money.

Out of my periphery, I notice two bouncers guiding my unwanted admirer through the gathering crowd.

I throw my hands up in exasperation. "Why do men always feel the need to lie? Do you think women are stupid? We always know when you're lying. For once, stick to the truth." I turn back to the barman who pretends to be busy rearranging bottles, but in reality he's staring just like everyone else in the vicinity. "Three more drinks of what I just had." The barman glances at me, then at Kade as though to get his permission. I'm so angry I could crawl up a wall. "Don't ask the prick. I'm the one buying," I mumble.

Kade sighs, sliding into the seat next to me. "Vicky, what are you doing? This is vodka."

"Good eye, Sherlock Holmes." I take a sip of my glass and grimace. This stuff is so bad, I can't believe people are paying good money to drink it. "I'm having fun, Kade. Join the party."

"This isn't fun." His hand stops me from taking another sip. "You're going to make yourself very sick."

Scoffing, I stab my finger in his chest, emphasizing every word as I say, "That's. Not. Your. Fucking. Business. Now, let me have my drink."

He lets go of my hand but doesn't back off. "You have to stop."

"I can't." Does my voice sound a bit slurred? Or is it this music that's made my head spin—and not in a good way.

"Fuck, Vicky. How many drinks have you had?" Kade asks.

I try to remember...and fail. "Two? Three? Four? Who's counting?"

"You're drunk." His statement makes me all defensive.

"I'm not. See, I can still walk straight." I jump up from my seat, and everything begins to shift and sway.

Kade's arms wrap around me just as I'm losing my balance. "That's it. I'm taking you home."

"Home?" I laugh so loud heads are turning to stare. "I don't have a home, but thanks for offering."

***

We're back in the limousine, and my head's

resting against the cold glass. But the coldness seeping into my skin does nothing to soothe the loud thumping sound hammering inside my head. Everything is spinning, and not in a rollercoaster fun kind of way.

There's a long pause as Kade opens the cabinet and pours himself a drink.

I stretch out my hand. "Can you get me one, too?"

"You've had enough for today," he says decisively.

"What's one more? I'm an adult. I can have as many drinks as I want."

"You're going to make yourself sick." His tone is still authoritative, but I can hear his resolve crumbling. I *am* an adult, and he can't tell me what to do.

I stretch out my hand again.

With a sigh, he hands me his drink.

"What's going on?" I feel his weight as he settles in the seat inches from me.

"I'm fine," I mumble.

"You don't look fine. You look upset, and I've had enough of not knowing what's going on."

"It's Bruce," I say after a drawn-out breath. "I think he's back with his ex."

"What makes you say that?"

"I just have this feeling." I shrug my shoulders

and look up, expecting him to start ridiculing my 'feelings' the way guys always do.

"Why don't you tell me about him?" Kade says. He looks tired, the way you do after a long night out, but his expression is earnest, interested.

I shake my head, not willing to talk about him.

"It's not my business," Kade says. "But I think this is a question you should ask yourself, and you obviously haven't done it yet. So, I'll ask it for you. What's so special about him?"

"He's an ice hockey player."

He doesn't even blink. "And?"

"And he's going to be famous," I say in one breath.

I expect him to be impressed. Maybe even a little jealous, but Kade still doesn't even blink.

Eventually he says, "That's a hobby or a profession, Vicky. While being a celebrity may only apply to a fragment of the population, it certainly doesn't make him more special than the rest of us." I open my mouth to dispute his statement when he holds up a finger, silencing me. "I'll put it the other way around. It's like you asking me what's my profession and me telling you that I'm a good person. Get it?"

I stare at him as I let his words sink in. I never

saw it this way.

"His profession is all that's special about him?" Kade prompts.

"No, he's also hot and I love him," I stammer.

His brows shoot up. "And?"

"And nothing." My temper's flaring at his inquisition, which doesn't seem to go anywhere.

"Why don't I believe you?" he says. "He treats you the way only a jerk would do."

"How do you know? Have you gone through my search history?" I can't help but sound accusatory.

"No. I wouldn't do that." Kade pours himself another glass. I watch him take a few sips.

"Do you think I'm attractive?" I ask as he puts his glass on the table.

"What?"

"You heard me." My voice comes out low but determined. "Am I attractive enough for you to want to fuck me?"

He eyes me warily. "Why are you asking? Is this some kind of test?"

"I've just been wondering if there's something wrong with me, that's all."

"There is nothing wrong with you, Vicky. Anyone who says so should get his eyes checked." His tone is soft, almost intimate. "Did Bruce tell you that you weren't attractive? Did he?" He doesn't look at me, but I can tell he's pissed.

"No."

He stares at me, his gaze ablaze. "Tell me the truth."

I shake my head. "No."

He doesn't believe me—I can tell from the way his mouth tightens.

I take a sip from my glass and let the alcohol burn its way down my throat.

"He never said that I'm unattractive or anything like that, but..." I stop, grasping at words to communicate the ugly truth.

"But what?" Kade's voice is soft, encouraging. I feel my inhibitions crumbling.

"We've never had sex." The words are out before I can stop them.

I cringe at how strange it all sounds—two adults in a relationship who've never had sex with each other.

"He's never had sex with you?" he asks in disbelief.

"Nope, we've never done it. He's always been good at finding excuses. He's never gone down on me, ever. He says it disgusts him, but demands that I be generous with the BJs." I close my eyes as mortification begins to course through me, making my skin tingle. "So, no, he doesn't seem to want sex with me." I close my eyes for a moment to escape his probing gaze. I couldn't bear to look at him and see the pity he surely feels for me. "I'm sorry. I don't know why I'm telling you all this."

"Because you trust me."

He sounds so understanding, I open my eyes and take a deep, steadying breath, unable to stop. "And then there's this woman...I think he really likes her. More than me."

His eyes narrow. "You suspect he's cheating on you?"

I shake my head. "I'm not sure. Not with her, anyway." I meet his questioning glance and decide I've told him so much, why not go a step further and spill everything? "I've created a fake profile. Now he thinks he's talking to this model instead of me. But if things were different...if it wasn't a fake profile...I don't know if he'd go for it for real. It sure looks like he would."

I feel ashamed at admitting that, yes, I was insecure enough to set up a trap. At the same time, I don't regret it.

"Want to show me?" Kade asks.

There's no judgment, no shock.

I take my time. Finally, I retrieve his phone and pull up the fake account. Kade takes his time reading Bruce's comments and messages.

I hold my breath as I wait for his reaction. Eventually he says, "This doesn't sound right."

"What?" I lean into him to glance at the tiny screen.

"The part where he's flirting with your fake account. It sounds like he's playing mind games." He holds up the cell phone to let me see.

"He isn't playing mind games." I don't know why I'm defending Bruce. Kade looks at me dubiously, and I cringe at the way I must look to him. "Here I am, protecting him and taking all that shit for him, and how does he repay me? By trying to hook up with a model and posting photos of him and his ex for everyone to see. Is something wrong with me? Am I not sexy enough? Should I start starving myself so I can compete with whatever it is he likes? I'm so fucking sick of this bullshit. I just want it all to stop. Come on, say it. I'm a pathetic stalker."

Smiling bitterly, I brace myself for his hard reply, for his judgment. When none comes, I search his face, trying to read the signs that aren't there. He's staring at me intently, listening to every word.

"Is that why you were upset back in there?" His

question takes me by surprise.

I laugh. "You just won't drop a topic, will you?"

"Never," Kade says, returning my smile. "You see, I'm trying to understand your circumstances."

His fingers brush mine gently. I peer down at our hands and feel the heat rushing to my face.

"I don't think you're unattractive at all. I think this guy is a goddamn idiot for not seeing how sexy you are," Kade says quietly. "No man in his right mind would turn you down. There's something wrong with him."

"He probably thinks I'm bad in bed," I mutter. "That's what's going on."

He frowns. "Don't take the fucking blame for this motherfucker. Guys like him disgust me."

"You have no idea what he's going through, Kade. You don't know him. He's had a lot of stress in his life." I don't know why I'm back to defending him.

"I almost give a fuck, but only almost." Kade lets out a laugh. "Is he sick? In prison? Does he have any balls at all?"

"Stop being sarcastic, Kade." I close my eyes, wishing I had never started. My anger's returning, but it's not addressed at Kade. It's addressed at myself and my inability to stop finding excuses for Bruce's behavior.

"You know, the more you talk about him, the more he sounds like a motherfucking coward who doesn't deserve one part of your body, let alone the entire you." Kade leans forward. "This guy doesn't deserve you, Vicky."

"You don't know him," I repeat and take a deep, shaky breath.

He sighs. "Alright. We're going around in circles. You didn't answer my question. What's so special about him?"

Ah, why won't he just drop that stupid question? I want to say "everything," and yet I can't because it's not the truth. When I don't reply, Kade asks, "How come someone as confident as you fell for this piece of shit? Do you enjoy people treating you like crap?"

His statement makes me feel as though a rug's just been pulled from under my feet. My hands begin to shake. I press them between my knees to hide it. "Shut up."

"Vicky," Kade says, his tone softer as his hands clasp around my chin, forcing me to look at him, "why would you want to be with someone who doesn't treat you the way you deserve to be treated? Just answer the question."

"I have no idea. I guess I love him."

His eyes pierce into me, reaching the parts of my heart I don't want him to see. "Ask yourself. Do you really?"

I meet his questioning gaze with a layer of ice. "What are you getting at?"

"Love isn't supposed to be this way."

"Like what?"

"Hurting. Addicting."

I laugh. Wow. He's just turned into an expert on the matter. "You have no idea what you're talking about. Why don't you stick to your own fucking problems? You and your sex addiction."

He nods his head patiently, ignoring my attempt at delivering a low blow. "Exactly. I'm addicted to sex. You're addicted to love. Our addictions are our own hell, but we're here to break them, run from, and free ourselves from them. Does that make us bad people? Does that give others the right to treat us like shit? Open your eyes, Vicky. We're not controlled by our addictions. We can control them. You, only you, have the choice to decide who to love. And if he's not worthy of that love, then it's not love at all."

I stare at him coldly. He has no idea what he's saying because he doesn't know what true emotions are. "What the fuck are you talking about?"

"Addictions do not happen. They are caused," Kade says slowly. "If you had attended group therapy, you'd know. Somewhere along the way, we cross a line we were never meant to cross."

My heartbeat spikes and anger surges through me.

That crap theory of his doesn't apply to me because I'm not addicted to anything. I've just had the misfortune of falling in love with someone who isn't completely honest about his feelings. Or maybe Bruce is just not ready to settle down yet.

"Stop the car," I shout. "Stop it right now."

"Where do you want to go?" Kade says, his tone nonchalant but cold.

"I'm going to be sick." Bile rises in my throat. I press my mouth against my lips, but it's too late. Before I can help myself, I puke on his shoes.

Shit.

"I'm so sorry." I wipe my hand over my mouth, feeling disgusted with myself. "So...so sorry."

Kade peers from me to his shoes, speechless. I expect him to be angry, throw a fit, feel as disgusted as I feel. Instead, he starts to laugh.

"What's so funny?" I can't help but ask as I fight another surge of mortification.

"Your expression." He winks at me. "Stop looking

so mortified. They're just shoes, Vicky." He opens a drawer, revealing tissues, and starts to wipe the vomit off his shoes.

The motion moves me to tears.

Bruce would never have cleaned up for me.

The last time I spilled soda in his car, he got so mad I had to reward him with a good BJ to calm him down.

"Let me help you." I inch closer and reach for the tissues when I realize he has some on his shirt, too.

"You should get out of your shirt," I say, my voice low and shaky.

"Why? Because you want to see me naked?" he jokes.

"Yes." I'm shocked at my honesty.

What the hell!

When he says nothing, I move closer to unbutton his shirt.

His fingers circle around mine, stopping me. "What are you doing, Vicky?" His voice is low, hoarse, a little heavy with the unmistakable. His dark eyes are two puddles of want.

"I feel like a complete failure," I whisper to him, avoiding his gaze. "My sister's getting married. I'm not jealous of her or anything, but I want it, too. Someone who loves me and wants me." I glance at him. "I'm terrified at the prospect of being alone for the rest of my life."

"Being alone isn't so bad."

"Not for you. But for me, it is." My fingers continue to fumble with the buttons. "I need to know if I'm bad at sex."

"And you want to find out how?"

I hesitate.

The truth is, Kade was right.

Love isn't supposed to be addicting. Love isn't supposed to hurt.

And yet it does. It freaking hurts to be away from Bruce. To not know. To not be able to see him. To keep guessing what's going on inside his head.

Not being able to call him, with the knowledge that he probably won't return my calls, makes me feel sick to the core.

Missing him makes me feel lost. And desperate because there's nothing I can do to escape this madness. And then there's so much anger I feel for everyone: the counselor, the judge, Bruce's ex, for Bruce because he's the one who's been putting me through this misery.

Only Kade can help.

"I want you to sleep with me." I stare into his eyes, begging, pleading. "Please."

15

Kaiden

MY HARD WORK'S paying off. One night out and she's already asking for my cock—albeit for all the wrong reasons. My cock is pulsating with excitement at the prospect of having Vicky in my bed. Feeling the effects of her touch, I ball my hands into fists. Judging from my past, it won't take long before sex is all I'll be able to think about. Whatever I want, I usually get.

Right now, I want Vicky.

More of her lips to find out what she tastes like.

More of her body, naked and at my disposal.

More of her as a person.

I'm filled with a longing to know more about her, about her life, who she is deep down, after all the walls have crumbled and she is laid bare.

"What are you doing here?" I ask for the umpteenth time. "Has Bruce fucked up and now you've decided you want to get rid of him after all?"

"Not funny." She smirks, but the skin around her eyes crinkles a little.

"What's the story then?" I prompt.

"We're going through a rough patch. I'd rather not talk about it, if you don't mind."

Usually, I wouldn't care and would leave it at that. But she looks like she needs someone to spill her heart out to.

"No, I actually want you to tell me what happened."

"I can't," Vicky says, her tone imploring. Her eyes are staring at me, pleading. "Please don't ask me to tell you."

"Tell me or nothing's happening tonight." I don't know where that just came from. But it feels right. I want her to want me, not a revenge fuck.

She rolls her eyes. "Oh, please. Don't tell me you don't miss sex. We both know you only invited me along so you could fuck me. So, here I am." Her honesty hits me hard and fuck, it makes me sound like a weak jerk who can't get a woman unless he's broken her will with the help of a couple drinks on a night out.

I want to fuck her.

And, yes, I invited her along in the hope of getting closer to her.

But I'm not sure it's the same thing she's just described.

"What are you waiting for?" She presses my hand against her breast and makes a moan-like sound that I'm sure is supposed to entice me. She's so drunk, I doubt she'll remember a thing come tomorrow. I doubt she knows what she's doing. This isn't going the way I imagined at all. I could fuck her and be done with it, but the prospect of being her rebound, of taking part in her little revenge sex plan, isn't appealing.

I'm not going to fuck a woman who's so drunk she can't think straight.

"I can't." I withdraw my hand.

"Are you honestly saying no to them?" She shakes her breasts in my face. I stare for a moment, wondering whether I'm making a stupid mistake.

"That's not the point." I shake my head and turn away from her. "The point is that you're in a very vulnerable frame of mind, and I don't want to take advantage of you."

I feel bad saying it.

My wish is about to come true, and I'm being an ungrateful jerk.

But, fuck. I don't want to be one of those guys who need to resort to alcohol to get a woman. That's never been me, and I'm most certainly not turning into one right now—no matter how hot she looks in that dress of hers.

"Look, I'm your friend, Vicky. I do care about you, but I can't just say yes to your request." Fuck, even my balls are hurting as I speak those words.

She stares at me for a long time. "Can you get me another drink?"

"No more drinks." I shake my head and peer at the time. We're skating toward our morning counseling sessions. If she continues like this, she'll barely be able to walk, let alone make it through a session without falling asleep.

"Why?" She pouts. I peer at those luscious lips of hers and can't shake off the image of them wrapped around my cock.

"You can barely sit straight," I point out.

"Alright, Daddy." She kicks off her shoes, then pulls up her legs, resting her chin on her knees. "I'm going to tell you something. But if I tell you, you need to promise me that you won't judge. Not me. Not him. And not one single word about it in the future. When I'm done, I want you to fuck me because I really need to know how I rate." She stretches out her leg and drapes it over mine. "Promise me."

I brush my fingertips over her ankle, up to her knee, marveling at how soft her skin is.

"We'll talk about your secrets later." I rest my hand on her knee and inch a little closer. "I want to hear your story first."

"What's my story?" She lets out a laugh. "Um, let me see. I was born, grew up, the usual stuff. What's really important is that I'm sick and tired of hearing about people getting engaged. I'm tired of being alone and fighting an uphill battle. I feel like I'm counting on something that may never happen. There's just too much I want. I want a family, a home, kids. I want true love and someone who loves me. And Bruce?" Her body begins to shake slightly. "It all seems possible with him. We spent most of our first date talking about family, marriage, all the things I want."

I cock my eyebrow. No guy ever does that—unless he wants to score. That he got the chance and didn't take it is strange.

Her gaze meets mine. "He told me that he needs a woman who wants to take that step."

"He told you that on your first date?"

"Yeah." Nodding her head, she turns to stare out of the window, her eyes lost in the darkness. "I don't know what happened. I thought we wanted the same things from life. But obviously, that's not the case. Or maybe he just doesn't want them with me, or why else would he insist that we keep our relationship a secret?"

I listen in silence as she goes on to explain how the restraining order happened, and why it's limited all contact.

It's a clear game of push and pull—as old as relationships—but the only thing that doesn't make sense are his motivations.

For the life of me, I can't imagine why Bruce would talk about marriage, unless he wants to sleep with her or he's after her money— which she doesn't seem to have a lot of.

The more she talks about him, the more I get the feeling that he's using her. But how can I ask without hurting her feelings?

Eventually, I can't bear it any longer. "Does he stand to inherit something if he marries?"

She stares at me blankly. "I don't think so. He's already rich."

Okay, scratch that off the list.

It clearly still is a game to him.

My hands ball into fists. The knowledge is there, hidden somewhere at the back of my mind. I just can't grasp it yet.

Vicky notices my reaction.

"You promised not to be angry, Kade."

"I'm not angry. I'm pissed." My tone is sharp, livid. "This guy's a total asshole." The statement shuts her up.

She turns back to the window, and her shoulders are slightly shaking. Her face is turned away from me, and for a moment I fear that she's crying silently.

Maybe I've been too harsh.

"Don't cry. Please. It's not your fault he's—" I break off as she turns to face me. That's when I realize she's laughing.

I frown.

Didn't she hear what I just said about her beloved Bruce?

"Do you think this is funny?" I ask.

"I'm sorry," she says, her entire body shaking now. "I know this is supposed to be a serious conversation, but I just can't help myself." She laughs, nearly falling into hysterics. "My whole life's this big mess. It's like I'm performing on a stage and any minute now someone's going to pour a bucket of water over my head. So, can we get on with it and just have sex?"

"That's it." I knock on the divider.

The glass slides down.

"You've taken us far enough," I say to the driver. "Stop the car."

"What are you doing, Kade?" Vicky asks between laughs. "Are you going to throw me out? Because if you are, make sure to give me one of those bottles to last me through the night."

The car halts. I grab Vicky's hand, her bag, and pull her out of the car. She doesn't put up much of a fight but keeps laughing as I tip the driver.

"You're making too much noise," I whisper. "I need you to keep quiet before someone notices us."

"What the hell?" The limousine speeding off seems to sober her. "How are we supposed to get home?"

"Quite simple. We walk." I sling her handbag over my shoulder and wonder what the fuck she's carrying in there.

"I'm not walking." As if to prove her point, she

stomps her foot and stands her ground.

Sighing, I turn to her. "You'll have to because there's no way in hell I'm carrying you." I point up the winding street and the lights shimmering in the distance. The sun will rise soon. It's only a matter of time until everyone's up. "That's a twenty-minute walk. We can make it in fifteen if you can keep up with me. The fresh air will help you calm down a bit."

"I'm calm," she protests.

"No, you're not." Our eyes lock in a fierce battle. For such a small person, she sure knows how to stand her ground.

The moonlight is shining on us, bathing her in a silver glow. It looks like her whole being is encased in fire and her red hair is a burning mane. For a moment, I'm honestly convinced that I've got things under control when she starts giggling again.

"It was a mistake to bring you along." I start to walk, not waiting for her to follow.

The air's cooled noticeably. The night's as silent as a grave; the only sound is the thumping of her footsteps. I hasten my pace because I can hear her getting closer, catching up with me.

"Talk to me, Kade."

So close to the rehab center. I can't have her in

hysterics again, so I keep quiet.

"Are you still angry with Bruce?" she asks. "I don't think he's ready yet. That's all. We're going through a rough patch. It won't last forever."

We're back to square one.

I shake my head grimly and keep going. "True love isn't about two people fighting an uphill battle right from the beginning of their relationship. Everyone who's been married for a long time will tell you that. That's not you two. I'm sorry, but you know it's true."

"I love him, Kade." She sounds so desperate to believe her own lie, I want to turn around and kiss the life out of her until she realizes that nothing she feels for that asshole even remotely resembles love.

"Who are you fooling?" I ask instead.

"Who the hell are you to question my feelings?"

She's getting angry again.

"I'm the man who cares about you." I stop and turn sharply. She comes dangerously close to bumping into me. Even though there's no need, I wrap my arm around her waist, pulling her close enough to feel her breath on my lips. "Like it or not, I'm the only one who's honest with you."

Her eyes narrow, but she doesn't pull away. "Honest about what?"

"You think you're in love with him, but the truth is that you're deluding yourself. You deserve someone better."

She cocks her head. "How would a sex addict know?"

"What? You think I was never in love?"

"I don't think someone like you is capable of loving." Her eyes widen and she takes a step back, as though shocked by her own remark.

"It's okay. I'm not offended," I say. "Look, I'm a lot of things, and that includes not wanting to form any sort of commitment. But I'm not incapable of loving. I was in love once in my life. That happened a long time ago, and I hope it stays that way."

"I told you my story, and now it's only fair that you tell me yours, Kade."

I consider rejecting her request. Ah, what the hell? "Fine. It's not like you'll remember any of this." I hold her hand as we resume walking. "I was twenty, and I was in love with this girl, alright? She meant the world to me. Back then, I truly believed we had a good thing going. At some point, even the word marriage came up. As you can probably guess, something happened." Taking a deep breath, I realize something. Old wounds might have healed, but the scars are still here. No one ever leaves your life without leaving their footprint in the sands of your being.

"Did she die?" Vicky whispers.

I shoot her a sideways glance and scoff. "You think I would be telling you this story if that was the case? No, she didn't die, Vicky. She cheated on me. With my then best friend."

The sudden silence is heavy.

"Cash?" she asks eventually.

"Not Cash. Someone else I never thought would betray me. But friends are like that. You never really know someone, until you do, and then it's too late." I shake my head. "I thought I could trust them. I was so naïve to believe that the only reason they spent time together was to plan a party for me. Fuck, even my uptight brother told me they were fucking, and I didn't want to believe him. That's how much I trusted them." I pause to gather my thoughts. The turmoil is still there, but it's numbed, just like the rest of me. "As things stand, my brother was right. I couldn't forgive, so I cut all ties with my so-called best friend. Three months after their little affair, he moved on to someone else and she was back on the market."

"Did she try to sort things out with you?"

"Not that I know of." Her betrayal hurt so much,

for months I jumped whenever the phone rang, thinking that she might be on the other end of the line. "That's the strange part. I thought she loved me and that she'd want to get back together, realizing that she made a mistake. But she didn't. She moved on to the next guy even though I tried everything to win her back despite the hurt she had caused. I was willing to forgive her. Fuck, I even tried my damnedest to give her time and space, but you know what they say? You won't make it work if only one's trying. There are two people in every relationship. My relationship didn't work out because I was the only one in it."

"I'm so sorry, Kade," Vicky whispers.

"Looking back now, I can tell that I was obsessive. I gave her so much and she wasn't happy. Today, there are days when I think back and reflect on how young and stupid I was." I turn to look at her. "My point is, do you understand that what you're feeling isn't love?"

"What do you call it then?"

"Obsession." My eyes search hers. In spite of the darkness surrounding us, I can glimpse an awareness that tells me my story has reached a deep part of her. "Obsession, Vicky. I had this perfect idea of love, and I wanted her to be that one woman worthy of my worship. She had the looks, but not the personality. I needed someone who completed me. But all she did was fill a need. As soon as I learned to be happy with and focus on myself, I realized where true happiness comes from. Thinking back, it's hard for me to imagine that I truly believed I was in love with her." I laugh. "It's actually strange that we're talking about her today out of all days."

"Why?"

"Because I ran into her at a party this time last year."

"How was she?" Vicky asks.

I shrug my shoulders and we resume walking. "She was nice, very impressed by my success. Told me she had been following me online for years but was too afraid to get in touch. She still looked good. Her hair was all done. Same weight, same style. But it still took me two minutes to remember her." I grin at Vicky's horrified expression. "It's as if a part of me had forgotten her, pushed her back into the deepest recesses of my mind. The moment she told me her name and I recognized her, I felt this huge surge of relief. Relief that I had absolutely no feelings left for her."

"None at all?"

"None," I say. "I was surprised. But I still had to

make sure I was completely over her, so I fucked her all night, and then I left. The feelings I thought I had for her never came back. Worse yet, and I feel bad saying so, but I didn't give a crap about what she had become. I don't care about her at all. She could have died, and it wouldn't have mattered to me."

We stop at the clearing to stare up at the building before us. Most windows are illuminated now. We need to make it inside as soon as possible before someone spies us out here.

"Come on. We need to get going."

"Wait." Her hand finds mine, squeezing into it, fitting perfectly. "You're saying it was just a phase, an obsession," she starts, resuming the conversation.

"Nothing that is real or lasting. It's something that passed the moment I decided to move on. That's why I know you don't love Bruce. When I look at you, I see myself many years ago. I see you making the same mistakes I made. And that's why I'm so angry, Vicky. Not at you, but at him." My finger settles beneath her chin, raising it a little until I'm sure I have her full attention. "You might think you love him, that this is some rough patch that will pass and he'll come around. But make no mistake, he knows what he's doing, just like my ex knew what she was doing when she cheated with my best friend.

So, no, true love doesn't hurt. It doesn't break you. It's all too easy to mistake obsession for love. Once you step over the brink and leave that insanity behind, you'll realize there's no good reason why you'd want to suck it up. There's no good reason why you'd want to keep making excuses for someone who's not worthy of them."

16

Vicky

I WAKE UP TO the merciless rays of the sun spilling through the window. Groaning, I cover my eyes with my pillow to get a few more seconds of sleep. My head is pounding like a sledgehammer has been hard at work. My pulse is thudding against my temples. Nausea has settled in my stomach, warning me that I need to get to the bathroom, but I'm too tired to leave the comfort of my bed. Flipping onto my side, I pull the sheets up to my chin when a cold breeze reaches me and I realize—

I'm naked.

I jolt upright and press the sheets to my chest.

Why, for crying out loud, am I butt naked?

Fighting against the sun blinding me, I scan the room. The window is on the wrong side. The desk seems misplaced. A black jacket is draped over the back of the chair, and clothes are scattered across the floor.

Why does the air smell like *him*? His aftershave— the scent I've grown to seek out whenever I use our shared bathroom.

That's when it hits me.

I'm in Kade's room.

My gaze roves wildly over everything, searching for some sign that this isn't happening.

What am I doing in Kade's room? But even as I ask myself the question, fragments of memories come to me. They are blurry, disjointed, but they all seem to circle around one thing: our night together.

I can't believe I asked him to fuck me.

"Oh, my God." I bury my head in my hands for a long moment, then wrap the sheets around my body, ready to storm out when I realize there's no way in hell I'm leaving my clothes behind.

As I push up to my feet, the room begins to spin. I wait a few seconds and then try again. There's no sign of Kade, no sign of my clothes. Maybe I left them in the living room. I head for the door when I stumble over something hard and almost take a tumble.

My heart gives a little jolt as I realize what it is.

It's Kade, sleeping on the floor, a blanket spread out, and oh, my God, he's naked, too.

A little yelp escapes my lips as my hands spread to halt my fall, but my equilibrium is way off. I tumble on top of him.

"Please don't tell me you want it again," he mumbles, his eyes closed.

Again?

My whole body heats up as I scramble to my feet, desperately trying to cover up with whatever I can find. My hands tug at the sheet, but as I pull it up, I also grab his sheet, exposing his body.

All the parts that count.

It's really one huge cock. And there's a real chance it's already been inside me.

"You didn't answer my question." He opens his eyes groggily, his lips twitching as he catches my glance. I drop his sheet and busy myself with covering his modesty.

"Did we..." I swallow hard, unable to speak out the unthinkable.

"What?" His brows shoot up in mock confusion.

He knows *exactly* what I'm talking about. He just wants to hear me say it.

"You know what." I gesture between us, fighting hard not to gawk at the huge bulge forming beneath the sheet. Fuck, I can't even say the word now that I've seen it again in all its glory.

He cocks his head. "Did we fuck? Is that what you want to know?" I nod my head. "You can't remember? Nothing? Not at all?"

I shake my head as my cheeks begin to catch fire.

Oh, my God.

Please don't tell me I slept with him.

His voice draws me back. "Relax. We haven't."

"Then why are we both naked?"

"I don't know about you, but I always sleep naked." His lips twitch.

"I don't." I stare at him, confused. "Why did I take off my clothes?"

"Because you stripped...a little. Mentioned it was too hot and that you had to remove your dress and underwear."

I stare at him. That's not me. I never do stuff like that.

"Why am I in your room?"

"You didn't want to sleep alone. You said you were scared, so I offered you my bed." My jaw drops.

The skin around his eyes crinkle, and I realize he looks so damn delicious in the morning, I feel the slightest bit of regret that we *didn't* do the deed.

"What was I supposed to do?" Kade asks.

"Say no?"

He lets out a laugh. "Do you have any idea how often I had to say no last night? Damn, woman, you're the most stubborn person I've ever met. I was about to give in when you finally passed out. Thank God for that."

He can't be serious.

"So, you just let me sleep in your bed while you chose the floor?" If what he says is true, I can't help but feel offended that he felt the need to reject me so many times.

"What was I supposed to do? Throw you out of my bed? You invited yourself in, and before I could stop it, you fell asleep."

I cock my head, a part of me wanting him to lie. But his expression is honest. Even his smile is gone.

"So, nothing happened?" I ask again.

"No."

I bury my face in my hands. "God. I must have looked like a complete fool."

"It wasn't that bad." I look at him and find him smiling again. "Just do me a favor and never drink vodka again. You were lucky nobody heard the ruckus you caused outside when I had to carry you inside. You put up quite the fight."

"Sorry." Cringing, I try to fathom when it all started to go so wrong last night. Then I remember the Facebook account: Bruce and the picture of him and his ex.

"How are you?" Kade asks softly.

"The term train wreck jumps to mind." I smirk. "I just want to cut off my head."

He lets out a laugh. "Go take a shower while I'm getting us breakfast."

Even though I shouldn't, I stare at his naked butt as he grabs his clothes and strolls out of the room.

Damn! He looks hot. Muscular, but not too much.

Before he closes the door, he turns and winks, catching me staring a little too intently.

My face catches fire, but I don't avert my gaze.

I embarrassed myself so much last night, what's a little more, right?

***

I don't know why, but I like Kade.

He's the first guy I feel like I can fully confide in. And he's hot.

Damn.

He's really hot.

Like cover of a magazine, Photoshopped hot.

He's sitting in front of me, half-naked, his upper body exposed. I can see the tattoo on his shoulder, snaking down, and can't help but wonder what the design means.

"You're staring at me," he says, raking his hand through his hair, as though I'm making him nervous.

"Sorry." I peel my gaze off of him. "I still feel like a fool. I'm so sorry about last night."

"Stop apologizing. We had a lot of fun. That's important." I smirk. He catches my glance and laughs. "Not that kind of fun. But fun, nonetheless." He points to my plate. "How are the eggs?"

I stare at the fried mess he calls breakfast. "Good." Fidgeting in my seat, I take another bite of my omelet, pondering how to put it so his feelings won't get hurt. "A bit salty, maybe."

"I have a confession to make. I didn't really make this."

"I reckoned that much. We don't have eggs in the fridge."

"While you were in the shower, I dashed down to the cafeteria and scraped together all the leftovers I could get," he says just as I'm about to stuff another forkful into my mouth. "How bad are they?"

"Disgusting?" I peer at the fork, unsure whether to eat the stuff or go hungry until lunch.

"You know..." He lifts his fork and helps himself to the remnants on my plate, then grimaces. "One day I'm going to learn how to cook." His chocolate eyes meet mine.

"Maybe for the right woman?" I laugh at his expression. "This is really disgusting, but thank you anyway."

"No need."

As we eat, the sudden silence makes me aware just how comfortable I feel around him. I haven't even thought of Bruce yet. I still have the phone, but the thought of checking up on him hasn't even occurred to me today.

"How can I repay you, Kade?"

"By having coffee with me?" He pushes a mug of some milky concoction toward me.

"You know what I mean." I lean back and brush my hair out of my face. "This place sucks. I don't think anyone wants to be here. You took a risk by inviting me along even though you didn't have to. You don't even know me."

He shrugs his shoulders. "I like your company. You're fun."

"You mean fun as in acting like an idiot."

"It wasn't that bad," Kade says. "The way I saw it, I could leave you behind and risk you exposing my temporary escape. Or drag you along and be partners in crime."

I smile at him. "I really enjoyed our night out even if I don't remember a great deal of it."

"We don't need to keep it at just one. We can sneak out whenever we want."

"You want to go out again?" Even though my head's still spinning a bit and my stomach isn't quite ready yet to digest solid food, I find the idea appealing.

"Sure. You don't?"

I let the thought sink in for a moment. "What if someone sees us?"

"Won't happen because we'll be even more careful." His eyes soften. "The next time you're upset and you feel like hitting the bottle, I want you to tell me. Do you think you can do that?"

"I'll try," I mumble. Telling him, that is. The controlling my alcohol intake part won't be too difficult because I hardly ever drink.

He stands and begins to busy himself with clearing the table. As he turns around, I get a few more seconds to look at him. There is another tattoo on his back, spreading across his upper back almost like wings.

"Still staring." He turns around and refills his mug, then mine.

"Not really," I lie. "I was just wondering what your tattoos mean. I've never seen something like it before."

"This one?" He points at his upper arm. "It represents the countless times I made mistakes. Patterns tend to repeat themselves. To break a habit, you need to step out of the picture and listen to what others have to say, even if you don't want to hear it."

"That's one long-winded explanation." I frown. "Are you making it up as you go along?"

He laughs. "You caught me. In all honesty, it represents all the crossroads I've been at in my life and the times I had to cut ties to achieve something."

I think I'm beginning to understand him and his motivations. With Kade, it's all about change. "Like the ex you told me about?"

He looks at me, interest striking his face. "Out of all the things you could have remembered, that's the one you chose to retain?"

He's so right about that. "You said I'd forget, and I just couldn't let you be right."

He sits back down opposite from me, and stretches out his long legs, nudging my foot. "What about you? Do you have any tattoos?"

His eyes brush the front of my top, lingering on my breasts. "You tell me. You've already seen me naked."

"I didn't look."

My lips twitch. I don't believe him. "Not once?"

He shakes his head, his eyes feign innocence. "Nope."

"You expect me, in all honesty, to believe that you didn't look?"

"I swear." He crosses his fingers in front of my face. "On my Scout's honor, I promise that's the truth. I didn't look at you while you were naked." He lifts his mug to his lips, eyeing me with an amused grin.

"You were a Boy Scout?"

"Yeah." He laughs. "If you want, I can show you some cool things."

I narrow my eyes, not trusting him one bit when he smiles that lopsided grin of his. "Like what?"

"Like how to build a tree house."

"Here?"

"On the island, yeah. Obviously we'll have to go with a miniature version of it."

I shake my head, both to signal that I'm not interested and also because I realize his words have stuck with me and I'm pissed.

"You didn't look?" I ask.

"I didn't take advantage of your drunken state," Kade says, misinterpreting my sudden irritation.

"Why didn't you?" I hold his gaze.

"Because you deserve someone who cares about you. That's why," he says matter-of-factly. "I'd feel like I violated your privacy, and to be honest, I don't want to jeopardize our relationship."

"Our relationship?"

"Yeah," he replies, cocking his left eyebrow. "The relationship between two friends."

Right.

What the hell did I hope to hear?

"You know, this place isn't so bad once you get the hang of it," he continues. "Join the group session today."

I don't know what to say to that. I can't just tell a bunch of strangers my most intimate thoughts. "How do you know I haven't been there?" I ask.

"I don't ever see you." He regards me intently. "You know there are mixed sessions, right?"

"Is it working for you?"

"I don't think anything's working here." He

winks. "But when I listen to other stories, it actually makes me feel better knowing I'm not going through their shit. So, in some way, you can say that I'm relishing in the fact that others have it worse."

I laugh. "You're so bad."

"I know, right? Join me, Vicky. You'll have so much fun. It's one big soap opera after another," he says. "There's this girl who's in love with someone she's never seen, never spoken to. And, get this. She hasn't even seen his photo, meaning she doesn't know who she's been chatting with. But she's convinced that she's in love."

"I don't believe you."

He raises his eyebrows and gives me a deadpan face. "Why don't you join us and see for yourself? This is real-life stuff. Even better than *Catfish.*"

I stare at him. *"Catfish?* Seriously? You watch the show?"

"Is that so hard to believe?" He smiles and his eyes flicker with something. "We have a lot in common, don't we?"

His words catch me off-guard.

"Yeah, I guess we do," I say softly. My feel-good bubble is slowly bursting as something dawns on me. "How late is it?"

He glances at his watch. "Past eleven."

I'm so late.

The last time I checked, it was shortly before nine. I realize we've been together for more than twelve hours.

How did my time with Kade fly so fast and I didn't even notice?

"I've got to go." I jump to my feet and run out the door before he can say anything.

17

Kaiden

THREE THINGS I'VE learned about my new roommate the past few days:

1. She's hot.
2. I have to fuck her.
3. She's going to be the death of my cock. I know it with the certainty some people know that it's going to rain, which brings me back to point number two: I have to fuck her and get her out of my system.

Ever since meeting her, I can't seem to stop thinking about fucking her. But just thinking about it is no longer enough. At night, I'm lying awake, knowing full well that my honorable commitment of not fucking her when I had the chance will keep coming back to haunt me.

I know I could get her drunk again, wind her up by talking about Bruce, and then let that asshole boyfriend of hers do the rest of the work. But there's one tiny problem.

I do like her.

I really like her.

Maybe a bit more than I should.

When I set up the 365-day, non-stop sex calendar, I had one rule:

Not to fuck someone I care about.

I never wanted to let a woman get close to me, and yet I've encouraged Vicky to tell me so much about her life that I feel like I know her.

I've told her secrets about myself. And now she knows me.

We've gotten close without even having sex.

Vicky Sullivan is a strange girl with even stranger manners and the strangest mind. She's like a caterpillar, both fragile and beautiful to look at.

She's sitting opposite me, her face turned to me

as we've been listening to the stories around us. She's next in line.

I'm holding my breath, waiting for her words to spill out; for the transformation to come through, knowing that it doesn't take much for her to wrap herself in a cocoon and bounce hard with fragile wings against the hard shell that is her reality.

But she remains evasive. Almost indifferent.

Her arms are crossed over her chest, her face absent. Her whole posture screams 'I don't care what you think of me,' except she hasn't even uttered her boyfriend's name.

"Vicky, how would you feel if—" Mary, our counselor, lowers her gaze quickly to search through her notes, "—Bruce were dating someone other than you?"

The entire group's staring at Vicky, giving her their full attention. It's Vicky's third group meeting, and my ninth.

"I wouldn't be happy, I guess." There's no expression on her face; she isn't even blinking. She's reached the stage that's called defeat, maybe even acceptance.

"Despite him getting a restraining order against you?" Mary asks carefully.

"It wasn't him," Vicky says defensively. "It was his

ex together with his mom. He would never do that to me."

I set my jaw. Acceptance, my ass. She's just being stubborn while getting nowhere.

"Never?" I ask, raising my brows. Everyone turns to look at me. The glances are reproachful. This isn't my battle to fight. I'm only supposed to listen, not throw my two cents out there. It's the first time I have spoken today, but damn, I'll make it count.

"No, Kade. He would never," she says, giving me the kind of look that screams 'shut the hell up.' "He loves me."

"You sure?"

If looks could kill, I'd probably have an arrow embedded deep in my chest. "Yes, he does."

I smile. "Not to burst your bubble, because it's riveting and well-constructed, but can you set something straight? He's inviting you over to his place and he expects what? That you enter through the walls? Hide in some Harry Potter cloak and move past his mom?"

Her eyes narrow dangerously. "What are you getting at?"

She thinks she can shut me up with that venomous look. I can see it in her arrogant stance.

Good that I'm not one to easily hold my mouth.

I'm too angry for that.

Last night, after she returned my phone, I peeked at the history to see why she was upset again.

She had not logged off her Facebook account, and I found a vacation snapshot of Bruce with his ex. They were obviously spending time together, rekindling their romance. And yet Vicky insists that her relationship with Bruce is still going strong.

Maybe the lie serves the purpose of deluding herself. Or maybe she just doesn't trust me enough to tell me.

Either way, it pisses me off big time.

"He's a worthless piece of shit, Vicky," I say.

The room's dead silent. Everyone's jaw has dropped. Every gaze is turned to Vicky, waiting for her reaction, waiting for an outburst.

"It's not like that." She's surprisingly quiet and composed. "I could have always said no, but I didn't. I wanted to see him just as much as he wanted to see me."

"Why didn't you refuse his demand?" I ask, ignoring the latter part. "Is your life so boring that you need a guy who treats you like a spare tire? Is it the lack of attention that makes you seek out the wrong kind of attention? You're so full of faith he'll come around and rescue you from the mundane.

Think again. This guy will always remain a worthless piece of shit, and no love from you or anyone is going to change the fact that he's a momma's boy."

"Kade," Mary whispers. If it's supposed to be a warning, it doesn't scare me.

Vicky's body is shaking. Anytime now she's going to throw a fit about it being none of my business. I know it because we've been there before.

"He has problems."

"Issues. His own, you mean." I laugh. "And plenty of them."

Mary claps, the sound ringing through the tension. It's clear she's trying to end this conversation. "Great job. Great job, everybody. Let's give Victoria and Kaiden a round of applause. We'll resume our session tomorrow, same time, same place, in case you don't know."

Everyone laughs and begins to pack up whatever they've brought with them.

Vicky continues to stare at me, her chest heaving as she tries to control herself.

The room begins to clear. As soon as I step outside into the hall, a hand tightens around my upper arm and pulls me into the storage room next door.

I blink against the sudden darkness, and then

blink again as the light goes on.

"Are you crazy?"

I stare into Vicky's livid expression.

"Maybe a bit." My expression matches her anger. "Does it matter?"

"You just exposed me."

"You thought I would keep my mouth shut?" I ask. "Why didn't you tell me that he's back with his ex?"

The silence lasts all of two seconds.

"What the hell, Kade? Did you go through my search history?"

"You lied to me," I say. "I think that's the point we should be discussing."

"It's private. It doesn't concern you."

"Nothing's private on my phone."

She purses her lips, waves of anger wafting from her. "You still had no right to tell others all that I confided in you."

"I didn't really get the chance to say a lot." I shake my head grimly. "You lied, Vicky. What the hell? I thought we had reached the point where you could trust me. Why didn't you confide in me that he was back with his ex? I could have been there for you."

"Because I wasn't sure."

I frown. "There is a picture of them at the beach

on vacation. What's there to doubt?"

"Fine." She lets out a sharp breath. "What do you want to hear? That my relationship isn't going anywhere? That I'm a failure?"

I stare at her, at a loss for words. "He's a grown man who's still living with his parents, and you're the failure? You know what they say about men who are attached to momma's apron strings?" I don't wait for her reply. "I'll give you a clue. It starts with P and ends with Y."

"Stop it, Kade. This is not the time for jokes." In spite of her attempt at looking annoyed, her lips twitch.

"Why not?"

"You're making me angry." She grabs the handle but doesn't open the door. I press my open palm against the door, planting myself before her.

"If making you angry is the only way to make you realize you're wasting your time with this guy, then it's worth it."

"Why do you even care?" Her voice is soft now.

I don't understand the anger I'm feeling or the fact that I do care.

I don't understand why I need to protect her while shaking some sense into her.

"I would hate seeing you wasting your time over

this loser. I hate knowing that this piece of shit makes you feel bad about yourself." I grab her chin, forcing her to look at me, fighting the sudden urge to kiss her. "No woman deserves to feel the way you do. I don't know what his fucking problem is, but Vicky, I do know that you're hot. I have to restrain myself around you, and it's not easy."

"You find me attractive?" she whispers, her eyes wide.

"Yeah. Without a doubt." I brush my fingertips over her lips, tracing the contours. "You're weird but sexy as hell. Do you have any idea what you're doing to me? How much you leave me in want? I don't think you do."

She stares at me in silence. Seconds pass. Her proximity is both beauty and agony. I want to crush her lips with mine. I want to push my tongue into her mouth and find out whether she tastes as sweet as she looks.

At last, she pulls away from me, breaking our eye contact.

"Then why do you keep pushing me away?" she asks quietly.

The words hang heavy between us.

It takes me a full three seconds to understand what they mean.

She still remembers that night. The night I thought the alcohol would wipe her memory.

I let out a shaky breath. "I'm not pushing you away, Vicky. But I don't want to hurt you. You're too fragile for what I can give you."

"Oh, please." She laughs. "It was you who suggested we hook up. We both know what it means."

What it used to mean.

Outside the door, the hall's getting busy, and I realize only a piece of wood separates us from the world. And yet we couldn't be farther away.

"You're right, but it was before…" I break off, unsure what the hell I was just about to say.

"What?"

"Before I got to know you better. I don't want you to do something you might regret."

"What if I don't care?" She lifts on her toes, bringing her lips close to mine. "What if I want us to hook up?"

"Is that really what you want?" I ask.

She nods her head. "I want to feel it. I want to feel you, Kade. You're the only one who understands. The only one who doesn't judge me." Her arms wrap around me, and even though it's stuffy in here, I can feel her shivering through her thin dress. "Please.

It's been too long. I need to feel normal again." She leans her head against my chest and her fingers start to unbutton my shirt.

I can feel myself hardening. If she doesn't stop, I know I won't be able to control myself.

I press my fingers against hers, stopping her movement.

Every fiber of my being demands that I take her, right here, right now.

If only it didn't feel so wrong.

I know what she wants, but I can't give it to her. She's too fragile, too important to me. I don't want to break what we have, but I also don't want to miss the chance. "I'm a sex addict, Vicky."

"We're all addicted to something that makes us feel good, Kade." Her hand pushes my shirt aside and begins to draw circles on my chest. "Talking about addictions, my addiction's more fucked up than yours."

I shake my head. "I don't think so."

"Let's agree to disagree." She flattens her palm, and her gaze searches mine. "Are you going to kiss me now?"

I hesitate.

It's not confusion that's clouding my mind. I know I want her. I'm hesitating because this feels different from the countless hook-ups I've had before. I should never have challenged her. Now I have no choice than to go with it and see where it leads us.

I cup her face and bring my lips down on hers, whispering, "I was going to kiss you, anyway."

Without wasting a second, my mouth is on hers, demanding.

Her lips are softer than expected, reminding me of flower petals, the touch of a soft, winter breeze. She tastes of roses, too. It's her skin. The same scent that lingered on my pillow long after she left my bed. It sets my whole body on fire. I let out a groan as her hands move down my chest, past my abdomen.

It's a game of fire and lust.

I'm about to guide her fingers to my hard-on when the lights go out.

We're engulfed by darkness.

"Did you just switch off the lights?" I ask, peeling my mouth from hers.

"Yeah?"

"Why?"

"I don't know," Vicky whispers. "Habit, I guess."

I set my jaw, knowing that she can't see me. I reach across her shoulder and pat down the wall until I find the switch to turn the lights back on.

"When we're doing it, I want to do it on my terms." I lift her arms over her head. "I want to see you. The real you. With all your faults, your mistakes, your baggage. Not some woman I'm kissing in the darkness. I want you to know that it's me who's here with you, at the worst of times, in the worst of all places, about to make the worst mistake."

Her lips are swollen, her eyes hooded with desire. "You aren't a mistake, Kade."

"No, Vicky." I shake my head. "But you might be one to me. If anyone finds out about this, I started it. Got it?"

She nods her head and lets out a shaky breath as my hands circle around her small waist. In one swift motion, I turn her around. Her back is turned to me, her chest heaving with excitement. I kiss her neck softly. She lets her head roll back against me and tilts her head to accommodate me.

I let my tongue trail down her neck to her collarbone, then move upward again, tasting her skin. She smells of the intoxicating scent that's been lingering around our apartment since her arrival. She tastes of roses and strawberries and cream and *her*.

I press my growing hardness against her ass

while my breath grazes her ear as I whisper, "I want to taste you. All of you."

Her breath catches in her throat—I can hear it, I can feel it in the way she freezes against me. An instant later, her pulse quickens against my lips and she pushes her ass against me, grinding slightly, as though eager to feel me inside her.

"Kade." She says my name—half protesting, half imploring. It could go either way now.

I let my hand trail down her back until I reach her hips and push up her dress. Her skin is feverishly hot against my fingertips. Only a thin pair of lace panties is standing between me and what I want. What I've been aching to touch and feel and taste.

"Is this what you want, Vicky?" I part her legs with my knee and push her panties aside. She draws in her breath the moment I touch my fingers to her entrance.

She's hot and wet for me.

The thought drives me crazy. Unable to control myself, I let out a low, feral growl.

I have to have her *now*.

I want to make her writhe and quiver. I want to see her come with my name on her lips.

Turning her around, I lower myself down on my knees. She doesn't protest as I push up her dress and gather it around her hips, guiding her hands to keep it up.

Her panties are damp, dripping with want. I pull them down her legs, letting them fall to her ankles, then guide one leg up around my shoulder. She's now captured between the wall and me, at my mercy, just the way I want it.

"Kade?" Her voice is questioning. Pleading.

"You know how long I've been waiting for this?" I want to look up into her heated gaze, but I can't peel my eyes from her swollen lips.

She's tight. Perfect. Made for me.

I brush my fingertips against her entrance, parting her lips in the process, and then press my mouth against it, inhaling her scent.

Her breath catches in her throat, and her fingers catch in my hair, half pulling me to her, half pushing me away.

She wants to protest, I can feel it, but I don't give her the chance. I grab her wrist and hold it in place as I begin to lick her up and down, taking my time to encircle the tiny bud.

"So good." I groan into her hot pussy and slash my lips over her before I release her hand.

The moment I dive two fingers into her she's gone. She's so tight I can feel her vibrating around my fingers s she begins to seek her own pleasure, all reasoning forgotten.

"Kade." My name spills from her lips, carried by a raspy breath.

That's what I wanted.

My dick's so hard I don't think I'd last a minute. I want her around it, riding it, filled to the brim. But I can't peel my mouth off her burning core. She's too close. So damn close. I want to taste her when she comes, and then we'll take care of my dick.

"I'm—"

"Yes, sweetheart. Come for me." I work my fingers faster, deeper, reaching that one point I instinctively know she's going to like while my tongue keeps its pressure.

Her breathing flutters as fast as the wings of a butterfly as she comes, clenching and unclenching hard.

I stare at her as she unravels beneath my touch. "You're beautiful," I say gently.

"Thanks." Her cheeks flush as she lets her hand trail down my pants. I stop her before she can reach my crotch.

"What are you doing?"

She looks up at me, her gaze questioning. "Finishing this."

"No, Vicky." I shake my head to get my point across. "Not here. Not now."

"Why?"

"Because." I hesitate.

"Fine. Not today." Pulling her panties up her hips, she lets out a laugh. "But I'm warning you and I'm serious. If you don't fuck me by the end of this week, I'll ask someone else."

My brows shoot up. "Is that an ultimatum?"

"No. I'm giving you a choice."

"What about Bruce?"

There's a short silence. When she looks up, her eyes are glinting with something.

It's not sadness. It's fury. The same look she gives me when I challenge her.

She wants to get even with him.

"What about him?" she asks. "Kiss me one more time and then ask me if I care about him."

She sounds serious, as though she's challenging herself.

I want to believe her, but I can't.

Too much is at stake. Someone like her can go from extreme heights to even greater lows. There's never a middle ground with her.

I have to be cautious not to rekindle her obsession with her ex, which could easily happen if I don't tread carefully.

Doing the real thing as opposed to giving oral pleasure is different.

At least, I like to think so. If we have sex and she realizes it's a one-time thing she might run back to Bruce, which is the last thing I want for her.

"As much as I want to fuck you, you need time alone, Vicky," I say and almost kick myself the moment I do.

She laughs. "What are you? My therapist?"

"No. I'm your friend." I smile softly. "Look, I'm just trying to help. Doing something that we might both regret isn't going to help any of us. We're different, Vicky, but not *that* different. We both need a fix. For me, it's sex. For you, it's love. You think by fucking me you'll feel better, but trust me, you won't. If anything, you're going to feel worse because it won't change a thing in your life, and the last thing I want is for you to hate yourself." I pause, taking in her reactions. She just looks at me, her face a mask that betrays none of her emotions. "Give yourself at least a week to process his betrayal."

She remains quiet for a while, letting my words sink in. "Why one week?"

"I want you to be sure that you really want this. And also, I don't trust myself around you." I don't know how to put this, so I go for being straightforward and blunt. More blunt than I've ever been before. "You're beautiful, Vicky, but you deserve someone who wouldn't hurt you."

"And you would?"

I smile sadly. "I might. Look, it's not something I'm proud of, but many women I've hooked up with have been left disappointed because they harbored the foolish hope for more, which I can't give."

"And you think I'm like those women?"

I cock my head to the side, regarding her amused expression. "You aren't?"

"I can assure you that I understand what I'm getting into, and my answer's still yes, I want to."

"One week." I lean into her, my lips grazing hers in one final kiss, and then I open the door. "Think it over. If you still want it by next week, then we'll take the next step."

One week.

Plenty of time for her to think about it. Plenty of time for her to really want me or push me away forever.

18

Vicky

"I can't help but notice that you like someone."

"What?" My head snaps to Sylvie who's sitting in front of me, her blue eyes scrutinizing.

"Look at the ten o'clock hottie. That's who I'm talking about." She gives me a gentle nudge and I turn my head to follow her line of vision. The cantina's overcrowded today—it might even be the busiest I've ever seen it. Something about a new chef arriving has everyone curious. Nothing exciting ever happens so someone's arrival is the attraction of the week.

"Great," I mumble and am about to turn my attention back to my plate when I see someone standing in line, filling his plate.

It's a newcomer to the cantina.

Kade.

I don't know when he ever eats, but apparently not at the same times as I do.

His back is turned to me, but I'd recognize his broad shoulders anywhere. Wearing a black shirt, the sleeves rolled up to his elbows, he looks even sexier than on the day we first met.

A burning flame erupts in my abdomen and settles between my legs, gathering in a delicious pull that reminds me of what we've done in that closet.

It's only been a few days, but the memory's still fresh. I can still feel his lips on mine; I can still feel his fingers inside me and his tongue between my legs, doing unspeakably sexy things to me. No man has ever made me feel so wanted. Even though we've overstepped the threshold of friendship and entered friends with benefits territory, nothing has really changed between us.

We still talk about everything. Except about the closet event.

And Bruce.

He hardly ever enters my thoughts now, but there

are still times when I feel hurt.

Only Kade can make me feel better. Watching him now, I'm reminded just how much I look forward to our evenings together.

"That someone," Sylvie whispers. "I have this kind of sixth sense about romantic relationships and their outcome—unfortunately, I suck at predicting mine."

I turn back to her, hoping that the heat covering my face isn't a major blush.

"I don't like him." I put on a fake smile. "I mean, not the way you think. It's just..." How do I explain to her that Kade and I have spent a lot of time—a lot of nights—together and we've become really close? "...we went out."

"He took you out for a date?" Sylvie asks, aghast.

"It wasn't a date, per se. It was only clubbing and I didn't even spend time with him. I sort of looked up with Bruce and then got drunk."

Which is only half the truth.

"Oh, my God, Vicky. Why would you take such a risk?"

I shrug my shoulders. "I needed the change in scenery. I mean, look around you. Who can stay sane in this place?" I squeeze her hand, suddenly worried that I've just made a mistake by telling her.

"You won't tell anyone, will you?"

"Are you serious? I'm not a snitch." She leans across the table and whispers conspiratorially, "Was it worth it?"

Was it worth it?

"Only time will tell." I take a sip of my coffee, remembering the time I saw Bruce with his ex, and the feeling of disappointment returns. I thought he'd wait for me, but the bitter truth is piercing and harsh.

He moved on within days.

It's not helping that my therapist says things I can't even talk about. The statement she makes rings true and the seed of doubt has begun to grow, no matter how much I try to bury it.

Lately, I've been having thoughts like, 'He used me,' and 'He's never really been in love with me.'

It hurts like hell.

"Think your roommate wants to fuck you considering he's, you know?" Sylvie says.

I roll my eyes. "Of course, he would. He'd fuck anything that walks on two legs, but he hasn't offered yet."

"He hasn't tried to touch you yet?"

"Not even a peck on the cheek." I shake my head a little too vehemently in the hope that Sylvie will buy my bluff. "He's like a big brother."

"You don't date your brother."

"I told you. It wasn't a date, per se." Pausing, I sit back and think back to the night he slept on the floor. "He's a decent guy."

Sylvie lets out a laugh. "I wouldn't call someone who runs around naked decent, and particularly not when he doesn't care who sees him."

"Well, he is. He hasn't done it again." Which is a shame, really. I wouldn't mind seeing Kade naked a second time

She cocks her head to the side, her eyes narrowing. I look down quickly, realizing that maybe I shouldn't have defended him.

"Why do I have the feeling something happened between you two?" Sylvie asks.

I stare at her, unsure what to do.

She couldn't be more spot on, but if I deny it, she might not believe me. If I don't deny it, she might take it as a confirmation that she's right.

Basically, whatever I do, I'm in trouble.

Sylvie's expression reflects that she's growing more suspicious by the second.

I have to find a way to act like nothing happened.

Except, I can't. The whole situation is too ridiculous. Too complicated.

I feel embarrassed to even think that I was the one who did the chasing.

"You want to," Sylvie says matter-of-factly.

I bite on my lip, afraid to say the wrong thing. The right thing. *Anything at all.*

As if sensing my dilemma, Sylvie leans forward. My whole body tenses, and I brace myself for whatever discovery she might make next.

"Why don't you hook up with him?"

I stare at her, taking in her grin. "He's my roommate."

"And?"

"It's against the rules."

"Everyone's breaking at least one rule around here. You wouldn't be the first."

Is she joking? I can't tell.

"Are you saying you're..." My heart beats faster when she nods her head.

"It's a lonely place."

"Oh, my God. You scared me. I really thought you were going to tell someone."

She laughs at my expression. "Please don't tell me you didn't see it coming. You've been here for two weeks and haven't noticed that some people seem to be a little too friendly? I'm going to let you take a wild guess what's going on behind closed bedroom doors." She winks, her tone changing and dropping to a conspiratorial whisper. "Whatever they tried to achieve by pairing us up was a flop. Half of the love addicts are already sleeping with the sex addicts." She cocks her head. "But even if they find out, I doubt they'd rethink the program. Too much money has gone into it. At best, they'll declare us cured. At worst, they'll impose new rules, maybe even watch us twenty-four seven."

"You think so?"

"Maybe." She shrugs. "So what about him? Is he up for it?"

"Who? Kade?" I look over my shoulder, fearing that he might hear me speaking his name.

To my relief, I see him sitting at another table, engrossed in a conversation with a guy I don't know. His glance finds me, and our gazes meet.

And then he winks.

My stomach flips a little.

I turn my attention back to Sylvie. "No, he doesn't want to fuck me. He's absolutely not interested."

"Hmm." She doesn't sound convinced. "He asks you out but doesn't want to sleep with you?"

"Yes. That's about right." I purse my lips, ready to tell her what happened between us when a short ringing sound echoes through the hall.

"Is this a drill or something?" I stand up, watching everyone else push up to their feet and rush out the door.

"No." Sylvie slings her handbag over her shoulder. "It's visitation day."

I was so busy I had completely forgotten.

"Catch up later?" She leans into me and whispers, "He's checking you out."

Only after she's headed for the door do I dare to look.

Kade, standing near the table, holding a note pad in his hand, which he holds up as soon as he notices me looking. On it, he's written:

Do. Or do not. There is no try.

I grab my bag and head for him, smiling. "*The Empire Strikes Back*, right?"

"You know your movies." He leans into me to place a soft kiss on my cheek.

"What does it mean?"

"It's a mental note to remind you to return to the present moment by letting go of attachments, such as fear and limitations. By eliminating the word try, you have the choice whether to actively do something or not. You have the power to see it through. You're acknowledging that every act is sacred and you do what needs to be done while facing an obstacle."

My lips twitch at his implication. "And visitation time is an obstacle?"

"If whoever's visiting you stops you from completing something, it is," Kade says.

I laugh. "Thanks, Yoda. I'll keep that in mind."

He lifts his hand, offering it to me. "Shall we?"

I interlink my fingers with his. "Only if you stop the *The Empire Strikes Back* quotes."

"Not a fan, are you?"

"Can't say I am."

"Me neither," Kade says, laughing. "I just have a very good memory for quotes."

We follow the crowd into an adjacent building. The scent of grilled chicken reaches me long before we step into the hall that's been rearranged to accommodate the large number of visitors.

"I thought everything was closed for a mile down." I let go of Kade's hand and turn to him. "You knew about this, didn't you?"

"We even get ice cream." He points to a stand with a guy dressed in white, offering ice cream to whoever passes by. "I think they're trying to pretend this isn't like prison at all."

"Yeah. Treat us to candies when we have guests, and let the real torture begin tomorrow." I scan the room, not expecting to see anyone familiar because, to be honest, none of my friends know I'm here. That's when I see my sister. "I shouldn't be here," I mutter.

"Why?" Kade asks.

"Because I didn't go to group therapy until a few days ago and I feel like I'm not making much progress." My gaze remains glued to her. She's talking to someone and nods sympathetically.

"If it helps," Kade says, leaning into me, "I'm a work in progress, too."

I can't help but smile. "You're a goof, you know?"

"Life's already serious like shit." He follows my line of vision. "I have another good one."

"Yeah?"

"If you don't feel it, fake it," he says.

"Is that your new philosophy?"

"No, that's my survival strategy." He flashes me a grin. "I'm just roaring with the crowd. Doesn't mean I mean what I say."

"I thought you wanted to get help here?"

"How the hell did you come to that conclusion?"

I should claim that I was taking a guess. That I don't really care. But I do care. I want him to get help. "You know, I've been wondering, how the hell could you be so successful in your job with all the sex pop-ups and the dates and the meaningless sex?"

Probably a lot of that.

"What can I say? I'm a juggler."

His fingers settle beneath my chin and before I know it, his lips are on mine.

His mouth is both tender and wild—the kiss too short.

"It's all for a higher purpose," he says, taking a step back.

I stare at him, aghast. "You didn't just do that in public."

He laughs. "What can I say? I'm a rebel."

"You're not a rebel. You're insane. What if someone saw us?" My gaze sweeps across the room.

No one's looking.

They're all focused on their conversation.

"What could anyone possibly do to us?" Kade asks, drawing my attention back to him.

"How about serve us some jail time?" I say.

This shuts him up…for all of three seconds.

When I look up at him and see his lips twitching, I know he's about to say something stupid. "You'd look hot in orange."

I roll my eyes playfully. "Wow, first a nun, then

an inmate. You really have the strangest fantasies."

"I don't judge a book by its cover, and you shouldn't either. You should give me another try." His eyes twinkle with something. "Remember when I did that little flip with my fingers that curled your toes and you said—"

I clap my hand over his mouth.

Out of all the moments he could have chosen to mention our little oral sesh, he had to choose this one. "Please stop talking."

"You sure…"

"Hush." I press my finger to my lips and turn my back to him. "My sister's coming over."

19

Vicky

"SO, THIS IS where you're staying." My sister drops her handbag on my bed, her frown displaying her displeasure. Dressed in her business suit, with her hair styled into a bun, she looks as though she's here to make an investment rather than visit her sister.

"Where's Mom?" I ask.

"She's not coming."

My mood reaches a new low. "She is still upset, isn't she?"

Grace doesn't reply as she sits down on my bed

and crosses her legs. She runs her hand through her hair and shifts uncomfortably—the only two signs that this is a topic she'd rather not talk about.

She's strangely quiet today. Too quiet. Something's up.

"Aren't you going to answer the question?" I ask. "Mom promised she'd visit. She'd never break her word. So, where is she?"

"She can't see you suffering," Grace replies flatly. "She can't see you even more hurt."

I laugh. "That doesn't make any sense. I'm here to get help. That's why we have therapists and professionals available round the clock. The only bug I could possibly catch in here is from eating too much junk food. Or I could get pregnant." I catch her frown. "I'm kidding."

I expect Grace to laugh. But she doesn't. She looks guilty as hell, and that's not something I'd ever expect from my sister. My mom and I have always been close. That she doesn't want to visit hurts.

"Grace, you make me feel like I'm some kind of criminal. Is Mom ashamed of me?" The realization hits me hard.

"No."

"Then, what's going on?" I sit down next to her, my heart racing as I mentally go through all the possible reasons why Mom couldn't or wouldn't want to see me. "Is it Will? Did something happen?"

"Will's okay. Don't worry about him." She takes a deep breath. Then another. Then yet another, still not talking.

"You're making me nervous. God, Grace. You act like someone just died."

"Sorry." She grabs her bag, and I realize her hands are shaking. "I'm not even sure I should be giving you this. Mom told me not to. That she wouldn't come if I did, but..." She pulls out a letter. "It's from Bruce. She actually pleaded with me, but I really think you should know."

Her gaze pierces into me, her eyes imploring, apologizing, stubborn.

"Know what?" I mumble?

"I should give you some privacy while you read this." She grabs her handbag.

I take the letter from her outstretched hand. "What is this? Jesus, Grace. What's going on? Why's Mom not here?"

"He's getting married, Vicky," Grace says slowly.

"Who?" Her words make no sense to me. Who's 'he' and what does he have to do with Mom's decision not to turn up?

"Bruce." Her tone is soft, almost a whisper. "We

heard it from friends who were invited to the engagement party."

"What engagement party?" My brain fails to register the meaning of her words. Everything's racing: my heart, my mind. Even the ground beneath my feet seems to want to slip away. Inside me, I can feel a rift forming that threatens to rip me apart. Pictures begin to flash before my eyes. Bruce and Nat at the beach, clinking champagne flutes, cuddling with the sun setting in the background.

All so beautiful and romantic.

The big rock on her finger makes so much more sense now. I initially thought she had purchased it from an accessory shop because it looked so huge and fake.

I should have known the diamond ring was real.

"Bruce is getting married in two weeks." Grace's voice draws me back. "I just thought you should know."

I peer at her, taking in her expression. The concern is etched in her features, the tiny lines around her eyes.

"Get out." I choke on the words, so I try again. "Get out of my room."

For a few seconds, she just stares at me, unmoving.

"Grace." My tone is a warning. I need to be alone. I need her gone. She seems to realize this because she nods her head.

"I'm going to wait outside in case you need me."

I wait until she's closed the door behind her before I tear open the letter. Everything's shaking as I read it.

Dear Vicky,

This is my fifth letter and I still don't know how to say it. In the end, I've decided that being short and direct is the best way to go about this.

I'm going to marry Nat.

She isn't my first love, but she's the right choice. Marrying her is the right thing to do. My family demands it, and I'm going to honor their wishes.

Over the past few months, we had a lot of fun together; however, it's time to call it quits and move on.

Don't get me wrong, you're great. You're a good friend; maybe the best female friend I've had, but you aren't what I need. You deserve a person who's honest and who will see you as the caring human you are. I'm sorry that I can't be that person, but I hope we can still be friends.

> *Take care,*
> *Bruce*

Gasping for air, I fold the paper and toss it on the bed.

Fuck.

20

Vicky

LOVE IS AN ILLUSION.

It's a chemical reaction that makes you blind to what the heart perceives as real. As soon as the glasses are off, it shatters you and all the parts you gave of yourself freely.

There's no more us. No more tears. No more fights. No more breaks. No more second chances. Seconds of saying hello; months wasted on someone who wasn't worth the time. Someone who takes a heart too easily and breaks it in an instant.

What the hell did I think would happen?

How foolish of me to ever think we had a chance.

It's even more foolish that I ever thought he was great.

The mind replays what it cannot understand.

I expect the pain to hit me hard, but I find I'm only filled with emptiness—as if my heart's a shell, the edges roughened, the inner padding turned to stone. I feel like someone who exists but doesn't breathe. Everything in my mind is still, the inner clockwork laid to rest as if I've given up altogether.

I stash the letter in a drawer and grab my jacket in the hopes that a short walk might help me feel something.

Anything.

Because any feeling is better than the emptiness residing inside me.

I think of my sister, feeling bad for kicking her out, but really, it was for the best. For the life of me, I can't face her, can't listen to her apologies. Can't hear one more word about Bruce because he's dead to me.

There's only one path left for me to go—move ahead with my plans, get this rehab thing over and done with. The sooner I return to my old self, erase all traces of him, the better.

Black clouds hover in the sky. A soft breeze grazes

my arm, sending shivers through my body. It's going to rain soon. I close my eyes, savoring the sensation, breathing in the raw scent of the earth, the trees, the ocean that's close and yet too far away.

The numbness is still here, wrapped around me like a soothing cocoon.

Pretending that everything's okay has never been so easy.

I don't know how long I'm standing frozen to the spot, but at some point, the sky splits. Little droplets of water begin to fall, which form into rivulets, turning into a downpour soaking my clothes, my soul, washing away the memories of the special times that weren't special to begin with.

In the midst of it all, I think of Kade.

Kade is everything Bruce isn't.

Why can't I be with someone like him? He makes me laugh like no one can. He makes me feel good. Around him I can be my true self.

Kade's not only better looking, he's also kind and generous—at least in the between-the-sheets department. But he's a sex addict, and my friend, and that's all he's ever going to be.

Harboring any hope that I might ever be with him would be another big mistake. Once this is over, he'll forget me. We both might spiral back into the vicious circle that is addiction. That's what people say will happen. I'm going to fall in love with the next wrong guy only to have my heart broken again, and he's going to keep fucking his way through the female population.

That's how life is: full of mistakes, regret, and self-blame.

I let out a scream, pouring out all the anger, pouring out all I have. As my emotions rip through me, tears begin to fall.

I'm not crying because of Bruce. I'm crying because of all the mistakes I've made, because of what I am, what I can never be.

For months I thought I knew Bruce. Turned out I didn't know him at all.

My feelings for him were nothing but an illusion concocted by my heart. Now I'm paying the price, because I was too blind to see we were never going to have a future together.

Night has fallen when I finally return to the main building. I enter through the old entrance next to the dining area, avoiding the first floor lobby. The antique, mahogany, grandfather clock announces that it's midnight. Everyone should be either asleep or in the lounge room.

Kade said something about working on his

memoir at night, meaning he might still be up.

Changing plans, I head for the lobby, passing the large living room quickly, and reach the entertainment room.

I find him sitting in front of a computer. His back is turned to me, as he's typing furiously on the keyboard. To his right, three guys are playing cards, their conversation too low to understand. As I slip through the open door, they lift their gaze, eyeing me for a fraction of a second before resuming their game.

Kade isn't alone.

My stomach drops a little.

I spin around, ready to leave, and have almost reached the door, when his voice startles me. "Where are you going?"

My whole body freezes into place.

"Back to the apartment." I turn to face him reluctantly and find Kade frowning. He's wearing glasses, looking kind of sexy in a nerdy way. It suits him.

"Jesus, Vicky. You look like—"

"Shit?" I shrug, fighting the urge to scowl at him. "Yeah, I know. Moisture doesn't do my hair any favors."

I hate my curls. Add a bit of heat or rain, and my

hair turns into a curly mess. I rake my fingers through my hair and pull slightly in the hope that it might magically straighten into the smooth, glossy look everyone else seems able to achieve these days.

I don't need a mirror to know that it's not working.

Kade watches me in silence, his face a blank mask that keeps his emotions unreadable. Finally, he points at the seat next to him, pulling the chair out with his foot.

I take him up on his silent invitation and sit down next to him, avoiding touching him in the process.

"Actually, I was going to say that you look exhausted," he says. His expression darkens a little, as though his words don't please him, as he continues, "Can't sleep?"

"No, I was actually looking for you." As I speak out the words I realize I can't take them back. He'll want to know why, and I have no answers to his questions.

Why do I always have to blurt out the truth?

"For me?" He cocks his head to the side. "Seems like you've found me. Why were you about to head back to your room, then?"

I avert my vision, hoping that he won't see through my lie. "You looked busy. I didn't want to bother you."

"You're never bothering me. I needed the break anyway." He smiles, offering me his half-full mug. "Coffee? It's cold and stale but drinkable."

My pulse speeds up.

In the past few days, he's offered me a lot of things: his friendship, his assistance, the possibility of keeping my bed warm and my attention far away from Bruce. But offering me a sip of his coffee is a new thing. It's intimate and sexy, in a strange way.

I peer down at the white porcelain, imagining his lips on it.

The very lips I want to feel on my skin.

I should be staying away from him, from anything that makes me crave him more, and yet I can't.

"Thanks." My fingers encircle the mug. Feeling his glance on me, I lift it to my lips and take a sip.

Our gaze remains entwined for what feels like forever. His expression is unreadable, but his eyes speak to me, asking, wondering, worrying.

"Where have you been, Vicky?" Kade asks slowly. "After your sister left, I went looking for you. I couldn't find you."

"I needed some fresh air to clear my head." I force a smile to my lips, thinking of ways to change the topic without being too obvious about it. "How's the sex book coming along?"

He gets the clue to drop it.

"Writing it is harder than I imagined." He leans back and crosses his arms over his head. "Want to know what the most important perk of my book is?" He grins and continues, not waiting for my guess. "No real-life experiences. No drama. It's simply fiction. And the storyline's just changed."

"Changed how?" I narrow my eyes as I regard him, not getting where he's heading with this. "I thought you were going to recollect your sexual exploits."

"It's a little too late for that. I've turned it into fiction." He turns the screen so I can read a few paragraphs. It's a scene describing a woman stumbling into a bathroom. Judging from Kade's description of her, and the dialogue, there's no mistaking.

No, he didn't!

"You're writing about us?" I ask, flabbergasted.

"No. My story's about a guy who's a sex addict and he meets someone who's in love with the idea of being in love."

"That sounds like us."

He shrugs, grinning. "Coincidence."

I let out a laugh. "What are their names, Kade?"

"Kale and Viss." His grin widens.

"Clever." I return his smile. "Sounds like a coincidence, indeed. With those names, it would never cross anyone's mind that you might be writing about us. So, what happens next?"

"You tell me." His expression turns serious again. "Will she make a decision or not? That's the big question. What do you think, Vicky?"

The insinuation is unmistakable. It's clear he's asking about us.

It's been a few days since we made out.

A few days can be a long time.

I shift closer and lean into him, whispering into his ear so he's the only one who can hear what I have to say. "I think she wants to. Very much so. I came to a decision last week, Kade."

"I hope it's the right one." His eyes meet my glance, questioning, probing. At my nod, he smiles. "Is that why you're here?"

"Yes," I whisper. My heart's pounding in my chest. I don't know why, but the fact that my ridiculous attraction to him is out in the open makes me feel excited, almost anticipatory. As though I can't wait to find out where this might be taking me.

"Good. That settles it then." His fingers trail over

the back of my hand, the motion gentle. But there's a fire in it, a spark that's searing my skin. "Where do you think they would want to do it?"

My body begins to tingle all over. "Near the ocean," I whisper. "They would do near the water."

His lips cock into a sexy grin. "You sure? It might get a bit cold."

I ponder my choice for a moment. The image of my legs wrapped around Kade's naked hips drives a pang of heat to my face. I can almost feel his hard body against me, inside me.

"I think so, yes," I whisper, averting my gaze before he realizes just how much the idea intrigues me. "They would keep each other warm."

21

Vicky

THANKS TO THE GOOGLE maps software on Kade's phone, we reach the beach in less than half an hour.

A soft breeze rustles the leaves in the nearby trees. Even though it's too dark to make out much, we choose a spot behind a large rock, shielded from the street and hidden from anyone who might walk past. Kade spreads out a blanket, which I'm pretty sure he's helped himself to from the broom closet on our floor. I let myself fall on it and watch as he settles beside me. The rainclouds are gone, but the air's still carrying the scent of salty moisture and clean earth. I breathe in and hold it for a long moment before I exhale the air, feeling lightheaded from both the abundance of oxygen and the man lying beside me.

The crescent moon above us catches in the water, making it shimmer like countless black diamonds. The display is stunning, but it's not what amazes me. It's the stars above, twinkling in the night sky. I've never seen so many in one place.

"I can't believe we haven't been here before." My voice sounds haunted, surreal.

"I guess I never suggested it because I'm so used to it," Kade says.

I shoot him a sideways glance and stifle the groan building at the back of my throat. "To sex on the beach?"

He lets out a laugh—deep and hoarse and sexy as hell. "No. To seeing water. I live in California. My house is situated on a private beach."

This is the first time he's shared something meaningful about his present life. Even though it's barely anything, it feels special.

"You know—" I hesitate, wondering whether I'm making a mistake by communicating my thoughts so openly. "—you've barely told me anything about you while I've practically spilled everything about my life."

He shrugs. "I'm a private person."

I raise my eyebrows. "You know too much about me for that. So, start spilling. Relationships?"

He shakes his head. "I'm not a commitment type of guy."

That part was to be assumed, wasn't it? So why the sudden disappointment washing over me?

"Except for that one girl who broke your heart, right?"

He turns to face me. "You remember that but not the part where you stripped naked?"

I let out a laugh to hide the rush of embarrassment.

"Faintly," I whisper. "But only because I've been wondering if it never gets lonely."

He cocks his head, hesitating, probably considering his words carefully. "Having sex with someone is easy. It's the holidays that are hard. I never get involved with anyone, which means no follow-up phone call or date. No feelings, no drama." His eyes search my face, as though he's trying to read my emotions. When I don't give him anything, he continues, "But there are times when it would be nice to have someone."

"Are you going to be alone...forever?" It's not the most obvious question I could ask, but certainly the one that bothers me the most.

He shrugs. "Why would I have to be when I have a good friend like you?"

There's something beneath his statement—a meaning I cannot grasp.

I suck my lower lip between my teeth, too afraid to ask. But if I don't do it, I know I'll always wonder.

"Are you implying you'll still want to see me after this is over?" The words whoosh past my lips as quickly as a breath.

"I'm saying you have no choice." He laughs, the sound grazing my skin. "The program booklet says that once rehab is over, we'll still be required to check in with our roommate. There's even the option of becoming a sponsor, which I intend to use."

My lips twitch. Having Kade as one's sponsor is probably as bad as stocking up an alcoholic's minibar with vodka bottles. "You mean I'll have to endure more of you?"

"I figured you'd ask that." His fingertips graze the front of my chest, unbuttoning my jacket and spreading it.

My breathing is cut short. I turn to him, almost expecting him to pull himself on top of me and do what I've been wanting him to do ever since I laid eyes on him. His palm travels down my stomach and comes to rest just above my hip.

"Stop it. I'm ticklish."

"I know that." I let out a scream as his fingers squeeze a little. "I'm going to be tickling you until you ask me to be your sponsor. Call it blackmail tickling."

"I think you've just invented an expression." Laughing, I jump up and start running. I'm headed for the water even though I've no intention of jumping in fully dressed. I feel Kade's arms around my waist a moment before he spins me around. I collide with his hard chest and let myself be pulled into the soft sand.

He lands on top of me. And, wow. I feel like the temperature has just increased a few degrees.

From up close, he looks even more delectable with those skilled lips and the strange look in his eyes. He reminds me of a god—the bad and naughty kind. I'm holding my breath, marveling at just how perfect he feels against me. I try to look away, but I can't. His gaze has me captured, mesmerized. My heart is slamming against my chest. If he were to lean farther into me, I'm sure he'd hear it crashing louder than the waves against the store.

"Now, what was your reply again?" His voice is hoarse, and I swear it's not from the cool breeze. "Who will you ask to be your sponsor?"

"You." I can barely speak, let alone breathe. "You, of course."

"Doesn't sound convincing."

"That's because I'm not sure you can handle me and all of my addictions." I think of my therapist and the many moments of disagreements we had over the past two weeks. "I can be a handful, and I'm sure you'll give up on your first day."

"I like you."

"That's a good thing, because you need to like me as my sponsor. Right?"

"No, I like you, Vicky." His serious tone sends a tingle through my body. "I like *like* you."

My already shaky breath breaks as I realize that our conversation has turned in a different direction.

"You like me?" I can barely speak out the words. My voice is a strangled whisper, far more emotional than it should be.

I shouldn't care whether he likes me or not, and yet it matters.

Something changes inside me. Something takes hold of my chest, squeezing it tight.

"Yes, I do."

It seems as though his eyes stay on me for a long time, and then he kisses me as if every beat of my heart belongs to him. As if he really means it.

If only I didn't know any better.

22

Kaiden

NOW THAT THE words have been spoken, I know they can't ever be taken back.

I lean into her, breathing in the scent of her skin, wondering how the hell it happened that I started to like a woman who's in love with another guy?

It has to be the chase. To want something that's unattainable, because that's exactly what's she's been so far.

My first real challenge in years.

My personal prize for getting this rehab thing done.

My little emergency kit.

Cash's bet hasn't been much on my mind lately. I'd almost forgotten about it.

Until now.

All I can think about is all the ways I want to kiss every inch of her body to make sure she's branded for life. I want to bite into her skin to see if she tastes as sweet and delicious as she looks. I want her to ride up and down my dick, my hands buried in her hair, tugging as she screams with pleasure. But can I do that in good conscience when I know my motivations are corrupt?

I'm supposed to fuck her to win a bet.

And yet all I want is to take care of her.

"Vicky," I whisper. "I don't want you to do something you'll come to regret later."

The warning is there, hanging heavy in the air. I silently implore her to grasp it, to go and never look back. She deserves to be happy. Bruce can't give her that, but I'm not sure that I can either.

"It's too late for that." She shifts closer to me, pushing her hips against my thigh. "You have to finish what we started."

My heart speeds up. She's echoing my thoughts, but without my hesitation.

A soft smile's playing on her lips as she rises to her knees and positions herself in front of me until her lips are inches from mine. Her eyes shimmer with determination. I know what she's about to do a moment before she shrugs out of her jacket and removes her shirt. My gaze sticks to her chest and I lick my lips in anticipation.

Her tits are perfect. Round and full, but not too big. The rosy mounds beg to be licked and sucked.

She notices my staring and lifts her hands to cover up.

"You're beautiful, Vicky." I meet her gaze. "I want to see all of you."

She doesn't need much persuasion. I watch her as she strips. My whole body fills with want, sending tingles of excitement to my balls.

She *is* beautiful—that wasn't a lie.

I could just sit here, watching her until time stands still. Her body moves with the grace of a dancer, her hips swaying slowly as her panties gather at her feet.

Her fingers brush up her neck, and she gathers her hair in her fist, exposing her delicate neck. I know she's trying to seduce me.

And fuck, it's working.

As if sensing my thoughts, she touches my hand, guiding it between her legs. I shudder with want at how wet she is.

Her whole body is hot.

Hot to touch, hot to feel. Another shudder courses through my body.

I fight the urge to grab her and bury her beneath me.

I want her bad, but something's keeping me back.

Is this really a good idea?

I wet my lips, angry at that unreasonable part of me that keeps hesitating, dragging this out.

"You really want us to break the rules?" I ask.

"They're only rules."

She leans over me. Before I realize what she's doing, her fingers are busy unbuttoning my jeans.

"Are you saying you don't want to?" she whispers, her fingers coming dangerously close to the bulge I haven't been able to get rid of since the first moment I saw her.

Groaning, I close my eyes, feeling the familiar spin in my head.

She's about to do things to me that are far too familiar. Memories of my past experiences with women begin to flicker before my eyes. I can feel the usual rush of excitement.

There's no going back now.

I'm a lost cause. She knows it. We both do.

"I want you to fuck me, Kade. I'm not asking you.

I'm demanding that you do." Her tone is impatient, shaking with nerves.

"You know it's not going to mean anything?"

"Kade." She shakes her head and lets out a sharp breath. "I know what I'm getting into. Trust me. I'm not like your other conquests. I won't try to keep in touch after we're out of here. Unless you're my sponsor, which I hope you won't be."

She's not like my other conquests at all.

Maybe that's why her words sting.

That's the thing. I want her to keep in touch. I want to see more of her, whatever the fuck that might mean. Maybe I'll keep her in my life as a friend. I've never met a woman with whom I can converse so easily. Yet, at the same time the thought of seeing her after this is over scares me. I don't want a relationship with her, but I also don't want to never see her again. I want more of her, while at the same time I don't want to hurt her, because that's exactly what's going to happen.

My conflicting emotions confuse me.

My own body confuses me.

I'm attracted to her while being repulsed by the idea of knowing I could hurt her. Like I hurt all those other women I fucked.

It's not at all like me to stop and ponder. The old

me would have jumped right into bed with her. Heck, I would not even have needed a bed. A table, blanket, shower, closet—whatever—would have sufficed.

But the new me is considering, wondering, fearing.

Vicky leans forward, her mouth descending onto my dick.

I can't say no to *that*.

A groan escapes my lips.

Of course, I can't say no.

Not with those gorgeous lips ready to suck and lick. Not when I want her to do just that—desperately.

I lick my lips, feeling another shudder. She won't stop. I know it. Sooner or later, probably sooner than anticipated, she'll make me lose control.

I can feel the heat and the tug in my balls.

"Jesus, Vicky." I groan again.

This woman is everything I shouldn't want.

Her fingers circle around the base while her tongue begins to lick eagerly. She sucks me in, her mouth hot, tight, her throat making tiny noises that signal she's enjoying this as much as I am.

I fist my hand in her hair to hold her head, but I don't push. I want our rhythm to be hers to control.

Up and down she goes until I'm getting dangerously close to spill before the real fun's even begun.

Fuck. It's been two weeks since my dick's seen any action and Vicky's perfect little mouth isn't exactly helping my self control.

"That's enough." I push her away, gently but with enough force to let her know I mean it.

"What we're doing is just a little fun. Nothing more. Nothing less. Now are you going to kiss me or not?" she asks. "Or is it customary for sex addicts to wait so long."

My lips jerk at the tiny jab. "Let's not keep a lady in need waiting."

"Sounds like a great philosophy to live by." A sexy grin tugs at her lips. "I want you to touch me."

My eyes lock onto her tits hungrily. They look fucking amazing, soft and tight and way too delicious not to pay them the attention they deserve.

Maybe I'll play with them later. Now that sweet pussy of hers is all I can think about.

"I'll take it from here, sweetheart."

I grab her hips and place myself behind her, one hand settled at the back of her nape, the other forcing her legs apart. Her ass is sticking straight up in the air; her pussy's on full display.

I take my time running my fingers over her

swollen lips, spreading the wetness that's already there—for me.

"Kade." Her voice is a heavy whisper, imploring, demanding.

"Shhh. You are perfect in every way. I want to savor this."

My finger finds her entry, and I press it inside, curling it as I thrust it into her. She arcs her back, then sticks out her ass, wanting more. I add another finger, opening her, preparing her for me. Her walls clench and unclench, swelling around me as I thrust in and out, coating her in her own lube.

"I'm going to fuck you tonight," I say, even though it's pretty obvious where we're headed.

The little sound she's making is driving me insane. This is so good, I can barely think straight. My cock's pulsating with life and eagerness. My balls are hurting, tugging at the last remnants of my self restraint. All my nerves are firing. I can't wait any longer. I have to have her now, or else I'll come like a teen fingering his girlfriend for the first time.

I pull my fingers out of her and quickly coat my cock with her juices. Vicky glares over her shoulder. When she notices what I'm doing she smiles, her eyes shimmering in the moonlight around us.

"Yes. Finally."

Suddenly I know what I want. Feeling naked skin on skin isn't going to be enough. I need everything she can give. I need to give her everything I have.

I trail my fingertips down her spine, around her hips, to her glorious ass. It is glorious—all round and ripe. I spread her lips and brush the tip of my cock down her entrance to her clit.

Vicky gasps and pushes her hips out, silently begging me for more.

"Kade. I swear if you continue to keep me waiting, I'll—"

Her voice breaks off as I slide my entire length into her. Her body stretches to take every inch of it, but damn, she's tight. Her breathing comes out as a moan. She's struggling to fit me inside her just as much as I'm struggling not to come on the spot.

"Feel how hard you make me?" I manage between ragged breaths. "This is all for you, Vicky. Say you want it."

"I want it." She moans and rotates her hips, drawing me deeper into her.

I tangle my fist in her hair and push her head down as I begin to thrust in and out of her. I watch my cock plunge inside her, her milky skin glistening around it. I haven't been bare with a woman in years, but with Vicky it feels right.

"I want you to come around me." Changing my rhythm, I lean over her and trail my teeth over her naked shoulder. My hard shaft's rubbing against her front wall. Her breathing is barely more than tiny gasps intermingled with soft cries. I begin to thrust harder, faster, hitting the spot that rewards me with a high moan.

"Yes, Kade. Fuck."

She's on the brink. She's going to fall soon. I want to fall with her.

Closing my eyes, I angle my hips and surrender to the sensation of her pussy clenching around me. I can almost feel the electrical current surging through her as she comes. The tiny sound of abandon is all it takes to take me with her. I come buried deep inside her, lost in the pleasure of marking the one woman I truly want.

Once I'm done, I gently pull out of her and settle on the blanket, pulling her to my chest. I want to tell her just how amazing she is, but I can't. The words that usually find their way past my lips so easily seem meaningless now. So I remain quiet.

Through the waves of the ocean crashing against the shore, I can hear her heavy breathing, feel her longing. It mirrors my own.

We are compatible.

In a way.

Different, but still so much alike. She's like the female version of me. Maybe that's why the program hosts sex addicts with love addicts, because deep down love addicts just need a little fucking and the sex addicts just need a bit of love, each of us learning something along the way.

That sounds pretty convincing.

I feel like I'm getting cured already.

23

Kaiden

I WOKE UP AND found no sign of Vicky. No note. Except for the heavenly scent lingering everywhere in the apartment, there's no indication she's even been here.

Things between us have become a little weird. I haven't talked to her since that night on the beach. It's been days.

It doesn't take an idiot to figure out that she's avoiding me.

She's been ignoring my knocking, slipping out of the apartment as early as she can. Come night, she's keeping her bedroom door closed. I haven't heard the shower running even though I'm pretty sure she must have used it at some point. The only time I'm seeing her is during the group meetings, and even then she barely acknowledges me. It's as if she's ashamed. Or maybe she came to the conclusion she cheated on Bruce during our little trip to the beach.

But let's be honest, what kind of man would keep someone like her out of his bed?

The loser doesn't deserve her.

I see her with her friend, though.

The two hang out in the dining room or in the cantina, most of the time. I suspect Vicky's hiding in her friend's apartment.

She thinks I'm not noticing, but every time she's talking to her friend she's glancing my way, as if there's a part of her she's left behind with me. Sometimes our eyes meet, and for a split second something clicks into place—knowledge of that night. And then she looks away and acts like nothing happened.

My therapist's polite cough draws me back. She's sitting in front of me, her legs crossed over each other as she's cradling a large notebook in her hand on which she's scribbling. I realize I don't remember her name. Something like Jill or Jane, or was it Julie? Definitely first-name basis.

The soft, classical music playing in the background sips through the perception of my brain. It's probably supposed to calm patients, but it doesn't quite have the same effect on me.

Nothing has these past few days.

"How long have you been an addict, Kade?" she asks when she realizes that my attention's back on her.

"My obsession with sex started in my early twenties."

She nods, as if she saw my answer coming. More furious scribbling before she glances up. Something in her somber expression causes alarm bells to ring in the back of my mind. "Tell me... how is your relationship with Victoria Sullivan, at the moment?"

The question throws me off. Just hearing my roommate's name coming out of my therapist's mouth makes me think back to the beach and how glorious it felt to be inside Vicky.

"Who?" I ask, brows raised.

"Your roommate," the therapist clarifies with the same serious expression. "Victoria Sullivan."

"Right. Is that her name?"

Another nod.

I tap my fingers on my thigh, signaling my impatience and boredom with her. What the hell could I possibly say without sounding guilty in one way or another?

"I'm sure she's great, but..." I pause, looking for the right words. "I think she could do with being a little less hostile."

"Hostile?" She raises her brow.

"Metaphorically speaking, yes. Maybe even more social." I hold her questioning gaze. "See, we don't hang out much. She's withdrawn. Her nose is always stuck in a book. The few times we've exchanged a couple words, she's always made her priority to mention the library not having enough books. I'm worried that the lack of reading material might, well, make her...you know..." I spin my finger near my temple to imply she might be on the verge of going cuckoo.

"I see. Well, I'll see what I can do. Thank you for bringing this to my attention." My therapist pushes her glasses back, eyeing me with renewed interest. "You're making good progress here, Kade. We're all very pleased."

I smile at her. She has no idea.

"It's all thanks to you, of course. I couldn't have done it without your help," I say sweetly.

Her face brightens. Seriously, I could play this act forever, spoon-feed it to her and she'd be buying it like all the others.

"Oh. It's nothing. We're all trying to help." Her cheeks blush.

"I'm sure of that. But I'd still like to point out that I couldn't have found a better therapist than you."

The red stains on her cheeks darken. If she isn't careful, she'll soon resemble a tomato.

"So, you have absolutely no desire to fraternize?" she asks.

"Not one bit." I lean forward, resting my arms on my knees. "It's like a miracle. I've had a great deal to reflect upon since my arrival. I've come to the conclusion that sex isn't the answer to solving the pain inside me." More like the itch, but I keep that part to myself. "I've recognized, too, that my past has shaped me. It's taken me a long time to accept that moving from foster home to foster home didn't exactly help me in becoming the person I want to be."

I shouldn't be enjoying this as much as I am, but to be honest, it can be quite boring in here. Now that Vicky's ignoring me, this is the only fun I can have.

I've been playing the broken patient who's just had a big revelation, or my favorite—the perfect, humble and grateful patient—card for the past two weeks and it's been paying off.

It works this way:

She asks a question and I come up with the answer she wants to hear, then give her all the credit for helping me to come to the right conclusion. It's been working like a charm. She's sucking everything up.

My therapist nods. "A journey is like a sunrise. It's night at first, but it reminds you that every darkness becomes light, giving rise to new beginnings. A sunrise is never defined by yesterday's dawn. Every day is a new beginning." She leans forward, her eyes sparkling. "Life has shaped you but it hasn't broken you. Don't let your past define you, Kade." She puts her notepad down, hesitating before she continues. "It's probably a bit early to ask the question, but I'll give it a try anyway because I believe in you. What are your plans when you get out of here?"

I muse over her question for a moment.

Will I stop fucking? No.

Will I host a party? Hell, yes.

I'm going to host the biggest party in the city to celebrate my comeback, and everyone's going to be talking about it.

I let out a fake breath, dropping my tone until I've infused enough sadness into my voice to fool her.

"The first thing I'll do is find a support group and check in. Then I'm going to try to live in the present, take it one step at a time, one day after another, because I know it's going to be hard. And I'm planning to exercise a lot."

"Those are good thoughts, Kade." She nods enthusiastically, obviously pleased with my answer. "Exercise goes hand in hand with an increase in mental wellbeing. Our discharge coordinator will give you a list of local health institutions that could cater to your individual needs. The first step is to get a treatment plan and follow it through. An unhealthy environment can easily lead to a relapse. It might be necessary to cut ties with old friends."

"I understand." I draw a dramatic breath. "I don't want to relapse. If cutting old ties is the only way for me to succeed in my endeavors, then so be it."

"You have to think of yourself and yourself only. It's going to be a long process, but you can do it, Kade." She glances at her closed notebook, her hands running down the rim. Her hesitation is evident on her face. "I could help you with the transition and check in with you...for moral support, of course."

She doesn't need to say more because it's pretty obvious why she'd want to continue seeing me. Once

I'm out of this place and she's no longer my appointed counselor, there's no reason why she couldn't pursue more than just talking.

My lips curl into a soft smile. "I'll keep that in mind."

A knock at the door echoes through the room.

"I'm sorry." She smiles apologetically, then calls out, "Yes?"

The door opens.

"Your next appointment is here."

"Great." She smiles at me and rises to her feet. "Thank you for seeing me, Mr. Wright. When can I expect you tomorrow?"

"Same as always." I shake her hand, making sure to prolong the action for a second too long. "Two p.m."

"Oh, right." She laughs nervously, and I make sure to shoot her one of my lingering smiles.

Women dig the lingering look, the lingering touch. I do it out of habit, not because I enjoy it. She's nothing like Vicky. No one is. Vicky's actually the first woman who seems to be avoiding me now after we've had sex. The thought bothers me just as much as the realization that she's also the first woman I want to keep in my life.

24

Vicky

AN OPEN LETTER TO JANE AUSTEN

Dear Jane,

I still feel a lot of anger in my sessions, but my new bestie says it's a good thing. I'm not angry with Bruce's mom, or his ex. I'm angry with myself for wasting eight months of my life on someone who wasn't worth it. I feel anger that I was blind. Anger for being weak, for getting invested in something that was never real.

Him getting married was the push I needed to step back and contemplate my life, see things for how they really are. When I read that letter, I was scared of the big pain that I thought would hit me, for it to crush me, that I would become more obsessive. But none of it happened.

I just stopped caring. That's all. The only things I now care about are my family, my new friend, Sylvie, and Kade.

That's right. Kade.

This is the first time I'm mentioning him. Until now, I barely allowed myself to think about him.

Jane, I must confess something:

I like Kade. A lot. Like really, really a lot. And not just as a friend. I love his body, the way he smiles at me, as though I'm the one thing that brightens his day. I love the way his hands roam over my body, aching to touch every inch of me. It would be all too easy to fall in love with him. I'll need to guard my heart to stop preventing falling for him because I won't make the same mistake twice.

This morning, I found myself staring in the mirror. While I looked the same as always, there was something there—a change that hadn't been there before. I had thought I found love with Bruce, but now I don't think that's true at all. My obsession with Bruce drove me to the brink of insanity. With every bit of rejection, I became even more obsessed. The drama made me fixated. Every plea that escaped his lips turned into more damage to my being. At some point, it sent me on a trail of destruction where I began to hope and seek for the wrong things. All the turmoil and the feeling of desperation, that's not love. I recognize that now.

Sylvie recommended that I step back and try to focus on myself for a change rather than on a man. She's right, of course. I know that if I don't follow her advice, I'll end up falling into an even darker pit where confusion, obsession, and self-doubt continue to plague me. I refuse to be stuck in the hell my mind's all too ready to concoct for me.

I have to think about the future and protect myself. Not only to prevent myself from having my heart broken again, but also so I won't fall again for the wrong person. In here, for the time being, I feel safe. But as soon as I think of tomorrow, I worry about the future. I worry that I'll fall back into old patterns and get back to that one place where obsession is a big part of my dysfunction. I don't want to go back to my delusions.

Don't be mad that I'm no longer writing regularly but never has a future been so full of unknown roads. I'm not even sure I know who I am anymore.

Am I the one chasing love or is love chasing me?

Did I ever feel love at all?

Lots of love,
Vicky Sullivan

25

Kaiden

IT'S BEEN ALMOST a week since that night on the beach, and I still can't stop thinking about her little body shaking as my tongue slipped in and out of her. Was it five orgasms she had? Six? Maybe even seven? At some point, I think I was too wrapped up in her to continue counting.

I'm getting hard thinking about her naked ass, the swell of her breasts, the generous curves of her body, the flawless skin beneath my fingers, the way her hair bounced as she moved up and down on my cock, drawing pleasure from my body, taking all she could.

The memories are enough to make me go insane. No amount of treatment is going to erase the pictures replaying on a loop in my mind. The night I spent with her is still fresh in my mind, and yet it seems as though countless years have passed. It's not helping that she keeps avoiding me. I'm all too aware of the little detours she takes to stay out of my path, and that's getting me worked up even more.

I've decided to wait a few more days to see what happens. With a bit of luck, she'll start missing me. Or my cock. I'd take either one at this point.

If she's not seeking me out soon, I'll start working on a plan to get her back into my bed.

Rivulets of cold sweat are trickling into my eyes as I lift the bar a final time, holding it above my head, then begin to count.

Ten....nine...eight...

My back is drenched with sweat as I push myself to my limits, ignoring the burn settling in my arms, my chest. At last, I take a deep breath and with a groan I return the bar to the rack.

I wipe my forehead with a towel and take a swig from my bottle of water. Exercise is my way to relax. It always helps me wind down and forget whatever's bothering me. It's not doing its intended job today. Vicky's still clinging to the edges of my mind. Today, I haven't been able to shake off her memory, no matter how hard I tried.

As I gather my belongings, my mind keeps going back to our last conversation. There's something about it that doesn't sit right with me. Vicky enjoyed what we did—but it wasn't guilt free on her part. I had a feeling Bruce was the reason she kept a certain emotional distance from me. Instead of just understanding that what we did wasn't cheating, I should have made sure she shared my opinion on the matter.

Closing the door of the fitness room behind me, I sling my bag over my shoulder and turn to head for the elevator. That's when I notice her leaving the library. Her red hair shimmers in the light, the curls inviting me to push my fingers through them and pulling her mouth to mine.

She doesn't notice me standing, staring. Her attention is focused on something far away, her face drawn in concentration.

I know where she's headed.

This is my opportunity to finally get her to face me.

Knowing that she won't notice me until it's too late to avoid me, I reach her in a few, long strides.

I brace myself for contact as I let my body slam into her, not hard enough to hurt her but with enough force to startle her.

The books she's been carrying drop to the floor.

"Kade?" Her shock lasts for all of a second, before

it's replaced by disbelief and...is that fear? Annoyance? I can't place her expression.

I squat to help her pick up the books. "Avoiding me much?"

"I don't know what you're talking about." Definitely annoyance, and plenty of that.

I squeeze her hand, which immediately draws her attention to me. "Why are you avoiding me, Vicky?"

Biting her lip, she looks up and our gazes meet.

I don't like what I'm seeing in her eyes even before she's spoken the words. "Fucking you was a mistake, and you know it."

Oh, for fuck's sake!

"Was it?"

"Yes." Her voice is forceful, challenging, as though she wants me to prove her wrong. "I shouldn't have brought you into this situation."

"Sorry, I'm not following. What situation?"

She peers around her to make sure no one's tuning in before she says, "I demanded that you fuck me."

I can barely hide my amusement. "You hardly forced me, sweetheart. It sure didn't feel like you were assaulting me, more like—"

She rolls her eyes, and for a moment there's a glint of amusement in her gaze. "God, Kade. Stop it with the jokes. This is serious. I'm trying to have a meaningful conversation with you and you're not taking it seriously." Her eyes sweep around us once more. Even though there's no one around, she's paranoid that someone might be watching. I want to point out to her that after five the halls are always empty because most patients are attending music therapy, but my reassurances will most certainly not be heard.

Vicky's voice drops to a whisper. "You're a sex addict. It was wrong of me to ask you. I don't know what I was thinking."

"I can't say I regret it. To be honest, I felt good afterwards. Better than I have felt in a long time. And from the looks of it, you enjoyed our little session, too." I wink at her playfully. She frowns. A soft blush spreads across her cheeks, which makes her look even more endearing.

"For the sake of all that's sacred, can you please keep your voice down?" Her voice is so low I have to lean forward to make out what she's saying. "It doesn't matter whether we liked it. We can't let it happen again."

Meaning, she's enjoyed every minute of it and is now trying hard to come up with reasons why she shouldn't be joining me between the sheets again.

Tilting my head, I cross my arms over my chest as I regard her with amusement. "Why not?"

"Just because." She glances away, avoiding my prodding gaze. But her voice is strained, betraying her emotions. She's torn about us. "I want you to get over your addiction, not for me to make it worse or for you to relapse. I don't want to be the reason for you failing rehab. So, I'm going to take responsibility for what happened between us. I'm going to ask to be roomed with someone else."

My jaw sets and anger pulses through me.

As if avoiding me wasn't bad enough; now she wants to put even more physical distance between us.

I haphazardly arrange her books on a tray and grab her hand. She doesn't protest as I lead her back inside the library, to the farthest part where I'm sure no one will see us.

"Kade, I—"

Pressing my body into her, I push her back against the bookcase. My face is lowered to hers, our breath intermingling. She smells so good I want to suck her lower lip between mine until she moans my name.

I want to touch her, but it wouldn't be right. Not before we've talked. Settled things. Got her worries and paranoia out of the way once and for all.

"You want to be roomed with someone else?" My voice comes out sharp, threatening.

"Why are you offended?"

"I'm not offended. I just don't think it's necessary. That's all." Her proximity is all I can focus on. I didn't anticipate that being so close to her would be so hard...or so heady.

"I can't keep living with you, Kade."

"Why not?"

"I don't want you to hate me." Her eyes are half-closed, her breathing slightly labored. She's finding this as hard as I do.

"I could never hate you. No one could."

"You will. Trust me." She lets out an exasperated breath. "I know me. I'm a walking disaster, and I'll bring you down with me. I'm sorry, but we can't do this anymore. I can't continue things with you. Not with my issues. Not when your own issues are as grave as they are."

"They're not as bad as you make them out to be. I think we're actually making progress."

"Progress?" She lets out a scoff and squints at me incredulously. "Tell me one good thing that's come out of this."

"Well, for starters, you haven't mentioned Bruce

in a while. You used to mention him in every sentence."

"Really?"

She holds out her hand as if she doesn't want to hear more. Exhaling a sharp breath, she glares at me, but what I see in her eyes isn't anger. It's fear.

Her tongue flicks across her lips and her eyes shimmer with what I'm pretty sure are tears.

I frown.

Fuck.

Did I say something wrong?

"What's going on, Vicky?" I ask softly.

"I thought I could do this, but I can't." She shakes her head. Waves of tension waft from her. "I feel like I'm trapped in a corridor, walking from door to door, with no hope of ever getting out. I seem to make one mistake after another. I thought by hooking up with you my problems would be solved, but I've realized everything's getting worse. It's only a matter of time until I fall. And when I do, I don't want to bring you down with me. Don't take it personally, Kade, but everything I'm doing I'm doing for us."

"Why do you think you know what's good for us? Maybe I don't want to stop now."

She hesitates and her expression darkens. "We

have to. There's no other choice."

"That's not what you want, Vicky. Take a good look at yourself. Your body's speaking volumes."

She laughs. "Seriously?"

"You don't want to stop." I brush her neck gently, trailing my fingers down her shoulder. She tenses under my touch, but she doesn't pull away.

"Fine. What do you want to hear? That I want you?" Her tone is flat. She really feels lost. She doesn't know what to do with the attraction between us.

"I want you to say that you want to fuck me again."

"I can't say that."

"Why not? And don't claim that's not what you want."

There's a short silence. "I'm not going to lie," she says slowly. "But that's the thing. I always seem to want things that destroy me. That are bad for me. It's my illness, and I'm not going to let my addiction destroy our lives. We have to be realistic. Face the facts. This little hook up of ours is going nowhere."

I inch toward her, my hand going to the back of her neck, caressing it, forcing her to meet my gaze. I lean into her until our lips almost touch, but not quite. Her breath is hot, sweet, and inviting. I want it to mingle with mine. I want our breaths to be one. "To get over one addiction you have to become addicted to something else."

"To what, for example?"

"To me," I breathe against her mouth. "Become addicted to me."

Her expression darkens and her lips part, quivering, inviting my tongue into her mouth. "That's the thing. I already am addicted to you, Kade."

My heart skips a beat, then another. When I say nothing, she continues, "I'm addicted to the way I feel when you touch me. I'm addicted to the way you came inside me. You're in my thoughts, in my dreams. Fuck. You're everywhere, Kade. It's like I can't escape you because you're my drug. I've tried to stop it, but I can't. That's why we can't keep meeting. You're leaving me no choice but to tell them the truth."

I stare at her, expecting repulsion to hit me low the way it always does when women proclaim their feelings for me.

But all I feel is a wave of shock—shock at the fact that I actually want her to feel all those things for me.

I cannot stop this—not now, not yet.

Not seeing her for days was unbearable, but at least there was always the certainty that I could change her mind again. Exposing us is another thing. It could mean the end of us.

I shake my head. "You won't do that."

"Why not?"

"I'm not ready to let you go."

She frowns. "Didn't you understand what I just said? I'm damaged."

"So what? We're all damaged. We've all done things we're not proud of. We're all trying to learn from mistakes we seem to repeat over and over again. Life is the process of learning things we cannot understand and the acceptance of things we cannot change. That's life. Accept it and move on."

Fuck. When did I start sounding like my therapist?

Her eyes widen, shimmering with sudden understanding. She's listening to me, *really* listening, clinging to my words as if they're a lifeboat that could save her.

I suddenly realize I want to be the one who saves this beautiful woman who is capable of saving others but not herself.

"Just because you might get all obsessive on me, doesn't mean I want to stop seeing you," I add, in case I didn't make that part clear enough.

She cocks her head, regarding me through those beautiful eyes of hers. "But...I thought you said you hated closeness."

"I do. But it's not like you want to enter a lifelong commitment with me, right?"

She opens her mouth, drawing a slow breath, then lets it out slowly. "That's right."

"Look, Vicky." I let go of her face and brace my palms against the shelf, leaning into her. My weight's keeping her from shifting, but she doesn't seem to mind. "I don't care if you're addicted to me because I could just as well say I'm addicted to fucking you. I'll be honest with you, I want to fuck you—bad. I want it not just once, but again and again. That breaks the golden promise I once made to myself. I believe it breaks most of them."

"What are you saying?"

"I'm saying that I don't want to stop now. There's no way I'm giving up what we have. Not yet."

"You still want to continue despite knowing I'm obsessive."

I nod. "That's the thought, yes. We have a good thing going. What's the harm in that?"

She laughs, the sound bitter and sad. "What's the harm? We could get caught, Kade."

"You knew that when we started this. Why the sudden fear?"

"Because I feel like I'm moving into unknown territory," she whispers. "This addiction of mine represents everything I've grown to hate about me. There's this constant fear. Uncertainty. Since being here, I've realized my greatest mistake is that I tend to live in the future rather than the present. I used to pin all my hopes and wishes on people who never intended to stay around. As you can see, it didn't work out too well for me."

"It's a good thing you realized that because I want us to live in the present and not focus on tomorrow. I want us to focus on *us*." I stare at her, letting my words sink in. "You have something I need, and I can give you something you want. Call it a symbiosis. An intimate relationship with no commitment, but one that is of mutual benefit."

Her lips twitch. "Are you comparing us with trees and spores?"

"Something like that." I lean into her, brushing my lips against hers. "I'm into you, Vicky. I just don't do relationships. I never made a secret out of that fact. If there's a chance that we can help each other, then I don't think we should stop. I just think we should make our own rules."

"Rules?"

"Yeah. Rules." I trace her cheekbone with my finger, cupping her face again. "Rule number one: you need to be honest with me at all times." My thumb glides over her full lips that are quivering under my touch. "Rule number two: I want you to act on your desires. I honestly believe that sometimes the things that keep you obsessed are the things that might help you heal. If you want to touch me, go on and touch me. If you think of me, don't just think. Act on your urge. If sex is what you crave, then let me fuck you."

"What's number three?" she whispers just as short of breath as I feel.

"Why do you assume there's a rule number three?"

"Because the first two rules only seem to apply to me. You haven't mentioned yourself yet."

My lips curl into a smile. "This isn't one of my rules so much as a general fact about me, but I'm going to teach you that love is overrated and sex is a cure."

She laughs briefly. "That sounds wrong on so many levels."

"How can sex be wrong? Sex doesn't break your heart. Sex doesn't need kindness to work out. Sex is never patient. It rarely boasts, and it always makes you feel good."

"Did you just make that up?"

I look at her, wondering the same thing. "Maybe. All I'm saying is that I want you to let go of your limitations, fear, and expectations. Stop thinking about what's wrong and live a little."

"What about rehab?"

"What about it?" I shrug. "I am here voluntarily. I could leave at any time, but I choose to stay because my company's important to me. This is all a show I'm putting on. Doesn't mean I really have a problem."

As I say the words, I realize how empty and hollow they are. I might have believed them not too long ago. But something has changed. Yes, my company's important to me, but so is Vicky. I refuse to let her go just as much as I won't lose the very thing I built up from scratch. This isn't a show any longer, and my bet with Cash is no longer what drives me to pursue Vicky, which is why I haven't yet mentioned to him that the deed's been done.

Vicky regards me for a few moments. "I knew you'd say that." Her words sound strange. Maybe a bit bitter but not angry. I don't know what to make of them.

I wrap my hands around her waist, pulling her close. "I do feel a great level of attraction to you. What you see is how I feel about you. I want you. I desire you. I crave you in any way I can have you. Right now, I'm thinking of tearing this thing off your body and fucking you on the spot. I want to go on a journey inside your body, discover the world with you. I want to be your favorite place. I want you to be your true self with me."

She's changing her mind right before my eyes. I can see it from the way she's chewing her lower lip, sucking it into her mouth. I want her like I've never wanted anyone else before. But admitting that part to her is never going to happen. If the very idea of getting involved in a sexual relationship with me scares her to death, admitting my level of fondness for her would drive her away forever.

"What happens after this?" she asks warily.

I don't know that. I don't know what I'm feeling or thinking. I just know that I crave her. Everything about her. And it pains me to see just how hesitant she is to the possibility of seeing me again after rehab's over.

"Who cares? I want you now and don't give a damn about tomorrow." I cringe at the words. Cringe at the fact that she's nodding her head in agreement, as though I'm saying all the things she wants to hear from me.

The realization feels like a punch to my stomach.

This isn't me. I barely recognize myself. Barely recognize my reactions to her blatant emotional aversion to me.

As if to regain some of my old self, I move my hand between her legs, stroking her pussy over her dress. "I want to find that hidden spot inside you and mark it as mine. I want you to know how much I want you and find out if you're brave enough to want me back."

At least that's the truth.

"Kade, what are you doing?" She throws her head back and swallows a moan as my fingers find their way beneath her dress.

Her panties are soaked with want. That's all the invitation my dick needs. I take in her expression—a mixture of fearfulness and excitement.

"What do you think?" I pull her panties down her hips and unzip my jeans. My hard shaft jerks to life, demanding that it finally finds its way home, as a hurricane of need and desire spreads through my entire body.

"We can't. What if someone sees us?"

"We'll think of something." I slowly thrust my

finger inside her and curl it to find her sweet spot. "I love how wet you are."

"Kade." Moaning my name, she closes her eyes and throws her head back. My teeth graze her neck as my finger finds its rhythm inside her. "I know what you need. I know how to heal you. Let me be the one who fixes you."

My mouth finds hers in a slow kiss, our tongues entangled in a slow, erotic dance. She tastes like cinnamon and sunshine. Like all the things I love and cannot have.

I thrust deeper, my whole body coming alive as I drag her into another kiss. "Is this what you like?" I whisper into her open mouth.

"Yes," she moans in that sexy voice of hers and grinds into my hand. "More."

I want to give her more. So much more. I'd love to give her more every day of the week.

Slowly, I pull out my fingers and spread her moisture to prepare her.

"No. Don't stop." Her eyes are glazed over, her lips pouting, mirroring her displeasure.

I suck her lower lip into my mouth as I position her against the door and myself between her legs. She doesn't need any invitation to spread them apart.

I place both of my hands under her ass and lift her up, splaying her wider open than she's probably ever been.

Her eyes meet mine. "Kade, I—"

I don't give her doubts enough time to get in the way of things. Before she can protest, I stroke my cock between her swollen lips, up over her clit, and then back down to her slit, sliding into her—all the way in.

She gasps and grabs onto my shoulders for support.

"You make me so fucking hard, Vicky," I say and start to rock my hips.

My hand fists in the hair at the nape of her neck as I pull out of her and thrust back in. Between my tight grip and the door keeping her in place, she's completely at my mercy, but she doesn't seem to mind.

"Yes." Her lips part and she throws her head back, moaning. Her pussy clenches around my cock. I can feel she's close to the edge. Seeing her beautiful face lost in her lust for me sends tiny explosions through my body.

I cup her ass and lift her just a little higher, letting me dive balls deep into her.

"I promised myself it would only be a one-time

thing," I groan and bite the tendon at the base of her neck. She gasps for air. "But I can't get enough of you."

"Fuck, yes, Kade. Don't stop." The sounds she makes sets me on fire for her. I force myself to fuck her slow and steady. Her nipples are standing on end, poking through the thin fabric of her dress. I want to suck them into my mouth, to make her squirm and scream my name. But I'm in no rush. There's time for that later, in the privacy of my bedroom, where I'll have her tonight.

"You're so tight and wet, baby. I love it."

Taking her lower lip between her teeth, she looks up at me. The expression in her eyes reveals her desperation for finding release. As much as I want to prolong our little session, someone could come in any second. We can't risk being found out; not as long as I haven't had enough of her.

I thrust into her hard and stay there, rocking barely an inch in and out of her. Her pussy muscles clench around me. I move my hand between our slick bodies and find the little nub. The combination of my hard cock inside her and my fingers brushing over her clit does the trick. She erupts with a cry of pleasure that makes me plunge into my own orgasm. I pump into her with a groan, spreading my load as she continues to clamp her pussy around me. She angles her hips to meet my last stroke and plunges into another orgasm.

Even though we're both panting and spent I take my sweet time setting her down and pulling out of her.

I arrange her dress around her hips. "Are you okay?"

She nods and smiles. "Better than in a long time."

I lean into her to kiss her lips. "I want you in my room tonight. I expect you right after dinner."

Her eyes narrow on me and that suspicion of hers is back. "Why?"

"Because I have plans for us. And that involves being naked and lots of screaming."

She opens her mouth to protest when I place my finger against her lips, silencing her. "And don't be late, unless you want me to tie you to my bed and torture you until you'll beg me for release."

26

Vicky

IT'S A CHILLY SUNDAY afternoon. I'm taking my regular walk, lost in thought, when I get the distinct feeling that I'm being followed.

I spin around and almost bump into Kade.

"Whoa, there." His hands go around my waist to steady me, pulling me a little too close to him.

"Jesus." Pressing my hand against my chest, I exhale a sharp breath and peer around us to make sure no one's seen us. "You scared the life out of me." I want to be angry with him, but I can't. He looks so carefree with that lazy smile on his lips and the sun catching his eyes, that for a moment I almost forget who we are and why we're here.

For a moment, it feels as though he's someone I've known forever.

Someone I've started to like way more than I

should. I don't even know when it happened. Maybe the feeling's been here all along. Or maybe it started the moment I realized that even though he only wants my body, during those moments together he made me feel as though he treasured it.

As though he treasured me.

"I thought I'd take a turn being a stalker. You know, shake things up a little." He guides me to a nearby tree and presses me against it. We're shielded from the rehab building and the windows overlooking the back, but that doesn't mean people walking by couldn't see us.

Even though the weather's been rainy, a few rays of sun are shining through the heavy curtain of gray clouds. Squinting, I reach up to brush Kade's hair out of his eyes and marvel at just how right it feels to have his hard body press into me.

This won't last.

My mood drops a little at the thought, but I won't allow myself to go there. All that counts is the present.

"Don't tell me you've been following me all the way up here."

He laughs. "To be honest, walking isn't really my thing." He tilts his head to the right. I follow his line of vision and notice a mountain bike leaned against a tree.

"Where did you get the bike?" I watch his lips twitch and frown. "On second thought, don't answer me if it involves anything illegal. I won't be your partner in crime."

"Anything that doesn't carry a lock and an explicit warning, can be borrowed."

I gape at him, unable to decide whether to laugh or be shocked.

"How about we take a trip around the island and visit the local museum? Group meeting's been canceled, so we might as well enjoy the day together."

"I'm pretty sure most tourist attractions are closed."

"We can still look around, spin our own stories about the early settlements." He wiggles his eyebrows. "I bet we'll see some interesting things inside."

I let out an exasperated laugh. "You're not seriously thinking about breaking in."

"Who says anything about breaking in?" Kade says gravely, but his tone can't fool me. "Come on. It'll be fun. We'll have a bottle of cabernet sauvignon and maybe watch the sun set on the beach."

"You brought wine?"

He points at the bike again. "The most expensive...available in rehab, which is a ten-dollar bottle."

"I'm impressed. How could a girl possibly decline?"

"You have to promise me something first. Don't get drunk on me again. My arms are still aching from carrying you back to our apartment."

He had to bring that part up. Slapping his shoulder, I look at him. Really look at him and realize it comes as no surprise women are throwing themselves at him. I mean, everything seems so easy with him.

"You in?" Kade prompts.

I close my eyes. "Kaiden Wright. You're going to break me."

The breaking part is meant as a joke, and yet it isn't.

"Your will?" He steals a soft kiss that feels like my legs have just sped off in the distance—leaving me behind. I lean into him, wanting more but he pulls away, continuing, "There's no chance I'll let that happen. Before I break you, you'll have to rip me to pieces first, because I would rather lose my heart than be without you." He looks at me before adding softly, "As a friend, of course."

Of course.

He's made that part clear on so many occasions that it shouldn't come as a surprise. And yet a heavy weight grows inside my chest, cutting off my air supply.

But what choice do I have?

His words are sweet as honey, and yet meaningless. Even though I shouldn't, I want to be close to him. I simply can't stay away.

"Okay. Let's do this." I turn to head down the narrow path when his hand clasps around mine, stopping me.

"We're taking the bike."

I shoot a wary look at the bicycle. That thing doesn't look like it's made for two people. In fact, I doubt anyone should be riding on it. "Are you kidding me? It can't carry us both."

"You're scared." His eyes are glinting with something, and his expression softens. "I'll teach you. It's not hard."

"What if I fall off?"

He lets go of my hand and cups my chin, tipping it back until I'm forced to look at him.

"If you fall, I'll be there to catch you. There's no way I'd ever let you get hurt." He kisses on the corner of my lips, lingering on my lower lip. His touch is soft, gentle, his soul fused with mine. His fingers trail down my back, kneading the knots in my muscles.

"Ready to give it a try?" he asks, pulling away.

I nod, still intoxicated from his kiss. His strong hands hold me steady as he lifts me onto the handlebars. I long to hold on to them, to stay in his arms for a little longer, but like everything else that's too good in life, his embrace is over too soon. My whole body tenses as he gives the bike a push and settles onto the seat.

As the bicycle rolls down the path, I jerk forward, my legs dangling in the air. A startled yelp escapes my throat, followed by a shriek of relief and laughter.

"I can't believe we're doing this." It's both fun and exhilarating. Having conquered my fear, I feel like I'm on top of the world with Kade right beside me.

"You're doing great, baby," Kade says, joining in my laughter. I love the sound—deep and manly, the waves carrying through my body and leaving a delicious tingle behind.

I want to peer at him over my shoulder, but my confidence is not there. For one, I could still fall off. And then there's also the fact that I might like what I see a little too much.

We circle around the island in silence while the wind's playing with my hair and my body's relaxing more and more with every passing moment. For the first time, I really feel alive and free, as though we've escaped the web of time.

I only notice that we've reached the historical site—a red brick building—when the bicycle comes to a halt and Kade jumps down, catching me in his arms.

"We're here," he says, needlessly.

I nod and stare up at him. This is the moment I should be prying myself away from his arms, but all I can think about is that he smells of the sun and the woods around us. The nerves inside my body fire all at once, and my insides clench in response. I want to snuggle up against him and run my hands up and down his ripped torso. Beg him to take me to a secluded spot and guide him inside me so he can fill the space that's always empty without him.

"You sure this is a good idea?" The question is addressed more to myself than him. I'm not sure how long I'll be able to enjoy his presence without ripping the clothes off his glorious body.

"Now it is." He jiggles the handle and pushes the door open. "Please." He gestures for me to enter and follows after me.

"Why? So you can pretend I was the one breaking in and you were merely an innocent bystander?" I laugh at his fake-innocent smirk.

"You caught me there."

I watch him spread a blanket across the hardwood floor of the reception hall and pour us two glasses of wine as I settle on the blanket.

"Wow. You really thought of everything." I take the glass from his outstretched hand.

"I always please."

For that I can vouch.

"Here's to your first ride with me," Kade says, holding up his glass.

I let out a laugh. "And here's to you for being pushy. I've most certainly never met anyone like you."

"And here's to you seeing Bruce for who he really is."

I stare at Kade. Barely two weeks ago, I would have thrown a fit at his audacity, but something's changed inside me.

I agree with him.

"You really can't stand him, can you?" My voice comes out as a whisper. I'm not even sure the words are addressed at him and not at myself.

"That's an understatement. I actually hate the

guy's guts, and I haven't even met him yet. Anyone who treats a woman the way he treated you deserves a good ass whooping."

"Why?"

He hesitates, choosing his words carefully. "I can't explain it. I just have this strange feeling that he's more than a cheater. You're in rehab because of him, and how does he repay you? By taking a damn cruise with his ex. Who does that?"

That's not even half of the story.

I think back to the letter and that I haven't yet mentioned Bruce marrying his ex.

"If you were with me, I'd love you the way you are," Kade says, wrapping his arms around me. I lean into him, inhaling his scent, wondering what it'd be like to be close to him outside, in the real world.

His words are sweet and heavy, like the wine coursing through my body.

Staring at the old ceiling, I wonder how much I can open up to him.

I peer at him. His eyes are clouded, his thoughts shrouded in mystery, miles away. From so close, I can feel the heat radiating from his body. The strong, male scent of his aftershave carries over and for a moment I remember every detail about last night. Every breath, every word, every thought feels as though it happened just a moment ago.

"I'll be sorry when this is over," Kade says, breaking the silence.

His intense gaze is on me. There's something in it—something sharp, ferocious.

"Me, too." A smile tugs at my lips. "We could always relapse and return to live here, happily-ever-after."

It's a joke—only, not quite.

"Yeah, we could. Except, we'll have to find a new place because they're closing this place down in a few months."

"Really? Who told you?"

"My therapist."

"No one tells me stuff like this," I mumble. "Am I the only one who doesn't get along with her therapist?"

"I always get the scoop. It certainly helps that she likes me." He looks at me, poker-faced, and then we both erupt in laughter.

"Why's every woman into you?" I ask. I mean, I get why. He's hot. He's successful. And he seems like a great catch.

But does every woman *have* to be into him? When you have the entire female population to choose from, there's no way you'll ever settle for one.

"I don't know." He falls silent for a moment. "They see what they want to see. The troubled bad boy who needs the right woman to change him. What they don't realize is that I'd never change for anyone—unless I did it for myself."

"Nobody should change for anyone." I smile at him. "I like the way you are."

He grimaces. "I'm not sure you would if you knew the things I've done."

"It doesn't matter. The past can't be changed. Deeds cannot be undone. Memories can't be unwrapped. I've known you for a few weeks, Kade, and I think you're amazing."

"Amazing, huh?" He leans over me and brushes a stray lock out of my eyes. "I'd take amazing every day, almost as good as perfect."

"Don't get cocky on me," I manage to whisper before he rolls on top of me, his weight pinning me down. "Obviously, I was just trying to be nice. That's not to mean—"

My breath hitches as he cuts off my words with a kiss. It's only a kiss, but it's the most beautiful one yet—soft and smooth and filled with unspoken promises—and for the first time I can't help but wonder:

Could there ever be more?

Could more become forever?

With him, I feel safe. Safer than I've ever felt before.

When the traps of life keep you tied to rigid things, you appreciate that one special moment.

This is my special moment.

I don't know why, but I kind of like Kade. I like everything about him. He makes me laugh and stands by me when everyone has been judgmental. He's shown me how to breathe again after I thought I'd always live in a state of suffocation.

But why does it feel so wrong to want him and so right to need him?

I peer into his eyes nervously.

He looks at my lips and my heart flies as if it's a bird discovering the sky for the first time. He takes a breath, and I suck it in. He's so close that I could get lost in him forever.

"Am I making you nervous?" he whispers and brushes his thumb over my lower lip.

"Sometimes."

"Did Bruce ever make you nervous?"

"I don't know." I want to lie that he did and yet I can't.

"How can you not know?" Kade asks. His hand

tightens around me possessively. "You know what I think? I don't think you ever loved him. Do you think of him now as much as you did on your first day here?" I open my mouth, but he holds up a hand, silencing me. "Think before you answer. I want you to be honest with yourself. Because true love doesn't just go away."

I bite my lower lip, thinking. This is the one place I don't want to revisit, mainly because I fear I might go back to a state that wasn't healthy for me. "I don't want to talk about him. Please, just drop it."

I try to wiggle my way out of his stealthy embrace, but my attempt is a feeble one. Truth be told, I enjoy his touch. Enjoy everything he does to me. I know it. He knows it. The silence that follows is awkward, but not uncomfortable.

Kade leaves me to my thoughts, which I realize is probably just as bad as forcing me to talk about my demons.

Me never in love with Bruce?

If someone had told me that weeks ago, I would have said that was impossible.

But Kade has been close to the truth. I never truly loved him. I know it now because what I'm beginning to feel for Kade is what love really feels like.

It's honest and beautiful. Accepting and giddily exhilarating. It makes me feel more beautiful than I've ever felt before.

"Why did you have to bring up Bruce?" I whisper. "You've ruined the moment."

"Have I really?" Kade lowers his lips to my neck, his hot breath grazing my skin as his hand forces its way beneath my clothes.

Moaning, I throw my head back as I realize what he's about to do and the lust from before settles deep in my core.

27

Kaiden

OUR BEACH HAS BECOME our very own private resort. Far away from the rehab building, it's our safe haven. We've visited it every day after rehab, sometimes twice—so many times that I've lost count.

It's been endless hours of talking and lovemaking. I can't even call it fucking any more because it would cheapen the experience. It would cheapen *her*.

Those are my beautiful moments.

I don't think you can count them. I don't think you can measure happiness. Every breath I take is with her.

It's become our breath.

Vicky lifts her hand, intertwining her fingers with mine.

In the lightening sky, she looks more

breathtaking than ever, with her hair wild and her cheeks still flushed from my kisses.

"You know, I never expected things to turn out this way," she whispers. "It seems like my whole life I waited for something to happen. But this rehab thing wasn't it." She laughs softly, the sound dark and sad. "My poor mom—I hate to disappoint her after all she went through with my dad."

Pulling her to my chest and the blanket over her shoulders, I prop my arm underneath my head and wait for her to continue.

She remains quiet for a few seconds while her fingers are tracing circles across my abdomen. Every touch makes me breathe hard. I want to kiss her, to take her again, claim her body as many times as I can. But there's something in the silence surrounding us that keeps me from doing so.

Vicky's relaxed, on the verge of falling asleep in my arms. Those moments are so rare that I can't let it slip.

Above us, the night is turning into dawn. The red rim of the sun is stretching over the purple-blue shaded horizon.

Suddenly, I want her to talk. I need to know more about her.

"When you were cutting my hair, you mentioned

something about your father. You talk about him like he's not in your life anymore," I say.

"That's because he isn't." She pulls away from me and flips onto her stomach, placing her hand under her chin as she looks up to me. "He ditched my mom when I was fifteen. I haven't heard from him since. I have no idea where he is or what he's doing. My best guess is that he has a new family and has forgotten about us. Rumor has it he got someone knocked up while he was still married to my mom. She's still paying off his debts."

"I'm sorry."

She shrugs. "It's no big deal. I'm a big girl now. I can deal with stuff like that. My mom believes that my father's walking out on her is to blame for my mental breakdown. Is she right?" She pauses, grimacing. "I don't know, but it was hard for us, more for me, because I was real close to my dad. His sudden decision to cut ties with us left me feeling depressed and guilty. I try to hate him for all the pain he's caused my mom, but I can't. My therapist says that my love addiction is a coping mechanism. That the feeling of having lost my dad got to me so much, it's become normal for me to get attached to a new guy to try and replace the connection with my dad."

"She might be right."

She cocks her head to the side, a soft smile playing on her lips. "Hey! Aren't you supposed to be on my side?"

"I am." I roll one of her perfect curls around my finger, tugging gently. "But as your friend, I'm also supposed to tell you the truth. What about your siblings?"

"My brother's great. He spends all his time playing video games with his best friend. But my sister? She's a real pain in the ass."

I let out a laugh and she shoots me an annoyed look.

"Trust me, that's the kind of sister you don't want to have. She's annoying as hell, and competitive, but she knits a damn great sweater to keep you warm, and I love her to bits."

"But it's nice to have family." My words come out a little too bitter and envious. I realize that too late.

"Yeah, it is. What about you? Do you have a good relationship with your parents?" She regards me intently, her beautiful eyes two dark spots that penetrate the walls I thought were impenetrable.

"The two people I call my parents are dead," I say.

Her easygoing expression slowly disappears. "I'm

sorry."

"Don't be," I whisper. "Unfortunately, we can change the past just as little as we can predict the future. My parents adopted me from an orphanage when no one else would. You see, it's hard for orphans to be placed in new homes. More so for boys than for girls. You see your friends go, then make new ones, only to see them leave, too. After a while you begin to feel unwanted. Like nobody gives a fuck about you." I grimace as the memories I thought I had left behind come back to haunt me. "I tell myself that both of my biological parents were drug addicts. That's the only excuse I can think of as to why anyone would abandon their three-day-old child."

"Did you ever try to find them? Your biological parents, I mean?" her voice is choked, afraid to ask.

I shake my head. "No, and I never will. They abandoned me. They don't deserve to have me in their lives. The way I see it, they're not worth meeting. I'm not sure how I'd feel about seeing them, clouding my memories, letting them in. Too many years have passed. What happened can't ever be changed. They're strangers and I want them to stay that way." I pause to choose my words carefully. "That my biological parents gave me away hurt me for a long time, but it was nothing compared to the pain I felt when I lost my adoptive parents. They're the ones I'm still grieving, because they were the parents I thought I'd never have. They raised me as if I were their own. To me, people like them are more of a parent than some name on a birth certificate."

"What happened to them?"

I sit up to ease the tightening sensation inside my chest.

The night sky is breaking to make room for dawn—just like when my mom slipped away.

"My father got targeted by some guy. He lost his business, all of his money. Over the span of a few weeks, we lost everything he had fought for over the course of thirty years. And then my mom became ill. He couldn't afford to get her the best treatment. He was so desperate that he killed himself so she could claim his insurance policy and we wouldn't end up homeless. His death hit my mom hard. She died a few weeks later. Any form of treatment would have come too late anyway." I close my eyes, the memory hitting like little sharp spikes piercing every part of my body. "I still miss them. At least I'm close to my brother. He's the reason I'm here. I gave in to the board's demands because of him."

"I'm sorry," Vicky whispers. I open my eyes to take in the pained expression on her face. Probably for the first time in my life, those words aren't meaningless. She truly feels them. "I'm sorry," she repeats. "I feel so stupid talking about my father when you...I don't even know what to say."

Under different circumstances, I'd feel uncomfortable with people's pity. But Vicky looks at me like I'm part of her soul. What she feels doesn't look like pity; it is compassion.

Tears are shimmering in her eyes. I lean to wipe them away and realize just how much I love the kind of person she is. Her kindness is probably the reason why she feels the need to take care of everyone but herself. It's probably also the reason why she gets attached so easily.

"It took me years to get over it. For a long time, I could only feel anger for the people responsible for my father's business going bust. I wanted revenge and I got it, but along the way I realized as sweet as revenge might be, it doesn't bring back the people you love." I cock my head to the side as it dawns on me that I've never opened up to anyone the way I seem to open up to Vicky. I also realized that it feels good, as though after such a long time I've finally found the right person to open up to. "You know what's the strange part? My brother, Chase, married the woman whose stepfather ruined our parents."

"You can't be serious," Vicky says.

"I tried to hate her, but she's not her stepfather's sin. She thinks he killed her mother."

"Did he?"

I take a deep breath and hold it for a moment as I consider my words. "I don't know. I guess we'll never know the truth. All I know is that my brother loves her very much and I'm fine with it."

Vicky squeezes my hand, and I smile at her. In the soft light, she looks like an angel.

"Love does strange things to you," I say softly. "I've never seen Chase happier. It all goes to show that you can't choose love. Love chooses you. You don't have to seek it. It comes to you." I brush a finger over Vicky's cheek. "Speaking of relationships, have you decided what you're going to do about Bruce?"

"Bruce." She draws out the word and grimaces.

"You'll have to make a decision soon, Vicky. He won't be in your life forever. The sooner you get him out of your head, the better."

She casts her glance down. I sense something, but I can't tell what she's thinking, feeling. Eventually, she gets up and moves a few steps away from me, leaning her back against the wall.

"Did I say something wrong?" I want to close the distance between us, draw her in my arms and tell her that everything's going to be okay. But this is her fight. I can't force her to get rid of a pattern that's not good for her.

"I've been wanting to tell you," Vicky says slowly. "You're right. He isn't going to stay in my life for long. Not single, anyway. He's marrying his ex this summer."

Oh, fuck!

I stand and reach her in two long strides. My fingers itch to touch her, to give her the comfort she needs, but I hold back. The fragments of her soul seem too fragile to touch. Only she can hold together what can be so easily broken.

"When did you find out?" I ask.

"My sister told me when she came to see me. She brought a letter from Bruce. Like the coward he is, he broke up in writing. Couldn't even tell me in person."

"Vicky." She doesn't look at me as I place my hand on her shoulder, gently forcing her to look at me. Her face is a mosaic of emotions. But there are no tears. No pain.

I frown, unsure what to make of it.

"Why didn't you tell me sooner?"

She shrugs. "I didn't want you to think that I'm damaged material."

"I would never think that of you. I never have." Every muscle in my body is tense. I want to punch this guy, kick the shit out of him, for hurting her. As soon as I'm out of this place I'll make sure he gets to walk down the aisle painted in purple and blue.

Maybe I'll throw in a bruised and swollen eye.

"How does that make you feel?" I repeat my therapist's standard question.

"I don't know. Stupid doesn't even cover it. I feel used, I guess. I put so much faith in him only to find that he was engaged to someone else the entire time. The hardest part is lying to my therapist. She still thinks we're together. I can't bring myself to disclose the truth out of fear that she'll sense my anger, and then I'll be forced to talk about it even though all I want is to forget."

"You're better off without him."

She nods. "I know, Kade."

"You never lost him, Vicky. You just learned that he wasn't real to begin with."

"I know that, too." Her voice is low, thoughtful. "But I still feel like I wasted my time and energy. Eight months of my life will forever be wasted. Eight months I could have put to better use."

"I wouldn't look at it that way."

"Yeah?" She regards me, weary. "How *would* you look at it?"

"I would always find a reason to grow. Sometimes, the smallest mistake turns out to be the biggest step in your life. Your experience with Bruce might not have been pleasant, and it most certainly was a kick to your ego, but you know what they say. Better a short pain than a long, excruciating one. In the end, he would have brought you more pain, so he did you a favor." I squeeze her hand gently, forcing her to listen, to trust me the way I trust her. "Even if he wasn't dating someone else, the last thing you'd want is to marry into his family. I wouldn't let you."

Damn! Where did that part come from?

She stares at me, her eyes narrowed. "You wouldn't?"

"Obviously, I couldn't stop you in any way," I add quickly, eager to backtrack and rectify my mistake. "I'd probably give you a wakeup call."

"And how exactly would you do that?"

"Let me think. You might want to close your eyes."

Vicky groans and rolls her eyes. "Why don't I like the sound of that?"

"Probably because a wakeup call might not be what you'd ever expect." Before she's even registered what's happening, I cup her face between my hands and capture her mouth in a soft kiss.

"I could get used to your kind of wakeup call," Vicky whispers against my lips.

"To the cold ones, as well?" Before she can register what's happening, I've scooped her up in my arms and am headed for the water.

"Kade, let go of me," she shrieks.

Laughing, I head into the ice-cold water, making sure her feet aren't touching the surface. The first wave hits me so hard, I almost topple over.

"Don't you dare," Vicky says, misinterpreting my hesitation. She kicks her leg and it's a great kick, causing me to lose my balance.

We both tumble into the water, and it's so freezing cold, that for a brief second, I fear she might pass out.

"Fuck." I let out a shuddering breath as I pull us both up. "We should have gotten undressed first."

"Seriously? That's the one thing you think we should have done?" She grimaces at me, and before I can come up with a remark, she splashes water in my face. "Jerk. I told you to put me down. Not to drop me."

"Actually, sweetheart." My lips switch. "Your exact words were to let go of you, and that's exactly what I did."

I inch closer to her. Her chin is trembling as she stares up at me. She looks as though she might be about to launch another attack. And then her expression changes and she begins to laugh.

"God, Kade. Your phone!"

Fuck!

I pull it out of my pocket quickly and try to switch it on. All I get is a blank screen.

"There goes our little escape plan." I throw the little device onto the beach and wrap my arms around Vicky, realizing I'm completely cut off from the real world now...and it doesn't matter.

"I'm sorry." I nuzzle her neck. "I've just ruined your chance at continuing to spy on Bruce."

She cocks her head, granting me better access. "Are you?"

"Not really. On a side note, we're completely alone out here." I look at her to take in her reaction and realize her lips are slowly turning blue. "I shouldn't have thrown us in. That wasn't my brightest idea."

"It's not so bad," Vicky says. "It'll get warmer in an hour or so. By the time we get back, our clothes will be dry." She's trying to paint the entire thing in a positive light, but her body's betraying her. She's clinging to me, seeking my warmth. Up close, she smells amazing. I want to bury myself in her and ignite her heat from within her little body. I want to make her shiver from want and hear her moan my name with the waves crashing against us.

But she's too fragile to be out in the cold for too long, and I wouldn't want to see her harmed in any way.

Drawing her closer to me, I brush a stray strand of hair from her forehead as I take in her face. She has gorgeous lips. Everything about her is beautiful. Holding her feels right, the way it should be.

I wonder if she would let me hold her like this forever, shield her from whatever the world might be throwing in our path?

"I want you naked," I whisper in her ear because that's all I can demand from her.

"Why? So you can fuck me again?"

"Would it bother you if I said yes?"

She laughs. "It would bother me if you didn't."

She snuggles into me and wraps her arms around my neck. We're both shivering. It's so damn cold, I know we need to get out of here before we both catch pneumonia, but the moment is too special.

I want to hold on to it as long as I can.

Above us, the sun is slowly rising in glorious shades of red, building a beautiful backdrop to the twinkling stars. Rubbing my hands up and down her back, I whisper, "If you're not amazed by the stars, your heart has no place for beauty."

Vicky nods in response.

"Let's get out of here." Without waiting for her reply, I lift her out of the water and carry her back to our little spot. She doesn't protest as I undress us both and then sit down, drawing her into my arms as I wrap the blanket around us.

The sun is rising in the distance, bathing the water in a shimmery hue of gold.

"It's so beautiful here." Vicky's breath is hot against my cheek. Her skin is deliciously soft and warm against mine. I place a soft kiss on my mouth and pull her just a little bit closer to me.

"No. You know what's really beautiful? You are," I whisper. "You are beautiful, Vicky, in every sense of the word."

She throws her head back, and our eyes lock.

The stars are magnificent, but compared to her, they pale in beauty. I know it now; I knew it the moment I laid my eyes on her.

I don't just want to just see her happy. I want her

to stay. In my life. In my heart. In my breath. In everything I have to give her.

I realize my heart isn't just beating faster whenever she's around; it beats for her.

She leans her head against my shoulders. I can sense that she wants to say something but can't bring herself to.

"I wish I had met you before," she says eventually. "I bet I wouldn't have ended up here."

"Maybe. But under different circumstances you might not have liked me."

"Why do you assume I like you now?"

"Because you do. You have to," I say. "At this point, any man is better than Bruce."

She nods, and after a while, she says, "While reading his letter I wished I could make him disappear."

"Disappear, huh?" I nudge her. "I know a good place to hide a body."

"Kade, that's not even remotely funny." In spite of her sober expression, her lips are twitching. "I meant disappear out of my life so I'll never have to see him again."

"I can't help you with that. But I'd kick his ass in a heartbeat."

"You don't have to say that," Vicky says.

I shrug. "It's the truth."

"You'd do that for me?" She raises her head and our gazes lock knocking the breath out of me.

"That, and much more. You know what? When we get out of here I'll dare you to crash their wedding and introduce me as your boyfriend. If he so much as breathes a wrong word, I'll show him how to treat you right."

"We can't." She smiles sadly. "He wouldn't believe us."

"Why not?"

"Because you're far hotter than he—" She breaks off before she can finish her sentence, as though she's just realized what she was about to say. "You know what I mean. I'm sure I don't have to spell it out for you."

"Actually, I don't. Please spell it out." I shoot her a sheepish look. "You mentioned that I'm good looking, sexy, clever, and you also said something about my...?"

She rolls her eyes. "My mouth is sealed shut."

"Come on, say it." I lean into her and force her onto her back, placing myself strategically between her parted thighs. "You said something about my—"

"There's no way I'm saying that." Her breath is coming in tiny rasps. Slowly, she grinds her hips against me—the movement so tiny, I'm not even sure she's aware of it.

"Why not? You already mentioned my magic cock once." I push slightly into her, rubbing my hard shaft against her hot core. "You're better off without him, Vicky. You wouldn't be happy married to a guy who can't satisfy you. Beauty fades. But love? Love is a fire that needs sex to be burning strong. What good is a man who doesn't own a match to light your fire?"

I let my hand roam over her body, caressing her breasts, her abdomen, her swollen clit. Closing her eyes, she shivers under my touch and a moan escapes her lips.

"Let me make you burn for me, baby." I kiss her softly. One kiss becomes a thousand kisses and it strikes me that she hasn't replied to anything.

I need to tell her so much more, but now's not the time. I can't destroy what we have just yet, not before I've had her body one more time.

28

Vicky

AN OPEN LETTER TO JANE AUSTEN

Dear Jane,

The rehab experience has turned out different than I could have ever imagined. Every morning, I wake up energized, excited to see Kade. He has become the reason why I don't want this to end.

I don't want us to end.

But as night comes, I can no longer silence the voice of reason that this will not, and cannot, last.

Nothing will last.

Not the peace. Not the fake harmony. Nor the little things that have etched his image into my heart. I'm waiting for that one defining moment when everything starts to fall apart...where ties are severed.

Layers removed.

Rose-colored glasses taken off.

Walls made of lies destroyed.

I really dread the day when one of us will leave this place. I know I'm going to miss him, miss what we have, for a long time.

When I look in the mirror, I see me. The true me. And it's a different me from what I thought I saw before. It's become impossible to see what enticed me about Bruce in the first place. He wasn't even a good kisser, not at all like Kade whose lips are to die for. I cannot help but wonder what I ever saw in Bruce. I find myself forgetting him more and more, as if he's being wiped from my memory, while I find myself falling more and more in love with my roommate.

When Kade kisses me, countless butterflies are fluttering inside my abdomen. They're beautiful and vibrant—nothing like the moths burning to dust whenever Bruce touched me.

My therapist mentioned one's ability to actively love without being in love. Isn't that something Kade once mentioned, too? I'm not sure how I feel about it, but a part of me keeps thinking they both might be right. Could it be possible that I used to love the idea of Bruce loving me, because I needed it and so I unconsciously decided to actively pursue it? That I was in a rush to love someone because my sister got married and I couldn't bear the idea of being alone? Or maybe it was the disappointment of my father's leaving that pushed me to pursue the first guy I came across?

If love with Bruce wasn't real, what is this thing I have with Kade? Do I love him because he's helping me and makes me feel good about myself? Or does my body love him because he's good at what he does?

I don't know, Jane. All I know is that my feelings are turning into something I've never felt before. For the first time in my life, I don't feel the need to stalk a man. I just want to see him happy, be that happiness with me or with someone else.

Love,
Vicky Sullivan

***

The sun is high above us, warming the beach, ending another perfect night that means we have one day less together.

Keeping a safe distance in case someone sees us, we walk back to the main building. The morning and afternoon pass quickly. I breeze through my mandatory behavioral therapy session and return to the apartment.

All is quiet, meaning Kade's not back yet. I head for the bathroom to freshen up, content that I'm alone with my thoughts. The conversations with my therapist have become less heated. I think we've even started to get along. There are times when I talk about my feelings, masking them as best as I can, pretending it's all about Bruce when, in reality, everything has become about Kade.

My therapist is adamant that I need some time alone.

I don't necessarily agree with her.

I strip and twist my hair into a bun before taking a shower.

Closing my eyes, I let the warm water cleanse my body, and gradually, I find myself relaxing as the thoughts in my mind are reduced to a distant hum.

"Mind if I join?" Kade's rumble wakes me from my reverie.

I turn slowly.

He's standing in the doorway, fully dressed, but his presence is enough to send an electric current down my spine.

My body begins to tingle all over. In the last few days, we've barely slept. My core's still pulsating from his touch, my clit's still swollen from his tongue, and yet I find myself longing for him.

Always more of him.

"You forgot to lock the door," Kade says, misinterpreting my silence, but he makes no move to leave. The way he says it, it sounds as though I did it on purpose.

My breath hitches, rendering me speechless, as he slowly peels his clothes off and inches toward me, his eyes roaming over my naked body, taking in every inch of skin.

And he seems to like what he sees because a small, wicked smile tugs at his lips.

I don't think anyone has turned me on like he does. The water keeps pouring over me, burning my skin. Or maybe it's the intensity of his gaze that scorches me.

He stops mere inches from me. Flooded by

memories of us together, I try hard not to stare at his perfect body, at the strength and familiarity of it.

The silence is unnerving.

"Kade?" My voice sounds shaky, nervous as I try to break the silence. I need him to say something, anything, before I lose myself in those eyes of his.

"You're beautiful, Vicky." His voice is soft and serious, with a hidden meaning I can't grasp. It doesn't fit the scene of two naked people who clearly want each other in all possible ways.

"Why does your words sound so heavy and meaningful?" I ask.

"Because one day you'll find someone who says it to you and you'll fall in love with him."

I regard him for a few moments, wondering what brought on the sudden change in tone.

"Don't choose someone who's no good for you," Kade says slowly. "You deserve someone who looks at you like he's just won a galaxy with all its stars."

"That's impossible, Kade." My eyes turn moist, but not from the water pouring over me.

How can I tell this beautiful yet unreachable man that I could never go looking for the person he describes because I've already found him?

"I know." He sighs and turns the faucet off. "No one will be good enough for you."

"I don't understand." I shake my head. "Do you want me to end up all alone with only a few cats for company? Don't you want to see me happy?"

"That's the thing, Vicky. I think *I* can make you happy. That's why we need to talk."

I stare at him, unsure whether I've heard him right.

He can make me happy?

For a moment, I'm so paralyzed, his words keep replaying in my mind. Like in a loop, they keep swirling around, too fast to understand.

I do feel like I can make you happy.

My heart jumps into motion as realization dawns on me. If there's one thing Kaiden Wright can't do, it's commitment.

It's like he's allergic to it—he joked about it.

I take a deep breath and let it out slowly as I gather my thoughts. "My therapist says we'll relapse, Kade. Not necessarily now, but it will happen eventually. She says that friendships, relationships, any form of bonding formed during rehab never lasts."

"She's right. People relapse. And then they get their shit together and get better," Kade says slowly. "But that's not us."

I raise my brows. "And you know this how?"

"Because we don't belong here." He pulls me into his arms, skin against skin, his heat warming me, his eyes piercing into mine, filling me with the kind of hope I shouldn't allow myself to feel. I look up at him, sucking in every word as though my life depends on it. "You're the most beautiful woman I've ever seen. You make me feel like I've only just now started to live. Like everything before you was just existing, floating with no meaning. I'll never get enough of you. And I sure as hell won't ever share you with anyone."

Sweet words...so meaningless, so much hope.

I don't know what his game is, but I don't feel up for playing, and yet I can't walk away.

Everything inside me is trapped in a storm wreaking havoc.

"I'm not telling you that I love you. I'm saying that I crave you so much I cannot imagine you being with someone else," Kade says.

My heart sinks, breaking just a little bit.

He presses his lips against mine.

"Love is not an accident. It's a verb. You don't wait for it to happen. You make it happen. And I have every intention of making you mine," he whispers into my mouth.

"You don't do commitment, Kade. We'd be

friends with benefits."

"You would be my only friend."

I should feel offended that he'd ever proposition something like that to me, but all I can feel is hurt and want. I want him so much even though it hurts. And it hurts like hell that he doesn't want me the way I want him.

When did things take this turn?

When did our little uncomplicated thing become so messy?

"I don't want to lose you," he whispers.

I press my mouth against him, taking everything he can give me, even though I know it's never going to be enough.

Could I keep on seeing him without actually being with him? Could I ever kiss his lips without wanting them to be mine—and mine only?

I can't let him into my world, only to feed my obsession, which would lead to stalking, then to misery—a never-ending circle I couldn't possibly break on my own.

Things with Bruce started out the same way. Except, Bruce never saw me the way Kade does.

Kade makes me feel wanted while still keeping me at arm's length. He created feelings I never had before while doing nothing. His kisses are like soft breezes and roaring hurricanes, his touch a warm rain shower and a cascading waterfall.

"I think it's time we change things up a bit," Kade says as he begins to trail soft kisses down my neck. "How about I take you out to dinner? Just the two of us."

I shake my head. "You don't have to do this."

"I want to. I want a date with you."

I frown. "You want a *date*?"

"Something like that." He grimaces, as though the very notion pains him.

"But I thought you don't date?"

"There is an exception to every rule."

"I don't understand." I take a step back to regard him. "What changed your mind?"

"You," he says softly. "And the fact that we only have a few days left. It seems like there's never enough time for the good things in life."

My heart starts to pump a little harder, stupid fool that it is.

He wants to be something like friends with benefits, but exclusive, and also take me out on a date.

Only Kade could be so complicated.

"I can't wait to see what you have in store for me." I smile at him, suppressing the sadness that hovers on the bridge of my soul.

"Let me see what I can do, given the circumstances."

As I watch him get out of the shower and gather his clothes off the floor, I realize the only reason he's offered to take me out on a date is that he doesn't want to hurt me. People say one thing, and maybe they mean it in that one moment, but as soon as they step into the real world, all plans turn to dust.

"Where are you going?" I ask, also realizing that this is the first time we're both naked and he's not taking advantage of the situation.

"Workout." He pecks my lips absentmindedly and heads out, calling over his shoulder. "I'll pick you up after the group session tomorrow. Don't be late."

As soon as the door closes, I turn the shower back on, shaking my head at my own stupidity.

Kade Wright doesn't date; he only fucks. And right now I'm not even getting that.

29

VICKY

"VICKY," KADE SPEAKS MY name in his sleep.

He says it softly, as if my name carries a special meaning to him. Even though I don't want to, I know I'm falling hard for him. Falling for a man whose heart I may never possess. A man who has become my drug.

When did love become so complicated? How can someone go from loving one person to moving on to the next? Since when do I have to resort to lying that I don't have feelings for him when he's all I can think about?

People use the word love, but do they understand its meaning? The power behind it? Do they realize that to love means to lose oneself in a tangled forever with no way out?

Love isn't a drug.

The actual drug is another person's touch. Being kissed by someone. Granting him access to the pieces of your heart that could destroy you.

Loving Kade feels like I'm falling into a safety net I never want to leave.

Even though Kade Wright is still a player, it feels right to trust him.

Maybe too right.

But he's the only person who understands. The only one who doesn't judge me. I might have only known him for a short time, but he's given me more than anyone else before.

He is everything Bruce isn't, except Mr. Future, so I call him Mr. Present.

There is this attraction between us. We're like two polar opposites glued together by the foundation of what we have built.

The program's supposed to end in two weeks. I dread the day I'll be forced to return to a life without him.

But a deal's a deal.

A present with him is all there is, no matter how much I crave a future.

Kade is sleeping next to me, our bodies intertwined between the sheets. My fingers itch to touch him, to brush the dark hair out of his face and kiss him like there's no tomorrow.

I'm going to miss him. The imminent threat to be without him fills me with dread. I can't bear the thought of being away from him. Of belonging to his past.

"Remembering you is easy. It's letting go that's the hard part," I whisper.

As though hearing me, he stirs and opens his eyes. He really has the most beautiful eyes—a rich brown, like melted chocolate, like everything that's good in the world.

"What did you say?" He sits upright and glances around.

"Nothing." I smile at him. "It's going to be a hot day."

"Good thing I got us ice cream." He catches my confused expression. "I bribed the kitchen staff. It's in our freezer."

Our freezer.

He makes it sound like we live together for real, and my heart believes the lie.

Stop it, Vicky. Stop getting invested.

"Want some for breakfast?" Kade asks.

"How could I say no?"

"Yeah, let's be bold. Let's break the rules." He gets up and winks at me. "Don't run. I'll be watching the door."

I laugh. It's the first night we've slept in his bed. We've been intimate in our apartment, but until now, I refused to sleep in the same bed. I watch him as he heads out, butt naked.

He looks like a prince. Royal and sexy.

As if sensing my thoughts, he peers through the open door. "I could pose for you if you wanted." He flashes me another cocky smile and then disappears again.

I wrap the sheets around my body, feeling the familiar heat gathering in my core.

No amount of ice cream could stop the fire he's ignited inside me. My clit's pulsating to life at the chance of him spreading ice cream all over me and then licking it off.

Maybe he'll let me do it to him, right before I suck his cock into my mouth and reward him with the kind of attention he usually lavishes on me.

"What did you get?" I ask when he returns with a large container and two spoons.

"Chocolate and pistachio with crushed M&Ms. Your favorite."

I never told him that. "How do you know it's my favorite?"

"Your sister told me."

He settles next to me and hands me a spoon.

"My sister?" I can't help but roll my eyes.

"Yeah. She kept asking everyone if they knew where you were."

"What did you say?"

"That your therapist called you in. That your session's always on a Tuesday."

"You didn't have to lie."

"Should I have told her that you ditched her?" He shrugs. "I didn't see the need to tell her the truth."

I watch him dip his spoon into the tub and scoop up a good amount of ice cream.

"What else did she tell you?" My body stiffens as I think of all the things my sister could have revealed about me. My failed relationships, my not-so-proud moments, all the things I started and never finished.

"Not much," Kade says. "I told her that we're roommates and that we're kind of supporting each other, after which she invited me to her wedding." He catches my wary glance and gives me a reassuring smile. "Don't worry. I haven't accepted. I won't be jumping into your life if you don't want me to."

Not want him to?

That's everything I want. But I can't tell him when he has no intention of staying.

"Did she suspect anything?" I ask, changing the subject.

"That we're a thing?" He shakes his head. "I don't think so. Maybe she didn't show it." He watches me with a sly grin on his face, and there's that naughty glint in his eyes again. The temperature rises a few degrees, and the ice cream isn't the only thing melting.

He scoops up some ice cream and lifts the spoon to my mouth. When I open my mouth, he grazes my lips with chocolate, then leans forward to kiss me.

His tongue slips slowly into my mouth. He tastes of chocolate and want.

"I want to cover you in this and lick you all over," he whispers.

"Sounds like something we should be trying." Sliding my leg over, I straddle his lap and thrust my hips against his hard erection.

"Let me be your plus one," Kade says.

I stop in my movement. "You want to come?"

"Why not? We're friends, right?"

"Yeah."

Friends with benefits.

That's what we are. Maybe throw in the odd date, but nothing more.

"Why are you so nice to me, Kade?"

There is little distance between us and yet it feels like there's an invisible barrier.

He frowns, watching me with a puzzled expression. "Why shouldn't I be? You're great."

I shake my head. "No. I mean why are you like...this? Talking as if we're really going to see each other again in the future. We both know that's not going to happen. It's all pretense."

"Is it?" His gaze burns me. It's that deep. "I like you, Vicky. I like being around you. Is that so hard to understand?"

"Yes, it is," I whisper. "Nobody has ever looked at me the way you do."

"When I'm with you I don't feel like I have to pretend to be anyone or anything. I feel like I have known you all my life. I like being around you because you make me want to be a better person. And, let's face it, nobody has made me laugh harder than you have, so yeah, I like you, Vicky." He shrugs. "But that's not what you want to hear, is it? The question you actually want to ask is if I have feelings for you."

I swallow past the sudden lump in my throat.

"No." My answer comes out too shrill. We both know I'm lying.

"Tell me what you want to know and I'll answer

your question."

I want to tell him that I want him. I want to ask whether he feels the same way, whether he wants me as much as I want him, body and soul. I want to tell him that I've fallen in love with him, that I want everything he can give, and more.

But how can I ask whether he feels the same way when I know the truth already?

"What time is it?" I get up from his lap and begin to gather my scattered clothes.

"Ten. By the way, you suck at changing the topic."

"Crap." I ignore his remark and squeeze into my clothes. "I'm so late."

I'm almost out the door when his arms wrap around my waist, forcing me to stop.

"You forgot something."

Pulling me back against him, his lips press against the nape of my neck. His kiss feels intimate, loving. A surge of emotion instantly chokes me, and I realize Kade is like quicksand, drawing me in, killing me softly.

I turn and offer my mouth to him, stealing a few more moments together. He kisses me as if he wants to drown me in the depths of his passion.

He kisses me as if he won't ever let me go.

I melt into him. If all kisses are like this one, then

I want him to kiss me forever and never let me go.

Eventually, he lets go.

Taking a couple of deep breaths, I try to remember what it was that was so important.

"You're late, Vicky," Kade reminds me, reading my thoughts. "Don't make any plans for tonight. We need to talk."

"About what?"

He winks, but his expression is dead serious. "You'll see."

30

VICKY

IT'S BARELY LUNCH, but the day already feels like it'll never end. Minutes feel like hours, and hours like centuries. I try to focus on the morning session, and the cognitive behavioral therapy following right after, but all I can think about are Kade's words. Kade's lips. Kade's touch. It seems as though he isn't just occupying all my thoughts; he's in every part of my body.

Of course, he couldn't have possibly meant what he said, yet a part of me can't help but wonder what could happen between us if his feelings were real.

Sylvie nudges me, drawing my attention back to her. "Are you attending the dance therapy?"

I stare at her, absentminded for a few seconds, as her words slowly sink in. I used to love dancing, not just because it used to be my outlet and the only way I could ever forget my worries. Maybe it'll help me take my mind off Kade. "Count me in."

Kade wasn't at the group session. He didn't get lunch. The day's finally coming to an end while the growing uncertainty in the pit of my stomach seems to be increasing. The more I think of him, the more I'm not sure what to think and make of him.

"You're crushing, aren't you?"

I blink. "What?"

"It's so obvious that you two are an item," Sylvie says matter-of-factly. "You need to be careful. Someone was transferred yesterday because they did it in the lounge room and the staff saw them."

I don't feel like denying the obvious. For one, Sylvie would never believe it. And then there's also the fact that I trust her. "I thought you said everyone does it."

"Of course. Doesn't mean it's allowed though. The worst place you could ever choose is the library."

I almost choke on my drink. "What?"

"They have hidden cameras in there, probably to keep people from stealing books. Some people apparently didn't know and did it anyway. The hooking-up part, not stealing books. No one wants those."

All the blood rushes from my body.

I feel so faint, I might pass out.

"Since when does the library have cameras?"

She stares at me like I'm from outer space. "Duh. Like forever." Her brows shoot up. "I've heard someone's about to get into a lot of trouble."

"How do you know?" I whisper.

"Why are you so weird?" Her expression turns suspicious. I open my mouth to lie when awareness flickers in her eyes. "Wait...Don't tell me... you..."

I nod, closing my eyes.

When I open my eyes again, Sylvie's staring at me.

"Please don't tell me you did it in the back of the room."

"We did."

"Fuck." She shakes her head. "What are we talking about? First base?" I shake my head. "Second base? Shit. Third base. What the hell!"

My cheeks flame up. "We went all the way, all the bases covered. And probably more."

"You're going to be in a shitload of trouble."

"Are you sure the cameras are real?"

"Absolutely positive."

"Oh, God." I draw a deep breath, but no oxygen seems to be reaching my lungs. "Someone must have watched the video."

Sylvie's fingers wrap around my hand, forcing me to face her. "That's not the worst. There's going to be this huge announcement."

"How do you know?"

"My therapist hinted at it this morning."

"Right." This is getting worse by the minute. "Did he tell you how to get out of this one?"

"I can't ask him without him getting suspicious."

"I have to warn Kade." I jump to my feet when Vicky's hand stops me.

"It's too late."

"Why?"

"I saw him in the main office earlier today. The doors were open, so I didn't think much of it. I thought he was picking up a parcel or something. But now I'm pretty sure that's why he was there. Other people were with him. To be honest, it all looked pretty strange."

My heart jumps into my throat. "Then I should be there with him."

"That was before the group session. It's probably over now."

That was probably the reason why Kade didn't attend.

I plop back down onto the chair. "What am I

going to do?"

"Nothing. You just wait."

"But I'm as much to blame as Kade. I have to tell them. I have to explain the situation."

"Hey, look at me." She squeezes my arm hard. "I don't think that's a good idea."

"He'll probably try to take the fall. I can't let him do that." The moment the words leave my mouth I know they're true. I know it's the reason why no one bothered to call me in to explain myself.

"Are you sure?" Sylvie asks.

I nod and force a reassuring smile to my lips.

"Good luck, then."

"Thanks," I mumble. "Sounds like something I might need."

31

VICKY

THE DOOR TO THE main office is closed. I stare at it for a few seconds, undecided about what to do. My heart is slamming so hard, it takes every ounce of my willpower not to run away.

The decision is taken from me when steps sound and the door is thrown open.

I find myself face to face with the redhead from the bus.

Marlene Elijah.

"We were just talking about you." She glances at me with pity. "Come in."

Shit.

They know.

Of course, they do. Sylvie warned me already, but it didn't feel real...until now.

I follow Marlene in, and she motions to a chair.

"Please, take a seat. They should be done soon."

"Shouldn't I go in?" I ask.

She shakes her head. "Kaiden Wright has already explained. We just need to confirm a few details with you."

I frown. Kade has explained what? I want to ask, but Marlene stops me by grabbing my hand and forcing me to sit. Keeping my hand in hers, she says, "Don't you worry. You're safe now. He's being transferred as we speak."

I stare at her, dumbfounded. "What are you talking about?"

"How he befriended you—" she makes air signs, "—and then demanded things from you. We had no idea he would go as far as assaulting you. We know you're scared, but rest assured we're dealing with the situation."

"What?" My lungs constrict, choking me. "But he didn't do anything."

"We know everything, Victoria," Marlene says, ignoring me.

"Know what?"

"You had no choice. He forced you to engage in sexual activities because of the phone. We'll understand if you decide to press charges."

I've never felt so faint in my life.

"No, you don't understand. Kade never assaulted me; never forced himself on me. I don't know why you'd come to such a conclusion."

I try to push my way past her.

"You can't go in there," Marlene protests.

Ignoring her, I throw the door open.

Five people are sitting at the table: four male and one female. Kade's not among them.

"This is all a mistake," I say. "Please don't transfer him. It's me you need to send away."

All heads turn to me. This is when I notice the television screen. The image is static, but there's no denying that that's Kade and me, caught up in the moment of our lovemaking.

How anybody could ever believe that he's forcing me needs their eyes checked.

A hot blush covers my face and neck. I can still remember Kade's hand between my legs, stroking my clit as his cock plunged in and out of me.

"It's not like that," I whisper.

Oh, who am I kidding?

This is so hot, I want it again. I don't regret any of it. The only thing I regret is the fact that we got caught.

"We've already made our decision. Kade is leaving tomorrow," the woman says.

411

"It's not his fault. None of this is."

"That's what he said you would say," a guy says.

"And you believed it?" I shake my head. "Why did no one call *me* in to explain?"

One of the men motions to the chair. I feel nauseous to the core as I take a seat and fold my hands in my lap.

They're all staring at me now.

"He's a sex addict, Victoria," the same guy continues. "He knows that what he did is wrong and so he agreed to make a formal statement. We didn't ask you to explain yourself because we didn't see the need. The situation is as uncomfortable for us as it is for you, what with you being a victim and Mr. Wright taking advantage of your fragile state of mind."

"But he didn't do anything."

"You're ashamed, which is a natural response among victims," the woman chimes in.

I shake my head vehemently. "I haven't been sexually assaulted."

As my words begin to sink in, their expressions darken. I can see the disappointment written on their face, like I'm some kind of failed experiment. The room's silent. After what feels like an eternity, the youngest guy seems to take charge.

"Mr. Wright has testified. He's even provided a witness who knew about his plan. His best friend showed us the call log and some text messages as proof. That's all we needed to believe him."

"He pursued a plan right from the start," the woman says. "He preyed on your vulnerability."

"Is that what he said?" I ask feebly. As much as I don't want to believe their claims, I can't help but wonder whether there's a seed of truth to them.

"Why don't you see for yourself? We've gathered a formal statement for you in case you want to take this to court." The woman types on her laptop and the image on the screen changes.

My mouth goes dry as I stare at Kade explaining how it all started as a bet and how important some sex calendar was to him. He goes on to explain the great length he went to to get me into bed, even though I turned him down countless times. He finishes with a recount of how he discovered that I had smuggled in a burner phone—information he saw as his chance to blackmail me, culminating in the library event, during which he claims to have forced me to have sex with him.

My heart skids to the halt.

I know most parts are made up, but there's also truth to his version of events.

As soon as the video ends, I can feel all eyes on me, but my gaze remains glued to the screen while Kade's words keep echoing in my mind.

"Needless to say, Mr. Wright won't be staying in your apartment until his transfer." The male voice speaking sounds as though it's coming from the far side of a tunnel.

"What about my therapy plan? Will it be affected in any way?" I don't want to ask the obvious: will any of this affect my court order in any way?

"That's up to your therapist," the woman says. "She might want to keep you in here a little longer."

My heart sinks. Staying without Kade is the last thing I want to do.

"We're very sorry for everything you've been through," a guy says.

I turn to the window, ignoring the empty apologies that follow. It all started out as such a beautiful day. I can't help but think that they ruined it. They ruined everything I had with Kade.

***

My whole body feels numb as I leave the office, closing the door behind me. Sylvie's standing a few feet away.

"You were in there for almost an hour. I thought you'd never make it out alive. How did it go?" she whispers even though there's no one else in the hall.

"Not well. Kade's being transferred." I turn to her and lower my voice. "He lied to them to protect me. God, I can't believe he took all the blame."

"What did they say?"

"Some bullshit about Kade forcing me to sleep with him." I shake my head. "Actually, they used the word 'blackmail.' I feel so bad because it's all my fault. He was moved to another apartment. I need to find him before he leaves."

"I'll ask my roommate. He always knows what's going on. When's Kade leaving?"

"Tomorrow." The word sounds ominous in my ears.

I have a little more than twelve hours to find him. Twelve hours I could spend with him before he's gone forever.

"Don't worry," Sylvie says. "We'll find him."

32

Kaiden

I'M RESTING ON a stranger's bed, staring at a poster of "The Scream" by Edvard Munch. I've never been a fan of old, famous paintings, but this one talks to me. Fear has been plaguing me since I was called into the main office this morning. The fear inside me has grown to new proportions when I was told to pack my bags and move out of my apartment. My fear's now turned into panic at the prospect of leaving Vicky behind.

In retrospect, I could have handled that meeting differently. I should have kept my mouth shut or called my relationship with Vicky a one-time thing, but as usual, I went overboard. I revealed everything, bathing myself in a very bad light to protect Vicky, which might not have been necessary.

Despite my willingness to confess, my request to continue the program was denied. So, here I am, fearing the hours that are quickly passing by, waiting for the car to pick me up, as I'm staring at a print of an old painting.

At least, I could convince them that Vicky was in no way to blame. That knowledge will be my only solace after I've left this place. That and the hope that I might see her again.

I hope she'll want to.

There's a rap at the door. Soft at first, then a little firmer. I choose not to respond because it can't possibly be anyone I want to see—and the only person I want to see is Vicky.

Footsteps retreat.

Good!

They can leave me the fuck alone.

Another rap that resembles scratching, this time urgent. The sound comes from the window.

I jump up from the bed and pull the curtains aside. My temporary bedroom is situated on the second floor overlooking the front yard. It's dark outside, the light of a single streetlamp too weak to illuminate the path leading up to the entrance.

Even though everything's silent, I open the window anyway and scan the area below.

I spy Vicky standing near the tall bushes, holding a tall, wooden stick in her hand. Her face is bathed in darkness but I can't help but notice her beautiful hair falling past her shoulders in flowing cascades.

"Vicky?" I whisper.

Before I can tell her to wait, she starts to climb up the rose trellis under my window. And fuck, she looks hot doing it. I stretch out my hand to get a grip on her and pull her up.

"Why are you here? Do you want to get kicked out, too?" I wrap my arms around her and hold her close.

"I needed to see you before you left."

There's something in her tone. Her face is pale, her eyes swollen as if she's been crying, which is impossible.

Vicky never cries.

"I'm sorry," she whispers.

I frown, taken back by her state, by her words. I close the window, drawing the curtains closed, then turn to face her. "It's not your fault."

She takes a deep breath, struggling with whatever she wants to say.

"Kade." Her lips are quivering as she speaks my name. "What you did—you probably saved me from violating my restraining order. The calendar…I don't know what to say to that." She breaks off, searching my gaze. "It was certainly very inventive."

I cringe.

This is the time.

Even though telling her the truth is the last thing I want to do, we can't have secrets standing between us.

"They told you everything."

Vicky nods her head, her expression still soft, but her insecurity is etched in her features. "It was a good excuse. How did you get your friend to play along?"

Silence fills the air as realization dawns on me.

She thinks it was all a lie.

I stare at her, taking in her bright eyes, the hope, and the faith I'm going to take away.

I wipe my face with my hand. "No, Vicky." My eyes meet hers. "That's the thing. We need to talk about that."

It takes her a split second to understand before her eyes go wide and she takes a step back from me.

"You really have a sex calendar?" Her tone sounds so hurt, my whole body tenses.

"I *did*."

She shakes her head. I see suspicion in her eyes, followed by disbelief, then suspicion again. When I don't go on to explain myself, she shakes her head again.

"So, it was all true?"

I sit down on the edge of the bed, unsure how to proceed. It was never my intention to hurt her, but I know what I'm going to say next will do just that. "I started it last year. It's the reason why I'm here. A sex scandal went a little out of hand and my company's board decided that I needed to get help." She looks at me like she doesn't know me, which is worse than any screaming and shouting. "I guess I needed help," I add.

Her hands fall to her sides. She looks defeated, as if all her power has poured out of her.

"Why didn't you tell me before?"

"It's complicated."

She cocks her head to the side. "How so?" I don't answer. "Kade, how is something like aiming to fuck a different woman every day for a year more complicated than you telling me you don't do relationships?" Slowly, she inches closer until she's standing before me. I fight the urge to pull her into my arms, to touch her, to tell her that things have changed, that none of it matters, but I dare not, afraid of her reaction.

Her disdain, even though she might not even

know her role in this game.

"I'm the last one." There's no doubt in her voice. No hesitation. Just a simple statement. She sits down beside me and tucks her hands between her knees as she exhales a slow breath.

Her body's so close I can feel it burning.

"I thought we were being honest with each other." Another statement. "Did you really think it would have bothered me?"

I regard her, expecting to see pain. But all I see in her eyes is indifference.

"You don't mind?"

"No, I don't." She looks serious. I can't detect any lying either. "Why would I? You told me from the beginning that you only do hook-ups. What?" She catches my glance, scowling. "You really thought I believed you were a saint? Come on. Let's be real here. If there's one thing this institution has taught me is that you can't trust feelings." She falls back against the cushions, staring at the ugly painting— just like I did barely ten minutes ago. "Honestly, I expected it, Kade. I'm a magnet for the kind of guy who'll never settle for one woman, who'll never choose the little house with a white picket fence in the suburbs kind of life. I don't even remember a time when someone wanted me for who I am. Bruce never even wanted to fuck me."

I grimace as I remember that I still haven't told her everything. She catches my expression and frowns.

"What?"

I sigh. "I haven't decided whether I should tell you."

Her body tenses as she pushes up on her elbows. "Tell me what?" Her voice is high-pitched. Definitely nervous. "Don't tell me you're married or—" She scowls at me as she's thinking of scenarios worse than cheating.

"It's nothing of that sort. It's about Bruce." The words render her silent. "I thought I could keep it from you a little longer, but now that I'm leaving you deserve to know."

"Know what?"

"Bruce is gay. That's why he never wanted to touch you."

She stares at me for a few moments. Eventually, she exhales sharply. "Bruce is not gay."

"I thought you'd say that." I head over to my suitcase and retrieve an envelope, which I pass on to her.

I watch her expression as she peers at the photos inside.

The first shows Bruce with some guy, both wearing red Christmas-themed underwear while making out in a dimly lit room that looks like a bar. She peers at the next one, then the next.

The last one's so explicit, she claps her hand over her mouth and looks up. I expect her to cry, rage, anything but—laugh.

"I can't believe I was so blind. The thought never even occurred to me. And I thought you were married with two kids and I was going to hell for breaking up your marriage."

I don't get this woman at all.

"You're not angry?" I ask warily.

"Angry? Why would I be? I'm over him. I wish him nothing but the best. Maybe one day he'll find the strength to be himself." She stares at me as if she can't believe what she's just said. "I'm over him. In fact, I don't see what attracted me to him in the first place." She points at the explicit photo. "I don't know what to say except, holy crap. And who's the other guy? He looks familiar but I can't place him."

"Probably because his face is buried in Bruce's lap. It's his ex's brother. Or maybe I should say his fiancée's brother. They bought an apartment together a few weeks ago. That's how my brother found out about them. He's a lawyer. He knows where to dig."

"You knew, didn't you? That's why you looked into him."

I take the pictures from her outstretched hands and throw them in the waste bin.

"I suspected it. Seriously, no guy in his right mind would say no to you. But that's not why I asked my brother to investigate him. I just didn't trust him."

She lets out a laugh. "You would fuck everything that has boobs, Kade."

"Absolutely not."

She slaps my arm playfully. "Why don't I believe you?"

"That was before I met you, Vicky," I say softly. "No woman ever meant anything to me. It was all a challenge. Until you came along."

"Until I came along?" Her lips twitch. She's clearly not believing me.

"I know how crazy it sounds." I cup her face between my hands and look into her eyes, wondering whether she can hear how hard my heart is pounding. "But it's the truth, Vicky. I don't miss the kind of life I led before. But you, I miss you whenever you're not around. I want you."

More than she knows.

She isn't a nameless conquest on my list. She

broke all the rules by piercing her way into my heart.

"What are you saying?" Her voice is hoarse, barely a whisper.

"I'm not the same person. Can you forgive me?"

I know I'm expecting too much. She should be pushing me away, let me earn her forgiveness. Instead, she interlocks her fingers with mine and squeezes gently.

"Kade, there's nothing to forgive. You never made a secret out of not wanting a relationship, so I knew pretty much from the beginning what I was getting into."

"You were never a fling, Vicky."

"I would like to think of myself as one."

I frown. "Why?"

"It makes life easier." Her mouth tightens. "It'll make it easier for me to forget you once you're gone."

It strikes me that she isn't just the first woman to reject me and avoid me after we've had sex; she's also the only person who's ever accepted me for who I am.

This goes beyond friendship.

I don't want to lose her.

I have to make sure she knows that.

"The sex calendar was nothing, Vicky," I start. "It

started out as a stupid bet. Nothing more. Nothing less. But your friendship means everything to me. Hurting you was never my intention. I want you know that."

"You never hurt me, Kade," she says. "You saw a challenge, and you pursued it. Your past doesn't define you. What you did, what you were, is none of my business. I'm just glad we met." She searches my face. "You helped me and for that I'll always be grateful."

"I did nothing."

"You did, even if you didn't realize it," Vicky says slowly. "You were my light in the darkness. You helped me see things for how they were, not how I wanted them to be. I was blind and foolish. I couldn't have gone through it all without you, Kade." There's something in her eyes—sadness, regret, I can't tell. "You helped me get over him without ever judging me. How could I possibly judge you based on your past when you accepted me so willingly?" She smiles, but it's a sad smile. "You made a difference in my life. But why are we even talking about this? It doesn't matter. Nothing does. What matters is that you're leaving and it's all my fault."

I wrap my arms around her, feeling the magnitude of her emotions. Of what it could mean to be without her. Seconds pass, but I can't think of the right words to make her feel better.

"Will you stay with me one more night?" I hook my finger underneath her chin and lift her lips up to me.

"Only if we stay here. In this room. In this bed."

I grin, getting the hint. "Good, because last time at the beach I thought we might lose our toes to frostbite."

She lets out a laugh, and as I hug her I realize I can't get enough of it.

I can't get enough of her.

33

Kaiden

I'M ON THE BRINK of falling asleep, but somehow rest just won't come. The soft moonlight is streaming through the window, bright enough to illuminate contours of the woman snuggling in my arms. It must be around four a.m.—only four more hours until I'm expected to leave.

Vicky and I are both silent, lost in our thoughts. We've been drifting in and out of sleep, too afraid to fall asleep, too afraid to lose those final moments together. At some point, she stirs, her voice a mere murmur as she speaks.

"I'm sorry. I had no idea this would end so badly."

"Shit was prone to happen."

"I know, but I'm still sorry. You're leaving because of me."

"To be fair, you did warn me." I wrap my arms around her body and pull her closer to me. She smells like she always does—of sweet roses and warmth. "Come on, Vicky. This isn't so bad. I'm not dying. I'm just getting out of here. You should be happy for me. I'll get some change in food, and they're even throwing in a free plane ticket to London to get rid of me."

"You're not funny." In spite of her reproachful tone, a soft smile's playing on her lips and her eyes are sparkling. "You're risking your company. No man's ever done something like that for me."

"Then you haven't met the right man."

"What you did..." She shakes her head.

"Whatever happens, I did it for you. You're worth it."

"I want to be mad at you."

"No need for that." I kiss the tip of her nose gently. "A simple thank you would be appreciated but not required. Maybe you have a good parting gift in mind, something to remember you by when I lie awake alone at night."

"Alone, huh?" There is a short pause. "God, Kade. Why the hell did you have to lie that you blackmailed me?"

"You know why. I'd rather be the perpetrator

than you getting in trouble. Though truth be told, we both know you have a little crazy streak."

"I don't think I do," Vicky protests half-heartedly.

"You climbed up the rose trellis in the middle of the night."

"It's not the middle of the night, and I'm really good at climbing." Her laughter is quiet, but it's the most beautiful laughter I've heard in my life.

"You should demonstrate those skills by climbing on top of me." I wink at her, even though I hope Vicky will honor my request rather than see it as a joke.

"They asked me if I wanted to report it," Vicky says.

"And did you?"

"Of course not. I tried to convince them that you weren't to blame but they wouldn't listen."

"I bet you did. Seriously, it's not a big deal, Vicky. I'm expected to do six more weeks in London, and that's it. No one can force me to stay. No one can keep me away from you forever. I don't have to attend court-mandated rehab like you, so I'll be out sooner than you think. And I've been told the London institution is a piece of cake compared to this. I'll get a phone and even have access to the Internet."

"I bet they'll supervise every step."

I laugh. "Now don't be jealous, baby. I bet I'll have a blast." I turn to take in her beautiful features. She looks serious, thoughtful. "Are you going to miss me?"

"Never. I don't know how you'd even come to the conclusion that I might miss you."

"Maybe you will after I'm done with you." I switch on the nightstand light and walk over to my packed luggage.

"What are you doing?" Vicky asks warily.

"Close your eyes."

"Absolutely not. You can't be trusted. You'll do something stupid." In spite of her protest, she does as requested.

I find the blue box hidden between my clothes and place it into her hands.

"What's this?" She turns the box around, then looks up to me.

"A gift. I wanted to give it to you after finishing therapy, but I guess it's my parting gift now." I gesture at it. "Come on. Open it."

She takes her time looking at the box, turning it in her hands. I can sense her hesitation, as though she can't make up her mind whether to open it or not. Eventually, she puts it on the bed beside her, ignoring the small note that's attached to it. I tense, unsure what to make of her reaction.

Why does every moment I spend with her feel like it might be the last?

"I'm going to miss this. You," Vicky says. "I'm going to miss every little thing that we have."

"I'm going to miss you, too. More than you'll ever know." I brush her hair back from her face and plant a soft kiss on her forehead. She closes her eyes, breathing hard.

"I'm sorry that you have to leave. It's too soon, unexpected."

"Don't be." I kiss her cheek, my lips brushing gently over her skin. "You, Victoria Sullivan, don't need to be sorry for anything. Every moment we shared was worth it."

"Yeah. We had a great time." As she nods her red hair falls into her eyes, and I realize she isn't just incredibly sexy. She seems haunted. There's so much about her I want to know. She isn't any woman; she has become a part of my existence.

"I keep wondering what would happen if things were different." This is it: that one step I've been wanting to take but didn't dare. I suck in my breath, waiting for her reply.

"Different how?" Vicky asks.

I look into her beautiful hazel eyes and notice how deep they seem. If her eyes were her soul, I would want to lose myself in them. Her soul. Her mind. Her heart. I'd take them all to hold and guard forever.

"I can't imagine you not being in my life anymore, Vicky. Now that Bruce is out of the picture, I want us to have a fresh start."

"Bruce was never really in the picture. He was never much of competition to you. Not now. Not four weeks ago."

"I wouldn't have cared either way. I want to see you again. Meet me at the Four Seasons in Portland on August the fourth." I fight the urge to repeat myself to make sure she won't forget the date.

She looks at me, open-mouthed. "For real?"

"For real. A real date outside this place."

Her body stiffens, as though the word 'date' doesn't resonate well with her. "Sounds like something that might violate at least one of those rules of yours."

"True. But the beauty of rules is that they're made to be broken."

Her expression softens a little, but the mistrust doesn't completely disappear. "Why do you want to see me?"

"I think I've made myself pretty clear. I want to continue things." I wrap my hand around hers, forcing her to really look at me. "Even if we hadn't been found out, one more week together wouldn't have been enough. We would have wanted to find a way to see each other again."

"I don't know." She shakes her head and lets out a long, drawn-out breath. "It's probably not a good idea. We'll never work out." There's regret in her eyes, but also hope. Her feelings don't match her words, which ignites more determination in me. I want her. I want this.

"My therapist says that relationships and friendships formed during rehab don't last. They're a temporary phase that's not real. Whatever we have, whatever we think is real, it's short-lived."

My eyes narrow. "I don't believe that."

"But I do, Kade. Why should we be the exception?"

"Because to us, their rules never applied. I might have needed a bit of straightening out, but I was never an addict. Neither were you."

"Look, Kade. For the first time in my life I feel free. Free from worries. Free from expectations. As much as I want to claim that I didn't learn anything from this place, I can't because it's not true. While I still want a relationship, marriage, kids, I don't want to go back to a place where I can't trust myself, where I'm repeating the same mistakes over and over again."

"You wouldn't," I cut her off.

"But that's the thing. I might. We have to be realistic," Vicky says grimly. "We both want different things from life because we're different. As much as we both want to believe that we don't have issues, the truth is that we do. We're just too afraid to admit it." She pauses for a moment during which her expression hardens. I know instantly she's mentally preparing for the big blow. "If we had met outside in the real world, in a real place, you would never have fallen in love with me. You wouldn't have paid me a second thought. I would have been one of your numbers. Just like all the other women in your life, I would have waited for a call that would never have come. You would have ignored my texts, which in turn would have fueled my obsessive stalker streak. A week later, and you might not even have been able to remember my name or face."

She closes her eyes, probably to hide the waves of hurt wafting from her. As much as I want to pretend otherwise, her words ring true. Yes, that jerk was me, a few weeks ago. But that's no longer me.

"Vicky—"

"No." She holds up her hand, stopping me. "Please. Let's just enjoy this moment as long as it lasts."

"I thought you were addicted to me." As much as I'm addicted to you I want to add, but for some reason, can't.

"That's the thing. I am, which is why we can't see each other again." Her tone is earnest, resolute. "There's a difference between allowing yourself to fall in love and loving obsessively. Between fantasy and reality. I can imagine myself falling in love with you, but that would probably turn into your worst nightmare."

"Maybe I want you to. Loving hard is not wrong; it's not an obsession, no matter what other people say."

"I can't let myself go through all of that again." She gets up, hesitating.

"Are you leaving already?"

"That might be the best thing to do. I don't want a confrontation tarnishing my memory of us." Her shoulders slump under the weight of her decision. "Look, I appreciate everything you've done for me, but that's as far as it goes."

Fuck!

This isn't going as planned. "Forget the date. I'm not asking for a relationship. I'm just asking to see you again, as a friend." I meet her resolute gaze. "I just want to know that you're okay."

"I'll be okay. Goodbye, Kade. And thank you." She heads over to the window.

I curse under my breath.

"Vicky."

She opens the window. I jump up from the bed and in a few steps I join her. I want to touch her but sense that she might not welcome it. She meets my gaze, and that's when I notice the tears shimmering in her eyes. Realization dawns on me.

Leaving is not what she wants.

The prospect of never seeing me again hurts her as much as it hurts me.

She smiles bitterly. "I can't see you again."

She doesn't protest as I wrap my arms around her and pull her against my chest. "I won't give up on you. I won't give up on us. Agree to meet me, Vicky, and we'll take it from there."

"You'll give up eventually." Rising up on her toes, she places a soft kiss on my lips. For a moment, her heart's beating against mine, and in that instant, I know I'll fight to win her heart. Maybe not today. Maybe not in the next six weeks. But there will be a right time.

"Goodbye, Kade," Vicky whispers.

This time I don't stop her because for the time being there's nothing I can do to change her mind.

I watch her as she climbs out the window and I linger there long after she's disappeared in the darkness.

It's only after she's gone that reality hits me.

She hasn't agreed to seeing me again. Not because she doesn't want to. Not because we're different. But because she's probably right—to some extent.

There's no guarantee that we'd work out.

I have to let her face the real world again before I can expect any promise from her. And there's also the fact that I still have to face my own demons—our demons.

The trouble is...I don't mind.

What I can't face is the possibility that she might never change her mind. I set my jaw and return to the bed as I ponder over possibilities.

But there's only one outcome that appeals to me.

I've never wanted a woman more than I want Vicky.

This is no longer a mission to fuck her.

I have only one quest now: to make her mine.

34

Vicky

WHAT HAPPENS WHEN LOVE gets complicated?

You love hard…and fall harder.

Gravity knows no boundaries. That's what Kade is to me: my gravity. The one thing I can't pull away from. He made it all so easy. And just as things were about to take a great turn, a single mistake tore him away from me.

But have the few weeks we spent together changed anything? Made him less of an addict? Less of a person who enjoys the physical side of a relationship, no feelings involved?

Everything feels hopeless. Depressing. Lonely.

I make my way back to our apartment, even though the knowledge that he's gone is crushing me. There's no more us. No more of his smile.

I'm going to miss him.

Miss us.

His body. His scent. His warmth. The thousand kisses we shared. The touch of his hand. The way he made me feel complete.

I've just left all of that behind, and it already feels like the biggest mistake of my life.

I make sure to lock the door behind me and kick off my shoes, letting my tears flow freely. My mind is broken, torn by my choice of what I thought was the right thing to do.

Refusing to see him again...how could I ever think it might be easy to forget him?

But I have to. For us, for myself.

For the first time in my life, I'm going to put away my feelings, bury them deep in the crevices of my heart. Put away all my hopes, wishes, dreams— anything that involves Kade.

Revealing to him that I was addicted to him was only half the truth.

I'm in love with him; it's crystal clear now.

At first I wasn't sure. This feeling of love can easily be confused with obsession or attraction or a need to fill a void. But there's more to it, and it goes beyond the physical. I fear losing him, but I also want to see him happy. I want him to go his way in life even though that path might not involve me.

My steps are hesitant as I head for his former room. I don't switch on the lights but let my eyes adjust to the darkness. The bed's still how we left it—tangled, a mess. The scent of us still lingering in the air.

The memory of us rolls before my eyes. His presence is so strong, I almost expect him to appear in the doorway, sporting his usual sexy smile.

I close my eyes and press a hand against my chest. There's a dull ache as I recall the look on his face when I said goodbye. I sink into the sheets and inhale his scent.

Kade Wright was perfection—everything about him was.

It's hard to believe that only a day ago we were living in our happy little bubble. We should have played by the rules, but instead made the night our day.

We never stood a chance. I should have seen right from the beginning that the outcome could only be shattering.

I brush my tears from my face and get up again, but I don't leave his room just yet.

It was the right choice, I tell myself.

I have to believe that.

Someone new is moving in tomorrow.

I don't want a new roommate—someone who'll replace Kade's scent. But I have no say in the matter.

How long will it take him to forget me? One day? A week?

How long will it take me to forget him? Months? Years? Never?

I have to head back to my room before someone finds me in here, but for the life of me, I can't find the strength to get up. I sink into the pillows and close my eyes. As sleep is about to engulf me, countless thoughts race through my mind.

I'll never be the same without Kade, and no amount of denial can hide the fact that I haven't just lost my heart to him.

I've become his. Heart, body, and soul.

35

Vicky

I STEP BACK FROM the suitcase, ready to give up.

The damn thing just won't close even though I've already thrown out everything I think I might no longer need which, granted, isn't much.

"Need help with that?"

I turn and notice Sylvie leaning against the doorframe, her long blonde hair piled up in a bun, an amused expression on her face. There's a suitcase at her feet, which is even larger than mine. She's dressed in sweat pants and a tank top, like she's going to yoga and not leaving this place.

"You happen to have a trick up your sleeve?" I point to her stuffed suitcase.

"Sit on the thing, and hope for the best." She lets out a hearty laugh as she slides to the floor and picks up one of my shirts. At some point during my struggle with the suitcase, the damn zipper broke, and I ended up scattering half the contents. My room, or the room that's been my home for the past six weeks, looks like a mess.

"I can't believe we're done." Sylvie begins to rearrange my clothes.

"It was about time."

I try to help by handing her a dress. It's the same red dress I wore for Kade. My heart fills with longing as I remember his approving look.

"This place wasn't so bad, was it?" Sylvie says, shooting me a meaningful look.

"It was alright." I cast my eyes downward, ignoring the sudden dull ache in my chest.

It's been seven days since he left.

Seven days during which I could barely get him out of my thoughts, let alone forget him.

"I wouldn't want to come back," I mutter.

The day after his departure was particularly hard.

Much harder than I anticipated.

I couldn't hold up a conversation, couldn't eat, could barely breathe.

Days have passed and I still keep wondering whether he's thinking of me. Whether his feelings—like mine—might be growing with each second apart.

For the first time, I'm not obsessed...like I-have-to-stalk-you obsessed. I don't feel the need to chase him. I think of the special moments we shared, and miss him the way you would miss a good friend.

"Are you okay?" Sylvie looks up from my suitcase and frowns.

"I'm not even sure why I packed half of this stuff. I sure didn't need it." I avert my gaze before she can read my expression.

Letting out a loud groan, Sylvie begins to tug at the zipper, and to my surprise manages to get the thing closed.

I lean back and eye my overstuffed suitcase warily. It looks like it might be about to burst at the seams. "I can't wait to get out. But to be honest, I also dread the long drive back home."

"Might be a while." Sylvie points at a top and jacket on the bed.

"No. There's no way we'll ever squeeze those in." I shake my head and groan. "This will never end."

"You still miss him, don't you?" Sylvie says gently. The sudden change in conversation takes me off guard.

"What makes you say that?"

"You watched him leave and returned to the spot every day for a week." Her tone is soft, accepting. It brings tears to my eyes.

I watched Kade leave through one of the windows on the first floor, half hidden behind the curtains. I didn't think anyone had noticed me. I didn't think anyone would notice me seeking that particular spot, reliving the memory of Kade getting into the car, his somber expression, the dark circles beneath his eyes.

"I happen to like that window." I nod, eager to believe my own lie, if only I could.

"So you say. I have something for you." Sylvie hands me a bag I didn't notice before.

"What is it?"

"It's yours. I mean, it belongs to you."

My heart skips a beat as I peer in and realize it's a large blue box—the same one I left on his bedside table, unopened.

"Why are you giving me this?" My voice breaks. My body's shaking.

I can barely breathe.

"Kade," she says as if the name's explanation enough. "He asked me to give it to you Told me to hold on to it until the last day. I didn't ask what it was or why." She eyes me expectantly as I lift the box out of the bag and turn it in my hands.

"Don't you want to open it?" Sylvie prompts.

"I can't."

"Why not?"

Because it hurts too much that he's gone.

There's nothing that could change our circumstances.

"I can do it for you," she says.

I take in her eager expression.

It's only a gift.

Except, it's his, and whatever it is, it means the world to me.

A gift that will make me want him even more than I already do.

My first impulse is to ask her to take the gift back and never talk about it again, but instead I find myself holding my breath, hesitating, wondering, wishing.

It's only a gift.

It can't hurt me more than I'm already hurting.

"I can see what it is and then decide for you whether you'll like it," she suggests.

I nod. "Alright." I hand her the box and turn away as she opens it. Holding my breath, I wait for her reaction. Something. Anything. Sylvie remains quiet.

I turn around, frowning. "What is it?"

"It's...a book," she says somewhat incredulous, as if he's gifted me a goat. "An *old* book."

I take the box from her outstretched hands and

peer inside, instantly laughing.

It's not just any old book.

It's a first edition of *Pride and Prejudice,* in pristine condition.

Definitely a collector's item that must have cost a fortune.

How did he even get it?

"Someone should tell him that chocolate and flowers are the way to go. I'm so sorry. He really has no taste," Sylvie says. "It even smells bad."

I laugh and wipe at the sudden tears filling my eyes. "No, it's perfect."

"Perfect?" She sounds so aghast I let out another laugh.

"Yes." I turn to her, and for the first time I hug her—really hug her with tears spilling down my cheeks.

When I cried for Bruce, I cried for the months I had wasted on him. Now I'm crying because my heart is bleeding to be with Kade.

I crave his touch, his smile. It feels as though my soul's missing the sound of his voice, his laughter, everything about him.

"It's the perfect gift." I press the book against my chest, thinking that his hands touched it before me. That his thoughts were with me when he left. That he knows me so well, maybe better than anyone else.

"I miss him," I whisper. "I miss him even though I don't want to. Why does it hurt so much that he's gone?"

"Because you're in love with him," Sylvie whispers, smiling.

"What am I going to do?" I take a tissue from Sylvie's outstretched hand and begin to dab at my tears.

"That one's easy. You two are going to see each other again."

"I can't."

"Why not?" Sylvie asks.

"Because friendships formed in rehab don't last."

"But we both know what you and Kade had wasn't exactly friendship."

I grimace. It was friendship...and a lot of other things. "You know what I mean."

"He cares about you, so if you're happy about this—" she points at the box, "—book—"

"It's a first edition," I cut her off.

"I get it." She rolls her eyes, not getting it at all. "What I'm trying to say is that he makes you happy and that's all that counts."

"Let's pretend I wanted to get in touch with him. I don't have his number."

"That's not true." She points at the book. "He told me to tell you to look inside."

I open the book, my fingers lingering over the old print. As I turn the page, I stop breathing.

It's a note in Kade's handwriting, written on a piece of paper.

Vicky,

Our past doesn't define us. Your past doesn't bother me.

Call me when you change your mind...be it tomorrow or next year.

Call me when you're ready and I'll be there, waiting. Assuming they let me out, otherwise I insist you visit me, making use of your amazing climbing abilities.

And remember:

Do. Or do not. There is no try.

In the end, there's only us because we're one of a kind.

Kade

My fingers brush over his writing as a tear rolls down my cheek. My lips curl into a smile and I realize the tears that follow are tears of happiness.

I don't *have* to see him again.

But I can, and most importantly, I want to.

"He gave you his number for a reason. People don't do that unless they want you to call," Sylvie says.

Maybe.

I shake my head. "You told me that I needed therapy."

"That was six weeks ago when you still had that unhealthy obsession with your ex. You're different now."

I regard her for a long moment. "What changed your mind?"

She takes her time replying. "When you fall in love, you react a certain way when you hear the other person's name. Like you don't want other people to speak it out loud. Like it's sacred to you. Whenever I say his name, you give me that strange look." She shrugs as she considers her words. "Like a warning to tread carefully. Besides, I saw the way he looked at you. It's as if...I don't know." She shrugs again and gets up. "Just give it a chance, Vicky. You have nothing to lose. You two should stay in touch simply because you're in love with each other. You don't even need any other reason because your feelings are reason enough."

Why does she make so much sense today?

"Okay." I draw out the word. "What about my counselor's advice that addicts should never get involved because it doesn't turn out well?"

"She was probably quoting statistics," Sylvie says. "Look. Numbers are nothing. Maybe ninety-nine percent of people fail, but what if you belong in that minority who make it work? Don't you want to see for yourself whether you're up to the challenge? Last I checked you're not a number. You're breathing and living and have your own free will. Make use of it."

I stare at her as her words echo through my mind yet I'm unable to grasp them. "What are you saying?"

"I think you should get in touch with him."

"I wouldn't know what to say."

"Just ask him whether he's settled in. Shouldn't be too hard. Come on." She pulls me up with her. "Let's go."

I glance at the watch. "We still have a few hours."

"Why wait?" She gestures at me to get up. "Let's get our phones *now*. Time to shine."

I don't ask what she means by that because Sylvie looks like someone who knows how to get her way. And then there's something else on my mind.

A feeling that doesn't make sense.

It's growing in the deepest pit of my stomach, cold and heavy.

I can't wait to get my phone back, if only to find out whether Kade's changed his mind about us.

***

"You really think we'll be getting our phones back already?" I peer at Sylvie as we stop in front of the closed office door.

"They have to. The program's over so—" She shrugs. "But just in case, leave the talking to me, alright?"

I want to trust her, but I'm so anxious to resume communication with the outside world that I'd rather do this myself. "What's the plan?"

"You know how you always said that my counselor is much nicer than yours? Guess what? You were right." She flashes me a grin. "He's always offered his help, even let me borrow his phone once."

I can't help but laugh. "We all know he has a crush on you."

"A girl can use her charms." She shrugs again and knocks, shooting me a 'wait here' look.

She's in there for what feels like an eternity.

Maybe she's not the teacher's pet after all.

This can't go wrong. I'm about to knock when the door's thrown open and Sylvie steps out.

"So?" I prompt.

She peers at me and all my hope perishes. Her face is pale; her expression guarded.

Something feels wrong.

"What happened? Didn't you get our phones back?"

She shakes her head and retrieves my phone from her pocket, handing it to me.

I peer at it, then at her. "What's going on? Did he do something?"

She clutches at my arm and pulls me down the hall to the backyard. My heart's slamming in my chest with certainty that something is wrong. She only stops in the far corner where a tree's hiding us from anyone's view.

"Something happened." Her tone is cagey and her eyes are avoiding my gaze.

"What is it?" I scan her expression but can't read it. "Don't tell me we can't go home."

"No, Vicky." She shakes her head grimly. "I don't even know how to say this. It's about Kade." My breath hitches in my throat. She shakes her head again. "This is so hard."

Every part of my body tenses. I want to shake her, to force her to tell me what's going on. But all I can do is stare at her until she looks up.

Our eyes lock, and my heart sinks.

"There was an accident on the way to the airport." Her voice breaks. "I'm so sorry, Vicky, but he might not make it."

That's all I hear.

Kade had an accident two weeks ago and no one told me.

A scream escapes my chest. Or maybe it's just in my head—cruel and silent. Piece by piece, my heart begins to crumble, the pain as sharp as being cut.

Sylvie presses a note into my hand. "It's the hospital where they've taken him. That's all I know. I'm so sorry. I wish there was more I could do."

Tears begin to roll down my cheeks.

I can't be without him—that's the only coherent thought I can form.

36

Vicky

I'M NEVER GOING to sleep. I'm never going to feel happy again. Even though I've known Kade for only a few weeks, it feels as though his departure has ripped a piece out of me. I knew the time for saying goodbye would come. That eventually we'd separate and move on with our lives. The knowledge that it would end was always there.

But I never expected our ending to take such a tragic turn.

After hearing about the accident, I was in shock, my heart inconsolable, parts of it broken—sharp like shards of crystal glass.

I couldn't utter a word, afraid that even speaking his name would make it worse.

I haven't spoken a word since.

Not to my mom or to my sister whose questions about my treatment have been bordering on obnoxious, so much so that I've decided to ignore their text messages.

It's only after I've arrived back home and seen all the pictures of Bruce in my apartment that I realize I have to find a way to see Kade again.

I have to know more.

He's done so much for me by just being there when I needed someone. He never judged me when everyone else did; he also never sugar coated the truth.

I pack another suitcase and call a taxi, clenching the little note Sylvie handed me before we parted.

"Call me," she said, her tone imploring me to do so.

Kade had uttered the same words the night before stepping into the car that was supposed to drive him to the airport.

If only I had stopped him.

Spent a little more time together. Made plans. Discover the world together. Do as much as possible before what we had eventually turned sour.

If only.

I never got a chance to contact Kade, but I did ask Sylvie for help to find where Kade is. I skim her latest text message one last time before I toss my cell phone into my handbag.

The hospital where he was moved to is in Greensboro, almost three hundred miles from Roanoke Island. Getting there is the easy part. But how will I persuade the hospital personnel to let me see him if someone stops me?

I arrive before midday.

Stepping through the broad doors of Moses Cone Hospital, I breathe in the familiar scent of disinfectant. After years of working as a nurse, it's become a part of me, just like the steady buzz of people living, surviving, healing, and sometimes even dying. This time, the rush of familiarity doesn't instill confidence in me, which doesn't make any sense.

To my relief, the hospital is unusually busy and no one stops me. No one wants to know where I'm headed.

As I pass floor after floor, the waiting rooms, the maternity ward, I realize being here as a visitor isn't the same as doing my job.

All my life, I've known that death is a natural process. I've always believed in the advice of doctors and the progress in science. I've always shown compassion to patients and visitors. Now I realize I never truly felt the magnitude of it all.

I never understood the powerlessness people go through at the prospect of losing a loved one. And there's also the guilt that I'm to blame for what happened to him. If we hadn't gotten involved, he would never have left. He would never have stepped into that car and crashed on the way to the airport.

I reach the right floor and stop for a moment to orientate myself. His room number is on the left. As I head toward it, I can't shake off the feeling that Kade needs me.

Maybe it's just wishful thinking, but I need to tell him that I'm sorry one last time, even if he can't hear me.

I reach his door and my chest tightens, as if a string is wrapped around it and someone's tugging at it. My stomach recoils at the thought that I might be too late.

I push the door open and stop.

Kade's lying on the bed, surrounded by whirring machines.

He's not alone.

Sitting in a chair beside his bed is a woman, her brown hair falling into her face as she's busying herself with her cell phone. She's sitting so close she might be his girlfriend, or at least someone close.

I'm frozen to the spot, unsure whether to say something or head back out.

As if sensing my presence, she raises her head and frowns.

"I'm sorry," I whisper, taking a step back. "I shouldn't be here."

She's beautiful, I can't help but think. We're about the same age, but she looks glowing and sophisticated. Her skin is tanned, as if she's recently been on vacation to some tropical island. And she's wearing nice clothes.

Definitely girlfriend.

"Stupid," I mutter, realizing I've just spoken out loud.

"Who are you?" a male voice asks behind me.

My body freezes. Slowly I turn around and look up, tilting my head back to meet the guy's gaze.

Definitely hot.

Definitely not a doctor.

Definitely not Kade.

Of course, it's not him.

But there's something about this guy that has me on edge. For some reason, I feel a need to make him like me.

"I'm Victoria."

"Victoria? As in Victoria Sullivan?" The guy asks,

brows raised. I regard his expensive, fitted suit and the briefcase in his hand which makes him seem out of place here.

"Yeah, that one. Kade..." My voice breaks. "We met at the LAA Center."

I force myself not to peer at the woman, even though I wish I could catch her expression. Kade had me convinced that he wasn't into relationships, and I was stupid enough to believe it.

"I know who you are," the guy says, drawing my attention back to him. "I'm Chase. Kade's brother. He told me everything about you. I'm not surprised to see you here. It just took you a while."

I don't know why his statement throws me off. I meet his piercing blue eyes and the reproach in them.

"Therapy finished yesterday. I came as fast as I could."

Chase frowns, and I realize that I might not be welcome.

"I should go." My grip tightens around my handbag as I consider whether to wait for him to move aside or squeeze past him.

"Please stay," Chase says. "There's a cafeteria downstairs. We'd like to discuss something with you."

We?

And what could there possibly be to discuss? I want to ask when soft footsteps thud behind me. I don't turn to regard the beautiful woman, but I can smell her expensive perfume.

"This is my wife, Laurie," Chase says.

I stare at her as she shifts past me, right into his arms. He places a soft kiss onto her cheek and for a moment all they seem to see is each other. There's so much love in their gaze, I feel like an intruder.

That's when realization finally descends.

Wife.

Chase's wife.

She's Kade's sister-in-law.

Suddenly everything he told me comes back.

I'm so happy I almost laugh as I remember everything Kade told me about his family. The adoption. Losing his parents. His brother marrying the one woman whose family ruined the Wrights. Kade's struggle to accept her.

"We finally get to meet the woman who's changed him," Laurie says, offering me the kind of smile that makes me like her instantly.

"I'm not so sure about that."

"Ready?" Chase asks.

I sense a certain impatience about him, so I nod

and let him lead the way.

***

The hospital cafeteria is a busy place. Chase chooses a relatively private table near the back and disappears to get us drinks. Laurie and I have barely settled into our seats when the blaring sound of an EMS vehicle carries over from outside. I imagine one bringing Kade in, the people inside fighting for his life. The thought is too grim to pursue, not least because the fight isn't over. I only glimpsed him for a second, but the bruises on his face were hard to miss. And there's also the fact that he hasn't woken up yet. That's all Sylvie could tell me about his condition. This is my chance to find out more.

Chase returns with our drinks and places a cup of hot coffee in front of me. I whisper a 'thank you' and wrap my hands around the cup, letting the warmth seep into me as I consider how to start the conversation.

There are too many thoughts, too many emotions. Too much fear to put into words. I want to find out as much as I can and yet I can't bring myself to ask.

Luckily, I don't have to.

"The doctors tried everything," Chase says slowly. "In the end we've decided that an artificial coma might be our best option to give his body time to heal."

I bury my hands in my face. "How did this happen? I know it was an accident but—"

"The car was on the way to the airport when a van crashed into it," Chase says. "The driver didn't make it."

In spite of the heat, my body begins to shake again as I prepare to ask the one question that's been keeping me awake at night. "Has he opened his eyes yet?"

He must have.

Silence.

As I look up, I instantly know the answer and a dull ache forms in my chest. The prognosis is poor then. His chances are slim.

Chase shakes his head. "I'm sorry, Victoria."

I take a deep breath to compose myself, but the glimmer of hope in me dies with every second that passes.

"What did the doctors say, exactly?" I whisper.

"That he needs a kidney transplant. And even then he might not make it," Laurie says softly. "Time will tell but—"

She breaks off, leaving the rest unspoken. She doesn't have to spell out the obvious. I'm a nurse. I'm familiar with the statistics.

Time?

There isn't much of that.

Maybe three weeks. Maybe a little more. But the more time passes, the smaller the chance that Kade will make a full recovery.

A tear rolls down my cheek. I wipe at it angrily.

"There has to be something they can do," I say even though I know better. "How can I help? What can I do? You said something about a transplant. I'd be happy to test whether I'm a match."

Chase smiles kindly.

"I really want to," I add, in case he thinks I'm not serious.

His gaze moves to his wife, lingering there, and then back to me. "That's kind of you, Victoria. We appreciate the offer, but my wife's a match. We've already prepared the papers."

That's a lucky coincidence. Finding a donor never happens so fast. A wave of relief pours through me, while at the same time I regard her intently. Even her eyes are the same color, which is probably nothing but a figment of my imagination. I seem to see parts of Kade everywhere, in everyone, in

465

everything I pass and do.

"So you're a registered nurse?" Laurie asks.

"I've been working in a nursing home for the past year."

"Before that you worked in the ER?"

I nod, surprised that she's familiar with my résumé.

"I'm sorry, I can't do this." I take a deep breath and shake my head, fighting the urge to get up and leave. "It was my fault that we were discovered and consequently transferred. I shouldn't have let him go."

"What happened wasn't your fault, Victoria," Chase says. "We know Kade better than you do. If he doesn't get what he wants, he'll chase it—come Heaven or Hell. He has the most stubborn mind."

I soak up his words, but the consolation in them doesn't quite reach my heart. "I want to help. I just don't know how."

"There is something you can do, which is the reason why we've been meaning to get in touch with you." He leans back, hesitating.

"Yes?" I prompt.

"Laurie and I can't be here all the time and we need someone we can trust. We've checked your credentials and feel that you're the right person for the job, not least because I think you care about him as much as we do."

"I don't work here," I mumble. "And even if I applied it would take forever to be transferred. And it might not even be to the intensive care unit."

"Say that you want to and I'll make it happen," Chase says.

"You can make it happen?" I repeat, suddenly filled with excitement.

He nods gravely. "I'll get it done by Monday. It goes without saying that you'll get paid for your work and we'll also take care of all living arrangements."

"We trust you," Laurie says. "We really do."

"But you don't know me."

"Kade does," Chase says. "We respect his choices."

I regard him for a few moments. His expression is unreadable but there's something in his eyes. Whatever differences the brothers had, I realize it never rattled their relationship. "How do you know that Kade trusted me?"

"He told me." He leans back in his seat, and for the first time there's the slightest hint of a smile. "Kade isn't just my brother; we've been best friends forever. While we might not always see eye to eye, he still tells me everything, even when he knows I might not agree." He cocks his head. "For a long time, we only had each other. Our past has made us stronger, has brought us closer together. So, what do you say?"

I don't need any persuasion. Being near Kade is what I wanted. There's no way I'd decline Chase's offer. "Yes, on one condition though. I don't want to get paid more than what I currently make."

"Deal. Laurie will call you. If you need anything, here's my personal number." Chase pushes his card across the table and gets up. Laurie follows suit, shooting me a weak smile.

I take a deep breath and release it slowly as I get up. I reach out to shake their hands when Laurie wraps her arms around me, drawing me in the kind of hug that makes me like her even more.

"Thank you for doing this. It means a lot to all of us," she whispers and pulls away.

I want to say that it means a lot to me, but my throat's choked up and I can't utter a word. So, I just not nod and watch them leave through the crowd.

It's long after they're gone and I've finished my second cup of coffee that I realize the magnitude of it all.

I'll get to be near Kade without worrying about

my job or any financial implications. I'll get to take care of him. Talk to him.

I've read the reports of patients feeling and hearing but being trapped, incapable of communicating.

For the first time, a glimmer of hope flickers to life.

Maybe he'll hear me.

Maybe he'll know I'm there.

Even if Kade can't hear me, I need to let him know how I feel about him.

37

Kaiden

I BLINK IN AN effort to adjust my eyes, unable to make sense of the unfamiliar, off-color ceiling that's in need of a layer of white paint. I wince as another wave of sharp, throbbing pain hits the side of my head, forcing me to close my eyes again.

Two more minutes.

That's all I need to recover from the pain.

Several minutes pass, yet the pain doesn't subside.

The sound of humming and whirring keeps piercing through my eardrums. Every sound feels like a sharp knife is piercing my skull open. Every flutter of my eyelids feels like cement is about to dry them close. Every thought feels like a truck is hitting me over and over again. As I lie with my eyes closed, trying to make sense of what's happening to me, I realize my thoughts might not even be my own.

Voices are overlapping. Somewhere, a child's crying. And then a woman's voice, soft and low, soothing. I latch onto her voice like it's my beacon of light.

"You need to wake up." Fingers, soft like butterflies, touch my arm, my face. "Please, Kade. Please. I need you. I love you. I want you, but more than that, I need you to wake up. If you leave, you'll leave my heart in pieces and it won't ever heal."

My heartbeat hastens, not at hearing my name, but at the way she says it...hurt, disappointed.

I'm the source of her pain. I could take it all away.

If only I could wake up. If only I could remember what happened.

Did I hook up with her, then dump her? Because that's the only reasonable explanation as to why she'd be crying at my bedside.

She makes me feel like a no-good bastard with only his own interests at heart.

"I wish you could hear me."

The urgency in her voice scares me. As if something terrible is about to happen and it's all my fault that I don't wake up to stop it.

I force my mind to remember what

happened...but nothing comes.

My mind's a black canvas, all color and images drained from it.

It's pathetic.

I am pathetic. Useless. Trapped in this endless loop of pain.

"Even if you can't hear me, I want you to know that I love you. I love you, Kade Wright. I don't know when it started. I don't even know why, but I know that I love you and I can't imagine being with anyone but you." She lets out a shaky breath.

I realize with dismay that she is crying.

"People say you can choose to fall in love with someone if you want, but I didn't just fall in love. I fell into you. Into your soul. Into your body and mind. I don't just need someone to hold me. I need to know that you're alive and well. I would do anything to see you smile. I need you to make it, so please, wake up for me. If not for me, then do it for your family. I could never forgive myself if you didn't."

Desperation.

Her voice is filled with it and I realize she isn't blaming me. She's blaming herself. But she can't possibly have done anything wrong. There's too much love in her voice, too much longing, that it's hard to imagine she might be the kind of person who'd inflict pain upon others.

My pulse thuds as I force my eyes to open. My body feels drenched in cold sweat from the effort. The pain hits me hard—harder than ever before—but strangely it becomes bearable.

I blink against the bright light.

It's the same off-color ceiling. No one's painted it yet, meaning not much time could have passed since I last saw it.

The throbbing inside my skull increases as I focus on the blurred images around me. I'm lying on a bed in what looks like a hospital room.

My throat is dry, the metallic taste making me want to puke. There's a glass of water on the bedside table but my arms feel too heavy to lift.

I turn my head to the side and glimpse the small shape of a woman.

She's sleeping in a chair with a book clutched to her chest. There's a blanket crumpled at her feet, and her features are relaxed, as though she's been asleep for a while. But her face is pale and dark circles frame her eyes, as though even sleep hasn't been quite able enough to wipe away her worries.

She's so beautiful I forget to breathe, and memories begin to play inside my mind.

Vicky.

She's here.

What the hell happened? Why can I remember her but not why I'm in the hospital, surrounded by whirring machines?

I take in the bouquet of flowers on the table, the iPod station, the bag on the floor next to her feet.

She's wearing slippers and her nails are painted a soft shade of pink. A jacket is draped over the back of another chair.

She looks like she's living here.

"Vicky." My voice is barely more than a whisper, but it's enough to wake her, though. Her eyes fly open and she jumps up, disoriented for a moment.

Her gaze turns to me and shock passes over her face.

"Oh, my God." She dashes for one of the machines and presses a button before turning back to me.

"Kade." Her steps are slow, measured, and there's hesitation in her eyes, like she's afraid she might be dreaming. "You're awake." She pauses to take me in. "Do you know who I am?"

"It would take a whole lot more than an accident to forget you, Vicky." I try to smile but even that's too much effort.

She stares at me. "You remember."

"I do. I think I even got the name right."

Finally getting my attempt at infusing humor, she laughs and a tear rolls down her cheek. I wish I could get up and wipe it away.

"You remember me." She leaps onto the bed, throwing herself on top of me as she settles into my arms.

I inhale her scent and moan slightly. Good thing some parts of me are still working the way they should be.

"You have no idea how much I missed hearing your voice." She pushes up on her elbow and places a soft kiss on my lips. "You were asleep for so long I thought you wouldn't make it."

I frown, unsure what she's talking about.

"Please don't ever go back to sleep. Promise me. We're all scared of losing you." Her voice chokes up.

"I must have taken a bad fall on those stairs." I suddenly remember that part. The stairs were slippery and I stumbled, right before getting into the car that was supposed to take me to the airport. I don't remember the fall, but that must be it.

"Stairs?" Vicky looks at me, confused.

"I tripped."

"Kade." She hesitates. "You didn't fall down the

stairs. You had an accident."

An accident?

I don't recall any accident, not even a fragment of it. But then I don't remember how I got here either. I only remember my last night with Vicky. Our last kiss. My promise to her. The goodbye.

As far as I remember I never got in a car. Or did I?

My mind's blank, but it feels like I'm missing something. The gaps are there, waiting to be filled.

"You said I was asleep. For how long?"

She doesn't reply.

"Vicky," I prompt.

"Ask me another time, when you're better. It doesn't matter anyway. All that's important is that you are awake now."

"How long?" I push up on my elbows, ignoring the nausea settling in the pit of my stomach.

"Don't." She pushes me back down onto the bed gently. I don't try to fight her. I can't. My body's too weak for that.

"Tell me."

Fear shimmers in her eyes.

"You know if you don't tell me someone else will. I'd rather hear it from you," I prompt.

She looks at me for a few moments, her eyes

shimmering with unshed tears. "You've been gone for weeks."

Her hand moves to her abdomen, and her gaze grows distant. The swelling of her tummy is prominent enough to notice. I don't know why I didn't see it before.

I smile bitterly, realizing she doesn't mean weeks. Months have passed.

The world has moved on without me. Including her.

I can't blame her.

A woman as attractive as Vicky, and with such a strong need for love, couldn't possibly stay single. She needs someone by her side.

"Kade," she whispers. "Please say something."

I stroke her cheek gently. "I envy the guy you're with. That's all there is to say."

I close my eyes before a wave of pain engulfs me—but this time it's my heart that's hurting.

A door's thrown open and feet shuffle in. The bed moves before I'm being lifted up.

It all seems familiar.

I can hear Vicky's voice, but it might just be a thought or a memory.

Blackness crashes over me again. I realize, it's a different kind of darkness. My perception has been sharpened, my senses heightened, hovering in a state between dreams and reality. Slowly, fragments of memories come back.

Vicky watching me from a window. Me getting into the car. A vehicle crashing into us.

And pain. So much pain.

I had no intention of letting her go. But I realize that I might not have a choice now that she's expecting another man's child.

I just hope he'll make her happy the way I know I would have.

38

Vicky

"I'M NOT TRYING to tell you what to do, but I think it's time you called him, Vicky," Grace says. I look at her in the mirror, but she's busy removing imaginary lint from her gown, obviously trying to avoid my gaze by seeming busy. "It's been far too long."

"Absolutely not."

"But...ouch." She shoots me a murderous look when the crochet hook pokes into her back.

"Sorry," I say and proceed to pull the loops over the tiny buttons.

"Tell him how you feel about him, now that he's awake. You heard Chase. The physical therapy's going well. He's recovering. He can walk."

I shake my head vehemently. "Not happening, Grace. Please respect my wishes that I need to move on."

She drops her shoulders with an exasperated sigh. "I know that, and I respect your decision. But I just want you to know that I've noticed the way you look at that book he gave you, and I wish you'd finally confess."

I stop for a moment to shoot her a wary glance. "Confess to what?"

"That you're deeply in love with him. I know that. Everyone does, but you keep denying the obvious. Now, I don't know whether you're just lying to us or trying to convince yourself, but it's getting old. Like, last week old. Besides, look at you."

She shoots a meaningful look at my belly.

I groan inwardly.

After Kade woke up from his coma, I left. It was hardest thing I ever did, but it was the right decision. He needed the distance to help him heal without the emotional baggage and pressure that comes with finding out your rehab hook-up is pregnant.

I wanted him to be able to focus solely on himself, and I could only achieve that by disappearing from his life.

"Why don't you focus on your life? In case you don't remember, today's your big day."

Grace pulls a face. "The beauty of being happy is trying to spread the joy."

Rolling my eyes, I finish the last row of buttons and slump onto the sofa, exhausted. "You're good to go."

She spins in a slow circle, swiveling her Claire Pettibone wedding gown. "What do you think?"

She looks like a princess in her flowing, cream gown with a tiny waist and her glossy curls cascading down her naked shoulders. I dab at the tears in my eyes, struggling not to mess up my makeup. I'm so proud of her and have no doubt the backyard wedding at our mom's house will be both beautiful and memorable.

"You look beautiful," I whisper and blink in succession against the onset of tears.

This is the moment we both dreamed of ever since we were little girls.

I'm happy for Grace, and yet I'm afraid. In less than two hours, I'm going to lose the closest person in my life My childhood buddy. The person who always cheered for me and laughed when I tumbled. In spite of our differences, we remained close through the years, so finding out that she's moving to Sacramento after the wedding hit me hard.

"I'm going to miss you, Grace," I say, choked.

"Both you and your ugly, silly, handmade sweaters."

"Admit that you secretly love them." She laughs and then tears gather in her eyes. "Stop it or else I'm going to cry, too. I can't ruin my makeup."

"I'm not crying. I'm just amazed how much you have grown. That's all. Can you believe that used to be us?" I point to the pictures on the wall.

Grace must have been about five years old, her face painted in blue because she wanted to be a Smurf, just like her favorite TV show.

"I had real aspirations back then," Gracie says, laughing.

"And now you're getting married. It's a little hard to grasp."

"Those were the good times." Her voice softens as she peers at my belly. "You know I'll always be there for you, right?"

I nod because I want to believe her. She means every word of it, there's no doubt about that, but can she possibly keep such a promise when she's moving to Sacramento and soon will be too busy with married life?

"I know that," I whisper. "Now hurry up before you miss your own wedding."

"Okay." She takes a deep breath and her expression turns anxious. "Let me pee before the photographer comes in."

After she leaves for the bathroom I take out my cell phone to check an incoming text message.

It's from the wedding planner.

Kristy: The photographer and his assistant just arrived. Want me to send them up?

"Gracie, hurry up!" I shout. "The photographer's here already."

No reply, so I type up a text.

Me: Send them up in ten. Did you make sure to put the homemade wedding sentiments next to the glass vase?

Kristy: Don't worry. I got it. Everything's running smoothly.

It's her standard reply whenever she gives an update, which happens about every half hour.

I toss the phone on the table when the door's thrown open, and Gracie returns.

"What if I'm making a mistake?"

I groan.

"Oh, Gracie! You can't be serious." I grab her in a tight hug. "Don't get cold feet on me. We've both been waiting for this moment for such a long time. You've been together for five amazing years, and I can't even imagine you guys apart."

Textbook material.

"You're just telling me what you think I want to hear."

"No." I shake my head. "I've always wanted what you have. I'm happy you found it, because you're amazing and you deserve it. I'm just telling you what I feel. You've chased your happiness. Now that you've found it, hold on to it."

Her eyes search mine, her gaze full of hope, soaking up every word. "Even knowing that I'm moving away?"

"Even if you were thousands of miles away, I would still insist you marry him."

Her eyes fill with tears. "I promise I'll visit you as much as I can. And I promise I will call you every single day."

"You promise?"

"I promise." A small smile lights up her face. "I'll be here for my nephew's birth."

My sister was the first person I told that I was having a baby boy. She was also the one who attended parenting classes with me. "I really hope so."

"Oh, no." Her forehead creases into a frown.

"What now?"

"I'm panicking. What if I forget my vows? What if I look stupid and everyone laughs?" She catches my eye roll. "What? It *could* happen."

"Gracie..." I shake her shoulders gently. "Everything will go just as planned."

"I hope you're right," she whispers. "Do you think Dad will be coming?"

I hesitate. Obviously, I don't want to lie to her but I don't want to ruin her day, either, by telling her the truth. "I don't know, Gracie. Maybe, but I wouldn't count on it."

"I'll never forgive him if he doesn't."

"Today's your day. You don't need him. You don't need his blessing." I smile with more cheerfulness than I feel. "No matter whether he turns up or not, Mom and I have it covered."

She nods, falling silent again.

"The photographer will be here any minute." I head over to the nightstand and retrieve her jewelry box. "Pearls or diamonds?"

"Pearls." She turns to me, her voice excited. "Oh, I almost forgot. There's someone here to see you."

"Not now, Gracie." I lift two sets of pearl earrings. "Which ones?"

"You won't believe me when I tell you who it is. Aren't you curious?"

I put the earrings back and release an exasperated sigh. "I swear you're the most unfocused bride I've ever seen. Alright, I'll bite so we can get back to this. Who is it?"

She grabs my hand and pulls me to the window overlooking the backyard. I scan the crowd below. The planner's people are still busy setting up the place, but they're almost done. The chairs have been set up. The tables in the tent have been decorated. Rose petals adorn the white rug leading to the altar. "If your fiancé is trying to hook me up with his drunk friend again, I swear I'm going to—"

I stop midsentence as I spy the tall figure.

Kade.

He's hovering a head over everyone else; his gaze is fixed on the rows of empty chairs.

Even though his back's turned to me, I pull the curtains shut before he notices me. "Who invited him?"

"I did." Gracie's voice drips excitement. "We got on so well, exchanged phone numbers and all. Aren't you happy to see him?"

I stare at my sister, for once rendered speechless.

Happy? Of course, I'm happy to see him. But for

all the wrong reasons.

"Why would you do that?"

"Someone had to. It's been weeks. *Weeks*, Vicky."

I place both pairs of earrings into her hand and start pacing the room. "I know that. But—"

"What's holding you back from talking to him?"

"This." I point at my seven-month pregnant belly. "If you didn't notice, I'm pregnant."

"It's his kid," Gracie says.

She was against my decision to keep Kade out of the picture right from the beginning, which is one of the reasons why I haven't told her about his countless phone calls. Calls I've refused to answer. And even more text messages.

"That's beside the point. The point is that I can't see him now. I'm not ready to face him. I can't talk about the future. You have to tell him to leave." I look at her, my gaze imploring. It's her wedding; I can't cause a scene. I can't ruin it by starting a fight. All I can do is appeal to her better judgment, even though we've had similar conversations countless times before.

"Vicky." My sister's voice grows quiet. Too quiet. "It's his child. Don't you think he has the right to know about him? To have the choice whether he wants to have him in his life?"

I turn away from her, avoiding her gaze. "He doesn't want a family. He's not that kind of man."

"This might change his mind. Expecting a child is a life-altering experience. It changes people. Maybe this is what he needs to become the person he truly is at heart. And you're keeping this amazing experience from him."

"Now you're being dramatic." I narrow my eyes as I realize she's about to embark on the guilt trip. "I know what you're doing, but it's not working. I can't believe you went behind my back and invited him to your wedding even though I explicitly told you that I don't want to see him. This is an act of betrayal."

"The only act of betrayal is hiding yourself from the man you love." She squeezes my hand hard, as though to get my attention. "Don't you see? Sooner or later, you'll have to face him. Why not now? He's flown all the way here. We both know tickets aren't cheap."

I let out a laugh. "As if he can't afford them. You realize he's rich? Like super rich!"

"So?"

I roll my eyes, mostly because Gracie won't get it. "He has a penthouse. A big company that makes gazillions a year. He's been voted sexiest bachelor of California, and this is just a tiny bit of the information I could find on Google. He's out of physical rehab now. He's probably back to his old ways."

She shakes her head. "He's not. He wants you."

I laugh again. She's no naïve it's almost painful. "You're being ridiculous."

"Look." She hesitates, choosing her words. "He wouldn't be here if he didn't care for you. I can't tell him to leave."

"Why not?"

"Because I can't stand seeing you like this. I love you, sis, but you've been a pain in the ass. Besides, I want my nephew to know his father. Now, where's that photographer?"

I watch Gracie as she picks up her champagne flute and takes a sip. With dismay I realize she's enjoying playing matchmaker. I should have known my attempts at persuading her to understand my position were going to be a waste of time.

"Things might not work out between you and him," Gracie says. "But maybe they will. You'll never know until you two talk." She smiles. "If I have to drag you out there by myself, then so be it. Now stop arguing with me or I'll uninvite you to my wedding."

"You can't do that. I'm already here."

"For which I'm grateful, but push me. Or you'll

get to watch from the window. Mom, Jason, and you are the most important people in my life. I'm not going to stand here and do nothing while you let your stupid pride ruin your chance at finding happiness." She glowers at me, which she always does when she's trying to get her point across. "Now, I want you to go out there and bare your soul. You'll tell him how you feel about him. And we both know you'll do as I ask because I'm the bride, and you want to see me happy."

"That's so—"

Someone knocks at the door, interrupting my chance to tell her that even though she's the bride she can't demand those kinds of things.

I stare at her, ignoring the strong need to shake some sense into her.

"Love you, too, sis." Gracie laughs and then shouts, "Come in!"

The door opens, and Kristy steps in with a bunch of people in her wake, taking up all the space with her bubbly personality.

Kade's here, and there's no way I'll be able to avoid him.

That's all I can think about.

Storming out, I head straight for my old bedroom because it's the only place where I feel like I'm not going insane.

I'm not going to miss the wedding, obviously. But I don't have the courage to face him just yet.

I'll do it today, in public, with lots of people around us. Maybe he won't even notice me...or my very pregnant belly.

Oh, who am I kidding?

39

Vicky

IT'S BEEN BARELY five minutes when a knock raps at the door. The only person who might need me is the wedding planner.

Kristy and I have an arrangement.

Whatever problem, issue, or trouble, she'll come to me first to avoid causing unnecessary panic between the Sullivan members of the family.

I glance at my cell phone.

Only ninety minutes to go.

She's probably ready to brief me in or has last-minute questions about the seating arrangements.

The problem is I don't want to talk to her because I can't focus on anything but the man I'm desperately trying to avoid.

My heart feels like it's about to burst at the

prospect of talking to him after such a long time. My body seems to tingle all over at the memories of his touch.

A flicker of hope ignites deep inside me.

A flicker of want travels through my core.

This could be the closure we both need.

But do I even want closure?

Maybe I won't have to face him at all.

Maybe he's here to thank me after which he'll leave.

Maybe this insane attraction is all in my mind, and all that I need is one good look at him, and he'll be out of my system for good.

Who are you kidding, Sullivan!

"I'm busy," I yell and step in front of the mirror.

I still have to change out of my old Mickey Mouse shirt and my hair which was all glossy, red curls barely an hour ago thanks to Gracie's amazing hairstylist, is now a dull, tangled mess. There's no way I'm walking out of my room looking the way I do.

Only, I need to get my dress from Gracie's room.

Another rap at the door before someone throws it open and my sister's head appears.

She's not looking at me as she calls over her shoulder, "She's in here. Hiding, obviously."

Before I can blink, she's gone again, leaving the door ajar. Something tells me I'm no longer alone— or as alone as you can be in a house full of people.

A lump settles in my throat, cutting off my air supply.

He's here.

I can feel him, his presence unraveling, his magnetism overpowering.

"You've been avoiding me."

Sweet mercy.

His familiar voice sends a shiver down my spine. I've been longing to hear it for weeks.

My breath hitches in my throat as I meet Kade's intense gaze. His expression is nonchalant, but there's a glint of anger in his eyes.

I want to tell him to leave. That whatever I'm doing is none of his business. Instead, I find myself closing my eyes as his presence slowly overpowers me.

He's here, together with all those memories I've been trying to bury together with our past.

I've completely forgotten how good he smells. How his presence makes me feel like I'm the only woman in his world. How my body gets hot and bothered, burning for his touch.

"I haven't been avoiding you." My voice is weak.

Liar. Liar.

"You're lying," Kade says matter-of-factly.

Turning my back to him, I head over to the window, which is a little too close to my bed. Heat rises to my face at the thought. I haven't been with anyone since Kade. I couldn't even look at another man. He's ruined that part for me.

I'm glad he can't see my face and read just how much I want him.

"Kade." I open my mouth, then close it again.

What else can I say?

This is the kind of situation I've been trying to avoid. I knew all along that my feelings would render me defenseless to the extent that I wouldn't be able to think straight, let alone deny what he's doing to me.

I want him too much, so damn much, but I can't have him.

"I haven't been avoiding you. Not just you," I say slowly. "I've been avoiding everything about you."

"Why would you do that, Vicky?"

The sound of his approaching footsteps is muffled by the rug beneath our feet. I want to get out of here, but to do that I'd have to turn around and face him.

But that's out of the question.

I press my lips into a grim line as it all comes

back a hundred-fold. My ridiculous attraction to him. The fear that this might be our last few moments together. The powerlessness and despair at the fact that he might not want our child.

"Why are you here, Kade?" I ask, ignoring his question.

"You know why." His hand touches my shoulder. "I needed to see you."

I don't protest as he spins me around slowly, giving me no option but to face him.

His eyes.

I had completely forgotten how beautiful they are. How his irises change to a darker color when he's angry or how warm they look when he's worried.

Right now, it's a mixture of the two.

I remember all the times I touched his face, kissed it, fell more and more in love with it while he was asleep.

They say distance makes the heart grow fonder.

That's not true at all.

My heart fell for him while we were together.

It leaped when his eyes fluttered.

It jumped out of my chest when he looked at me.

Now it's breaking at the sight of him.

Kade Wright is perfection. He looks so beautiful

he must be made of sin.

"Vicky." He speaks my name gently and I can feel myself melting. He closes the last few inches between us and lifts his hand to brush a strand of hair out of my face. "You're back with him."

His voice is calm, resolute, there's an undertone of anger.

I bite my lip hard, but the pain doesn't stop the heat gathering between my legs.

He's sexy when he's angry.

I can't help but wonder whether his lips taste the same, whether his touch could still send me over the edge.

"Look at me." His tone is harsher. "You're back with him, Vicky."

It's a statement. Not a question.

The words echo in my head. They don't make sense until I catch his glance. It's the same glance he used to give me during our group therapy sessions.

The implication is so ridiculous I can't help but laugh.

"You think I've run back to Bruce?"

"Isn't that why you've been avoiding my calls?"

I suck in my breath, wondering how he could possibly come to such a conclusion when all I want to do is to rip off his clothes and squeeze in a quickie before my sister's wedding.

It's been months since I even thought of Bruce. He's been erased from my mind, and someone else has taken his place: Kade.

His name, our memories—they're everywhere, around me, inside me.

"I'm not back with Bruce," I say. "I'm not with anyone. Why would you even assume that? He's gay!"

Suspicion reflects in his eyes. "You thought you were in love with him, and he might still be in the closet."

This is the time to tell Kade how I feel about him. But I'm not ready to admit my feelings, my fears, my hopes. Saying it all when he was in a coma was easy, because deep inside I doubted he heard me. Revealing my feelings when he can hear me would only make me sound desperate, particularly since I'm pregnant.

"I won't let you shut me out," Kade says.

"I wasn't planning on doing that."

There's a long silence.

When he speaks again, I'm amazed by the softness in his voice. "I know that you took care of me."

I saw that one coming. "It's no big deal. Anyone

would have done it."

"Not really. Not to the same extent." His fingers touch my cheek gently, the soft caress making my heart flutter in my chest. "Chase said you were by my side every single day. That you worked overtime and rejected his offer to get paid for your time."

"It's nothing, Kade." My breath barely makes it past my lips. I fight the urge to lean into his touch. "You didn't have to fly all the way here to thank me. A simple thank-you card would have sufficed."

"Chase said you were by my side day and night, reading aloud, keeping my senses stimulated, doing everything you could to wake me. You advised him not to listen to the doctors when they claimed I might not make it. If not for you, I might not have woken up. We both know that."

I blink in succession to fight the tears gathering in my eyes. I remembered those dark moments when my own doubts threatened to take over. Seeing him alive and well, I'm glad I didn't give up.

Kade's hands cup my face, forcing me to face the intensity of his eyes. "I know you were afraid that you might lose me, Vicky. I know your fears are the reason why you're avoiding me."

I let out a pent-up breath.

He's right. But only almost.

He's so close to the truth it hurts.

"You have no idea how hard it was for me to see you in that hospital bed. I've never felt so helpless in my life. The knowledge that I'm to blame for you getting into that car made it even harder. I'll never forgive myself for letting you go." My honesty surprises me, but Gracie's right. I need to be frank with him because he's the only man I ever loved.

The man I almost lost, because we were stupid and reckless.

After months of worrying, it feels almost surreal that he's alive and well. I feel as though any minute someone might pierce the bubble of my reality and I'll discover that it was nothing but a beautiful dream.

"None of what happened was ever your fault, Vicky," he says softly. "I know how hard it all was on you, because at some point your voice pushed through to me. I heard everything you said. Your feelings. Your fears."

"I didn't really think you would. I just needed to tell you how I felt." My voice breaks and my cheeks flush.

That only thing that kept me going was my own need to hold on to faith. It was all a coping mechanism in case he wouldn't wake up.

"I heard every word, even though it took me a while to grasp the meaning of it all." He falls silent for a few moments, his eyes glazing over as if he's thinking back. "I don't remember much, but I remember your voice. You were the light in the darkness surrounding me. I woke up because of you."

"You don't need to say that." I almost choke on my words.

"If only you could see the truth." He closes the distance between us. The immediate proximity is more than I can bare.

Our time together feels like it all happened yesterday. It's all still raw and sweet, and so very painful.

"You saved me, Vicky," Kade says gently. "You took a part of me and kept it safe. Why did you leave?"

"I didn't want you to thank me."

He leans into me, pressing gently into my pregnant belly.

His hands go on either side of my face, trapping me in between them.

"We both know that's not true." The seriousness of his voice cripples me. Something flashes across his face. Determination. Knowledge.

I know what he wants me to say, but damn him. I'm not going to be the one to speak the obvious.

"You're scared. Confused," Kade says. "I want you to know that I don't care whose child it is. I want to take care of you."

My heart slams hard against my ribcage.

"This child might not be mine, but it doesn't matter. If you had read my texts, you would know that."

He takes out his cell phone and begins to scroll through countless messages.

My breathing stops as I start to read.

You're my drug.

The thought scares me, and yet if feels so very true.

You will always be my drug.

I want to be there for you the way you were there for me.

You can count on me...always.

"Don't shut me out, Vicky. I care about you and your wellbeing. No matter what happens, I'll always care for you. Friends or no friends, I mean every word." He points at one of the messages. "You can always count on me. All that I ask of you is that you don't push me out of your life. Let me help you."

I look up at him, confused. "Help me?"

"To raise the child."

My heart skips a beat, then another, as the meaning of his words slowly begin to sink in.

He thinks someone else might be the father. That's why he wanted to know whether I had gone back to Bruce; whether I was seeing anyone. It probably makes perfect sense from Kade's point of view.

I take a sharp breath to brace myself for what I'm about to say. "There hasn't been anyone since you, Kade. You're the father."

He stares at me blankly.

I let the words sink in, watching his emotions change as everything falls into place.

There's shock, then disbelief, then shock again. "I thought you were on the pill."

"I was." I nod gravely, unable to make out what he's thinking. "I don't know what happened."

The situation is charged with emotions. I'm so nervous, I can barely think straight. I want him to say something, do something, instead of just stare at me.

His eyes shimmer, and in that instant I realize he's fighting with himself just as much as I am.

"I thought…" He breaks off and laughs. For some reason, he's relieved. I can work with that. "When did you find out?"

"I had to go in for a health test before I could resume my position with Moses Cone Hospital. They told me I was four weeks pregnant, which means you're the father. I…" My voice shakes. "And I chose to keep it."

"Why didn't you tell me?"

"Because…" I hesitate. What can I say? That I was afraid he might think I got knocked up on purpose? That I might be the kind of woman who'd try to tie him to her by tricking him?

I swallow nervously. "The day I heard about the accident, I felt like my whole world had just crumbled. I prayed that you'd wake up. But days passed that turned into weeks, and nothing happened. Eventually, I started to ask myself. What if he doesn't make it?" I pause to read his reaction. His face remains blank, so I continue, "I'll be honest with you, Kade. I didn't think you'd make it. No one did. But I had faith." My hands cup my belly and the life growing inside. "This child gave me hope. I figured even if I lost you, at least a part of you would always be with me. I didn't avoid you because I didn't want you in my life, Kade. It was the fear of losing you all over again that kept me away from you. I was afraid that you wouldn't feel the same way about me."

"Vicky—" His fingers settle beneath my trembling chin, drawing my mouth to him. But I'm not done. Now that I've started, I want him to know everything.

"No." I shake my head again. "Please let me finish. I want to be with you, and that goes against everything you ever wanted out of us. I'm sorry I didn't tell you about the pregnancy. But I couldn't risk you trying to persuade me to get rid of it. You see, if I thought if I couldn't have you, at least I'd have him."

He sucks in a sharp breath and anger mirrors in his eyes.

This is exactly the kind of reaction I feared he'd show.

Stupid me for ever hoping for something else. Of course, everything he said in those text messages were nothing but empty words. Faced with reality— the possibility that this child might be his—he was bound to change his mind.

"Don't worry," I say, smiling bitterly. "I've got it

all figured out. Mom's helping me raise him. I don't expect anything from you. There are absolutely no expectations, no—"

His lips crash against mine—wild and passionate, cutting off my words. It takes me off guard, and for a moment all I can do is stand rooted to the spot as I fight to grasp the meaning of it.

For the life of me, I've no idea what he's doing.

Is it desperation? Lust?

Because that's how it feels, and more.

He pulls back.

"No one but us is raising this child." In spite of his smile, his tone is sharp and decisive, but also full of unspoken promises.

I stare at him warily. "What?"

"You heard me. We're going to raise him together. We're going to be a family, dammit."

"I don't understand." I search his gaze for a sign that he's not saying what I just heard. "But I thought you didn't want a family?"

"You assumed wrong," Kade says. "I never said I didn't want a family with *you*."

"What changed your mind?"

"You." His lips touch mine gently as he pushes his phone back into my hand.

I start to read again.

I can't believe you're pregnant and left without telling me.

I want to take us to the next level. I'm asking you to give us a chance.

I love you, Vicky. This is the truth. And even though I've got my head banged up pretty bad, I knew that all along.

I shake my head in disbelief. How did this happen? Is it possible that I got it all wrong? That I was too blind to see that Kade honestly cared about me?

"We—" I gesture at us, "—we were never supposed to happen, Kade."

"Rehab was never part of my life plan, but it led me to you. For that I'll forever be grateful. Before I met you, I didn't really have a purpose in life. Now I realize this is my purpose—to have you, to have a kid together. Maybe more soon." He winks and laughs.

"I haven't even pushed this one out yet," I mumble.

Kade shakes his head and his expression become serious again. "My point is, so much has happened.

We happened. I'm in love with you and I want this more than I ever thought I could."

I look at him, unsure. This is exactly what I had been hoping for; maybe even more. But I've been burned before. I don't want history to repeat itself.

"I've never felt this way about anyone before," Kade says. "That's why I am here. I don't want to lose you." He laughs at my confused look. "You can't expect me to just leave and not fight for us. I want to give our relationship a chance. Please say yes because I'm not the same man I was when you met me. I can't live the way I lived before." His eyes shimmer. "You've stolen my heart, Vicky Sullivan, and I hope one day I'll be able to steal yours."

I take him in—all of him. His beautiful eyes, his soft smile, the gentle caress of his fingers on my skin.

How can I tell him that he stole my heart the moment I saw him? That it never belonged—and will never belong—to anyone else but him?

"So, what do you say?" Kade asks. "Do you want to give us a try?"

The noise of guests arriving carries over through the open window. Someone's going to come and get me any time now. My sister's nervous laughter echoes from down the hall. I know I need to change for the ceremony, and yet all I can do is stare at the man in front of me, wondering what if.

What if I did give us a try?

Could I handle having my heart broken by him?

"How would that work exactly?" I ask weakly, as my heart's making up its own mind.

As much as I have to protest myself, I doubt I could ever live with the decision of letting him go without taking a chance on us.

Kade smiles. "We'll start like every other couple. Let me introduce myself." He stretches out his hand. "My name's Kaiden Wright. I'm a former sex addict, but really, I never was. It was all a ploy to save myself from boredom. I went to rehab, where I fell in love with the most beautiful woman I've ever seen. She's been on my mind since the day she walked in on me taking care of some very personal business. I don't know everything about her, but I know that she's kind, patient, loyal, and that I can't imagine my life without her. She makes me laugh like no one can. She makes me want to be my better self. Through her, I found out that when you meet the right person, and you feel like you can trust them, that's something to hold on to because it's both rare and precious." He places his hands on my swollen belly, his warmth seeping into my skin. "I'm not going to let her go, neither her nor my child."

I smile at him as tears gather in my eyes. "I can't believe you decided it might be a good idea to pour your heart out before my sister's wedding." I sling my arms around his neck, pulling him close. "You know I'll tear up throughout the entire ceremony, right?"

"You look cute when you cry." He places a soft kiss on my lips.

"Vicky," my sister yells down the corridor. "What the hell's taking you two so long? Save the making out session for later."

"We're coming," I yell back, noticing Kade's mischievous smile. I narrow my eyes at him. "What did you two talk about before she let you come up?"

"Not much." He shrugs and looks so guilty I know he's lying. "She told me to never give up on you because you're a lost cause, and that I have to exert patience with a pregnant woman due to her raging hormones."

I raise my brows. "That's all?"

"Not quite." He hesitates. "If you really must know, she also said something about those raging hormones being insatiable for other things."

My cheeks catch fire. I mentioned being horny maybe once or twice because she asked me. Trust

Gracie to go and blabber it all out to Kade.

"I like her," he says. "She's fun and honest. Now it's your turn."

"Alright." I take a few moments to gather my words. "I'm Vicky. I'm a former love addict, but really, I was just a poor, delusional fool when I entered rehab. I thought I loved someone, but then I fell in love with my roommate the moment I saw him naked in front of a mirror, which really left nothing to the imagination. I fell hard, without any reservations, plans, and hopes." My voice is shaking. In fact, my whole being is. "He's been on my mind ever since that day."

He laughs. "I always knew that you had a soft spot for butt-naked guys."

I shake my head. "Not for every naked guy; just this particular one."

"We're going to be okay," Kade whispers, wrapping his arms around me and pulling me to his strong chest. "The future might not be fixed, but there's some certainty. I'll always love you. You can always count on me, Vicky."

EPILOGUE

Kaiden

One year later

IT FEELS NOW LIKE an eternity has passed since rehab, but Vicky's taste never left my lips. Every time I feel her mouth against mine, a new wave of feelings rise inside me.

Hope, love, pride?

Yeah, pride.

I'm proud of what we have achieved. Together, brick by brick, we left our past behind, setting the foundations of our future. After the birth of our child, we moved in together.

Persuading her wasn't easy, let me tell you that.

I had to ask her a thousand times before she finally agreed.

It was the statement that our child needed both parents in the same place that gave her the courage to enter that new phase in our relationship.

If you had asked me if I could imagine that one day I might be so desperate to have this woman near me, I would have said that's impossible.

Having a child, a home, a family, commitment...I guess the impossible has become real.

She has become real.

She is my new, favorite kind of reality.

Smiling at her, I pull the car into the driveway and hit the brakes. She's frowning at me as I lead her around the house to the backyard.

"I don't like surprises," she says with a scowl, but the delighted glint in her eyes tells a different story. Her enthusiasm is one of the many things I love about her. "The last one didn't work out so well."

"This one will be more to your liking." I take a long moment regarding her, marveling at the way the rays of the setting sun seem to catch in her red locks, giving them that fiery hue that fits her personality.

She's been away on vacation visiting her family. I insisted that she spend some quality time with them while I secretly built the tree house.

"What do you say?" I point at the trees, but don't

look away so as not to miss her reaction.

We have a huge backyard. Her gaze sweeps over the vast space, past the shrubs and the trees...and settles on the little tree house.

A gasp escapes her lips. "Holy shit." Laughing, she turns around. "Don't tell me you built that."

"Guilty as charged." I grin. "Do you want to see it from the inside?"

I don't wait for her answer. Holding her hand, I guide her down the path, eager to get to the actual surprise.

She eyes the small ladder warily. "You sure this is safe?"

"Safest place on earth." My hands go around her waist to steady her. "And if you fall I'll be right here to catch you."

"Heard that one before." In a minute we're inside. Her eyes grow wide as she takes in the table and two chairs set up in the middle of the room.

"This is huge." She picks up a rose from one of the flower arrangements and lifts it to her face to smell it. "It's so romantic. And completely unlike you, Kade."

There's a strange tremor in her voice, as though something as little as a bunch of red roses are enough to fill her heart with joy.

"I admit I had a little help. But the rest was all my idea," I say.

"The rest?" Her eyebrows shoot up.

"Yes. *The* rest." I bend down on one knee, and as my hand squeezes inside my pocket, her eyes narrow.

"Kade," her voice is a shaky whisper now. "What are you doing?"

"Only something I should have done a long time ago." My gaze interlocks with hers, holding it, bathing in its warmth and love. "Remember the day I said I liked you?"

She nods slowly.

"I was lying. I didn't just like you. I was falling in love with you. And I still am, Victoria, more and more, every single day." I clear my voice to get rid of the sudden hoarseness in it. "I want to brand you as mine. I want to be able to call you my wife. Treat you like my queen. Respect you not only as the mother of my child, but also as the one person I get to spend the rest of my life with. And I hope you want the same, but not because I'm the father of your child." I exhale a slow breath as I try to recall the speech I carefully prepared—but can't remember a single word. "I need to know that you want more of me in every way I can give you. That's why we're standing here. That's why I built this tree house. Because the god honest truth is, I can't imagine another woman by my side. Will you marry me, Victoria?"

She inhales a sharp breath and her expression changes before my eyes.

I take it all in.

Suspicion. Shock. Surprise. Wonder.

And happiness.

So much happiness.

"Yes." She nods slowly, then with more fervor. "Yes, I do."

I cock my eyebrow. "You sure? Because you haven't even seen the ring yet? And that might be a dealbreaker for some women." I wiggle the box in my hand.

"Yes, I'm sure. Very much so." She wipes at the delicate tears trickling down her cheeks, but as she does so, more seem to take their place.

I open the box, holding up the ring.

"I'm so happy."

"Because our very own love story has become true?"

"No." She shakes her head. "Because you just showed me that sex is overrated, and love is a cure." She catches my amused expression. "And of course, because this is the most beautiful ring I have ever seen and I so want it on my finger."

ANOTHER EPILOGUE

Vicky

AN OPEN LETTER TO JANE AUSTEN

Dear Jane,

Kaiden Wright and I were never supposed to live together.

I was clingy, he was a manwhore. I lived to love, and he lived to play. I dreamed of a white picket fence, and he strived for success.

We couldn't be more different. Me, a normal nurse, him a successful CEO. I wanted to love while he wanted to run.

Yet, despite all our differences, we had one thing in common. We both fought hard for what we wanted.

Kaiden Wright wasn't my future, and I wasn't his

past, but we had moments. Moments that defined us. Moments that felt as though the present was ours and ours only.

Maybe it wasn't about ending up together.

Maybe it wasn't about loving someone so deeply you would do anything for them without expecting anything in return.

It's been ten years since I last wrote to you.

Yes, ten.

Can you believe that?

So much has happened. Kade happened. At first, it felt too good to be true and I didn't think our relationship would last.

I never anticipated that he'd be in for the long haul.

But he's surprised me.

In the most unexpected way.

My life hasn't just changed; it's evolved and Kade's been there with me, loving me, encouraging me.

I never had to chase love. It came to me—with all its delays, turmoil, and mixed messages. Sometimes, the most important thing is right before our eyes, and we just have to open them to see it. Open our hearts, and see the truth without expectations, without judging.

I'll admit I judged Kade, and I did believe all the lies I had been telling myself to protect my fragile heart. My heart could handle him all along; it was my mind that was too fragile. It's all too easy to believe our own lies, to give up hope, and to settle for less. To believe the demons and succumb to one's fears.

It was never the pain that broke me.

It was the fear.

Fear stopped me from striving for the best I could achieve.

Fear was the first thing I gave up after Kade and I officially became a couple.

Today, I'm a different person. Stronger. The moment our son was born and I saw his innocence, I knew that happiness doesn't come in chunks. It comes in pieces. Sometimes, they are small, and sometimes, they happen randomly. They fall into place when we need them.

My therapist once said that relationships formed in rehab don't last, but she was wrong. Because they can and they do. Because, guess what? I don't think therapists are always right. People can help us, and they can teach us to sail, but they can't hold the ropes for us. We alone control the direction we take.

We're the ships that weather the storms. And love

is our storm.

We moved to Santa Barbara to be near Kade's brother and his family. I love it here. Love the balmy weather. The atmosphere. Our huge new home.

It's during my moments with Kade that I realize just how beautiful life can be. It's unpredictable. Full of surprises. Just like Kade Wright.

When we first met, we were both lost souls that needed to learn how to cope with life and find their way home. We needed the challenges. We needed each other. I see that now.

I see it in the way we're not giving up hope for a second child. (We've been trying for a long time but we have faith that someday it will work.)

I see it every day when I wake up in his arms and his eyes reflect his love for me.

When our bodies merge into one being, our hearts beating against each other, each of us drawing and giving pleasure in equal measures.

Today marks our ten-year anniversary.

I couldn't be more happy about that.

Who would have known? A sex addict and a love addict. But it's true.

We couldn't be more different in our attitudes, but when it's down to love, we both love hard. And that's not a thing I'd change. Not about us. Or him.

Because when it's down to love, you can't stop, you just keep falling. And falling. And I fell hard for him. Kade Wright is the most amazing man I've ever met, and I can't thank the stars enough.

Yours, always faithfully
Vicky Wright.

P.S. (Note the Wright? We got married eight years ago. We've lasted through all the challenges and the fights, and there were plenty of those. But our love never faltered, and that's all that counts.)

THE END

Interested to read more about Kaiden's best friend, the nightclub owner? Cash Boyd will get his own story.

Cash Boyd ➜ *WILD FOR YOU*

Don't miss their release. Subscribe to the J.C. Reed Mailing List to be notified on release day: http://www.jcreedauthor.com/mailinglist

Kaiden's best friend Cash will make his appearance soon. This sexy standalone is all about the arrogant, rich playboy.

Watch out for

WILD FOR

YOU

(A STANDALONE NOVEL)

BY J.C. REED

COMING LATE SUMMER 2017

Make sure to sign up to J.C. Reed' s mailing list

http://eepurl.com/bFUFVT

to be notified when it releases

ACKNOWLEDGMENTS

This book could not have been written without a few friends' support...you know who you are. Thank you for taking the time to share your experiences with us. Thank you for letting us take a glimpse into the life of an addict and for sharing the difficulties you go through on a daily basis. Thanks to you, writing this book has been an incredibly humbling and mind-opening experience, and we couldn't have done it without you.

A huge thank you to our fans and everyone who's supported us on our crazy ride as authors.

Thank you to all the amazing bloggers who have been part of our journey. Without your help and reviews we wouldn't have reached our amazing readers. And lastly, thank you to our amazing readers. We love you. Thank you for the love you have shown for our books.

We hope this book has been as close to your hearts as it has been to ours.

Love,

Jessica Reed and Jackie Steele

BOOKS BY J.C. REED:

SURRENDER YOUR LOVE TRILOGY

SURRENDER YOUR LOVE
CONQUER YOUR LOVE
TREASURE YOUR LOVE

NO EXCEPTIONS SERIES

THE LOVER'S SECRET
THE LOVER'S GAME
THE LOVER'S PROMISE
THE LOVER'S SURRENDER

AN INDECENT PROPOSAL TRILOGY

AN INDECENT PROPOSAL: THE INTERVIEW
AN INDECENT PROPOSAL: THE AGREEMENT
AN INDECENT PROPOSAL: BAD BOY

STANDALONE BOOKS

BEAUTIFUL DISTRACTION
COUNTING ON YOU

BOOKS BY JACKIE STEELE

AN INDECENT PROPOSAL TRILOGY

AN INDECENT PROPOSAL: THE INTERVIEW
AN INDECENT PROPOSAL: THE AGREEMENT
AN INDECENT PROPOSAL: BAD BOY

STANDALONE BOOKS

COUNTING ON YOU

KEEP IN TOUCH WITH J.C. REED

Jessica loves to hear from her readers and fans.

Newsletter signup: http://eepurl.com/bFUFVT

Website: http://www.jcreedauthor.com

Facebook:
http://www.facebook.com/AuthorJCReed

Twitter:
http://www.twitter.com/JCReedAuthor

Instagram:
http://www.instagram.com/authorjcreed/

Facebook Fan Group:
http://www.facebook.com/groups/8443138422820
95

KEEP IN TOUCH WITH JACKIE STEELE

Newsletter signup:
http://eepurl.com/bdwNpH

Website: http://www.jackiesteeleauthor.com

Facebook:
https://www.facebook.com/AuthorJackieSteele

Twitter: https://twitter.com/AuthorJSsteele

Note from the authors

While Vicky Sullivan and Kaiden Wright are made up characters, love addiction is real. This affliction affects many people in different ways. Vicky's story is romanticized, but real sufferers often face rejection, pain, self-hatred and as a result are often suicidal.

If you are the victim of love or sex addiction or know someone who could use assistance, please visit:

https://slaafws.org

Printed in Great Britain
by Amazon